"IF YOU'RE TRYING TO TELL ME THAT YOU CAN HAVE ANY MAN YOU WANT, I ALREADY KNOW THAT."

"I already know that I don't belong on your list."

He tipped her head back and lowered his lips until they were brushing her eyelids, her temples, and, damn him, someplace deeper she had planned on keeping safe.

"But I'm there, aren't I? On your lists and under your skin just as surely as you are under mine. And the thought of Benjamin Cobb touching you, running his finger down your cheek like this—" He stroked her cheek and she knew that had he not been pressed up against her so tightly, her knees would have buckled and she would have slid to the floor.

"The thought of him playing with your hair—" He did that, too, winding a strand around his finger until he was tied to her cheek by a silken cord. "The thought of him pressing his lips here," he whispered, kissing her temple. "Or here." He pressed a kiss just under her jawbone, and his moan drowned out her own.

And just as she thought she had figured out the way things worked between the sexes, her handsome knight's lips caught hers, came down and demanded that she admit with her touch what she would never admit with her words. . . .

Also by Stephanie Mittman

THE MARRIAGE BED

STEPHANIE MITTMAN

Sweeter than Wine

A DELL BOOK

Published by
Dell Publishing
a division of
Bantam Doubleday Dell Publishing Group, Inc.
1540 Broadway
New York, New York 10036

ISBN: 0-440-22180-3

Printed in the United States of America

Published simultaneously in Canada

March 1997

10 9 8 7 6 5 4 3 2 1
OPM

This book would never have been written without the love, friendship, and support of four wonderful people:

Alan, you are always my inspiration, but for this one you were much more. When you said you'd love me for better or for worse, I bet you never thought it could get this bad! I promise to see you through your crises too.

Sherry, you were there when I needed you, with love, advice, and ideas. Without you, and my mom, there would have been no Princess Sugarlips within the pages of *Sweeter Than Wine*. But now I'm ready for the bonfire.

Laura, the world's best editor and darn good friend! Talk about patience! Talk about faith! Thanks for both. Without them I couldn't have possibly gotten to the end!

Patty, you are simply the best! Even though the book is done, can we still do dinner on Mondays?

And to Annie and Noah, who just wouldn't go away, thanks for another story! (And could you send a pie?)

Chapter One

At long last, Ethan Morrow's buckboard stood ready and waiting outside Hanson's Mercantile. Nestled in it, along with all the tender seedlings and year-old saplings, the well-worn tools and make-do supplies, the cast-off furniture and mended clothing, was a small collection of carefully preserved hopes and one freshly dusted dream.

"I suppose there's no talking you out of this, then, is there?" Charlie Morrow asked his youngest brother, as if it was some crazy fool thing for Ethan to actually think he could make a life for himself. And that it was even crazier to think about going beyond the boundaries of Ohio again to do it.

"No, Charlie. It's my last chance and I'm going." He reached into the jar on the store's counter and handed a honey stick down to Miranda, Charlie and Risa's cute-as-a-button middle daughter, whose chubby arms were wrapped around his left leg.

"So this morning, then?" Charlie asked, coming out from behind the counter to peel Miranda from Ethan's limb. "You're going to just pick up and leave this morning?"

"No," Ethan said, strumming his fingers against his thigh to stop himself from balling his fists. "I thought I'd wait until the rush was over and there wasn't one damn piece of Kickapoo land left. That way I could just turn around and come back home and spend the rest of my life right here, working Noah's farm for him. That what you want, Charlie? Want me to just be good old

Uncle-ain't-got-a-pot-to-pee-in-Ethan? Could *you* load everything *you* own into one lousy wagon and still have room for your dog?"

"I haven't got a dog," Charlie said, picking up Miranda and nuzzling her neck with his nose.

"No, you got three kids and a wife and a half-interest in this mercantile. And you've got a roof over your head that you can call your own."

"And I wouldn't trade any of them." He tightened the hold on his daughter, accepting a lick of the honey stick she offered. "But still, look at what you've got. You're young, you're footloose, fancy-free. You could have any woman you want. Nobody's depending on you to bring home the bacon, keep the wolf away. . . ."

"Jeez, you sure can turn a phrase, can't you? And what would I offer this woman I wanted—saying there was one in Van Wert, which there's not?" Ethan reached out and tickled Miranda's little tummy with just one finger as she squirmed in Charlie's arms.

At the jingle of entrance bells, they turned toward the door expectantly. Risa, short of breath and long on belly, lumbered into the store. "They're nearly all out there, Eth," she said, attempting a smile. Then she asked Charlie, "The baby still asleep?"

"Not a peep out of her." Charlie turned to Ethan. "You'll wait until she wakes up so you can give her a kiss good-bye, won't you?"

Ethan sighed and let a short laugh escape him. "And while I'm at it, why don't I hang around for your After-Christmas Sale, and the party for your golden anniversary. . . ."

"All right, Eth. Let me just go get Cara and the baby," Risa said, biting her lip while her eyes welled with tears. "They'll want to say good-bye to their favorite uncle."

He was sorry they were having such trouble saying good-bye. Sorry, and maybe even a little flattered. But the truth of it was he was happier to be going than a short-legged grasshopper in a field of new corn. He truly was. Not that he didn't love his family—each and every one of them—but Van Wert was a small town with no stone left that he hadn't turned twice. Where was the adventure that quickened a breath, the surprise that made a heart pound? The only thing left for him to conquer in Van Wert was boredom.

Still, that didn't mean he was looking forward to placing that last kiss for who knew how long on any one of his nieces' or nephews' foreheads.

"Can I have a minute?" Risa asked, dabbing at her tears with the corner of her apron. "I don't want the baby to see me like this."

"Yeah," Ethan agreed. Jeez, they weren't making this easy. "But Risa honey, only a minute. I gotta go soon."

He paused a moment, savoring the taste of the word in his mouth. *Soon, soon, soon.* It had been a litany in his head for almost as long as he could remember. A litany that had gotten him through day after day of looking at the rear of a horse that wasn't even his, plowing a field that wasn't his, sleeping under a roof that wasn't his.

"Think you could get her now?" he asked, his impatience getting the better of him. It wasn't as if waiting an hour, or a day, or even a week would make a difference to his family. It had taken him six years to get from the wishing to the going. Six years of going no place and getting nowhere. And after six long years of sitting down to family dinners and setting up town picnics, of putting up this one's windwheels and putting in that one's crops, they still weren't ready to let him go. What good was another few minutes going to do?

"What's your rush, Eth?" Charlie asked him as Risa took Miranda's little hand and headed for the stairs. "The land won't even be open for another month."

Of course, Charlie could afford to feel that way. He was the third in the alphabetical family line that began with Annie, Sissy's given name, continued with Bart, and went on down to Francie. It was her birth that had

ended their parents' grandiose plans for the entire al-
phabet—Zena Morrow had fallen victim to some awful
birth fever and died within days of Francie's birth.

But even at third, Charlie couldn't wait his turn.

"Didn't you have to be the one to be married first?
The one who wanted to be a father first?" He looked
down at the clean white shirt with the frayed cuffs he
was wearing. "Believe this was yours first," he said,
pointing to the shirt. "Along with just about every other
shirt I own. I'm not taking leftover land, Charlie. I'm
gonna be there first, right up there in the front of that
line or at the starting gate or however they work it out
there, and I'm gonna pick me out the damn best piece
of ground a man can sink his roots into."

It was his only chance, damn it all, and he was taking
it.

The bell over the door jangled once more, and Sissy
and Noah came into the mercantile, Sissy sniffing as she
entered. "You about ready to go?" she asked, putting on
a bright smile. "The children are getting pretty restless
out there."

He was really going. Not next week, not soon. *Now.* A
few good-byes and he and Honesty, his pathetic black
mutt that drooled better than he did anything else,
would be on their way.

From the strained look on Noah's face and the way
he kept patting Sissy's arm and peeling at her fingers,
his sister was gathering strength from him to say her
farewell. Having been like a mama to him, she was
surely gonna be the hardest to leave. But then, leaving
any one of them was tough. Leaving them all was hell.

All right. Maybe not hell. Not when he thought about
his own cabin on his own land. Of breaking new
ground, building a new life in a new town. Over the
years he'd wondered, as one day blended into the one
that came before it and all the ones that would follow it,
if hell wasn't just the monotony of doing the same thing
day after day. It was the sense that he'd plowed that row

a million times, walked that path every day, patched that piece of roof already, and mended that stretch of fence before. And for all the miles he'd walked, and all the repairs he'd made, he'd gotten nowhere.

Until now.

"The whole family out there?" he asked, trying to see beyond the gewgaws and signs that nowadays cluttered the front window of Hanson's Mercantile and showed that Mr. Hanson had most definitely retired and left the store to his daughter and her husband.

"Well, a few of them are late," Noah said with an apologetic smile. Heck, there wasn't any reason for Noah to feel guilty. It wasn't his fault that their brother-in-law, Peter, never seemed to get to any family gatherings anymore. "Bart and Willa are out there with the boys. And Della, bless her heart."

"Della's here?" he asked, ducking to get a glimpse of her out the window. "She came out? With James?" he asked hopefully, knowing how angry his poor nephew was about his leaving.

"Not yet," Sissy said, a bright smile pasted on her sun-kissed face. "But I'm sure he'll be here soon, Eth."

It shouldn't have been much of a surprise that James hadn't come to say good-bye. Still, the boy's absence was enough to start that itch in the back of his throat. He'd have thought the child would at least want to bid good-bye to old Honesty.

"Yeah," he agreed without conviction. "You'll tell him, if he doesn't show, that I asked after him, won't you? And that I expect him to come visit me when I get settled. And that I just couldn't wait any longer. . . ." His voice trailed off. He was disappointing his nephew, joining the long line of people who had been disappointing the child ever since no one could save his twin brother all those years ago.

"Reminds me of when Francie left, doesn't it?" Sissy asked her brother Charlie, who nodded and stared at

Ethan as if he was trying to memorize his face. "Well, she's happy, anyways," Sissy added.

He supposed she was, living in New York with a husband rich enough to send Ethan a ticket to New York just so that he could bring Francie some of Sissy's home-baked angel cookies for Christmas.

New York.

That city had surely been something all right. But New York fit him like someone else's Sunday church suit and fancy gaiters, whereas Ethan was a man who belonged in well-worn work pants and boots caked with mud. Oklahoma was sure to fit him an awful lot better than New York. Oklahoma was something a farm boy like him would know how to handle.

"You probably should have gone a long time ago," Sissy said. "I'm glad you're going now, Eth. Real happy. You should have gone in the first rush probably."

"But then I'd have missed meeting Gracie," he said, remembering how excited they'd all been when Sissy had announced she was expecting a child of her own.

"And Miranda," Charlie added, his eyes watching the top of the stairs.

"And Rory and . . ." Ethan said, peering out the window at all the little ones he might never see grown up. All the children who were about to become specks in a family photograph sent once a year to a town where he didn't know a soul and no one knew him.

They'd all better visit him, that was all. And he'd throw open his home to them the way his whole family had always thrown open theirs to him.

"You should go," Sissy began again, opening the door to the mercantile and checking the sky, as if a cloud could stop him. Heck, a tornado wouldn't stop him now.

"I'll just give him another minute or two," he said, shooing Sissy and Noah out the door and turning to Risa, who was making her way down the steps with her girls, trying to see the stair treads over her rounded belly. Well, there was one baby whose birth he would miss. "Got something for me to snack on while I'm traveling?"

Five more minutes he'd give James. That was all. Then wild horses couldn't keep him in Ohio anymore.

* * *

"And the princess said, 'Will you play with me?' but the royal gardener was too busy," Sterling Phillips said as she and Worth walked down Chestnut Street toward the mercantile.

"What was the princess's name?" the boy asked, stopping to pick up yet another rock to consider for his collection and holding it up for her approval.

"That'll shine up nice," she told him, examining the very ordinary stone that for the moment had the ability to fascinate the three-year-old at her side. "Sugarlips. Her name was Princess Sugarlips."

"Oh, her." He shoved the rock into his pocket and took her hand. "Then the gardener musta said no, 'cause he was too busy planting those peenies."

"Peonies," she corrected. "But she didn't mind because . . . ?" She waited while he considered his answer.

He smiled up at her, quite pleased with himself. "It was raining, anyway."

"Good one," she said, giving his little hand a squeeze. "So she asked Cornelia, the upstairs maid, if *she* would play with her, but Cornelia had to make the beds, so Princess Sugarlips . . ."

". . . got a new Indian rubber ball to play with."

"Princess Sugarlips got a new ball? Or is that a cunning little boy who only has two pennies to spend and wants one of mine?"

"Could I? Just one, Ster, please?" he begged, as if she'd ever denied him anything she had. As if she ever would.

"Watch where you're going, honey lamb," she warned

as they wended their way through the throng of people milling about in front of Hanson's. Around them the street had the air of a party to which they had not been invited.

"Morning, Miss Phillips," Noah Eastman said, nodding pleasantly at her as she tried to pass.

"Morning," she responded cheerily, especially fond of the man ever since she'd seen him kiss his daughter's scraped knee right in the middle of Fountain Park. Her own father would have stepped over her and lectured her about her clumsiness. "Is something going on?"

"Hi, Miss Phillips," Julia Eastman said with a little curtsy. Sterling gave her a small bow in return. "How's that princess with the butterfly?" Julia asked.

Sterling cupped the girl's chin, looking into exquisite eyes that smiled back at her. "Why, she was riding on that butterfly just last night. Didn't you see her?"

"I saw the little lights, at dusk," the girl answered, slipping her hand into her stepmother's. "Uncle Ethan's finally taking off. Mama's real sad about it, but she's pretending she's as happy as Uncle Eth."

Sissy Eastman was doing a pretty poor job of pretending, standing there with her lip caught between her teeth and trying to smile. "Well," she said. "Even if I'm not his real mama, it hurts just the same."

"I'm sure it does," Sterling agreed, grasping Worth's hand so tightly that he whined and wriggled out of her grasp, striking up a conversation with Rory Morrow about the relative value of rocks versus stones.

"He's like mine," Sissy admitted sheepishly. The woman had raised her five brothers and sisters and was caring for Noah Eastman's two little girls before she'd even had any little girls of her own. "My little boy."

Sterling had never really thought about Ethan Morrow as anyone's little boy. Not the way he towered over half the congregation at the Pleasant Township Methodist Church. Not the way those broad shoulders strained his clean white shirts. In fact, though she'd never admit it even if they held her feet to the fire—and Worth didn't know it—Ethan Morrow was Sir Glad-I-am, Royal Knight of Princess Sugarlips's kingdom.

Of course, Ethan Morrow didn't know it, either.

"I don't have to tell you about raising siblings," Sissy said as she knelt down and put out her hand to Worth. "How do you do, young man? You get bigger every time I see you. Won't be long before your sister has tears in her own eyes." She pushed herself off her knees with considerable effort and met Sterling's gaze. "You know as good as me that when you raise them, there's not much difference between being their sister and being their mama, is there?"

Not much difference. There was all the difference in the world. And no one knew it better than Sterling. Why, a sister shouldn't just drop a kiss on her brother's head. She couldn't cuddle her brother to her breast. Would a sister weep at her brother's first tooth?

"Not a lot of difference," she agreed anyway, ordering the unwelcome butterflies that so often took up residence inside her to cease their frantic winging and allow her to draw a quiet breath.

No, there was only the difference between being a brother and being a bastard.

She brushed the hair out of Worth's eyes for him. "Come on, honey lamb. Let's get you that ball."

"I can do it myself," Worth said, forging ahead and leaving her to follow in his wake. Oh, but he was growing fast, barreling into childhood before his babyhood was over. Always in a rush to conquer the next challenge, to stretch farther away from her when all she wanted to do was hold him close, keep him safe.

"Tell my uncle Eth we're waiting," one of the children said as she opened the door to the mercantile and Worth slipped in under her arm.

"Yes, I will," she agreed, smiling at little Gracie Eastman and marveling at how she'd grown. Glory-laury, but the family seemed to have one of every age. She felt the familiar stab of envy, and pushed it aside. She had her baby, her wonderful son, and that one child to love was worth it—worth defying her father, worth being sent from her home in New York, and worth the lie she had chosen to live.

Not that she gave a flying fig what anybody'd think of her or the mistakes she'd made. She'd earned their scorn and she'd take it, too—if it was hers alone. But her son? She'd crawl to hell on her hands and knees before she'd let a body think ill of him for what she'd done.

"Cripes!" she heard Worth say, and hurried in the direction of his voice, nearly colliding with Ethan Morrow in her haste.

"Sorry," he said, steadying her at the elbow. "Guess I ought to look where I'm going."

He was as handsome close up as he was eight pews away in church. Handsomer, maybe. Church was where she'd dubbed him a knight. There, too, the Reverend Winestock had been given the job of Royal Magician. Several other members of the congregation were also cast into smaller roles within the dreams she wove for her son. Writing stories in her head was certainly more entertaining than listening to the sermons.

And it was a little late to be saving her soul, anyway.

"Miss Phillips?" His hand was still on her elbow. "You daydreaming?"

She felt the color rush to her cheeks, and fought for composure. Reminding herself that he had no idea that he was Princess Sugarlips's Royal Knight, she explained that she was just looking for her honey lamb before he dismantled the latest display.

Next to her, the knight smiled understandingly, as if he knew the damage a child could do given a moment alone in a mercantile. My, but the man even smelled good, like fresh laundry on the line, all bleach and breeze and grass.

He pointed over his shoulder at Worth, who appeared

mesmerized by a shiny red three-wheeled velocipede that was bigger than he was. "Seems pretty taken with that bike. Not that I blame him. I'd have looked just like that when I was his age."

He'd probably always been irresistible. No doubt, it was that errant curl of honey-colored hair on his forehead. It was an effort not to slip a finger against his forehead and brush it away from his amber eyes, where it caught on lashes longer than any man had a right to.

"It's red, Ster," Worth said of the velocipede, bouncing on his toes. He fingered the bell, and Sir Glad-I-am encouraged him to try it out. The cheerful clang bounced off the shelves and was lost.

"And red's your favorite color. I know, honey lamb. Now, how about that ball?" she asked, trying to steer him toward the counter but finding him impossible to budge. "Come on, love. Aunt Imogene started worrying about us before we even got past the front gate."

Her gallant knight tried, but failed miserably, to hide his smile at the way she pronounced her aunt's name, as if it rhymed with *progeny*. No doubt he'd seen the advertisement Imogene Harrington had taken out in the *Van Wert Gazette* the day she decided that everyone should pronounce the *e* on the end of her name. "Why else would it be there?" her aunt had asked. It didn't matter how many other words ended in *e*, Aunt Imogene was adamant, and they'd all had to adjust.

"Please?" Worth pleaded, his feet moving slowly toward the counter, but his eyes still riveted on the three-wheeler.

"Oh, buy the kid the bicycle." It was natural for him, just like everyone else, to assume she could afford it. Most everyone in Van Wert assumed a great deal, and she was more than willing to take the good along with the bad.

"It's too big for you, honey," she told Worth, wondering how much her mother's pearl-and-gold brooch might bring from the jeweler in Bellefontaine. And whether an all-steel velocipede (even one built to stand "a heap of racket," according to the sign) would be the right thing to spend it on. Why, much as she hated to think about it, at the rate her son was growing, Worth would be sure to outgrow it before they all blinked twice. Still, it was surely hard to resist those enormous blue eyes staring up at her, one little tear clinging to the corner pathetically.

"Your feet wouldn't even reach the—" She pointed to the metal bars. "—those."

"Pedals," Ethan Morrow said, encouraging her son without even realizing it.

"Did I forget to mention your whole family is waiting for you outside?" she asked, pointing toward the door. Any moment now Mr. Morrow would have Worth atop that velocipede, and she'd never get his feet back down on the ground again.

"I'm just waiting for a straggler or two," he said, glancing at the counter and raising his shoulders. "So, Charlie? Any sign of him?"

"Please?" Worth begged again, those shiny eyes threatening to spill over.

"You could put blocks on the pedals," Mr. Morrow told her, pointing at the bicycle.

"Couldn't he get hurt?" she asked. "I mean he's still so little, and I . . ." *And I'd die if he lost so much as an eyelash.*

"He is a bit of a thing," the man agreed quickly, chivalrously taking pity upon her. He held his hand above Worth's head as if he were measuring, then raised it six inches or so for an imaginary child. "Yes, now that I get a good look up close, I think you might have to grow some more."

Then he took a step back and looked her up and down, as if he were sizing her up as well while he was at it.

"Don't they feed you over there at the loony . . . Harrington Manor?"

So much, she thought, for chivalry. Whoever had said it was dead was right. While it was true that her aunt Imogene was eccentric at best, it was equally true that she was good and kind. And by now she was no doubt worried about what was keeping them. The dear woman worried too much about Worth, but then Sterling thought that was probably natural under the circumstances. "Get your ball now, honey. And say good-bye to the bicycle for today. We can visit it another day."

"No sign of him, Ethan," Charlie said after looking out the front door. "And much as I hate to admit it, I think the corn's ready for picking."

"I'm coming, then," Ethan replied, ruffling Worth's hair and nodding politely at her as he took his leave. "You have a good day, now, the both of you. I'll be looking for news of you riding that bike, young man."

"Here you go, son," Charlie said to Worth, handing him a black rubber ball, which her honey lamb had nearly lost interest in, and holding out his hand while Worth slowly counted the three pennies into it.

"If there's nothing else . . . ?" the shopkeeper asked. It was clear that he wanted to be free to see his brother off.

"No, that's everything," she said, pushing Worth toward the door and fumbling with her parasol.

"I forgot to say good-bye to the velo'pede!" Worth ran back while she continued to fight with the black silk umbrella she'd gotten when her mother died. If only she could get used to a hat to shield her fair skin from the sun, she could retire the old umbrella to the back of the closet, where the box full of memories of her mother, and better times, was stored.

Outside, she stood on the sidewalk waiting for Worth and watched as Ethan Morrow said his good-byes.

"So, I guess this is it." He shoved his hands into his pockets and checked the sky, all the while blinking furiously.

"If you're gonna go . . . ," Noah Eastman said finally, and several children groaned and rushed the man for one last hug or kiss or pat on the head.

". . . you'd better go," Charlie Morrow said with a laugh, pulling one child after another from Ethan Morrow's legs like leeches after a swim.

"Do you really have to go?" one of his nieces asked.

He nodded, pulling lightly on her pigtail. "Now, don't you go growing more than an inch or two," he warned her, wagging his finger in her face. "I want to recognize you when your mama and papa bring you down for a visit."

"Why can't you stay with us?" Julia Eastman asked, and her sister's groan indicated it wasn't the first time she'd raised the possibility. "What's so great about your own door?"

"Maybe he doesn't like chickens watching him get dressed," Hannah Eastman said, trying to steer her younger sister away so that the next in line could have a chance. "Julie, he's got to go."

"Now?" another little boy asked, running his hand down Ethan Morrow's thigh as if he didn't want to forget what his uncle felt like.

"But One Shoe's not here," one of the children said.

"Don't call him that," Risa Morrow said, grabbing the little girl by a pigtail and yanking. "Bad enough others do it. Your cousin's name is James and don't you forget it, young lady."

"Well, he isn't here," the girl said. "And they call him worse."

"Children can be mean," Sissy Eastman said, "but family is different. James knows his brother's gone. He doesn't need reminding."

"I don't want to hear from your mamas and papas that you're not being kind to your cousin," Ethan Morrow said, shaking his head at the children. "James isn't half a pair or one shoe or any such thing. That clear?"

Without exception, every niece and nephew nodded. In fact even Bart Morrow and his wife, Willa, nodded, but whether it was for emphasis or because they were properly chastised wasn't clear.

Then the handsome man with the honey hair and skin and amber eyes allowed himself to be passed along from sisters-in-law to brothers and brothers-in-law to sisters, while his niece Hannah narrated the whole event as if it was a fairy tale come to life. "He kissed everyone good-bye except James. And Uncle Peter. He's late— probably he's counting money. That's what they do in a bank."

"Well, you'll tell him I said good-bye, won't you?" he asked Della Gibbs, embracing her and kissing the top of her fading blond curls as she nodded against his chest.

She muttered something Sterling couldn't hear, and Ethan Morrow's shoulders sagged.

His oldest sister took Mrs. Gibbs into her own arms, freeing him to go. "He's got to leave before it gets too warm," she said.

"Going to goddamn Indian country," Bart Morrow said, his gruff voice breaking, then coughing to cover it. "Ain't even a state. What are you thinking, anyways?"

"I'm thinking that you already got your farm, Bart," Ethan Morrow said, apparently oblivious of the children hanging from his arms and legs while he gestured toward his brother Bart's two sons. "And your family. What've I got?"

"Mama's cookies." Gracie Eastman, one of the Eastmans' little ones, held out a bulging sack to her uncle as if her mama's cookies could fix anything. Sterling had heard rumors to the effect that they could. But then, anything Mrs. Eastman did was perfect.

"You'd better go now, Eth," Mr. Eastman said with a nod. "Or you'll never get going."

"Yeah, go, Uncle Ethan," one of his nieces ordered.

"Yes," Sissy Eastman said softly, nudging him slightly in the direction of his wagon and exchanging a look with Sterling that watered both their eyes. "Go."

He took a step or two toward his wagon, then turned

and reached out to his sister. "I'll miss you," he said, tucking a stray hair behind her ear. "I love you all." There was no scroll in his hands, but it was a proclamation nonetheless, and anyone within two blocks could have heard him clearly.

Sterling couldn't recall a man ever declaring his affection so openly. She dipped her head, pretending to be busy with her parasol, and allowed herself the luxury of pretending to be sent off by such a family, absorbing the warmth in her bones and storing the feeling in the fairy box in her mind.

It was past time for her and Worth to be heading back, but she granted herself a moment longer to watch and wish as, one after another, Sir Glad-I-am's retinue backed away from the wagon. Charlie Morrow swiped his cheek with the back of his hand and sniffed loudly. "And take your mangy cur with you!" he yelled. The big man then ruffled the animal's fur and gave him a gentle pat on the rump.

"Come on, Honesty," her knight yelled to the dog, who had shined the faces of every child too small to escape his loving tongue. The friendly mutt had just discovered Worth, black rubber ball in hand, and was including him as though he were just another member of the family. "Let's go."

Sterling could just hear her honey lamb telling Aunt Imogene about how his little suit came to be wet and sticky, and how brave he'd been when the giant monster had wanted to lick his face.

Meanwhile the mongrel, black and shaggy and covered with drool, jumped up into the wagon to a spot on the right that obviously belonged to him, settling down with his tail thumping against the hard wooden seat like a drumroll signaling the beginning of a momentous journey. From the way the wagon was piled and tied and outfitted, it appeared it was to be exactly that.

"Well, this is it!" Ethan Morrow said, more to the dog than to the crowd, which now stood on the sidewalk hugging one another and staring at the wagon as though it was a funeral hearse. He slapped the dog's flanks affectionately. "And stay off my vines, you stupid mutt."

"Bye!" Risa's littlest called, waving her hand from her mother's arms.

He took a moment to wave back, and then he was off, the pale palomino stallion already digging at the ground with his hooves, anxious for them to be gone and on their way. He picked up the reins and released the brake. "Lord, you'd think you never saw so much excitement, Buckshot. Well, fine. Let's go!"

"Uncle Ethan! Uncle Ethan, wait!" From down the block came a shout, and Sterling, along with everyone else, turned to see James Gibbs running toward them, his arms waving. Behind him several yards and panting, trotted his father, Peter, vice president of the Van Wert Bank and Trust.

She'd have liked to stay forever, on that spot, just close enough to everyone to feel the warmth. She'd have liked to go home with the Eastmans, or back into the mercantile with the Morrows. Mostly, she'd have liked to climb into that wagon with Ethan Morrow, and be off on a grand adventure.

Oh, to pretend, for just a moment, that the fairy tales she wove for Worth could come true. That there could be a prince for them who would take them to his castle where they could live happily ever after.

But pretending was the province of a child, and it was time she got hers home. Reaching down for Worth's hand, she felt nothing.

"Honey lamb?"

It took her only a second to find him, not among the Morrow children but chasing after his ball into the street.

And running right into the path of Ethan Morrow's horse and wagon.

The scream went right through his bones. He felt the

wagon lurch, the horse buck, his chest tighten. And still the scream went on and was joined by others. Afraid of what he might see, he gave in to the urge to shut his eyes for a moment, and was assaulted by the faces of every one of his dear nieces and nephews.

But the body lying just inches from Buckshot's prancing feet didn't belong to a Morrow or an Eastman or a Gibbs. Little Worth Phillips, his pristine white sailor suit already marred with a spattering of deep red blood, lay crumpled and broken in the street, his sister bent over him to keep him from harm's way.

By the time Ethan reined in the horse, set the brake, and jumped down from the wagon, shock had set in. The boy was still—at best unconscious—and the young woman was equally motionless.

He slogged on the road as though it were quicksand, each step a supreme effort, sucking the breath from his lungs, the life from his body. In his shadow, Sissy knelt beside the boy and put her arm around Sterling Phillips.

The girl wasn't a whole lot bigger than her brother— a slip of a thing, pale and fragile, dabbing gently at a trickle of blood matting the boy's nearly white hair.

"Honey lamb? I'm here, baby," she cooed while Ethan tried to swallow against the nausea that rose up his throat. "I'm here."

The child didn't stir.

"Worth?" she whispered, tracing the pudgy outline of his cheek with one finger. "Worth!"

Sissy laid a hand gently on the boy's small chest and then pressed her ear where her hand had been.

"Is he . . . ?" Sterling Phillips asked, obviously unable to force the word *dead* from her throat. She didn't need to. Not a one of them didn't have the same question burning their tongues.

"No," Sissy said, raising her hand to the boy's forehead, gently probing other spots as if she knew what injuries to look for, "but we'd better get him to the doctor." She glanced up at Noah, telegraphing the urgency to him with just the look in her eyes. "He isn't coming around, and . . ." She shrugged and stopped midsentence.

"Hannah honey, you watch after Gracie," Noah said, prying himself free from one daughter's hold on his thigh and another one's grip on his arm.

"Dr. Cobb," Sterling Phillips said, her tear-streaked face raised up at Noah. "Make sure it's Dr. Cobb."

"Let me take him," Ethan offered. "Dr. Walker's a little closer."

He knelt before the child and tried to slip his arms beneath his back.

Sterling's hand caught his wrist. "Don't. Oh God! Don't you touch him. You've got no right to touch him!" Her voice was high, thin, cracked. With wide, pain-filled eyes she stared up at him while trying at the same time to cover her brother with her body.

"I just want to help," he said, trying to reassure her. "It would be foolish to waste time when I can—"

Sissy stilled his arm. "Let her be, Eth. There's nothing you can do right now. It'd be better not to move him."

Of course, she was right. He knew better, but it was hard to think straight with a crumpled child inches from his horse's hooves. He smacked at the horse, who moved away and breathed heavily over them all.

"I'm so sorry about this," he said, kneeling next to the girl and her brother. He hardly even knew her, couldn't even address her by her given name or put an arm around her, offer her his shoulder to cry on. Not that she'd be likely to want it from him.

"*Sorry?*" she asked, raising tear-filled blue eyes to him. "You're *sorry*? Look what you've done! You ran him down. He could be—"

"He'll be all right," Ethan said. "I'll see to it that he is. I swear."

"If he isn't . . . I swear I'll kill you myself. I will." Frantically she looked around. "Get away from us. Please. Just go. Wherever you were going. Go!"

Though her voice was choked, he could still hear her ranting as he walked back to the wagon. He rummaged through the piles of supplies in the back of the buckboard as fast as he could while she continued her threats, interspersed with soft mewls to her brother. All the while Sissy's even voice kept trying to reassure her that everything would be all right.

"He's going to be fine," Ethan heard his sister say as he dug around until he found what he was looking for. "Look. Here comes Noah with the doctor now, see? Everything's going to be fine, just fine."

Corny Cobb, in one of his brown plaid suits, a plug hat on his head, hurried down the street on the same short legs that had made him last in every Arbor Day race when they were boys. Since he couldn't pick up the boy, Ethan was tempted to run and carry the doctor— anything to get them together sooner.

By the time Benjamin Cobb finally reached the baby and his frantic sister and knelt down beside them in the street, Ethan was ready to pull every hair out of the pointy little mustache Corny was twirling nervously while he assessed the situation.

"Is he all right?" Miss Phillips asked, fear closing her throat so that it was hard to hear her, even harder to listen to her. "He isn't waking up. I was afraid he was . . ." Ethan stopped what he was doing and held his breath. From where he stood by the wagon, he could see Cobb pull out his pocket watch and lift the boy's wrist, counting the beats his tiny heart could make. The doctor lifted an eyelid and let it drop.

A breeze carried the girl's whisper. "Why doesn't he wake up?"

Corny—Ethan had trouble calling him Dr. Cobb, and even more trouble thinking of him that way—placed a steadying hand on the girl's shoulder and waited for her to meet his gaze. "Pull yourself together. It would be a shame to fail him now."

"You know what he means to me, Dr. Cobb. Please

make him wake up! I'll take better care of him, I swear I will. Don't let him die!" she sobbed.

"Somebody ought to get Oliver Harrington," Ethan said to his brother Charlie. "Maybe you or Risa could . . ."

Charlie nodded and, after a word with Risa, headed up the road at a good clip. From what Ethan had seen of Sterling Phillips and her brother, the girl was practically raising him, the way Sissy had raised him and his brothers and sisters.

Corny got to his feet with a resignation that chilled Ethan to the bone despite the warm sunshine, and looked around at the crowd, reveling in his importance. Benjamin Cobb always had to be the biggest frog in the pond. He'd always been that way. "Well, let's get him off the street, anyway. Best to bring him to my infirmary."

"He *is* going to be all right, isn't he?" Sterling Phillips asked, finally raising her eyes from her brother to search the doctor's face.

He'd never given it much thought, but Ethan supposed that Worth Phillips was about all his sister had. He remembered clearly when they'd come to live with the Harringtons, the girl all dressed in black with that white, white face and that corn-silk hair; a baby held tight to her chest, who was nuzzling her as if he could find sustenance within her arms.

The good Lord only knew what would become of her if that little boy didn't make it.

And what would become of Ethan as well. This time he couldn't just run for the hills. Not that he would. Not ever again.

He reached into the wagon and pulled out the plank he was looking for. And after just a moment's hesitation he grabbed the rifle his father had given him. He returned to where Corny was once again crouched beside the boy, poking and prodding.

He placed the shotgun next to the girl and then laid the board beside the doctor. "Thought we could use this

to move him," he said in a voice so soft he wasn't sure
Corny heard him at first.

"You picked a fine field in which to finally step into
the manure, Morrow," the doctor said at last and then
nodded toward the board. The two of them eased the
unconscious child onto it. Noah bent down for the end
nearest the little boy's head, while Ethan raised the
other end.

He was such a small and fragile boy, so full of life one
moment, so still the next. And all Ethan had done was
look back for James. One stupid moment and the boy's
life might never be the same again.

None of their lives would be, and no one knew that
better than he did.

He looked down at the girl. Lord, she was fine-
looking, even in her despair. Fine and fragile and innocent, just like the boy. "Just let me get him to the
doc's," he told her, rising with his end of the board
before gesturing toward the rifle with a jerk of his head.
"Then you can use that on me, if you want."

Wide blue eyes, wet with tears, stared up at him in
surprise and doubt.

He nodded at her, his chest tight, his look assuring
her that he knew what he'd said.

And meant it.

Chapter Two

Ethan Morrow's family sat across from Sterling in Dr. Cobb's tiny waiting room, while the man she had mistaken for a shining knight paced back and forth, back and forth. Just like the first time she'd been at Dr. Cobb's, her heart pounded against her chest and she found it difficult to breathe. Sweat collected between her breasts now just as it had then.

Tears had filled her eyes back then too. But they'd been tears of shame, not fear. Then *she'd* been the one to be examined. *She'd* been the one to bear Dr. Cobb's clinical touch and the indignity of sitting nearly naked on his table while he probed and poked and easily surmised the truth of her situation. One didn't develop milk fever from contact with infants, he'd told her, but by bearing them.

It was to have been Dr. Prill, Aunt Imogene's trusted friend and doctor, whom she was to see. Instead his young associate had come into the examining room. She'd wanted to die, but he'd refused to allow it. With icy hands he'd lifted her aching breasts, seeming to weigh them in his palms. He'd pressed against her sore nipples, traced her blue veins, squeezed here, pulled there, all the while making appropriately sympathetic noises while she gasped and moaned.

While he'd clearly disapproved of her "tragic mistake," as he'd referred to her son, he treated her politely and listened to her plea for secrecy without shaking his head even once.

Tearfully she'd begged for dignity for her son, and

after only a moment's hesitation he'd agreed that her deceit was the only choice she had, both for herself and for her baby.

Of course, following the incident, he'd become the family doctor. And treating the Harringtons brought him other wealthy families as patients, until he had parlayed a tiny practice of setting farmers' broken bones into treating the town's richest and finest citizens.

Still, he'd kept her confidences as he'd promised, even on this dreadful morning, even as he'd refused to allow her to stay with her son.

"I really am sorry, but everyone knows that only parents or guardians are allowed in my examining room," he'd said, looking up from her baby's body meaningfully. "You'll have to be brave now and sit in the waiting room like a good big sister. I'll come for you as soon as I'm done."

"Please don't make me leave," she'd begged him, but he'd said it was best, and he'd shown them to the door, just as though she'd had no stake in her own son's welfare.

Ethan Morrow had wanted to stay too. She could tell from the way he gripped the edges of the cot, the way his feet dragged across the floor as he escorted her out, the way he turned his head for one last look before Dr. Cobb shut the door behind them.

For a second he stared at her, neither of them moving away from the doctor's door, as if there was something he wanted to say. Then he bolted toward the porch, pushing out the screen door with his foot and letting it slam with a smack behind him.

She heard him retching outside, over and over, and felt the spasms in her own throat. Long after she'd taken a seat in the waiting room, she was still shaking.

"You all right?" Sissy Eastman asked her brother after a while. "You're still as green as the sky before a storm."

"I'm fine," he said, shaking his head. "I'm not the one who's lying in that room all bent and—"

Sterling covered her ears with her hands.

Her baby was going to die.

The sins of the fathers shall be visited on their children.

And the sins of the mothers? Would they cost them their children? It didn't seem fair. It was her debt to pay, not her son's.

But then, what price would be more fitting?

"Sterling?" It was Aunt Imogene, her quivering voice soft, questioning. "Should I put my hands over my eyes and Uncle can put them over his mouth?"

Sterling lowered her hands from her ears. "No, ma'am," she said, uncurling herself from the ball she had been huddling in and reaching out to pull her aunt close. "It doesn't help."

"I didn't think it would," her aunt said while her uncle shook hands with Noah Eastman, his wife, and Ethan Morrow, pumping each one's hand in turn, shaking his head sadly, and introducing himself.

"Oliver Harrington. The boy's uncle. Any word?" He repeated it to each of them. Sterling thought she might even be next.

"Nothing, Uncle Oliver. Dr. Cobb's still in with him."

"Terrible thing," her uncle said, then said it again.

Aunt Imogene smelled of lavender. Sterling buried her head against the pale purple folds of her aunt's skirt and let the woman stroke her hair.

"I'm so frightened," she whispered into the satiny fabric that rustled around her.

"I'm always frightened," her aunt whispered in response. "So far it hasn't helped."

Real life was cruel.

Her mother had told her that once when Sterling had asked about why her fairy tales couldn't come true.

Real life was cruel and cold and unforgiving.

Her father had told her that many times, and had made it his business to prove it.

And so she'd been vigilant from the very moment she knew that a life grew inside her. She'd safeguarded that life from the doctor her father brought in to confirm it, protected it from the plans her father made to rid her of it. In all the months of waiting for Worth to arrive, the weeks of nursing his tiny body, the years of hiding the truth from everyone but her aunt and uncle and Dr. Cobb—she'd nurtured, she'd cherished, she'd tended. And then she'd simply stopped—stopped the nurturing, the cherishing, the tending—all to watch a touching farewell.

And in that one thoughtless, stupid moment she'd let go of her baby's hand, let down her guard.

"Ster!" Her baby's cry slid under the door, carving a piece from her heart.

The waiting room contained six grown people. None of them made a sound—not a breath, not a whimper.

Finally Sissy Eastman sighed for all of them. "He's alive, then." She gripped her brother's hand tightly until her knuckles turned white. "Thank God. He's going to be all right."

Her baby cried out again, louder, fear and pain bright in his voice. Sterling gasped and wrapped her arms around herself, fighting the onslaught of tears.

"You mustn't worry," Aunt Imogene said, shuffling her feet to tuck her little purple velvet slippers under her skirts. Apparently she'd come running when they'd come for her and never had time to get properly dressed. "Worrying means something could go still more wrong, and that can't happen."

Yet another, weaker cry crept under the closed examining-room door to tear at her heart. She looked accusingly at Aunt Imogene.

"No, dear," her aunt said, her head shaking even more than it usually did. "Silence would be worse."

"What do you think is taking so long?" Ethan Morrow asked, jumping to his feet and beginning again the pacing he had stopped only moments before. His white shirt, so crisp and clean in the mercantile, was now stuck to his body, rings of sweat stretching beneath his armpits and down his back. He swiped at his upper lip with a red handkerchief and mumbled something under his breath about *sweating like a damned animal.*

"Well," Mr. Eastman said, "I'm sure that the doctor has to check for broken bones and—"

His wife laid a hand on his arm and shook her head slightly, silencing him. Either she thought it was bad luck to state the obvious or she was trying to protect Sterling from the truth. "He's doing what needs to be done to make sure that the boy will be fine," she said with so much conviction Sterling almost believed her.

No wonder Sissy Eastman was nearly a legend in Van Wert. On the rare occasions when Sterling had done something exemplary with Worth (like that time when they'd made it to church in the worst snowstorm Ohio had seen in thirty years), she'd hear the women comparing her to Sissy Eastman. "Sissy'd have brought her charges," they whispered.

Of course, she hadn't the moral fiber of Sissy Morrow Eastman, but the town didn't know that when they made their kind comments about how good Sterling was, how helpful, how she was always the first to bring a basket to a needy family, the first to loan a book to a convalescent, the first to forgive a transgression.

And she had tried. Glory-laury! How hard she'd tried. Now it seemed she'd fallen short yet another time. Her father had told her she would. Had laughed at her when she'd said she'd take care of her baby better than her father had taken care of her.

But Cyril Phillips was never wrong, and this time Worth was paying the price.

As if to prove it, he cried out again. Inside her, fear tightened her heart, as it did her fists. Ethan Morrow crossed in front of her once more, his leg brushing against her gay striped cotton dress in the small confines of a room meant for two or three. She could smell his fear, pungent and manly, and he gave her a lopsided grin as if to apologize for it.

It seemed to her that he had a lot more to apologize for than the odor of his guilt. A man did have an obligation to look where he was going, didn't he? She might not be the best mother in the world, but there wasn't one woman in that crowd in front of the mercantile holding on to all of her children when that man's wagon had started to move. It could have been any one of those children, his own niece or nephew, that he'd hit.

Horrified at herself, she realized that she wished it had been. There were so many of them. So many children and sisters and brothers.

And she was all alone.

He marched back again for a second pass, his boot tip touching hers, the sound of his blue jeans whistling in the room as one leg passed the other. A short while ago she'd been standing in a store with Worth, denying him a bicycle he wanted desperately, and this man had interfered. He'd butted into their lives and then like a whirlwind he'd gone and blown them all apart.

If one of them had to suffer, why couldn't it have been he? Why wasn't he the one lying on the doctor's table instead of a baby who still willingly shared his cookies with the ants?

How had she ever thought he could be Sir Glad-I-am? He was just as reckless as the members of the young women's sewing circle had declared him while they quilted for the poor. He was just as wild as the ladies of the women's auxiliary all clucked as they prepared food for the sick. She'd thought them all gossips and she'd bent to her work and kept to herself. But hadn't he gone and proven their claims?

Hadn't he?

Her nails bit into her palms. Her bottom lip was raw. And still he paced back and forth, back and forth, a useless sentry outside the chamber of the crown prince. Each pass brought him closer and closer until, in an effort to avoid his brother-in-law's outstretched limbs, the black knight's leg hit hers. Before she knew what she was doing, she raised her fists and began pummeling his side.

Her hand hit his hipbone, his belt, his ribs. Her knuckles burned and she opened her hands and swatted at his chest and arms. Each blow cracked the silence in the room and embarrassed her, but still she didn't stop. And blow after blow, smack after smack, he just stood there, until she exhausted herself.

When finally she looked up at his face, he was staring down at her sadly, steeled to accept more punishment in the event that she wasn't truly spent. Covering her face with her hands, she swallowed a silent sob.

"Well, that's what you get for driving a rig on the sidewalk," Aunt Imogene said in the hushed silence that followed her outburst.

"I beg your pardon, ma'am?" Ethan Morrow's voice was very low, and there was a hoarseness that sounded as though his throat was clogged with tears.

"The sidewalk, young man," Aunt Imogene repeated simply. "Everyone knows you can't drive a buggy on the sidewalk. Why would they have built roads if—"

Uncle Oliver interrupted her. "Imogene dear, the roads came first. The sidewalks were built for the protection of pedestrians and to keep ladies' hems clean."

"Yes." Imogene sighed. "That's my point. That baby should have been safe on the sidewalk, but this young man purposely ran up on the sidewalk after him and . . ."

The black knight didn't say a word. Didn't deny it, didn't defend himself. Neither did his sister or her husband. Maybe they all just thought it wouldn't do any good to explain things to someone as crazy as Aunt Imogene.

Or maybe they were just waiting for Sterling to admit her guilt.

Well, she hadn't been the one to run over her son. She hadn't been driving a wagon with her head turned

clear around so that she couldn't see where she was going.

A whimper slid under the examining-room door, and
Sterling twisted in her seat and bit her knuckle. Damn
them all for making her be the one to tell the truth.

"He wasn't on the sidewalk, Aunt Imogene," she admitted reluctantly. "But if Mr. Morrow hadn't been so
busy with his own family, he might have noticed someone else's."

"Oh, I quite agree," Aunt Imogene said. "We can't
have young men driving their wagons on the roads in
Van Wert if children are going to run there, can we?"

"I should have been watching where I was going."
His fists clenched and he smacked one against his thigh.
" 'Cause I'm sure as heck not going anywhere now."
Mr. Eastman stood and put an arm around his brother-
in-law, attempting to lead him to a chair. Shaking his
head hopelessly, Ethan Morrow jerked away, then
seemed to realize he had nowhere to go.

As if going somewhere with the junk in his wagon
could have made a difference in anyone's life. Her son
was crying in pain on the other side of the door, and
this man was bemoaning a little trip.

"Indeed," Aunt Imogene said, looking as indignant as
her nearly five feet permitted. She took a shallow breath
and then another, and Uncle Oliver jumped to his feet
and started stroking her arm while studying her nervously. All they needed now was one of Aunt Imogene's
dreadful asthma attacks. Sterling and her uncle watched
her aunt. The Eastmans and Mr. Morrow watched
them.

With each breath shorter and more frantic, her aunt
continued with her tirade against the black knight.
"How you managed . . . to hit that tiny . . . child
and miss . . . dear Sterling is . . . a miracle. . . .
Imagine if . . . they'd both been . . . hurt!"

Sterling helped her to a chair while Uncle Oliver fumbled with his jacket flap until he could pull out the

small vial of bromide of ammonium from his pocket, open it, and wave it beneath her nose. With exaggerated slowness he breathed in and out, setting a rhythm for his wife to follow.

All that the rest of them could do was breathe in unison with her uncle, as if their collective breathing could fill her aunt's lungs with air.

"Should I get the doctor?" Sterling asked, taking a step toward the examining-room door.

Her aunt shook her head, working to control her breathing. "Not that idiot. Besides, Worth needs him," she managed to get out as her gasping subsided and silence once again filled the room so that they could wait in peace for the doctor to tell them whether the world would ever be right again.

As if in answer, a weak cry came from beyond the door. Like some sort of vine, it wound around Sterling's heart and squeezed her lungs with guilt until, like her aunt, she could hardly breathe herself.

"I can't stand this." She mumbled the words and found it impossible to drag her gaze from the closed door behind which her heart and soul lay battered and broken.

She'd been barely sixteen when Worth was born. He was the first and only infant she had ever taken in her arms, the first truly innocent and honest soul she had ever beheld. If he so much as sighed in his sleep, she was bereft.

Now he lay on a sterile white cot in the next room, and all she wished, with every fiber of her being, was that she could take his place, bear the pain for him, even die for him if it came to that.

*　*　*

Ethan was afraid to close his eyes again. All he could see was that tiny little body, all dressed up in navy and white, lying in a crumpled heap in the road, Buckshot's hooves dancing just inches away from his still form.

He'd taken his eyes from the road for only a moment or two. He'd been so happy to see James coming to say good-bye that all his attention had been focused there, and now the little blond boy was paying for it, instead of him.

And the boy's sister. Jeez, he'd always thought she was pale, but now she was whiter than his bedsheets. In just the way Sissy had taken care of him, this young woman was a mother to her little brother. And just like Sissy would be, she was in true pain for the boy.

So, for that matter, was he. But then, he knew well that that was what responsibility was all about.

A hundred times he'd heard one of his sisters wish she could take the pain for this child or that. Poor Della had wanted to die for Samuel. And, five years later, she was still asking the skies over his little grave why God hadn't taken her instead.

He knew just by looking at her that Sterling Phillips was promising God her very soul if he would spare her brother's life. And he had no doubt that she'd gladly serve tea to the devil himself if it would spare her brother a moment's pain.

And selfish bastard that he was, Ethan couldn't help but wonder what this accident would do to his own plans, his own life. If the boy was fine, it was one thing. And if he was . . . well, he refused to even think about that. But what if this was one of those slow-to-recover things? He couldn't stay in Van Wert indefinitely.

Hell, if the kid didn't recover, and quickly enough at that for him still to get to Oklahoma, he might just as well take that rifle back from Sterling Phillips and use it on himself. His life would be over anyway.

He'd never hurt anything in his life. He was a farmer—he brought life from the soil, tended his crops and his animals with equal care, went to church on Sunday, and gave his nieces and nephews piggyback rides. He'd always asked for so very little out of life.

Until now. Now he was praying with all his might for

a life he hardly knew. The life of a three-year-old. It was such a small life. Was that so much to ask?

Yet another moan slid under the door like a personal note addressed to him, and the woman who sat curled in the chair across the room seemed to draw into herself even farther.

"That's it!" he said, unable to just sit by, listening to one Phillips child suffer, watching another. "Come on." He pulled the girl up by the arm gently, afraid one good stiff yank might break her in two.

"What are you doing?" she asked, not really fighting him, but not eagerly following him either.

He nodded toward the closed door. "Going in there." He tried to read her face, but its perfection hid her wishes. "You coming?"

"But Dr. Cobb said we were to stay out," she said, following him so closely that he could feel her breath against the back of his neck.

"You always do what you're told?" he asked, and saw the first bit of color pinken her cheeks. It made her even prettier, if that was possible.

Of all the girls in Van Wert, she was the only one he could never manage to work up enough nerve to call on. Oh, her money would have been reason enough, but those looks and that fine air about her . . . she was so far beyond his means that he hardly even dreamed about her. There was nothing a girl like her could see in a man who lived in a barn and couldn't get the dirt out from under his fingernails, so what would have been the point?

And if this morning had gone the way it was supposed to, she'd have been a distant memory. The girl he should have at least asked to dance, to kiss, to . . .

He put his ear to the door just as one last mewl put them both over the edge. Cracking the door open, he slid in, pulling Sterling Phillips behind him.

Cobb, a white apron covering a brown plaid suit, looked up and frowned. Behind him were several open books, the thin pages flipping in the breeze. Ethan hadn't been in these offices since Dr. Prill had retired. Now blank squares of brighter white, each one with the nail still sticking out at an angle to mark where Dr. Prill's certificates had hung, were the only decorations on the walls. In the corner a plant stood dying.

"Sorry," Ethan said, putting up one hand. "I know you think it's best for the boy if you see him alone. Only thing is, he's gotta be a little scared. And so's she." He paused and then continued honestly. "Heck, I am, too, if you want to know the truth. We'll stay out of your way, but we're staying."

The little boy on the examining table moaned for his sister, and she gasped at the sight of him. Ethan surely didn't blame her. Taking up only a fraction of the cot, he lay still beneath the white sheet, his tiny head swathed in a bandage, his bloody clothes in a pile on the floor.

"Ster!" the little boy called, his voice raw with panic.

Fear crossed her features for a second, but she buttoned them up behind a mask of calm that Ethan couldn't help but admire. He worried that she'd bite right through that soft lip of hers before she finally got herself composed and took up a place across from the doctor.

"Haven't you done enough, Morrow?" Corny asked. "Don't forget who's in charge here."

Before Ethan could lift the man off the floor by his lapels so that he could look him in the eye, Sterling cleared her tear-clogged throat.

"Please, Dr. Cobb?" she asked softly.

Good old Corn-on-the-Cobb took his sweet time considering the request before granting it. Ethan marveled that the man was so full of himself that he could even consider refusing so fine and fragile a woman anything. If she were to ask Ethan for anything at all in that newborn-kitten voice, he'd find a way to do it.

"Oh, baby," she said, her hand hovering over her

brother as she looked for somewhere to touch him without causing him pain. "Do you hurt?"

The little boy's eyes rolled back and closed.

Being a farmer, Ethan had seen his share of harsh things—the slaughter of pigs, the paws left in fox traps, the accidents equipment could cause. But there had been nothing in his life that had prepared him for this moment. He clutched the foot of the examining table and fought the nausea down.

"He comes and goes," Cobb said, and Ethan found that he could breathe again, if uneasily. "It's a concussion to the brain. The books say that if he's alert when he's with us, there's reason to hope."

"Honey lamb?" the girl asked softly, and Ethan watched the child struggle to open his eyes. "Can you hear me?"

The boy smiled tentatively, though his eyelids still refused to lift. But the smile was enough, and Ethan's sigh filled the room.

"You're gonna be just fine," he reassured the child. Maybe he just needed to hear the words himself.

"Don't jump the gun, Morrow, the way you always do. The boy's got extensive injuries."

The child's eyebrows flinched, and any relief Ethan had felt evaporated like the dew in June.

Corny looked up at Ethan and backed away until he didn't need to tilt his head. Lord, the man didn't have an inch on Sterling Phillips, and she was a tiny bit of a thing. "It's not just the concussion to the brain. As I said, he seems to be holding his own with that. It's his spine that worries me. We're talking paralysis here. I want you to understand that from the outset. It's a question of duration—"

Ethan couldn't let the man finish. Not in front of the child, anyway. They weren't in the schoolyard anymore, but Corny was still a master of saying the wrong thing at the wrong time. Only, Ethan couldn't shut his jaw now the way he used to then.

"This little buckaroo'll be just fine," he said in as strong and steady a voice as he could fake.

Laying a hand on the sleeve of Cobb's plaid jacket, he added more quietly, "And it doesn't seem there's anything wrong with his ears, Corn pone, so I know you'll agree with me and give the boy the comfort he needs. Ain't that right?"

The man looked down at Ethan's hand on his sleeve. He waited until Ethan released him to answer. "They say impetuousness is a disease of youth. Something a person should outgrow." He studied Sterling Phillips as though he were waiting for her to agree.

"Don't put on airs with me, Corny Cobb," Ethan said, gripping the examining table so hard it moved several inches. "Not now."

"Then don't threaten me." Cobb realigned the table with the dust marks on the floor. "Not ever."

Silence filled the room, magnifying a sob from the little boy. Corny patted Sterling Phillips's hand. "Time will tell. It's the best I can offer. The best any doctor can offer. That in time—"

"Heck, anything worth getting is worth waiting for." Ethan moved closer to the child, leaned down near his ear, and whispered, "Like a nice red all-steel, coil-sprung velocipede with rubber wheels, huh?"

"I don't believe there's such an item of frivolity in this boy's future," the doctor said with the same grim expression he'd worn since he came home from medical college.

"Well, then, I think you'd better practice up on your tea-leaf reading," Ethan asked. "Because I think you haven't got it quite right. Just tell me who I take him to to get him fixed." He bent to pick up Worth's bloodied clothes.

"There is no place to take him." Corny's exasperation was as plain as a pikestaff. "The boy needs a hospital, and Van Wert hasn't got one."

"But we've got other doctors," Ethan said, handing

the clothes to Sterling Phillips. "Which one can help him best? Since you can't."

Corny narrowed his eyes at the girl. "You think there's a better doctor in town, *Miss* Phillips? If you do, be my guest. But I can't be responsible for what happens to your *brother*."

She stroked the hair away from her brother's brow with a shaky hand. "Could someone else help him?"

"I think not," the doctor answered with all the arrogance that his diploma and the respect of a small town gave him. "I did my training at the New York Post Graduate School and Hospital four years ago. You want someone who learned their stuff in '73? Dr. Prill, who was cutting off legs for the Union?"

"If there's a chance that someone else . . . ," she began, but stopped when the doctor put his hand on her shoulder.

"There's no one else," Dr. Cobb said softly, looking the girl up and down, stopping at her bodice and slowly working his way up to her eyes. "Didn't I help you before?"

Ethan did not like Benjamin Cobb, hadn't liked him as a boy, didn't like him as a man. Had silently cheered when Etta Hanes suddenly and without explanation had thrown him over and given herself and the proceeds from that fancy house of hers on Chestnut Street to Clyde Dow.

Three years older than Ethan, there'd been a time when the good doctor had fairly towered over him, terrorized him. Cobb had a way of making veiled threats with a smile. Charlie and Bart had told him it was his imagination, and it had taken Ethan years to decide whether or not Corny was actually threatening him at all.

During those years Ethan had grown, taller and taller until now he was sure to be the first to know when Corny started losing his hair. Not that everyone but a few women and most of the children weren't taller than him now. It was just a matter of degree.

And with every inch Ethan grew, so did Corny's resentment. When the girls began to prefer Ethan, even though Corny was older, richer, and smarter, too, Corny had gotten mean and ugly. His threats were clearer, and they always involved those who couldn't defend themselves, such as Ethan's sisters.

It was Ethan who had put the slight bump in Corny's nose that people said gave his face character.

Corny put one of those stethoscopes against Worth Phillips's chest. "I've been his doctor all along. I know his history. He's safe with me. There's no one else who can do anything for him."

"I'll take him to Doc Randall's," Ethan said, trying to move Sterling out of his way so that he could pick up the boy and get him to someone who knew how to hope.

"No," Sterling said, blocking him with a poor excuse for a hip. Lord, but she was tiny! "Dr. Cobb will do what's best."

"Yeah," Ethan agreed. "But for who? He's already as much as written the kid off."

"I've done no such thing." Corny tucked the covers up under the boy's chin. "I merely said that a velocipede was premature. Though I suspect time will bear me out and that intellectual pursuits may very well be more within his potentiality."

"And I say that every kid ought to ride a three-wheeler." Ethan crossed his hands over his chest, knowing that the muscles in his arms would strain his shirt.

"Not every one," Corny said, looking down at Worth. "Some will develop their minds instead." He tapped the end of his stethoscope against his palm.

"Fine, if that's what he chooses." Ethan pointed at the child on the table, whose drowsy eyelids sagged. "But this one wants to ride, and damn it all to hell but he will!"

Sterling Phillips looked from one man to the other and shook her head sadly, dismissing them both. "Do you hurt?" she asked the little boy.

"I've given him something for the pain already," Corny said, gloating at Ethan, who remembered the good doctor kicking him in his lower back as a boy and claiming to know where it hurt most. Despite the fact that it was twenty years ago, Ethan still couldn't forget.

"I want someone else to see him," Ethan said to Sterling Phillips, one hand on her upper arm.

She looked at the doctor before answering. "No." It was simple and to the point. "He's my responsibility and I want him to stay here."

"Look," he explained, "this is all my fault and I just think I should have some say in his treatment."

"First you run him down and then you want to tell me, and my doctor, how to take care of my own flesh and blood? Are you insane?"

He supposed it would seem that way to her. He shrugged, maybe admitting that he was, a little, but said, "Nah. I'm just a bit stubborn."

"I'm stubborn, too," the little boy piped up groggily. Ethan had thought he was asleep. "Right, Ster?"

"Does it hurt you very much?" she asked him, holding on to his hand and leaning down to put a kiss in his palm, then bending his fingers closed around it.

"I got it," the child said. "I won't let go."

"Not till you fall asleep, honey lamb." Two tears coursed down her white cheeks and teased the corner of her mouth until a small pink tongue came out and captured them.

In the waiting room, Noah and Sissy probably heard Ethan's swallow.

"Not even then," the boy said, his voice barely a whisper. And then his eyes closed and his breathing became even.

Keeping his own voice low, Ethan asked, "Don't you

think your aunt and uncle ought to have some say in this? Aren't they his guardians?"

"Is your uncle here yet?" Corny asked, looking toward the doorway and seeking out Oliver Harrington's face.

Mr. Harrington extricated himself from the crowd of onlookers. He came forward a step or two, but stayed well away from the table where his nephew lay. Behind him, Imogene Harrington stood on tiptoe and looked over his shoulder.

"How bad is it?"

"Head injuries are tricky things," Corny said. Ethan tamped down his temper, reminding himself that Corny had always been smart in school. He'd been a great student, exemplary. Somewhere, though he'd obviously not gotten around to hanging it up, there was a diploma that said he knew a damn sight more than Ethan. "Hard to tell just how extensive the damage is. He loses consciousness, but he comes back each time."

"Isn't life ironic?" Oliver Harrington said. He stayed in the doorway, shaking his head, apparently afraid to venture into the surgery. "Well, as long as he keeps coming back," he added.

"There are no guarantees, but he doesn't seem a candidate for coma. I suppose I could be wrong, but I highly doubt it. I've checked all Prill's books to be sure. But in cases like this it's hard to know what the biggest worry is." Corny ran his hands through his thick dark hair—which Ethan noticed with some disappointment wasn't thinning—examined his shoes, and then looked straight at Ethan. "But we've got another situation as well."

Ethan thought calling the medical problems of a three-year-old boy *situations* was not just clinical but callous.

"Watch," Corny told them, and returned to the boy's side, where he pulled back the sheets from Worth's little legs and ran his finger on the bottoms of the boy's feet.

Instead of the natural laughter or squirming that would be expected, the boy just lay there. Hiding what he was doing from the boy by holding up the sheet, the doctor took a thin needle from a tray near the examining table and ran the point against the boy's leg.

Again there was nothing.

"Flaccid paralysis," he said, casting an eye toward his books.

"Flaccid?" Ethan asked, but Corny ignored him and asked a question of his own.

"Permanent?" He shrugged in answer. "I'm afraid that's likely. There is a small chance it could be a concussion to the spine. There've been cases in the literature where recoveries have been reported. More likely the cord's been severed."

"No," Ethan said, grabbing the testing needle and stabbing his own palm with it. "It ain't severed."

The pain in his hand radiated down to his fingers and up to his elbow and he didn't know what he was trying to prove when he stabbed himself a second time and then a third. "Whatever it takes. You understand me?"

He hoped they did, because he didn't really understand himself. All he knew was that until the boy could feel it for himself, he would feel the pain for the child.

They all just stared at him. He felt the girl's scrutiny along with the others' and dismissed it. People like the Harringtons were always writing him off as some know-nothing farmer who was lucky to get his own shoelaces tied each morning. And that was before they'd had a reason to dislike him, before he had run their little boy down in the street. They had no reason to believe that his resolve could move a little boy's legs any sooner than it could move a mountain.

And, he thought bitterly, they were probably right.

"How soon before he can be moved?" Mr. Harrington asked, still shaking his head at Ethan as if there was a damn thing Ethan could do to turn back the clock, make it morning again, and put himself halfway to

Oklahoma before Worth Phillips and his sister even got to Charlie's store. Didn't the man know Ethan would give up his dreams to do it? Now he'd probably give them up anyway and not spare the boy a moment's agony.

Ethan heard himself groan, and Corny, assuming the pain was something he could treat, grabbed his hand, examining the thin trails of blood on his palm that seemed to spell out his future—a road map to nowhere.

"Well, this was foolish," he said as if he hadn't expected anything else.

"Permanent?" Ethan asked, then made a fist. "I think not."

"*Think?* I didn't know you did that," Corny said with a bored look on his face, which Ethan decided to ignore. His personal problems with Corny Cobb were just that—personal. They had nothing to do with little Worth Phillips.

"What happens now?" he asked, gesturing toward the boy on the table.

"Oh, yes," Imogene Harrington said. "When can we take him home? We can't go to California without Worthie, can we, Oliver?"

Oliver Harrington rolled his eyes.

"Are you giving her the medicine I prescribed?" Corny asked him.

Mr. Harrington patted his wife's hand. "It makes her very tired," he said apologetically.

"And dopey," Mrs. Harrington added. "I have enough trouble with that without the medicine. I have to be ready to leave at any minute. Don't I, Oliver?"

"Not just this minute," he said gently, looking everywhere but at his nephew's still form.

"But soon," Imogene Harrington said, ignoring her husband's hint. Her head shook slightly whenever she spoke, and her hat feathers seemed to dance around her face and make her look even more confused than she undoubtedly was. "We're moving out there, you know—to my vineyards. It'll be ever so much better for my health. Isn't that right, Oliver dear?"

Oliver Harrington studied the tips of his hand-stitched fancy gent's button gaiters as if he expected them to take him somewhere and he was just waiting to see where that might be.

"Moving? Really?" Corny seemed wholly disinterested.

"Well," Oliver Harrington hedged. "Perhaps someday, dear."

"California," Ethan said, allowing himself to taste the word on his tongue. As far west as a man could go and keep his trousers dry.

"Oh yes," Imogene said, her nod setting the feathers around her face flapping like a bird having trouble taking flight. "You know my dear Oliver has always wanted to grow grapes for wine. . . ."

"Never mind about that now, dear. We've Worth to worry about."

Imogene Harrington's face fell, terror filling her big violet eyes. Ethan looked again. Her eyes were purple!

"Oh, but the young man said he'd be fine." Imogene pointed at Ethan, obviously confused. If it was up to him, the boy would be—but of course if it was up to him, the accident would never have happened in the first place and he'd be merrily on his way to the Territory. "Won't he be fine?"

"I think it might be best if I kept the boy here for the next few days," Corny said, refusing to answer the woman's question.

Well, Ethan thought, that about settled it. He could just forget about the Territory. After the doctor's bill he'd be lucky just to keep his wagon. And that of course assumed he was right about the boy ever walking again.

At least she wasn't going anywhere either.

He didn't know why that gave him solace. Maybe, he thought, it was just that if he was stuck in Van Wert, then she ought to be as well. Wasn't what had happened just as much her fault as his?

Worth moaned in his sleep, his pale eyebrows coming together in pain, and Ethan tasted the sour bile of guilt as it crept up his throat and threatened to choke him.

This was all his fault, his and that white goddess who was blinking furiously and biting on her lower lip.

And even if they'd never meant to sow the wind, it was still that poor little boy drifting off to sleep who was reaping the whirlwind.

Chapter Three

"He's working himself to death," he heard Sissy tell Noah as he let himself into the house. Pulling himself erect, which wasn't easy since even the layer of grime that covered him was heavy, he headed straight for the kitchen.

"Supper's almost ready," she told him, letting her gaze take him in from his sweaty hair down to his dirty shoes. "You've got time to wash up and rest for a few minutes."

He closed his eyes for a second, long enough to feel the exhaustion fight to win out over the need to press on, and shook his head. "Could you just butter up a slice of that nice bread I smelled baking this morning? I'll take it with me and eat it on the way over to the doc's."

"You're not planning on skipping dinner?" Noah asked him. "What'll that accomplish except to put you in the bed next to that child's?"

"You see options I don't?" Ethan asked his brother-in-law. "That mooncalf doctor's bill adds up every day, and unless one of those vines I got on the wagon grows money, I don't know how else I'm gonna pay him."

Sissy came over and sat down heavily in the chair next to Ethan. She looked nearly as tired as he felt. Her honey-blond hair was tied back loosely and her tan skin looked gray with exhaustion. Still, when she smiled at him, she was the most beautiful woman on earth.

He supposed she'd been doing more for herself the last few days, what with him hauling ice for Mr. Hertel, cutting limbs for Mr. Hatch, patching the roof for Mrs. Weller, and spending every spare moment he had at Corny's place with the boy and his sister.

"You all right?" he asked her. "You haven't been hoeing or doing the milking, have you?"

She shook her head and smiled shyly at Noah. "He doesn't let me lift a finger. I'm just tired, that's all. What about returning some of the stuff you've got loaded on the wagon? Charlie'd give you your money back and—"

"I'm still going!"

He hadn't meant to shout, certainly not at Sissy. He was quick to apologize and to lower his voice, but it was too late. He'd already awakened the baby, and with a sigh his sister pushed herself up from the table and headed for the children's room.

"How's the boy doing?" Noah asked when they were alone.

"No change," Ethan admitted, keeping his voice down so that Sissy wouldn't hear. "Doesn't feel a thing. Little legs just hang there, doin' nothing. Cobb's doing nothing, too."

"Does he give him any hope?"

"If I can just find some night work after I finish repairing the Wellers' roof, then I could stay with the kid for some part of the afternoon, and maybe I could . . ."

Noah shook his head and rose to check the pot on the stove. "If money could fix the boy, don't you think that Oliver Harrington would see to it that it was done?"

"I'm the one that's got to do this." Ethan said. "I'm the one that made him lame, and I'm the one that's gonna make him walk. And then I'm gonna get in that wagon and finish what I started."

"Now you're the good Lord himself?" Sissy asked him as she came into the room carrying their youngest, Isabella, slipping the little girl into a high chair and handing her a wooden spoon to play with. "Even He only worked six days and allowed Himself a bit of rest on the seventh."

"He didn't have bills to pay." Ethan got up and made his way to the sink to wash up, stopping to kiss the top of Isabella's head, still damp from sleep, and inhale the scent of baby he'd come to treasure. That awful itch tickled the back of his throat again. Every time he took a moment's rest, it was there. Every time he put down the ice pick, or the hammer, or the shovel, no matter how hard he tried to push the thoughts away, he saw the boy in the street and both of their lives shattered all to bits.

"Gotta go," he said as casually as he could, hoping the rush of water from the pump would cover the cracking of his voice. "You gonna fix me up some bread?"

"How much time are you gonna save eating it on the way over there?" Sissy asked, reaching for a plate and spooning up some stew onto it. No matter what his heart and mind said, his stomach still grumbled and his mouth still salivated at the smell. She shoved the plate at him and grimaced. "Eat it standing up if it'll make you happier."

"Stop punishing yourself, for Christ's sake," Noah said, and winced when Sissy glared at him for swearing. "People make mistakes, Ethan. The best ones learn to live with them."

"What does it look to you like I'm trying to do?" Ethan asked. "I'm facing my responsibilities and you're complaining about it. I don't know what more I could do."

One thing was for sure. He couldn't run out. Guilt wore off slow, and he suspected that responsibility never did.

"You could ease up on yourself," Noah said. "No matter how hard you work, no matter how much pain you feel, it's not going to change a thing."

"It has to," Ethan said, finding Sissy's meal uncharacteristically tasteless and putting down his plate. "Or my

life is over. If only I'd been watching where I was going. . . ."

"Or if that sister of his had been watching him," Sissy
added, finally giving voice to the thought Ethan had carried within him from the moment he'd seen them
sprawled in the street. "If you're so eager to place
blame, what about her? Wasn't it her job to watch after
that child?"

"Why, Annie Morrow Eastman," Noah said, using
her given name as he always did, "that's the most uncharitable thing I've ever heard you say. Doesn't anyone
in this house know what the word *accident* means?"

"I know she's a good woman," Sissy agreed reluctantly. "Probably one of the best. But if she'd been
watching him—"

"She never takes her eyes off that kid, from what I've
seen," Ethan said in Sterling Phillips's defense. "Told
Jimmy Brent she couldn't go dancing with him 'cause of
the boy. Never sees any men because she's always busy
watching that baby."

"Well, she wasn't watching him last Monday, was
she?" Sissy asked, putting the remains of Ethan's stew
between two pieces of bread and wrapping it in a napkin. "Look what this is doing to you, Eth. You can't take
all the guilt. If you need to place blame somewhere,
then blame her for not watching the boy."

Ethan took the sandwich and kissed his sister on the
cheek.

"Thanks, honey, but I'm afraid her shoulders are too
darn small for all that blame. I'll just have to hold on to
some of it for her."

There was no point in reminding his sister that he
was the one driving the wagon and his was the horse
that had crippled a little boy.

He knew it, and that was more than enough.

* * *

"And the cook said, 'Oh, but Princess Sugarlips. I am so busy,' " Sterling said as she sat by his cot in the doctor's infirmary trying to get one more bit of soup into Worth's closed little mouth.

"But she could help," Worth suggested, and slammed his mouth shut again just as Ethan Morrow showed up at the doorway.

"That's right," Sterling said, nodding politely at him despite the fact that he was the last person in the world she wanted to see. He sauntered over and took the spoon from her, Worth opening his little mouth widely for him and swallowing greedily.

"So then the cook wouldn't play with her?" Ethan Morrow asked as if he cared.

"Oh, Cook always lets her help," Worth told him between spoonfuls. "Right, Ster?"

" 'Well,' the cook said, 'I do have to make some Madelines,' " Sterling said, wiping Worth's chin. "Now, Princess Sugarlips wasn't a very good cook, you know," she reminded Worth, who giggled and reached for a small cracker.

"The princess can't do anything so good," he told his new best friend, while outside a dog howled and scratched at the window.

"I think he wants to hear the story," Mr. Morrow said, rising and opening the window a crack. "Happy now, you stupid mutt?"

The dog woofed and then was silent.

"So then what did the princess do?" he asked, spooning the rest of the soup into Worth's mouth.

"Well, she followed the instructions to the letter," Sterling said, hiding a smile.

Worth smacked his forehead. "Oh no!" He dissolved in a fit of laughter.

"I'm missing something," Mr. Morrow said, looking from Worth to her and back again.

"The 'structions say *whole* eggs!" Worth explained.

"And *cup* of flour," Sterling assured him.

"And a *spoon* of 'nilla!"

By now they were laughing as much at Ethan Morrow's bewilderment as at the story of Princess Sugarlips and her passion for following things to the letter.

"Don't tell me," Mr. Morrow said. "Shells and all? Cup and all?"

Worth pounded the bed. "Good thing she wasn't making nut cookies!"

"But when it came time to serve the cookies," Sterling said, watching as Ethan Morrow pulled out yet another article from the newspaper and held it out to her, "Cook had substituted the world's best madeleines. . . ."

"And the queen probaly said she never tasted madeleines so good as the princess's," Worth continued, as Sterling glanced over the article without losing the thread of the story. "Because she thought that everything the princess did was perfect, didn't she, Ster?"

"Mm-hm." Glory, but that man just didn't give up. Each day he came, that hopeful look on his face, that guilt stooping his shoulders. Each day he asked her to let him bring in another doctor. He showed her another book about miracle cures. And he handed her yet another article like the one she was looking at now.

"What do you think?" he asked, producing a rock from his pocket for Worth, but directing his question at her.

It didn't seem to matter how many times she told him that Dr. Cobb said it was useless. He still wanted her to hope, and to place her faith in him.

And Dr. Cobb wanted her to face reality and trust in him.

Having lived in fantasies for as long as she could remember, she knew all too well that they brought only temporary respite from real agony.

"You know, a cowboy can start a campfire with a rock like that," he told Worth, studying the stone with her son as if it had great value instead of none at all.

It was a shame, an awful shame. But despite Ethan Morrow's warm smile and the gibberish he was feeding her son along with his supper, it was Dr. Cobb, who spent his nights in a chair beside hers, reading aloud from *A Tale of Two Cities*, in whom she'd had to put her faith.

After all, she was too old to pretend, and life was too hard to allow her any more imaginary rescues to castles in the air. In the end no one really lived happily ever after, and it was time she faced that one hard fact.

She closed her eyes and let the man she had mistaken for a knight tell Worth about cowboys and cooking and anything else while she took a moment's rest. She was tired. Too tired to face yet another argument with him about Worth's treatment. Daydreams and pipe dreams frightened her. Hope frightened her.

"Doctor check him?" he asked, startling her. "Oh, were you asleep?" He'd thrown back the blankets from Worth's legs and was cupping one of his calves in a strong, suntanned hand.

"Of course the doctor checked him," she said, jumping to her feet and trying to replace the covers. Didn't he think she would make sure her baby was being cared for? Did he think that just because she was maybe a tiny bit afraid of Benjamin Cobb she'd risk her son's well-being by placing him in the doctor's care? Not ever, not for anything. She'd ride down Chestnut Street Lady Go-diva–style with Hawthorne's scarlet *A* sewn to her skin before she'd let Worth go untreated. Of course, Ethan Morrow didn't know any of that. All he knew was that Worth still wasn't well. "He checks him twice a day, like clockwork."

Benjamin Cobb, she'd learned, did everything like clockwork. He ate, slept, and worked by the clock. Each patient was allotted exactly twenty-five minutes. He saw patients on the hour and the half hour and his nurse cleaned the examining room in the five minutes that were left over. Each night he sat with her from eight to nine, put on tea, and came back from nine-fifteen until ten, when he bid her good night and went up to bed.

"Don't," she said as Ethan Morrow pulled up the covers once again and studied Worth's legs as if he expected them to suddenly start swimming across the sheets.

"I'm getting so tired of fighting you," he admitted. "What are you afraid of? That his feet'll get cold? Be the best damn news I've had all week."

He turned his attention to Worth, massaging her son's calf gently. "So, when you're better, which would you rather learn to ride, a horse or a bicycle?"

Maybe there was something in the town's drinking water to account for it. This man was every bit as crazy as her aunt Imogene. Hadn't he heard a word that Dr. Cobb had said?

Still, there was no denying the light in Worth's eyes as he considered the options as though either were really open to him. Finally his face was split by his delicious grin, a grin she hadn't seen in five long days.

"Both!"

"Well, you're a greedy little thing, aren't you?" the man said, lifting Worth's leg and kneading the muscles rhythmically. "Okay. Which would you like to learn first, then?"

"You're not supposed to do that," Sterling said. "Dr. Cobb says that he should be kept perfectly still." Though in truth she couldn't see what harm it could do. If the cord was severed, as the doctor thought it was, then it was too late to do it damage. And if it wasn't . . . She was afraid even to hope.

"So, the bike or the horse?" he asked her son, ignoring her.

"I hardly think he needs to make that choice right now," Sterling said, wondering how the man could convince himself anything good might come from this tragedy.

Maybe it was that nothing bad had ever happened to

him before, so he couldn't believe that now it had. She remembered feeling that way when she lost her mother—that it simply wasn't true, hadn't happened. But it had, and it was only the beginning.

Now the only thing that surprised her was that she hadn't seen this accident coming.

"I think you should stop," she said. *Stop making promises to him that aren't in your power to keep.*

"Isn't there something you could be doing now?" he asked her.

"A bicycle like the one at Hanson's," Worth said, apparently still considering the question.

"Red?" As if the biggest problem they faced was what color bicycle her baby wanted. "They come in black, too, but I've always fancied the red one myself."

"Red's my favorite color."

Ethan Morrow looked up at her, his jaw twitching. "Why don't you go for a little walk?" he suggested to her. "Stretch your legs."

"Why are you trying to get rid of me?"

"Me?"

She almost laughed. Even Worth could lie better than he could.

"I'm not leaving."

"Suit yourself," he said, pulling a needle out from the collar of his shirt. "But stay out of the way."

"Oh, no," she started. "Dr. Cobb says that—"

"Dr. Cobb is a fool," Ethan said. "A pompous ass who won't listen to reason. How am I gonna tell another doctor what's wrong with the boy if I don't know where he feels and where he doesn't?"

"What doctor?"

"I wrote to my brother-in-law in New York. One of his boys was hurt bad in a carriage accident last year, and Francie swears that the doctor saved his life."

"You want to take Worth to New York?" The thought chilled her to the bone. New York was her father's home, his territory. When she left, she'd vowed never to go back. Of course, if it would help Worth, she'd walk there . . . barefoot . . . in the snow.

"He called Charlie this morning at the mercantile. The doctor needs to know just where the feeling ends, whether he can feel hot or cold or pain, a bunch of things." He pulled out a carefully folded piece of paper from his pocket and handed her the list his brother had written.

"Well, Dr. Cobb tested him this morning and could probably tell us most of this. I could get him. He's just next door. . . ."

Mr. Morrow reached out and grasped her arm gently. "I don't trust his tests. It doesn't seem to me that Corny wants him to get well. It will mean that I, some know-nothing farmer, am right, and he's wrong."

"That's a horrible thing to say," Sterling said. The doctor was doing everything he could and more. Despite the fact that he held out no hope. None at all.

"Can I test him?"

She nodded.

"You want to go for a walk so that you won't have to lie to the doc, should it come up?"

"No. I just won't tell him."

"Sin of omission?" he asked, dismissing it with a shrug and then turning his attention to Worth, who was looking out the window. "Okay, so about that bike. Ah, I see you've met Honesty. Think you can make him jump?" While her son made faces at the dog, Ethan ran the needle down the inside of his leg.

"How?" Worth asked, unaware that Ethan had touched him at all.

Disappointment painted Ethan Morrow's face, from the over-bright eyes to the tight line of his lips. Sterling hadn't expected her baby to feel anything. Not really. But if miracles happened, she thought they must happen to men like Ethan Morrow, who worked and prayed so hard to make them real. Who believed in them so strongly.

"Like this," Ethan said, making a motion with his hand and guiding Worth's arm to copy it. The dog jumped up by the window and yipped. "That's just right," he said, a big smile plastered on that face of his.

It was a nice face, devastatingly handsome, even when he was obviously so tired. But no smile, however winsome, was going to restore the use of her son's legs. As Dr. Cobb had warned her, it was better to face it sooner than later. Nothing was crueler than false hope.

"What about my bicycle?" her baby asked. "When can I ride it?" He searched first her face and then that of the man with all the promises.

"That's a good question," Mr. Mrrow answered, stalling for time. "Are you a fast learner?"

"Tomorrow?" Worth begged.

"Mr. Morrow," she said, fighting the tightness in her chest that threatened to cut off her air. "May I see you outside?"

"It's not a good idea," he warned her, shaking his head. "I'm tired and hungry and we all might be better off if I just stayed right here."

"Not all of us," she said tightly, throwing her glance toward Worth, who no doubt had visions of velocipedes spinning through his head.

She held the door open for him, assuring Worth that she would be right back and getting the distinct impression from her son that he was much more interested in Mr. Morrow's return.

"I know, I know," he said when they were outside on the doctor's porch. "You think it would be better not to give the boy any hope at all. Is that it?"

He was studying his hands, picking at callouses and scrapes, and she couldn't help but wonder how they had gotten so damaged. Probably from forcing his way into other people's lives.

"Dr. Cobb says that the chances of Worth ever walking again are slight." Actually he'd said "virtually nonexistent," but had hedged some when she'd been unable to stop her tears. "I think, considering that, it might be best if you didn't come here anymore."

"I'm sorry," he said sadly, jamming his hands into his pockets when he caught her staring at them. "About what happened, mostly, but I'm also sorry that I can't just go for my sake. As long as he's stuck, I'm stuck. And I guess as long as I'm stuck, you're stuck with me. Believe me, lady, I'd sure like to tuck my tail in between my legs and run the heck outta here. But there are some things you just can't run away from, no matter how fast you go or how far it gets you."

"So you keep coming here to make yourself feel better, no matter what it does to us. Do you have any idea what you're doing? At night I reconcile myself, and in the morning back you come to eat at my resolve. Don't you think you've done enough? You've crippled that poor little baby, and now you're making promises to him you can't keep. I can't let you."

"But you're resolving the wrong thing. Don't you see that?"

It was hard to see anything lately when days melted into nights and all of them were laced together with disappointment.

"I see a well-educated, caring doctor who tells me that my son will never walk again. And then I see, grasping at straws, the man who made him lame and who can't face the truth of it. But no matter how many bicycles you promise the boy, you can't change the facts. You crippled that boy for life." She dabbed at the corners of her eyes and pulled herself upright. "That's what I see. What is it you see?"

He pushed himself off from the porch rail on which he'd been leaning, and towered over her. "Look, I warned you. I'm tired and not in a good mood, so you better just back off, missy."

She took a step closer. He had quite a nerve, yelling at her after what he'd done. "The truth hurts, doesn't it?"

He shook his head. "The truth is just the truth. It's a

lie that hurts. Have you thought about if Dr. Cobb's wrong, Silver?"

Silver. The nickname had died along with her mother. And Silver, the young girl with the hope and dreams, had died soon afterward.

"Have *you* thought about if he's right?"

"No," Ethan Morrow said without apology. "I refuse to consider the possibility."

"I suppose it doesn't fit in with your plans. Do you have this miracle recovery on some sort of timetable so that it doesn't interfere with your leaving? You are planning to leave, aren't you?" She knew he was. His wagon was still piled so high, she'd have had to be clear back east in New York City to miss it.

"I'm not leaving until the boy is fine. But then, lady, all you're gonna see of me is my dust, I'll be outta here so fast."

"Well," she said, "now I've got two reasons to keep praying for his recovery. Even if it *will* put you out of your misery."

His eyebrows came down slightly, highlighting the stunned look that covered his face. "You want to see me suffer?" he asked with such incredulity it embarrassed her. But the man seemed to have no concept of what he'd done. Maybe he just wasn't listening when Dr. Cobb had spelled it all out.

"You ran the most important person in my world down in the road. All our dreams are gone. He could be crippled for life. Have you thought about when he's fifteen and he's still got a diaper on him? Have you thought about what he'll never be able to do? How does it feel to know it's all your fault?" She crossed her arms over her chest. "Now are you so sure you want to go back in there and promise him a bicycle or a horse?"

He closed his eyes and sank down onto the glider on Dr. Cobb's porch. His Adam's apple bobbed slowly as if he was having great difficulty swallowing. He licked his lips, sucked in a breath, and seemed ready to say something, but stopped short.

Finally, in the softest voice she'd ever heard a grown man use, he said, "I know you want to believe this is all my fault. I know some piece of you needs to hold on to that. But"—he looked up at her with honey-colored eyes that glistened with tears—"do you really, in your heart, believe that?"

"You ran him over, didn't you?" she demanded. She wished she'd never asked him to come outside, wished she'd never said aloud the things that frightened her most about Worth's injuries.

There was something different about the way he looked at her then, a coldness that sent shivers down her back despite the warm May breeze. "And what were *you* doing at the time, Miss Phillips? When you should have been watching after the boy? If my memory serves, weren't you standing there in front of Hanson's Mercantile, just gawking at me?"

There was no excuse for it. He knew it the moment the words were out of his mouth, even before her lip began to tremble. He'd warned her he was tired. He'd warned her he was in no mood for a chat on the good doctor's porch.

But damn it all, he'd never meant to say those words aloud.

Lord, he was afraid to touch her, afraid even to speak. She looked as though a breath in her direction would crack her into a million pieces right there on the doctor's porch. Each breeze that caught her hair seemed strong enough to knock her over.

"Ethan?" The little boy's voice drifted on a breeze to them, a plaintive, lonely call.

"I wish to God you'd used that rifle," he said before going around her with enough room for a Conestoga wagon to fit between them.

"Ethan?" the little buckaroo called again, the plea

hanging in the air like some chicken feather, drifting from one of them to the other with no particular speed.

"Can I go see what he wants?" He turned back to her, as though suddenly it mattered how polite he was.

She nodded, nearly imperceptibly.

"Can I tell him you'll be in soon?"

Again, the slight nod, the difficult swallow. Lord, he'd never seen anyone fight so hard not to just break down and cry. So much pride, and all of it on his account. Her efforts cut at him more deeply than any amount of tears could ever have.

"There's a place," he said quietly, turning the knob to the door, "just to the back of the shed. Because of the creek no one can hear you cry from over there."

One tear escaped from the corner of her right eye.

With a shrug that he hoped told her it was no big thing, he added, "Just thought you might want to know."

Chapter Four

It was late when Sterling finished tucking Worth into his own bed. Late, and hot. She thanked Abigail for helping to get the boy settled and told the maid to get some rest. Then she finally sat down in the chair beside Worth's bed, opened several buttons of her shirtwaist, and began fanning herself and Worth.

"Good to be home?" she asked, grateful to be there, where she could relax and enjoy enough privacy to let the lace of her camisole show. It had taken the doctor a week to decide that there was nothing further he could do at his infirmary, and he'd finally, reluctantly, allowed her baby to come home.

"You gonna finish my story?" Worth asked her, examining the tray that Abigail had brought up for him, picking the green beans off the plate and burying them in his napkin.

"Where were we?" Sterling asked, pretending not to see what he was doing. She didn't like green beans any more than he did.

"The princess was all lonely after the queen died," he reminded her.

"Oh yes. She was very lonely. And made to eat her vegetables." She winked at Worth and pointed at his chicken. "Now, with her mother gone the maids were too busy pleasing the king to play with her."

"What about the gardener with the peenies?"

"Oh, it was the queen who loved flowers. And of course Princess Sugarlips. But the king had no use for them, and he banished the gardener and the gardener's whole family."

"Even the children?" Worth asked. He was barely picking at his chicken.

"You've got to eat something, sweetheart," she told him, slathering some honey on the tiny bit of chicken.

Worth ignored the food. "Where's Eth?"

"You mean Mr. Morrow?"

"Right here, buckaroo," he said, breezing into the room as though he had a right to be there. "Sure was surprised to find you gone from Cobb's."

"You can't just walk in here whenever you please," Sterling told him, pulling her blouse closed and furiously buttoning it with fumbling fingers.

"Warm night," he said, turning his back and looking out the window while she straightened up this and tucked in that. Even with his tanned skin she could see the red creep up his neck. "Sorry about bursting in."

"What are you doing here, anyway?"

He turned around and his gaze locked on her buttons, then slowly rose to meet her eyes. A gentleman would never have made it a point to study her blouse. Neither would a knight. She supposed it was the first thing a cowboy would do. Not that it mattered. She'd bade good-bye to her fantasies, and a good thing too.

"May I see you in the hall?" he asked, gesturing with his head. Then to her son he said, "Back in a moment, Buckaroo."

"Where's the dog?" Worth asked, peering around Ethan.

"Lazy thing's home sleeping," he answered. "I'll bring him next time, if that's okay. Or maybe it's not such a good idea, with Mrs. Harrington's condition?"

"I suppose it's not." It was considerate of him to think of her aunt. "I'm sorry, honey lamb," she told Worth.

"The view from the window's not bad," he said, coloring again. "If we moved the bed a little, he could watch the dog outside."

Sterling came to the window to see. It was dark out, and the light inside the room was reflected in the glass, turning it into a wavy mirror. Worth's eager face was clear enough, as was the bedpost by which she'd been standing. She imagined that Ethan had gotten an eyeful. Some Sir Glad-I-am she'd picked.

"I see," she said with her arms folded over her chest.

"Yeah, well, so did I."

At least he couldn't look her in the eye.

"Why did you say you were here?"

"Oh yeah," he said, taking her arm in his warm hand and maneuvering her to the door. "Honesty tomorrow," he promised Worth before they both left the room.

In the hall he put his hands in his pockets and looked down at her.

"Well?"

"Spoke to Graham's doctor friend in New York this afternoon," he said, searching her face to see if she remembered him telling her that he planned to call him around three.

"And?" Beneath the folds of her sleeves, she crossed her fingers even as she told herself not to hope, not to listen, not to dream. Dr. Cobb had warned her that despite Ethan's promises, there were no magic potions, no wizard's wands that could help her son.

Ethan shrugged. "He says he's good, but not that good. Wouldn't even try a diagnosis over the telephone."

"Oh." Her fault, she thought, for hoping. She should have listened to Dr. Cobb.

"But he also said that a child as young as the buckaroo still has soft bones, and that that works in his favor."

"Oh?" Dr. Cobb didn't know everything.

Don't hope! Don't hope! Don't hope!

"And that sometimes there's swelling from the accident that makes it seem worse than it is."

"And if the swelling went down?"

It could. Certainly it could.

"Then feeling and movement would come back."

She covered the smile that she couldn't stop.

"*If* that's the problem." She didn't like the worry his face revealed, the warning his voice held.

"So how can we tell?"

"Your old friend Corn-on-the-Cobb's favorite medical treatment."

He raised his eyebrows indicating that she could guess. Together they said, " 'Wait and watch.' "

"Dr. Cobb says every day that it doesn't come back makes it less likely he'll—"

Ethan shook his head. "Not according to the doctor in New York. He said a year from now the buckaroo could throw his legs over the side of the bed."

"A year!"

Ethan was quick to add, "Or it could be tomorrow. He says the usual pattern is to feel a prickly sort of feeling first, and then maybe like a twitching. Then things would come back gradually—feeling, movement, control."

"And what do we do in the meantime? Just wait?" She wrapped the ends of the ribbon that belted her waist around her finger until she reached the bow, let it go, and started in again.

"We keep watching for any sign that he feels something, and we pray and we hope." He pulled out a carefully folded piece of paper and handed it to her. "We all hope," he said.

She unfolded the paper and found an advertisement for the velocipede Worth had seen at Hanson's Mercantile. Hand-drawn on the seat of the bicycle was a little boy that looked a little, or maybe even a lot, like Worth. The mutt by his side looked just like Honesty.

"I'll pin it up near his bed," she said, clutching it against her chest.

"You know, I never thought you'd be quite so pretty up close," he said, halving the distance between them with one small step. "I mean, I figured you looked better from a distance. That you'd have a pimple, or yellow teeth, or something."

He hit his forehead with the heel of his hand. "I sound like an idiot. I just meant that even up this close, you really are perfect."

She bit at her lip, a habit her father had always hated. He claimed that it was a trait of nervous people with something to hide. And naturally, in her case anyway, her father was right.

"And I like the way you take care of that little guy," he said. "You know, the whole town thinks you're like my sister."

"Della?" Della was suffering from nervous fits, and there was a rumor that she'd taken to drink.

He laughed. "No, not Della. Sissy. The way you dote on that boy like he was your own. Don't think everyone hasn't noticed."

"Mmm," she said, for want of anything better. Ethan was right about the town. All those notes she'd gotten full of good wishes—each of them commented on what a good woman she was.

"I'm glad that if something had to keep me in Van Wert a little longer, at least it gave me the chance to meet you. Now when I'm all alone out in some lean-to on the prairie, I'll have some fine memories to pull out."

So he was still going off to slay dragons. And all of hers were right at home. "When will you be leaving?"

"When the boy can run after me and that stupid dog of mine to say good-bye."

"Then you think he'll get well that soon? I mean, isn't there some deadline on that land?" She knew he was going after free land, and knew that it wouldn't wait forever for him to come and claim it.

"I'm praying I can leave real soon," he said, then touched her earlobe gently with one calloused finger. "I'm glad you don't wear those fancy earbobs. Not that they wouldn't look pretty on you for some special occasion or something. My mama had a pair, I think."

Warmth spread down her neck at his touch. She could smell the lilac water she'd put on earlier come to life and rise from her throat. She worked at breathing evenly. How would it look for her chest to rise and fall beneath his gaze?

"I'm praying you can leave soon too," she said, taking two steps back from him.

"Lord, but you are truly beautiful," he said, shaking his head as if he just couldn't believe it. "Like one of those porcelain dolls I buy for my nieces when they turn four. You even dress like 'em."

"You buy your nieces dolls?" she asked. It sounded like he even picked them out.

"Yeah, well," he said with a shrug. "It's gotten to be kind of a tradition, what with all the nieces I've got. Guess we better get back in there." He nodded toward Worth's door.

"He might be asleep," she said, putting her finger to her lips and opening the door just a crack.

Her son lay with his arms bent up, his little fists near his ears. His head was turned to one side and his thumb shined wet in the near darkness. Ethan peered over her, pressing gently against her back with his broad chest.

"He sure is a cute kid," he said softly, his voice ruffling her hair. "And good too. Like his sister."

"He's being so patient," she said, not wanting to go into the room and risk waking him up, but not wanting to turn and find herself in Ethan Morrow's arms either.

"Well, you told him it's only temporary, and he knows he can trust you." One of his hands rested softly on her shoulder.

"What if it's not true?" she asked, swallowing hard. "What if he doesn't get better and he hates me for lying to him?"

"He'll get better." He made circles with his thumb at the base of her neck, easing the knot that had taken up residence there. "I promise. And I never lie."

She knew she should pull away from him, this near stranger who was pressed up against her intimately. She should send him from her house with her handprint on his cheek, not let him continue to run his hands along the base of her neck the way he was.

But there was nothing to stop her from just leaning back against him and stealing this one moment. Reveling in it.

Nothing to stop her except the knowledge that she would prove her father right yet again.

He'd told her she was nothing better than a common gutter slut, a woman without decency, without morals, without the God-given strengths with which a woman was endowed. He'd looked at her with contempt and disgust as if he had read her very soul and knew that she hadn't simply endured a man's touch. She had needed it. Sought it out.

"Is that better?" he asked, a slight crack to his voice. She supposed it was just that he wasn't used to whispering, coming from so boisterous a family. It couldn't be that he was every bit as nervous as she was. A knight, errant or otherwise, didn't shake in his armor at the touch of a woman.

She nodded, her head tapping his chest as she did.

"I guess I'll be going, then," he said. "I've gotta unload some sacks of grain for Charlie, and it's getting late."

"You work a lot, don't you?" she asked as he gave her room to turn and they headed for the stairwell.

"Much as I can. Nothing's cheap these days except talk."

At the top step she paused. "How soon do you have to leave for Oklahoma?"

"I got a few weeks," he said, his tongue playing with the corner of his mouth.

"Think you'll make it?" she asked, staring at the door to Worth's room.

"I'm a great believer in things working out for the best," he said with a shrug. " 'Course it doesn't seem like they have so far, does it?"

"Not yet."

He smiled at her and touched the tip of her nose. "I like that. *Not yet.* "

"Thank you for the picture," she said, raising it up in her hand.

"It was nothing," he said with a wave.

"It may be the only picture I ever have of him on a bicycle," she said softly, studying the pudgy face he'd drawn, the wide bright smile revealing tiny teeth.

"Oh no, you'll have lots of them. And I'll expect you to send me one when he wins his first race."

She nodded, fighting back the tears.

"I'll see myself out," he said, racing down the stairs and out the door.

She looked down at the advertisement again. The dog appeared to be drooling, but it was her own fat tear that marred the page.

* * *

"Eth." Sissy's whisper startled him and he felt his body jerk. "You're snoring!" she whispered.

"Sorry."

He should have just skipped church. He'd unloaded at Charlie's until after midnight, when Risa had come down and politely asked him to just go home already. At four he was up and mending Noah's back fence so that their stupid cow didn't wind up over at the Webbs' place again. Then he'd milked Harriet, daughter to Harry, the old cow who'd finally dried up a couple of years ago. They all figured they owed her a free meal for making her go through life with the name that Ethan had given her as a little boy.

Little boy. That Worth Phillips sure was a cute . . .

"Eth!" He felt Sissy poke him in the ribs.

"I'm awake," he grumbled.

"Then get up. The reverend's done. Services are over."

"I'm getting up," he said, shuffling toward the back of the church with everyone else. He mumbled "Good sermon" to Reverend Winestock, who raised an eyebrow and said something about how he supposed that God wouldn't frown on resting on the Sabbath. Tessie, his wife, asked after "that sweet little Phillips boy," and Ethan was about to tell her when Dr. Corn-on-the-Cobb answered for him.

"I hold little hope for a full recovery."

"Luckily," Ethan said, squeezing Tessie's hand warmly, "the boy's recovery doesn't depend on the good doctor's hopes."

"Hope has no place in medicine."

"Now, there I'd say we have a difference of opinion," Ethan said, noticing they were gathering a bit of a crowd.

Corny smirked. "Yes. We have my medical opinion, backed by years of schooling and research, versus your scars-itch-when-it-rains experience."

"*My* scars itch when it rains," someone said.

It was Ethan's turn to smirk.

"I've seen hope do a body a lot more good than any tonic," Ethan said softly. "And I've yet to see a medicine that works where there's no hope."

"Carbolic acid doesn't care what you're thinking about when it cleans your wounds. Laudanum will put you to sleep with or without hope. You can hope a boil will go away, but a lance'll work a lot better."

"A healthy man's wife dies and two weeks later you're burying him." He looked straight at Seth Coleman, whose parents had both died last year. "Nothing to live for."

"Maybe the man should have come to see me," Corny said.

"Excuse me, Benjamin," Mrs. Lutefoot said, extending an armful of flowers. Corny would never be Dr. Cobb to her. She'd known Benjamin from the days before Ethan had given him his nickname, and he was Benjamin then, so he was Benjamin to her now. "Might you be seeing the Phillips boy today? I don't want to intrude on them, but I did want to send over these roses. Flowers do so much for a sickroom, and I don't know but they wouldn't cheer up that lovely sister of his, even if she does have the prettiest peonies in Pleasant Township."

"I wasn't planning on going over there today, no," Corny said, his hands in his pockets. "And Mrs. Lutefoot, dear, it's *Dr. Cobb.*"

"Oh, you're not going?" Mrs. Webb said. "That's too bad. I was hoping to give you a note for Miss Phillips. Just wanted her to know I haven't forgotten that lovely basket of sweets she brought over when Gwendolyn had that awful bout with tonsillitis. I didn't think she'd be needing any food, what with Leona Trencher there, but if there's anything . . ." The woman threw up her hands. "I don't know what I can do for her, but I'm willing."

"He's not going?" someone else asked. "That's too bad. I wanted him to bring them some lemons my son sent me all the way from Florida! What a lemonade they make."

"Well, I suppose that I could check on the boy," Cobb said, studying the faces of the people who surrounded them.

"Such a lovely young woman," someone said. "And so good to that brother of hers. It's a wonder some gentleman hasn't snatched her right up."

"Wouldn't she be a feather in some man's cap?" Risa

said, nudging Ethan with an elbow. "Pretty, wealthy—a good woman all around."

Someone held out a small stuffed bunny, someone else a card.

"I think I will check on that little fellow," the doctor said. Ethan could smell the wood burning in the furnace of Benjamin Cobb's mind. "I'll take those flowers, Jane. And the note, Paulette. Anyone else?"

"You can bring her a message for me, Corny," Ethan said. "Tell her . . ." He was going to say something about pulling the shades, but people might start thinking things they shouldn't. He was going to say he would be over later, but he didn't want to start tongues wagging.

"She's quite loved, isn't she?" the doctor admitted when his pockets filled with notes and small tokens for Sterling and her little brother. "I had no idea."

"I think you've got one now," Ethan said, sticking his hands in his own empty pockets and turning away.

"Did you give her the advertisement?" Risa asked, her hand rubbing his back lovingly. He had given her some piece of paper ripped from a catalog as though it were some sort of gift.

"She liked it very much," he said, wondering what she'd really thought. "Thanks."

"You going over there today?" she asked. "I could throw a few things in a sack for the boy—a sucker or two, a few toy soldiers."

Jane Lutefoot's bouquet filled the doctor's arms, the stuffed bunny dangled by the ear from one hand. Cobb was wearing a handsome suit, even if it was plaid, fancy leather boots, and a smug grin.

Well, he supposed that Sterling Phillips could do a lot worse than to marry the town's most successful doctor. At least she and the buckaroo would be in safe hands. Cold safe hands. Clinical safe hands.

Still, they didn't have callouses to catch on her silky hair, or dirt to mar her perfect skin. Ethan imagined that the living quarters above the doctor's infirmary were more than adequate. Everything Benjamin Cobb had was more than adequate.

"No," he told Risa. "I don't think I'll be going over there today. I've got too much to do to get ready to go."

* * *

"Flowers?" Sterling asked as Dr. Cobb came into the parlor, nearly hidden by the bouquet of roses he carried. "For me?"

"From Jane Lutefoot," he said, handing them to her and brushing the bits of leaves and debris from the front of his suit before smoothing his mustache, pulling at the ends until they stood just so. "I suppose I should have thought to bring some myself."

"Really? Do you always bring flowers to your patients?" He hardly seemed the type to bring them to his own grandmother on her birthday. He didn't seem the type to even *have* a grandmother.

"Certainly not. But then you aren't one of my patients, anymore, are you?"

"No." She felt him stare at her breasts, and crossed her arms over them.

"I trust you're fully recovered," he said. "From . . . before."

"Yes." He seemed to be trying to find the breasts she had come to him with, engorged with milk, several times the size they were now.

"Good. Then it's all behind you." He studied her hair, her eyes, her nose. Any minute she expected him to pull out a wooden stick and look down her throat.

"Do I have spots?" she asked, touching her hands to her face.

"Spots?"

"You're staring at me like I've a new disease you haven't seen yet. Or like I'm someone you've never met."

"Don't be silly. It's just that you've changed a lot

since . . . since I had a good look at you." He took her hand and appeared to be examining her fingernails.

"You've seen me every day for over a week. Ever since the accident. And I can't count the number of times you've had dinner with my aunt and uncle."

"Well, yes of course. Technically I've seen you, but I've been concentrating on your . . . *brother*." Every time he said the word, he paused, then emphasized it as if to remind her that he knew the truth.

"And I suppose it's Worth you've come to see now. You know, Mr. Morrow feels that he needs more exercise, but he's so tired all the time. He was just napping now, so I came down here for a little change of wallpaper."

"Mr. Morrow, huh? Well, naturally I do want to see the boy. But I've come to see you too." He pulled a small bunny out from his jacket pocket and laid it on the chinoiserie table. "For the boy," he explained, and pulled out a small bag, several envelopes, and a globe that snowed over some sort of animal. A deer, Sterling thought.

"What is all this?" she asked, peeking into the bag and pulling out a string of sugar-candy crystals. "Did you—"

"Mrs. Webb. Or was that Mrs. Whelan? The notes are from Paulette Goodwin and several of the other ladies. I'm afraid I didn't really pay attention to who was thrusting what in my face. And of course, this is from me." He felt in his pockets, patting one after the other. "What did I do with—"

Sterling tried to hide her smile. With the greatest difficulty she could just barely picture the very proper, highly formal doctor surrounded by women trying to use him as a messenger, Jane Lutefoot towering over him, Mrs. Webb half a head taller.

"You think it's funny, do you? That a man who prides himself on his dignity, his imperturbability, stood flustered in front of the entire congregation of the Pleasant Township Methodist Church?"

She couldn't control her lips, and the smile had its way.

"I think it's funny that anyone could pride himself on his imperturbability," she admitted apologetically. "Especially while carrying a rabbit in his pocket."

"You have a lovely smile," he said. "I don't remember seeing it before."

"Well," she explained, "you do have the habit of coming into my life at the most awful of times." She twirled the ends of the ribbon that encircled her waist.

"You do seem to have the most awful of times," he said, stilling her hand.

"Well, every life has its winter along with its summer."

"Yes, but yours has had a blizzard or two, hasn't it?"

"Spring comes every year, and I have to hope that it will come again." His hand still lay on hers, and he began to trace the fine blue lines that crisscrossed her tendons and knuckles. Then he ran his pointer over the third finger on her left hand.

"You know, I'm not keeping company with Etta Hanes anymore," he said, drawing an imaginary band where none existed.

"That's good," she said, a silly little laugh escaping without her permission. "Since she's married now."

"Well, yes. I suppose she is. In fact since I know your dirty little secret, I'll tell you mine." He said it so quietly that she thought for a moment that she had just imagined it.

"My what?" she asked when she could find her voice.

"I put that poorly. Forgive me," he said, patting her hand. "I only meant that you made a mistake, and I came very close to making one as well."

She pulled her hand away and rose, knocking the flowers to the floor in her haste.

"I've upset you. I'm sorry. I only meant that you can trust me. I've kept your secret, haven't I?"

She refused to look at him and busied herself with the fallen flowers.

"I have, haven't I?"

She stopped and looked up at him from where she crouched on the floor. "Worth is not a mistake. He's a child. My child."

"Well," he said with a shrug, "Etta was a mistake. I was lucky to find out before it was too late."

"I thought Etta was the one to call off the wedding." She placed the flowers in a pile on the table and perched on the edge of the couch, not altogether sure she wanted to sit any too close to a man who felt about her child the way Dr. Cobb did.

"Everyone thinks that. I allowed Etta her pride. I didn't know what else to do, considering the circumstances. After all, it didn't reflect well on me either."

"Didn't reflect well? I'm not following you."

He studied his hands and spoke without raising his eyes to her. "How would it look to the town if, with all my keen intelligence and schooling, she'd still managed to put one over on me?"

"Put one over . . . ?" Sterling asked. Was he saying what she suspected he was saying?

"Look. It's one thing to live in a house that was paid for by another man. It's a fine house, after all, worth quite a bit, and she swore the rest of it was behind her. I'm not one to point a finger. You know that better than anyone. But then, after all her promises to the contrary . . .

"Well, I'm a doctor, after all. No one's got to draw a diagram for me to follow, or shove a calendar under my nose so that I can count the weeks. And raising another man's child is a poison I simply refuse to swallow. Why should I?"

"Did Etta tell you she . . . ?" She let the words trail

off. They were too hard for her to say, sat too close to her own heart to let them pass her lips.

"Tell me? That's a laugh. Not with all she had to lose if I knew. But I'm a doctor. I know a woman's body. There are signs. In a woman's eyes, in the shape and feel of her—"

Sterling cut him off. "So then she's carrying." It was more statement than question.

He shrugged, palms up, as if the truth was too obvious to bother uttering. "I'm not one to carry tales. Again, you know that better than anyone. But I'm not blind, and I don't see why I should be expected to close my eyes when someone else was making deposits in her bank and the dividends weren't likely to be mine."

"But if she's . . . well, wouldn't it be your dividend? I mean your . . ." She left the thought incomplete at the shake of his head.

"So then it's Clyde's. . . ."

Again he shook his head.

"I knew all along our wedding night wouldn't stain the sheets. That was clear from just one look at her, my being a doctor and all. Still, her past was no business of mine. Some women are weak. . . ."

"Did you say you knew just from looking at her? A doctor knows if a woman . . . ?" she asked, feeling her cheeks redden at the thought that they could tell, just by looking at her, that she had sinned.

"A good one can. Women are easy to read. Sometimes the shadows under their eyes tell the whole story." He looked meaningfully at her face while she fought the urge to run to the mirror.

"Etta had shadows?"

He raised his hands. "What can I say?"

"Maybe she just wasn't getting enough sleep."

The doctor laughed. "I'm sure she wasn't, sneaking out with her very dear old friend."

"Well, if she was sneaking out, it must have been with

Mr. Dow, mustn't it? I mean he married her, didn't he?"

"Oh, no doubt she'll try to make him think it's his. With any luck it'll be small and she'll claim the bastard came a month early. I'm sure that was her plan with me when she tried to move our wedding up. When that didn't work, she must have figured Clyde would buy what I wouldn't. And then there was that nice house for an incentive. It's a shame, really. Etta's a sweet thing, but weak.

"Still, to pawn off someone else's by-blow . . . And to Clyde Dow? You'll never convince me that a man like Clyde—a good, upstanding farm boy—was seeing Miss Etta behind my back. No. And even if he was? Make no mistake about it, sugar plum—there isn't a farmer in the world that would make an easy woman like that his wife."

Sterling fumbled with the roses, gathering them into her arms. "I'd better get these in some water," she said, then felt the prick of a thorn in her finger. "Ow!"

Dr. Cobb took the flowers and put them down once again on the table. "You really should have been more careful," he said, pulling out a hanky and dabbing off the tiny dot of blood. "But I can fix it."

Chapter Five

Ethan tiptoed into the buckaroo's room slightly winded from the long staircase at the house on Washington Street. What a house, if number 204 could even be called that. That one little family could inhabit such an enormous place amazed him. The boy's room alone was bigger than Noah and Sissy's parlor. And all done up in yellow shiny stuff he supposed was silk or satin.

In the center of an enormous four-poster bed, Worth was propped up between half a dozen or so pillows, and Sterling Phillips was curled up next to him, moving little metal figurines around on his tray as she spoke.

"So Princess Sugarlips tried to tend the garden herself, but she was forbidden from climbing the ladders, or getting her royal dresses dirty, or touching the royal shears."

"So the garden kept growing and growing," the little boy said, holding one figure atop another and one on top of that. "Higher and higher."

"That's right," she said. "Until the vines covered all the windows, and Princess Sugarlips could hardly see the sun. And it felt like night all the time."

"I don't like the dark." He squirmed uncomfortably in the bed.

"Well, then I suppose someone will have to come along and help the princess cut the vines, won't he?" Miss Phillips asked.

"Who?"

"How about a knight?" she offered. It looked to Ethan, who was observing all this from just outside the doorway, that she had suggested this possibility before, since Worth shook his head unenthusiastically. "Well, there was the carriage driver."

"Was he nice?" Worth asked.

Ethan wished he could see her face, but her back was to him, and all he could watch was the rise and fall of her small shoulders changing the blue stripes on her dress to ocean waves. "Yes, very. Besides the cook, the carriage driver was Princess Sugarlips's only friend in the palace."

"Did he cut the vines?"

She shook her head. "But he lit lamps in his tiny room and made the darkness go away. Sometimes it even fooled the princess into thinking it was the sunshine that was so warm and bright, but it wasn't."

"The princess was sad," the little boy said. "Wasn't she? Did she cry?"

"This is becoming a very sad story, isn't it?" she said, sitting up and brushing back her brother's hair from his eyes.

"It'd be better if she got a friend," the buckaroo suggested. "Or a doggie."

"Well, soon she had something better than a friend," she said, tucking her feet beneath her. "She had a little prince, all her own, to play with."

"Did he have a doggie?"

"No. He had a wonderful velvet hat with a tall, tall feather. A turquoise feather that swayed in the breeze whenever he walked."

"Not a cowboy hat?" The boy looked disappointed.

"He was a prince, silly. Prince Perfect."

"I bet he wanted a cowboy hat. And a dog." He pushed the figures to the edge of the tray, and one by one knocked them over onto the coverlet, some of them falling to the floor.

"No, he wanted a royal scepter and a crown."

"A cowboy hat and a dog."

"A crown," she said, pushing herself to the edge of

the bed and looking up to find Ethan staring at her at the same time. Her little mouth dropped open and she quickly looked down to make sure that this time he hadn't caught her with her buttons undone, which sadly he hadn't.

"Don't you ever knock?" she asked, straightening out her skirts and covering the smallest bare feet he'd ever seen on a grown-up woman. "Or have yourself announced?"

"That guy in the fancy suit that answers the door—Carl is it? He said to come on up." He shrugged and directed his attention to the pouty child, who smiled at the very sight of him. "Are the princess's cooking skills improving any?"

The buckaroo laughed. "Uh-uh. They don't get better. That's what makes the story funny. You wanna tell a part of it?"

"No, he doesn't," Miss Phillips said as if she owned the rights to this particular fairy tale and wasn't about to share. Or maybe it was that she owned all the buckaroo's affection and that was what she didn't want to share.

And that was too bad, because Ethan had come for a small piece of it.

"Okay, my little buckaroo," he said, finally coming into the room and standing beside the bed. "You're good at stories. How good are you at keeping secrets?"

Worth nodded his head solemnly, and Ethan smiled. He was counting on the boy liking him better than he liked Corny. He didn't think that would take much.

"The doctor play any games with you?" he asked.

"Games?" Sterling Phillips, who had posted herself at the foot of her brother's bed like a sentry, bit nervously at her lip. Lord but she was a pretty one. If he wasn't leaving town just as soon as her brother felt the first prickle, he might offer to bite that sweet lip for her. He did like how she looked with a blush on her cheeks.

"This Little Piggy Went to Market? The Itsy-Bitsy Spider? The Soldiers on the Hill? You know."

"We've been doing Here's the Church," she said, clasping her hands and turning them inside out. "And I know the spider one, but This Little Piggy?"

"You never played This Little Piggy? Not your mama with you or you with the buckaroo?"

She shook her head. "We didn't have pigs. We lived in the city. And we didn't play many games."

He tried not to laugh at her. It was too sad, anyway, to think of someone growing up without games. "These are your piggies," he explained, gripping at Worth's toes through the thin white blanket with the cross-stitched blue bunnies on it. "Look."

He threw back the covers and wiggled Worth's big toe. "This little piggy went to market," he said.

It wasn't funny without the gales of giggles that the child was supposed to make.

He moved on to the second toe. "This little piggy stayed home."

Worth watched him, not even the trace of a smile touching his lips. Sterling Phillips winced.

"This little piggy had roast beef." His free hand traced the boy's sole. That drove Isabella into such peals of laughter they hardly ever got to the last line. The boy just watched him curiously. "This little piggy had none."

"And this little piggy"—he wiggled the boy's pinky toe, so small that his big clumsy hands could hardly grip it—"cried wee, wee, wee, all the way home!" He ran two fingers up the boy's leg, over his belly, and up to his midriff. At the contact with his chest, the boy laughed and squirmed. Ethan tried to laugh with him.

"What's the secret?" the boy asked.

"Well, it's really your sister's secret," Ethan explained. "I'm guessing she doesn't want Dr. Cobb to know that we're playing games here when we ought to be working."

She'd told him the doctor's reservations yesterday, but last night Dr. Cobb had explained it even better. "It's just that he thinks we'll irritate the inflammation. You wouldn't go walking on a sprained ankle to help it heal, would you?"

There was logic to her reasoning. He surely didn't want to be hurting the child.

"Dr. Cobb says that in a few months we might try letting him dangle his legs off the bed."

A few months. Ethan rubbed the sweat from his palms onto his jeans. He couldn't wait a few months. Even a few weeks would cost him the Kickapoo land. Not to mention what would happen to the buckaroo's muscles. Ethan had broken his leg once as a boy. When they'd taken off the splints, the calf was half the size of his good leg. It was still a little puny, all these years later.

"What if the doctor in New York says it's okay? Then will you let me work on his legs?"

"Dr. Cobb says—"

He cut her off. "This doctor in New York is what they call a specialist. Graham told me he only works with people who've been in serious accidents. Ones that have been knocked down or knocked out—serious injuries." He took a deep breath. Somehow he could never manage to mention accidents or injuries without a strong need for fresh air. "Corny goes about lancing boils off the bottoms of rich old men who sit around too much."

Sterling Phillips looked down that sharp little nose of hers at him. "Dr. Cobb is this family's doctor. He's seen us through a great deal, and he can see us through this. I hope."

It was those last two words that told him he'd gotten to her. "He doesn't seem to be having much success with your aunt."

"My aunt is as sane as you or me. She's just had a lot happen to her in her life that's made her . . . eccentric. He can't cure her of what she doesn't have, and her nervous habits are none of your business. So what if she does things differently than most people? Wouldn't the world be a dull and boring place if everyone was just like the Morrow family?" Her hands were on her hips and her chest was heaving. He waited to see if the tirade was over.

When he was sure it was, he said quietly, "I meant that her asthma seemed pretty bad."

"Oh." Lord, he could spend a lifetime embarrassing her and watching the pink crawl across her cheeks. Finally she said, without looking up, "That's the weather."

He'd have polished his shoes if he knew how long she'd spend studying the tips.

"So then she'll be better when you move to California?" he asked, gently rubbing the buckaroo's legs. If there was swelling, the doctor said it would be in the spine. He didn't see how keeping the blood moving in the boy's legs could hurt him, and not doing anything was just eating Ethan up inside.

She kind of half smiled and shook her head. Even that little half smile lit her face. "Moving to California is just my aunt's Princess Sugarlips story."

He liked the way she said that, making the fine distinction between hope and wishful thinking. "Is it that your uncle doesn't want to go? It seems like he practically has those attacks along with her. Doesn't he want to see the Pacific Ocean? To plant his crops in a field where he doesn't have to fight nature for every grape he can get to grow? Wouldn't he like to just pluck a sweet grape off the vine and . . ." For a moment, he imagined the lips that faced him opening for a grape, and lost his train of thought. What was the matter with him? He knew better than to daydream about the likes of Sterling Phillips. "I'm sorry. It's none of my business."

"You really love your work, don't you?"

"No," he said while he massaged the boy's tiny calves with just two fingers. "I hate it. Oh, I like the plowing and the tending and the reaping. And I like being out in the sun, and even the rain doesn't bother me. But the growing season's short, and when I hear the wind howling in the winter, I think it's laughing at me because it's beaten me again. Stolen another year without me getting away." He couldn't believe he'd said that last bit out loud. He'd never told anyone, not even Noah, how he felt.

Lord but a room could go silent. He felt like a fool, pouring out such silly gush to someone who never did battle with Mother Nature, who couldn't possibly understand the stormy marriage every farmer had with her.

"Sometimes," she said softly, "when those first crocuses come up out of the snow, I think they're just for me. I think someone's trying to tell me that spring is coming, everything will be all right."

"Crocuses?" Ethan asked, wondering which ones they were. It would be nice to see something break through the snow and let him know he'd made it through another winter.

"They're little purple flowers," she said. He noticed that she was rubbing Worth's right leg while he rubbed the left. "I suppose that's what they're doing here. Aunt Imogene does love purple."

"I love purple, too," Worth said. "Ster says that purple is what princes like. Do cowboys like purple, too?"

Ethan remembered the story of a gambler who always wore a purple brocade vest. He didn't know exactly what brocade was, but he could tell Worth, with authority, that cowboys liked the color purple.

"Will I be all better when you're done?" the boy asked, moving on to more important matters.

"When we're all done," Ethan said. "But that might take a while."

"Later?" he asked, tracing the patterns the sunlight made on his sheets.

"Did you remember to thank Mr. Morrow for the

picture he made for you?" she asked, pointing to the bicycle advertisement that was pinned to the wall.

"Thank you, Mr. Morrow," the boy parroted.

"I told you, son. You can call me Ethan."

"Or cowboy," the boy added.

It had seemed like a good idea at the time, but now with the girl there, it seemed foolish.

"You do seem to favor cowboys, Mr. Morrow. Why is that?"

"Read a lot about them, I guess," he said and quickly added, "when I was a boy."

"Didn't you ever read about King Arthur and his Knights of the Round Table?" she asked.

He was a barely educated man whose reading matter as a kid had consisted of the little books he could hide under his shirt to both steal and return to Hanson's. He'd only heard of King Arthur once, and from the description, he hadn't considered himself Round Table material. He worked on the boy's legs without answering her.

"Well, I think you'd like the stories," she said, straightening out the little metal figures on her brother's night table. "Not that the cowboy hat doesn't suit you," she said with a nod toward the dresser where Ethan's black secondhand Stetson rested.

"That's probably enough of that," Ethan said, patting each leg and then replacing the covers. "I'll try to talk to the doctor in New York again. See what he says to do next."

"You know, this really isn't your problem," she said, playing with a purple ribbon that accentuated how small her waist was. Lord, he thought his big paws could span it twice. "I know you've got to be leaving for Oklahoma."

"What do you mean it's not my problem? I'm the one responsible for what happened to him."

"Not really," she said. Now she was staring at his boots and playing with that ribbon again. "You were right that I should have been watching him. If I'd been—"

He put his finger against her lips, silencing her. "My fault."

"Even if that were so, he's my responsibility. You've got plans and you've really got to see them through."

"You tellin' the cowboy to leave?" Worth asked. He'd busied himself with a snow globe, stuffed his mouth with candy, and was now busy scribbling on notes written to him or his sister on pretty flowered cards.

"She may not be, but I am."

Pig Feed Cobb stood in the doorway, a small bouquet of flowers in one hand, a box in the other, and a plaid suit that could wake the dead, in case his cures didn't do the trick.

"These are for you," he said awkwardly, holding out the daisies and pink stalks to Sterling. He eyed Ethan and added, "To thank you for last night. It was very enjoyable."

The man had all the subtlety of a brick over the head. If Ethan had really been a rival for Sterling Phillips's attention, it might have bothered him that she'd spent an evening with the illustrious Dr. Cobb. It might have grated at his gut that despite how tired she looked, she hadn't gotten to bed early. Too, it might have rankled that the doctor had thought to bring her flowers, something that had never occurred to Ethan.

But since he had no interest in Sterling Phillips beyond seeing her brother get well and bidding them both good-bye on his way out of town, he let it pass.

Corny put the box he was carrying, marked Goodyear Union Syringe, on the table next to the bed.

"You know what that's for?" he asked Sterling.

She nodded, and blinked furiously.

"Good morning to you too," Ethan said. "How are you, Cornykins?"

"Morrow," the doctor said with a slight nod. "Miss Phillips told me you feel that I'm not poking and prodding the boy enough. More stimulation, she said you recommended. And hope. I'm supposed to be doling that out in bigger doses, too, I understand. Are we practicing medicine without a license now?"

"Why don't you try practicing on someone else and come back when you're perfect?"

Ethan couldn't tear his eyes from the white box with the blue lettering and the small red cross. Just before his father had gone into the hospital that last time, Ethan remembered him telling Sissy he'd just as soon die as have her give him another bag's worth. He remembered him screaming in pain and Sissy coming out from his room, tears streaming down her face as she leaned against the wall and sank to her knees.

"You aren't thinking of using that, are you?"

"There is nothing more important than regularity," the doctor said, taking off his jacket and looking for a hanger as though they came down from the ceiling whenever he needed them.

"Let me take that," Ethan said as he watched Sterling busily pulling back the curtains and fluffing them just so. Just so that his drawing of Worth on the velocipede was hidden in the folds.

Corny handed him the jacket, and Ethan controlled the urge to drop it on the floor between them. Instead he hung it from one of the posters of the bed, wishing the man were still in it.

As Corny began rolling up his sleeves, Ethan felt the slight itch of sweat breaking out on his upper lip. Sterling looked like she was going to be sick.

"Are you sure that's necessary?" she asked him.

"Hasn't been done since I released him, has it?" he asked.

Sterling shook her head.

"And has the need *eliminated* itself?" He smiled at his own cleverness, which was good, because no one else did. Then he looked at Sterling, eyebrows raised, and waited.

"No."

"You must understand," he said. "There are poisons in the body. We call them . . . well, you wouldn't understand anyway. At any rate, these poisons collect in the blood and the organs, and they weaken the body. They could actually kill a person. Since the boy can't eliminate these poisons on his own, we've no choice but to cleanse his bowels. Twice a day. Every day. Nine in the morning. Nine at night."

"You that regular, Doc?" Ethan asked. He knew that he was going to have one heck of a hard time allowing the doctor to force some hard rubber nipple into that tiny child.

The doctor ignored him. "I assumed you have some petroleum jelly? Carbolized would be better, as I suspect that with repetition there will be tears and fissures."

He thought that Sterling Phillips might faint. She was like a clean sheet on the laundry line—bleach white and swaying back and forth.

"Can we put this off one more day?" Ethan asked. "Sissy's got some preparation we used to call blasting powder when we were kids. If it doesn't do the trick by the morning, I'll take care of this myself. All right?"

"I can do it," Sterling said, her voice as shaky as her knees. The constant movement of the blue stripes of her dress was making him seasick. "I've been seeing to Worth since he was born. I don't see any reason for that to change now."

"Gotta change sooner or later," Ethan said, hoping he could spare her this extra pain. "Don't think Noah would take too kindly to his wife still bathing and feeding me."

"Yes, but he's still just a baby," Sterling whined.

"Am not!" The buckaroo's eyes were wide and he clutched nervously at the blanket that covered him.

"Of course you're not," Ethan said, fuming that Corny had brought the damn box in the first place, then had let the buckaroo see it and hear them argue over it.

"Idiot," he muttered, wishing he could take that rubber tube and . . .

"You think I'm rigid, Morrow, don't you?" Corny asked in his own defense. "That I am coldhearted and callous. You, a farmer who kills off the runts of a litter to give the others a better chance. A man who prunes away the saplings so that the tree grows straight. Haven't you ever had to hurt an animal to help him? Would you do less for a little boy?"

He hated Corny for being clinical and unfeeling. And he hated him even more for being right.

"Can we try Sissy's dynamite?" It wasn't easy letting Corny call the shots, but Ethan was a farmer, not a doctor. And a stake wouldn't make Worth Phillips grow straight and tall.

"Another twenty-four hours?" Corny asked, checking Worth's eyes, pressing on his stomach with what Ethan could see was a gentle hand. "Willing to try Mrs. Eastman's medicine?" he asked the boy, who looked trustingly at Ethan and nodded.

"Well, Morrow, you're on. You try your remedy. If it doesn't do the trick, we'll try mine."

"Agreed."

The doctor rolled down his sleeves, refastening the cuffs, and reached for his jacket. "And Morrow, I hope Sissy's dynamite works."

"Yeah," Ethan agreed, his eyes glued again to the white box. "Me too. Thanks, Doc."

"Be still my beating heart!" Corny said. "He called me *Doc*!"

"Don't let it go to your head," Ethan said with a laugh, reminding himself that Corny wasn't the same awful bully from the playground, any more than Ethan or his sisters were the poor victims of his jokes. If they were going to work together to heal the buckaroo's broken body, it was time to acknowledge it.

He walked the doctor to the door and then out into the hall.

"I guess you're not the same kid who got paddled for looking up Risa's skirts," he said, smiling at the memory of where they'd been and how far they'd come.

Corny brushed at his lapels, the wax from his mustache leaving a residue. "No. Now I get *paid* to do it," he said with a wink. "I always was ahead of my time."

"Can you help the boy, Corny?" he asked.

"I can help them all. Just stay the hell out of my way, will you?" He looked up at Ethan as if he was some boulder it was impossible to get around or over.

"I'm hoping to be gone in a few weeks," Ethan said, turning toward the boy's room.

"I'm looking forward," Corny replied, heading for the stairs.

Why was it everyone seemed as eager for him to leave as he was to go?

When he came back into the room, Worth was staring at the box, his fat little lower lip trembling. "Does it hurt, cowboy?"

Ethan nodded. "But it won't hurt you." He looked up at Sterling, her face blurring as he blinked. "You won't feel a thing."

"Why don't you get some rest now, honey lamb, and then we'll feed you a little dinner," she said, putting the box away in a drawer without opening it.

"Ster?" When he pursed his lips like that, he had dimples that went right through his cheeks like someone had tufted them—two tiny dots as deep as could be. And his chin had one long line that he could store his pennies in. The kid was irresistible.

"Yes, honey lamb?" She stroked the white-blond bangs out of his eyes and smiled the best she could, squeezing Ethan's heart.

"Will you stay with me?"

The boy's eyelids were drooping. Ethan supposed he could spare a few more minutes. "Why don't I do that, buckaroo, and give your sister a little time to herself. Looks like she could use some rest."

The girl looked quickly in the mirror, studying the purple smudges beneath her eyes.

"Don't suppose you got much sleep when he was at the doc's," Ethan said.

Pinching her cheeks so hard Ethan winced, she turned the biggest, brightest, phoniest smile he'd ever seen on him. "I did have trouble sleeping," she said with a cheerfulness that belied how tired she was.

"You go ahead," he said, then put on his Stetson, rotated the chair beside the boy's bed, and straddled it. "So, howdy there, pardner," he drawled.

At this rate he was never going to get the Wellers' roof done, never get the doctor paid off, never get to Oklahoma. But then that was life, wasn't it? Too much work, too much debt, and not enough time.

"Howdy," Worth squeaked back, beaming at him. "You bring rope, cowboy?"

"Partner? Cowboy? Buckaroo? What is all this? A private code?" The boy's sister stood with her arms crossed against her chest and her foot tapping like she was sending a Western Union telegram with her toes. If not for the small smile on her face, he'd have taken her for angry.

"Like with the knights, Ster. But better. There's cowboys and Indians and guns and all. And I'm a buckaroo, 'cause Ethan says *honey lamb* is a baby name. He says I gotta be a fighter if I'm gonna get well, and all a fighter needs is a lasso and a good strong name."

"And Worth isn't strong enough?" she asked, directing her question not at the boy but at him. If her eyebrows were raised any higher, they'd be lost in her hairline. She wasn't smiling anymore. Who knew she'd be so touchy about a name?

"Your mama let you choose his name or something?" he asked. "Whatever happened to normal names—like Thomas or Abigail? Sterling's a metal, and Worth— worth what?"

"Worth everything, *Eth*," she answered through gritted teeth. Lord but she could make his name sound like it was one with four letters instead of three.

"Humph," he said, grimacing. "If I was born in this family, I'd probably be named To."

"To?" Worth asked.

"To Morrow," he said with a laugh. "Get it?"

Sterling Phillips rolled her eyes, but he'd put that smile back on her lips. "In *this* family," she said patiently, just in case he was too stupid to follow her point, "that would make you To Phillips."

"Hey," he said, smiling at Worth with just a quick glance at his sister. "Kind of like a Christmas present. 'To Phillips, From . . .'" He'd like to be a present to Sterling Phillips, but if he was honest, he was more like the booby prize.

"Or maybe a sir or a prince," Worth said, looking to Sterling for confirmation. "You warm, Ster?" he asked as her cheeks turned as red as those candied apples Sissy made for the church fair. And as ripe for tasting.

"He's got to eat and he's got to rest," she said, trying to regain her composure. "Maybe some prunes would be good, or—"

"Cowboy'll give me my grub," Worth said, obviously proud of himself for remembering the new word Ethan had taught him. "And he could tell me about those nights on the prairie."

"There were no knights on the prairie," Sterling said.

"Only days?" Worth asked, his nose scrunched up so much half his lip had followed it.

"Nights on the prairie were hardly ever dark," Ethan started. "'Cause there aren't any vines tall enough to cover the moon."

"And . . ." Worth prompted when he stopped.

Ethan knew as much about the cowboy life as any farmer who'd never been west of the Mississippi. Which was to say, he knew fables and tales and had read every dime novel Hanson's ever carried about adventure. They were what had fueled his dreams for the future as soon as he was old enough to recognize that he had none. But he'd be damned if this little boy would be robbed of his dreams, even if Ethan had to tie him to a horse to see them through.

"And they ate their meals there, just like people do here in this nice museum you call a house." He turned to Miss Phillips. "I'll be happy to get him fed. Seen to enough nieces and nephews in my time to have gotten the basics down pretty good."

"We really couldn't impose on you," she said in that same voice Sissy used when she wanted to do it herself in order to be sure it was done right.

"You sure do remind me of my sister," he admitted, though everything about Sterling was more refined, more fragile, more feminine. Something about the whiteness of her skin made him want to keep her sheltered in his shadow. Something about the thinness of her body made him want to make sure to fill her up. Something about those huge blue eyes made him want to appear better in them.

And something about how gentle she was made him ache—low and deep inside him. Ache with wanting and with regret that he was just some farmer without a field to plow, some man without a thing to his name that he could offer her beyond help and friendship. And even if that was enough for her, he was realizing quickly it wasn't enough for him.

"Ster can't make them cookies," the boy said sleepily.

"I hope she doesn't put in the eggshells like Princess Sugarlips," he said. "And I'm sure that sister of yours has plenty of other talents."

He didn't know what possessed him to say a thing like that. He surely couldn't imagine what made him follow it with a wink in her direction. Maybe it was the blush it brought to her cheeks.

Or maybe it was just that he wondered what other talents it she possessed.

* * *

Well, she was a great liar. She was sure Sir Glad-I-am would admire that wonderful talent. And she could pretend better than just about anyone. So what if sometimes the lines blurred a little between the two?

Oh, and she read a lot and knew how to fold paper to make little birds whose wings flapped when she pulled their tails. And she'd learned, thanks to Worth's books and his collection, to tell quartz from mica, and fool's gold from the real thing. Yes, she was a very talented woman indeed.

Of course none of those particular talents seemed to suit the moment, so she plucked from the air the first appropriate thing she could think of. "I studied the violin at the New York Conservatory of Music."

The man's eyebrows rose, though to his credit he resisted smirking. What had ever made her think that was an appropriate response? What value was a little music to a man who fought with the soil for his very existence?

"I'd like to hear you play sometime," he said, tipping her head with a single finger to see the underside of her chin.

It was no wonder Worth wanted this man to lift and carry him. She didn't really understand herself how a touch could be so gentle and yet so firm, like solid silk.

"I don't play anymore." He ran his fingers against her jawbone, feeling for the callus a violinist developed. Hers had finally softened and now was just a memory. "I'm busy running after this one," she said, and then quickly covered her mouth as though she could pull the words back in.

"I bet he'd like to hear you play some while he's mending," the would-be cowboy said, letting go of her chin and turning his attention to Worth. "You know, when cowboys are out on the trail, and they settle down for the night, ain't but a few minutes that go by before one of them takes out a harmonica or a fiddle and starts playing. Cowboys, and knights too, I hear."

"Really?" The boy was all ears and dimples. "Cowboys play on the trail? What about Indians hearin' them?"

"Well," Ethan said. He spoke in a faraway voice like he was remembering a dream. "Life's different out there—freer. A man can dream a dream and make it come true just by putting his back into it."

" 'Tending things don't make 'em so," Worth told him.

"Pretending," she corrected him, wondering where he'd heard that. Certainly not from her.

"There's a big difference between hoping and pretending," Ethan said, his big hands hanging clasped between his knees, the sun glinting on the sun-bleached hairs and giving the illusion they were gloved in gold. "Just like there's a difference between pretending and lying. Pretending never hurt a body, and neither did hoping.

"Maybe you and me ain't cowboys yet, Bucky, but there's nothing stopping us from hoping and wishing. My mama, God rest her soul, used to say that if you wished hard enough and long enough, what you're wanting might just come true."

"I wanna be a cowboy," Worth said sleepily.

"Me too," Ethan Morrow whispered.

But he couldn't be a cowboy, because he was already a knight. Sir Glad-I-am.

And I want to be his lady.

Thank the good Lord she hadn't actually said it aloud!

Making those kind of wishes just went to prove that Benjamin Cobb was right. Wishing would never make it so. And just as some things were better left unsaid, some wishes were better left unwished.

Especially when the one that was being wished about

was two feet away, staring at her as if he could read her very thoughts. She shifted her weight and looked away.

It wouldn't do at all for him to know what she was thinking—not when it concerned him, and how being in the same room with him eased the muscles in her neck and warmed her insides. Not when she'd begun to wonder what those enormous hands that gently cradled her son's head would feel like cradling hers.

She'd worked very hard since the days she'd lain in Henry's arms to make herself into the virtuous woman her mother could have been proud of. She'd done all the things that the good women of Van Wert did, and none of the bad. She'd kept herself locked away in her tower that was Harrington Manor lest temptation rear its ugly head and bite her with its wicked venom.

But all Ethan's kindness and gentleness, all his caring and concern, had tricked her into lowering her guard ever so slightly, a little more each time he came. He was, without question, a very dangerous man, and not just when he was high on a buckboard behind a wild horse.

He rose again and pushed the covers off her son's still-pudgy thighs. "I don't think you're supposed to do that. Maybe you should at least wait until you've spoken to the doctor in New York again."

"I suppose that's fair," he agreed, tiny beads of sweat dotting his upper lip. He put down Worth's leg and wiped his mouth on the shoulder of his shirt. "I'll try to get an answer from him as soon as I can. I don't want those legs weakening from the wait."

That wasn't something Dr. Cobb had mentioned. But then, she had the uneasy feeling that Dr. Cobb was giving up on Worth. He hadn't even checked him earlier, or tested him the night before, even when she'd suggested it. Instead he'd told her it was in God's hands and that a recovery would be a miracle.

Ethan Morrow had said he believed in helping miracles along.

Given both men's assessments, she knew the doctor

was probably right. And more than that, he'd told her
he'd be there to take care of her boy, and he'd implied
that he'd take care of her as well.

But somehow she still couldn't stop her fair knight
from testing Worth's legs, and she couldn't help hoping
when he did. And worse still, she couldn't help her disappointment when Worth failed to feel anything again
and again.

It hurt. It hurt so bad that she wanted to scream and
cry and bang her fists until they bled. Her baby had no
idea that he might not get well. "When?" he'd ask her.
"When can I get up and play?"

"Well," she said now, pushing up her sleeves and
brushing the hair off her forehead. "I've really got to get
this little one cleaned up before he begins to smell like
some barnyard creature."

"Tell you what," Mr. Morrow said. "You let me get
the boy washed up, and I might even take a little birdbath myself."

"A birdbath?" Worth asked, looking eagerly at her for
her permission. There was so little that excited him
these days, so little that could capture his attention, and
she was tired to the bone of entertaining him herself.

Would it really do any harm to let this nice man help
her, just this once?

"Haven't you ever seen a robin take a bath?" He rose
to his full height, which looked quite tall against the
small furniture of Worth's room, and looking wholly
undignified, imitated a bird in a puddle. "Splash a little
water under this wing. Splash a little . . . well, you get
the idea."

And undignified or not, he was one hard man to resist. Especially when Worth smiled at the very sight of
him. Even when her sweet baby had still been too dizzy
to eat and Dr. Cobb didn't want to let her take him
back home, Ethan Morrow had gotten food down him.
And now maybe the man's sister could find a way to
avoid the syringe.

"I'm sure you've someplace to go," she said, offering him a way out and hoping he'd take it.

Not that sending him away helped. Even when he wasn't around, her thoughts were on him. Even in her sleep, he was there. Her dreams were wanton, depraved. She was in his arms, beneath his body, within his soul. If only there was a way to wash a mind out with soap.

But if there had been, her father would have found it.

"It can wait. Why don't you get a little rest while my pardner and I get rid of some of this trail dust, huh?"

She thought of the years she had taken care of Worth alone, diapered him, powdered him, seen him through the croup and three winters of colds, chased a million monsters from beneath his bed and inside his cupboards.

"Yeah, Ster. You go lie down, and me and Eth'll get ourselves rentable."

"That's *presentable*. I suppose," she said reluctantly, "that I could go check on Aunt Imogene." Her son's big blue eyes lit up and there was nothing she could do but relent. She gestured with her head toward the highly polished eight-panel door in the corner of the cheerful yellow room. "You'll find everything you need in the bathroom. There's a basin beneath the sink you can use."

She waited a minute to make sure that Mr. Morrow would find everything he required.

"Hot water on the second floor. I'll be damned!"

"Damned? Oh no, not you," she whispered as she closed the door behind her and headed down the stairs where she could hear her aunt and uncle's voices coming from the fernery parlor.

* * *

"It's very warm in here," her uncle was saying as Sterling entered her aunt's domain. The room was a favorite of Sterling's in the winter when the sun came filtering through the stained-glass dome and the flowers and ferns thrived despite the snow that lay just outside the door.

In May, however, it was hot.

"Oh, Sterling dear! How's Worthie doing this morning? I peeked in on him earlier, but he was asleep. That nice Mr. Morrow says he's got him sitting up every now and then."

"It's quite humid in here," Uncle Oliver said, mopping at his brow with a hanky.

Sterling pulled the collar of her dress away from her neck and fanned herself with her hand. "Have you and Mr. Morrow been talking, Aunt Imogene?" she asked, trying to appear calm. Glory, Aunt Imogene could give away the family secrets as easily as last year's dresses.

"Oh, yes!" Aunt Imogene said. "He's a most interesting man, dear. And I know the two of you will be very happy together."

"Hot, even," Uncle Oliver said, unbuttoning the top button of his celluloid collar and pouring himself a glass of iced tea. "Tea anyone?"

"Happy together?" Sterling asked, wishing Aunt Imogene didn't always draw her into conversations she didn't want to have by making her ask questions she didn't want to ask.

"Of course, dear. Why else would he have hit Worth?"

"Because I wasn't watching, and neither was he, Aunt Imogene," she said, blowing upward at her own forehead in an effort to cool herself.

"Really, Sterling, do you think he would have come into our lives if he wasn't meant to be here? Dear, he's a farmer."

"Damn hot!" Uncle Oliver said.

"Why are we in here anyway?" Sterling asked her uncle, taking the crystal tumbler full of iced tea he extended to her and pressing it against her chest.

"Practice," he said, taking his head in his hands and

then peeking out at her from between spread fingers. "You know. For when we move?"

Of course. They were humoring Aunt Imogene. Why else would they be sweltering in the hottest room in the house in the summertime?

"Aunt Imogene," she said, making an effort to sound as casual as possible. "You haven't told Mr. Morrow anything that isn't any of his business, have you?"

"He's a farmer. What would I know about his business?"

"No, Aunt Genie. *Our* business." If her aunt had told Ethan anything, he'd probably never be able to decode it anyway. Maybe she was the castle spy.

"Who's *our*? You don't mean your father, do you?"

"My father?" Sterling couldn't even say the word without feeling the blood in her veins run to cold and send chills out from her frozen heart. "What would make you mention my father?"

"I wouldn't mention your father," Aunt Imogene said.

"You just did."

"To whom?" Aunt Imogene asked.

"That's what I want to know."

"Know?"

"Then you didn't?"

"You said *no*."

"I said not to . . . never mind, Aunt Genie." If Ethan Morrow had had a conversation with her aunt, he'd never even know it.

Her aunt gave her a wide-eyed, innocent stare. "I'm sure I don't know what you could be thinking, Sterling."

Ethan appeared suddenly at the fernery door, and Sterling's heart lodged in her throat. Had he overheard anything? She reminded herself once again that it wouldn't have mattered.

"I'll be right back in," he said, smiling a little wanly.

"Oh. And if you hear anything—don't pay it any mind."

"What?" Sterling asked, beginning to go after him but feeling her skirts caught behind her. "Aunt Imogene . . . let go, please," she said.

"Let him be. He'll be back. After all, you're going to marry him."

"Oh, Aunt Imogene. Don't you think that poor man has troubles enough? He's had to postpone his trip, and he feels so guilty about what happened that he's nearly working himself to death. And soon he'll be gone because he's going to the Oklahoma Territory and he doesn't have much time left to do it. Della Gibbs told me that herself."

"Oh, that Della Gibbs," Aunt Imogene said, dismissing her as if Della was the one who was crazy. "What does she know?"

"Della's his sister, dear," Uncle Oliver said. "What is that noise?"

"It's a dog, sir," Uncle Oliver's butler, Carl, said, coming in with a fresh pitcher of cold tea. "It's doing some kind of tricks under Master Worth's window, I believe."

"Oh, and we'll even have a dog!" Aunt Imogene said, and clapped her hands together. "Isn't life perfect?"

Worth was upstairs, unable to feel anything below his waist. Uncle Oliver was looking decidedly faint. Sterling was fighting feelings decent women didn't feel about the most decent of men. And Aunt Imogene was getting crazier by the day.

And her comment only proved it.

"Just going to settle him down for his nap now," Ethan said, tilting his head across the doorway so that he appeared disembodied. "Then I'll be on my way for a while. I'd like to be back after supper. I have a feeling Sissy's making him Boys on Crutches for dessert."

"How lovely!" Aunt Imogene responded.

There was no doubt about it, the castle had bats in the belfry and they were tolling the bell for her.

Uncle Oliver, sweating to death while he humored his wife, smiled politely but said nothing.

"Boys on Crutches?" Sterling heard herself ask. Oh, fine! Now he had her asking him questions the same way her aunt did.

"She makes these cookies that have special meaning for whoever's eating them. She used to stick them in custard and we'd have Cowboys on the Range, or Dancers on the Moors, or whatever suited the occasion. When my pa was sick and in a hospital in Cleveland, she used to make my youngest sister Nurses on the Ward. But Noah's little girls liked to save them, and they got kinda messy with the custard on 'em, so she just makes the cookie part now." He turned to leave.

"Don't you think it's a little callous to make him boys with broken legs, or whatever they're called?" she asked, surprised that Sissy Eastman, the *sainted* Sissy Eastman, would be so cruel.

"Heck, Silver—he knows his legs aren't working. And won't it be something when she gives him Boys Riding Bicycles?" He grinned, and took the stairs two at a time.

Well, she had to admit that bicycle cookies beat eyes of newt or whatever magic potion her fantasy might have called for. She gave Sissy Eastman the apothecary's hat and considered the possibility that she was now truly insane.

She figured if she was, Benjamin Cobb would be the first to tell her, so she decided not to worry about it and sat back with her eyes closed for a moment or two.

At some point Ethan was back at the doorway. "He's asleep. That's some boy you've got there, Mrs. Harrington. True to his word. Said if he could just see the dog, he'd go right to sleep, and sure enough, he did."

"Would that he were mine," Aunt Genie said, a far-away look coming into her eyes. Poor Ethan was about to feel awful, and it wasn't even his fault. "Lost seven, you know. All before I ever got to hold them." Her voice was a whisper.

"No, ma'am," he answered her quietly. "I didn't know. Must have been more hurt than a heart could bear. Weren't you blessed, then, when Miss Sterling here and the little buckaroo showed up?"

Sterling held her breath. She'd been so afraid that she and Worth would send poor Aunt Imogene right over an edge from which she'd never return. But her aunt and uncle had more than taken them in, more than welcomed them. In their own odd way, always from a safe distance, it appeared that they treasured them.

"Oh yes," Aunt Imogene agreed. "A blessed event. And so long denied. You know, it's even worse when you get to know them. Losing them, that is. I mean, should that ever happen, I wouldn't want to glue back any more pieces."

"Didn't you have somewhere to go?" Sterling said, trying to save him some discomfort.

But Aunt Imogene, bless her heart, put her hand on Ethan's arm and waylaid him. "You know, we really are going to California," she said as if no one but the two of them were in the room. "It's my land, sure as the business is mine, and it's just waiting there for us to come and plant it. Ask Oliver if that isn't so."

Oliver shook his head at Ethan, all the while saying, "Yes, dear."

"And don't you wish you owned a winery instead of just importing the stuff?" Aunt Imogene asked her husband.

"Yes, dear," he agreed again, but this time he looked rather wistful as he nodded.

"And all it would take is a man who knows farming, wouldn't it?" Aunt Imogene asked.

Oh, Lord! Sterling knew just where her aunt was heading.

"I told you that Mr. Morrow was on his way to the Oklahoma Territory," she said. "And that if he doesn't hurry, he'll probably miss out on the best land. Remember?" She turned to Ethan and knew how sorry she would be to see him go, but how genuinely he deserved it—the land, a good woman, a family of his own. Somewhere there was a Mrs. Glad-I-am, whereas Sterling was only Lady Wish-I-was.

"I suppose I will," he admitted. But for the first time it looked like Ethan Morrow's faith might be wavering. And Sterling didn't like the look at all.

"Oh, but how could he go now, with poor Worth a cripple?" Aunt Imogene asked.

Tears came from nowhere to nestle in her throat, and she barely choked out her words: "Don't call him that."

"And besides, the man hasn't any money," Aunt Imogene added. "Not since he paid Worth's doctor bill."

Ethan had paid her son's bill? She had no idea he'd done that. Men like Ethan Morrow didn't have reserves for emergencies. Lord knew how long it had taken him to save enough money to leave Van Wert. And now it was gone.

Wasn't it enough that she'd gone and ruined her own and Worth's lives? At least when she'd been thrown out of her father's house, she'd managed to protect Henry.

"Well, couldn't you please give him back his money and let him go?" Sterling begged her uncle. If she had one red cent, she'd pay him herself. Again she wondered what her brooch would bring and decided that even if it was the right thing to do, it surely wouldn't be enough.

"Oh no, dear. I don't think so," Aunt Imogene said pleasantly, not understanding that Ethan Morrow had to go—for his sake, for her sake, for everybody's sake. Getting to her feet slowly, her aunt put out her hand to Uncle Oliver. "I think I need a little lie-down. All the heat, you know."

Uncle Oliver rose and accompanied her from the room, Ethan standing by and smiling pleasantly as if everyone he knew was as odd as Sterling's aunt and uncle.

"I'll get you back your money," she told him when they were alone. After all, a farmer deserved a fair maiden just as surely as a knight did. "And then you can go."

Staring at her, he shook his head as if he couldn't quite understand what she was saying.

"I said 'I'll get you the money back and you can go.' "

"I know what you said." He looked at her as if she'd taken down the moon. "You think I'm deaf, too . . . or just heartless?"

Chapter Six

"I can't hear you," Ethan shouted into the telephone that stood in the corner of the mercantile. His ear stung from how hard he was pressing the receiver against it. For three days he'd tried to reach Francie or Graham, and managed to miss both of them every time he called. Now that he had Francie on the line, he could hardly hear her.

"Europe!" crackled over the line.

That he'd heard twice.

"What about Europe?" he shouted back. Risa, standing at his side, parroted his question. She rubbed unconsciously at her belly, which seemed to grow by the hour.

"We're going," Francie yelled. "Tonight. I'll write you from there."

Europe. His baby sister was sailing to Europe with babies of her own. He shook his head in amazement.

"They're going to Europe," he shouted at Risa, realized she was only a fist away and could hear him just fine, and then tried again. "Francie, what did the doctor say?"

"He's fine," she yelled back. "Just a cold, not that awful croup again."

"Who?" he boomed.

The line sizzled.

"Francie?"

". . . steam and hot compresses on his chest."

"For Worth?" There was nothing wrong with his chest.

"Who?" Francie yelled back.

This phone call was costing him half a day's pay, and all they were doing was imitating owls.

"Worth Phillips! The boy I hit with the wagon!" Two heads turned, and Risa put her hands where her hips once were and raised her eyebrows as if to tell Mrs. Webb and Mrs. Turner that his conversation, despite the volume, was none of their business.

". . . misunderstanding. Thought he was younger. But exercise is still the best thing you can do for him."

"He's sure?" Ethan asked, the heart lodged in his throat softening his words.

"What?"

"I don't want to hurt him, Francie. Any more than I have already." Risa rubbed her hand back and forth against his back.

"Dr. Steinway says that it's like a concussion to the brain. You have to get the nerves to wake up. And he says if you let the muscles atrophy, they might never recover."

He'd known he was right not to let the boy just lie there.

It was all he needed to know.

"Cobb thinks otherwise," he said.

"Corny Cobb's treating the boy?" Francie asked. Ethan could just see her face, a thousand miles away, her nose scrunched and her pretty lips turned down.

"He's the family doctor," Ethan explained.

It sounded as if Francie said, "Ugh."

"Well, have a good trip, Francie honey," he shouted. Risa nudged him. "Risa sends her love."

"I wish you were coming with us," Francie said softly. Somehow, despite the noise on the line, her love came through loud and clear.

"Me too," he answered without thinking. It was the expected answer, especially from him. He supposed it was just that Europe was cities and towns, and he wanted wide-open spaces. He supposed it was that he had an obligation to Worth Phillips. More than likely he was just too tired for any kind of adventure, working three jobs and visiting the boy every spare moment he had.

But for the first time in his life he wasn't ready to hop a train, climb aboard a wagon, or even find out if his sea legs were worthy.

"Give my love to Graham and the kids," he said. "And the dog."

"Tell Sissy and Noah and everyone I love them," Francie said.

With the cost of the phone call nearly breaking him, he was glad she didn't list them all.

"Good-bye Francie!" he said over a hum that grew louder and louder.

And then the connection was broken, but the warmth remained, lodged in his chest in the special place his sister occupied, nestled next to Della and Bart and all the rest of the people he loved.

"Gotta get going now," he told Risa, picking up the sketch he'd made of the buckaroo on a horse with a lasso high above his head.

"You want to take something along with you?" Risa offered, waddling toward the counter, where jars of candy fought for space with soap and chewing tobacco. Something for everyone. "I just got in some pretty paper fans from Elite Bouquet."

"Now what would a little boy do with a paper fan?" he asked her, strumming the counter. "Probably much rather have some of that Adams's New York Rubber Gum."

"A three-year-old can't have gum, honey." Risa showed him the fan, demonstrating how well it worked by waving it in front of his face. "They swallow it and it just sits in their little tummies forever."

"Then give me some licorice," he said. "And a couple sticks of that Rubber Gum just the same."

"What about a nice little bit of fine hand soap?" She stuck it against his nose. "Smell."

His nose tingled and he fought the urge to sneeze. "The buckaroo isn't going to want soap."

"No, I'm sure *he* won't. What about some lotion? She always tries that nice Eau d'Bouquet when she's in with Worth." She opened the cap for him and waved it under his nose. It smelled faintly like vanilla, maybe mixed with rain. Like one of those ice-cream cones during a sun shower.

"It's only forty-nine cents," she said, "retail. You could have it for a quarter's worth of work."

"I'll take the licorice and the gum," he said. "And some of those little liver pills."

"You having stomach trouble? It's no wonder, the way you're working so hard and eating on the run. But Sissy's got some Earling Fig Laxative. She bought that and some other stuff just a couple of days ago." Risa put a hand against his brow.

"Sissy's stuff didn't work," he said quietly. Mrs. Webb and Mrs. Turner stood poised at the end of the counter like two dressmaker's dummies showing off their clothes. Apparently they intended to spend the entire day in the mercantile, shopping for gossip. It must have been a habit of theirs, for Risa didn't offer them any help or seem to take note of them at all. Not even when Mrs. Webb cupped her hands around Mrs. Turner's ear and whispered something. Self-consciously Ethan whispered, "And could you lower your voice?"

"I think you should bring that lovely girl something, as long as you're going over there. Once you're feeling better." She put the roll of liver pills on the counter and leaned toward him. Quietly she said, "These work real fast, Ethan."

"Good. And the licorice and gum, too."

Mrs. Turner whispered something back to Mrs. Webb.

"Don't you give that child this gum, Ethan Morrow," Risa said with a wag of her finger.

"Tell you what," he said, reaching for the bag of goods, "how about I give the boy the liver pills and let his sister chew the gum? She old enough?"

Mrs. Webb tittered. Mrs. Turner pretended she was looking for a hairbrush. Ethan knew she was just pretending, because the poor woman had only a few strands left.

"She might like bonbons," Risa suggested.

"Get it out of your head, Risa," he said, knowing full well that the old ladies were listening too. "Your matchmaking days are over. At least until Cara's old enough to go fishing for a husband. All my sisters and brothers are seen to, and I'll be on my way by the end of the week."

He clutched the bag and headed for the door, listening to Risa complain to the old women. "Men! Why is it when Cupid aims for their hearts, he always seems to lop off a piece of their brains with his arrows?"

"He gets 'em in the eyes," Mrs. Turner said. "Can't see what's plain as the nose on their faces."

"I heard Benjamin Cobb brought her flowers," Mrs. Webb said.

Ethan heard himself snort. There was no way Sterling Phillips could be seriously considering Benjamin Cobb. No amount of flowers could make that man appeal to her, could they?

"Talk about blind," Mrs. Turner replied. "Why, that Etta Hanes was fooling around right under his nose!"

"How did he suppose she bought that house? With her sugar-jar kitty? And Clyde Dow's an even bigger fool than the doctor!"

"That's really none of our business," Risa said as if Ethan's life was public property, whereas Etta Dow's affairs were her own. "You ladies seen the new bolt of blue serge that came in last week?"

* * *

"Oh, another picture!" Sterling took the drawing from him and cuddled up with Worth on the bed, showing it to him. They'd worked out a system, she and Ethan, for giving her baby his cleansing. She lay on the far side of the bed, her arm around Worth so that he stayed on his side, and told him stories or showed him one of Ethan's many pictures. She talked as much as she could, keeping her son's attention on what was in front of him, and not what was happening behind.

Not that it bothered him at all. But oh, what it did to Ethan. With glistening eyes and a gentle hand he did what had to be done, and cleaned up afterward, all the while contributing to their conversation.

"So the awful troll that lived under the bridge that crossed the moat—"

"—that made the castle on a island . . ."

"—where no one could come or go . . ."

" 'cept Prince Perfect," Worth said, studying his fingers as though he'd just grown an extra one.

"Prince Perfect could come and go?" Ethan asked. His eyes watched as the rubber bag that hung from one of the posters of Worth's bed emptied. One of his big hands held everything in place. The other stroked her son's back, every now and then rubbing against her arm. "I'm not hurting you, am I?"

It was hard to know what to hope her baby's answer would be.

"Yeah, the prince could come and go 'cause the troll can't see him, right, Ster?"

"Right. But the princess could only get over the bridge if she paid a toll to the troll."

"Ah. The old troll toll," Ethan said with a nod.

"Sissy make me crutch cookies?" Worth asked. "I bet they'd be a good troll toll. Trolls love eatin' little boys."

"No," Ethan answered. "She fell asleep in the middle of making 'em, Bucky. Found her with her head on her arm at the kitchen table snoring away like a dull saw on an old white oak."

"Isn't she sleeping well at night?" Sterling asked.

He chuckled softly. "I'd say there was one night she didn't."

Sterling didn't know what was funny about that.

"Give her another seven months or so and she won't be sleeping through the night for quite a while."

"Oooh." Her heart did a little flip-flop at the thought of nursing an infant in the darkness of night.

"Why not?" Worth asked. "What happens then?"

"Then I get to be an uncle yet again," Ethan said, closing off the clamp and replacing Worth's diaper.

Sterling couldn't imagine what it would be like to walk away from a little one. She hadn't been able to do it herself once the time had come. No wonder Ethan had plans to get going before yet another niece or nephew claimed a piece of his heart. "I guess they'll send you a picture."

He rubbed his forehead with his forearm and sank into the chair beside the bed. With a deep sigh he rested his forehead against the back of his hand.

She didn't need to say it aloud, but she did, anyway. "You're not going."

"We'll see what tomorrow brings," he said, getting to his feet and moving over the basin to clean up after her son.

"I'll do that." She got up from the bed and came around to his side.

"Don't be silly," he said. "I'm here."

Worth twisted toward them.

"Really, you'd do me more good over there." He gestured with his head and she reluctantly went around the bed and sat down on the edge. "So what did she pay the troll with?"

"Peenies," Worth said. "Right, Ster?"

"Absolutely. She had to give him her beautiful purple peonies every time she wanted to cross the bridge."

"And she crossed it a lot, right, Ster?"

She stretched out her back and agreed. "Right."

"And she gave him every last peeny," Worth told Ethan. "Till she was unflowered."

"Oh dear!" Ethan said, trying to hide the smile, contain the laughter. "Poor Princess Sugarlips! Unflowered by a troll!"

"Now how's she gonna get across?" Worth asked while Ethan tried to get over the humor he seemed to find at the princess's dire predicament.

"Well, what does the troll want?" Ethan asked, his eyebrows suddenly coming down and a scowl darkening his face.

"He likes to eat little girls," Worth said, and Sterling knew something was terribly wrong when Ethan made no silly comment in return.

Instead, he sniffed, and when she lifted her eyes to meet his, he was shaking his head, his eyes closed, the tip of his tongue caught between his lips.

There was only one thing it could be. Dr. Cobb had warned them that her baby would bleed. Naturally, as with the paralysis, they'd convinced themselves that Dr. Cobb wouldn't be right.

She eased off the bed and came around to the other side, where a trickle of blood made its way toward the clean white diaper Ethan had placed beneath her precious child.

It was time to face reality. Her father had been right. Sins do not go unpunished. Dr. Cobb had been right. Neither Sissy Eastman's homemade cures nor Ethan's hopes were going to fix what was wrong with her son. No one was going to live happily ever after, least of all her, or more importantly her son.

Behind Worth's back she carefully took down the drawing of Worth on the velocipede, the one of him flying the kite, the one of him playing leapfrog with the dog. She also took the sketch of him riding a horse and put them all in the top drawer of his dresser.

"There's nothing to keep you here," she said, handing the man his ridiculous cowboy hat.

"You giving up?"

She busied herself with straightening up the dresser top, the curtains, the sheets on the bed.

How could she answer him when her heart was in her throat?

He supposed she wasn't used to fighting, or she'd know that there were always a few lost skirmishes. It didn't mean the war was over. "Seems there's more reason for me to be here than ever," he said, turning Worth onto his other side and putting a pillow behind his back for support.

In the silence he searched for a way to reach her.

"You grow peonies, too, like Princess Sugarlips, don't you?" The front yard was filled with lavender ones and pink ones and white ones with deep purple edges, and he'd bet she'd been the one to plant them there for her aunt.

"Ster grows lots of stuff," Worth said, and Ethan remembered he'd brought the boy some candy.

"Give me that bag," he told her, pointing toward the table on the far side of the bed. "And stop moping. You get bugs on those peonies?"

She handed him the bag at arm's length, still not speaking. The last thing she wanted was a lecture.

"Of course you do," he continued in the absence of any response. He decided that talking to Worth would be preferable to talking to the wall. "So then your sister just gives up and lets all those bugs and ants eat her pretty flowers, right?"

Scrunching up his nose as if Ethan was being silly, Worth said, "She picks 'em off."

"Each one?"

The buckaroo nodded. Sterling watched them out of the corner of her eye, the ends of that sweet soft mouth turned down.

"Must take a long time."

"All summer."

"I see. But three and a half weeks is long enough for a body to heal. That's all the time it gets, huh?" He handed the boy a stick of black licorice.

She set that pointy little jaw determinedly, but still she didn't speak.

"She prune those peonies?" he asked Worth.

"Yup." He put the end of the licorice stick in his mouth and twirled it around.

"She water 'em? Stake 'em?"

"Uh-huh." The stick went in and out. He held one out to Sterling, but she refused even to look at it.

"And in the end all she gets is a few flowers that last a couple days each, right? All that work, months of it. For a few flowers."

"Dr. Cobb will be coming soon." Sterling straightened her shirtwaist, retied the ribbon carefully at her waist, and smoothed her hair back with both hands. "I think it would be best if you weren't here when he comes."

"I'll just exercise him a little and be on my way before the good doctor gets here." He wiped the boy's mouth, which looked like he'd been sucking coal, and shoved the hanky into his pocket.

"No. I think you should go now."

"Look, if you see him coming up the front walk, I promise to run out the back, all right? I've gotta get these legs moving." He pulled the covers away from the buckaroo.

"No. No exercise. Dr. Cobb says he's to stay still."

"I don't want to have this argument in front of him," he said, gesturing toward the buckaroo.

"We're not having an argument. I said no. I've tried it your way. I can promise you that if I feed my peonies, if I water them, if I prune them and pick off the bugs, they'll bloom and flourish. What can you promise me?"

"I can't promise you anything, princess. Not a thing. I can't promise the sun will come up tomorrow. I can't promise you that this house'll be here. But if it does, and if it is, then I'll be here. And I'll be working on that child's legs. Tomorrow and the next day and the day after that. No matter how long it takes until he walks and runs and plays. And I won't rest until he does. And then I'll leave you alone. Has Cobb promised you better?"

Something crossed her face that made him think that maybe the doctor had done just that.

Chapter Seven

It had taken him a week. A whole precious week to convince her to let him test the buckaroo again. A week that had put Oklahoma off the map and softened Worth's muscles and broken everyone's hopes.

And even then she'd only let him visit because the boy had refused to eat unless he was there. And then there was the nine-in-the-morning, nine-at-night routine that had to be taken care of.

Visiting four times a day wasn't exactly fattening Ethan's meager bankroll. It wasn't easy to shingle a roof or lay fencing around a little boy's meals. But it kept him in Harrington Manor, irritating the heck out of Corny Cobb and wearing down Sterling Phillips's defenses until she'd been forced to admit that all he'd done was what the doctor had told him to do.

It hadn't been the exercising that had her son bleeding. It had been the cleansing, and even though he'd have liked to blame Benjamin Cobb for the blood, they all knew it was no one's fault and that it had to be done.

He noticed that as of two days ago she was slipping and referring to the good doctor as "Benjamin" every now and then. Risa made sure to tell him that the pair had had dinner Tuesday night at the Marsh Hotel dining room, and again on Thursday, this time at the DePuy House.

They made a fine pair, she and "Benjamin." She was quickly proving herself to be nearly as obstinate as the doctor himself.

But now that she'd agreed, and he was standing at the

foot of the buckaroo's bed, the blankets thrown back, ready to stick a pin in him, he found he wasn't all that eager anymore.

"Go ahead," Imogene Harrington said. She was peeking in the door, half in and half out, smiling encouragingly at Worth. "Hurry, before Oliver finds out I'm in here and I have to miss the moment."

That was what he needed, all right. An audience. He'd pushed and pushed for the opportunity to test the buckaroo, and now he wasn't so sure.

Maybe none of them was ready for this moment of truth. This moment when, just like fledglings wobbling on the side of some cliff, ready to either take off and soar or plunge down to a bloody end, the future of each of them hung precariously.

Feeling both Sterling's and Imogene's eyes on him, he slipped the pin from the collar of his shirt and touched it to the bottom of Worth's foot.

"Hey!" Worth yelled, pulling his hand away from his sister. "Let go, Ster. You're squeezing too hard."

He supposed his wasn't the only heart that refused to beat at the boy's shout. It wasn't only his breath that stopped, staggered by hope, only to become a sigh. His weren't the only dreams lying shattered at the foot of the bed.

But there was no solace to be found in company, no matter what they said about misery loving it. Each of them stood alone, and while he knew that Sterling's pain was as real as his, and that Imogene's was tied up with all her other losses, his was increased threefold. He had disappointed each of them.

He didn't know what to say, so he said nothing at all.

Sterling gently replaced the sheet, letting it fall over the buckaroo's feet the same way someone covered a dead man's face.

"Oh, no," Genie said, her head shaking with a rapidity reserved for hummingbird wings while she gulped for a breath.

Silver began fanning her aunt, one hand bracing her under the elbow as her breathing became more and more labored.

Ethan raced around them and grabbed the fancy chair from the hall, easing it behind the older woman and lowering her into it.

"What do I do?" he asked while Imogene struggled to draw in air.

"Her medicine." Sterling was kneeling in front of her aunt, their eyes locked. Her breathing was deep and deliberate and she was trying to make her aunt do the same. "Find Uncle Oliver."

Ethan ran out in the hall and down the stairs, searching for Oliver Harrington's office. He followed the man's voice toward the back of the house and found him standing beside a small table, a telephone in his hand.

"You gave up that right when you tossed her out on her ear, man. Don't think you can waltz in here and—"

"Your wife's having an attack," Ethan said, knocking on the wall at the same time since there was no door. He lunged, reaching for the pocket where he hoped Imogene's miracle cure was nestled. "Have you got her medicine?"

Oliver Harrington signaled for him to slow down. "Won't help if we come apart ourselves," he said, but he wasn't fooling Ethan, who saw the color drain from the older man's face and get caught in his throat, where it nearly suffocated him. There was shouting from the other end of the phone line.

"Go find someone else to persecute and leave her alone!" he shouted into the phone, replacing the receiver and then gesturing for Ethan to lead.

"She's in your nephew's room." By now the gasps seemed to fill the entire household. They could hear them clearly all the way at the bottom of the stairwell, like timbers bending in a big old ship. While they climbed the steps, Oliver Harrington got out the bottle from his pocket and put several drops on the hanky he apparently kept ready for such emergencies.

In Worth's bright yellow room he fell to his knees in front of his wife, holding the cloth to her mouth and nose, sweat beading his upper lip and dripping down from his temples. "Easy, love," he kept repeating. "Easy now. You shouldn't be in here. You know better than that. Just breathe, now, Genie. Dear God, breathe!"

* * *

They'd put her aunt Genie to bed the moment the attack was over. Sir Glad-I-am had scooped her aunt up in his arms and carried her from the room after Sterling reminded her uncle that if his back went out again, he'd be no good to anyone. Uncle Oliver had shrugged and mumbled something about being no good to anyone as it was, but Sterling supposed that watching the woman he loved fight for the same air that everyone else took for granted took a lot out of a man.

While he waited with her aunt in his arms for Sterling to remove the spread from her aunt's bed, the gallant knight of her wishes had spoken softly to her aunt as though it was a child he held. And yet there was nothing patronizing in his words or tone. Only a gentleness that one usually reserved for children.

"I bet it scares you some," he said softly. "I know it would scare me. You handle it so well. I'd be proud, if I were you. How did you learn not to panic and cry out?"

He kept up a steady stream of words without allowing her to answer until he finally set her down gently on the bed and asked, "How's that?"

Aunt Imogene hiccuped a few times and then calmed herself, to everyone's relief. Two attacks in one day took about as much out of those attending to her as it did of Imogene herself.

"It's okay," her aunt said, letting them pull the covers up to her chin and fuss with her pillows.

"Anything I can get you?" Sterling asked her.

Her aunt shook her head and pointed at Ethan. "You. You like ice cream?" Before anyone could warn him, he stepped with both feet into her trap.

"Yes, ma'am, I surely do."

Sterling liked the way he called her "ma'am" as though he really meant the respect it implied.

"Then it's settled," her aunt said in the same cryptic way she said everything else.

"Tuesday?" Ethan asked, just like that.

She should have expected that. The man had managed to form a special bond with her aunt, as he had with her son, and in only a matter of minutes. Here he was clearly following her aunt's loony brand of logic, just as she could. It made it seem as though the rest of the world was being obtuse, and left the three of them with a language all their own.

"Oh," Aunt Imogene said, clapping her hands together like a small child. "Tuesday would be ever so wonderful. Just us?"

"Just you and me," he said, bowing slightly. It was a wonder his armor didn't pinch him. "If you'd do me the honor, and your husband doesn't suffer from jealous rages and won't come after me with a long sword or a short pistol."

"Oh, Oliver's harmless," Aunt Imogene said with a wave of her hand. "You can sleep easy in your bed."

"Tell that to the cow and the chickens and Honesty," he said with a smile.

"The cow?" she asked when Aunt Imogene didn't.

"I sleep in the barn at Noah and Sissy's."

The smile was gone. With an apologetic shrug he shoved his hands into his pockets, but they would only go so far, being so big and all. Did a man's hands grow with hard work? His were huge. And yet when they cradled Worth's head to raise him from the pillow, they were more gentle than hers. They must have been, because Worth cried out or complained when she tried to help him sit up, but when his cowboy did, her baby was quiet and trusting.

"It was part of the pay when I started working for Noah," he explained. "Not that I needed a roof over my head or his housekeeper's cooking, but he didn't have much else to offer. And being a kid, I wanted to exercise my independence from Sissy." And then being a knight, he had to live within the palace walls, didn't he?

"Missed her cooking, though, I imagine," Uncle Oliver said. He'd been studying Ethan from the corner of the room, looking him up and down and drinking him in with his eyes. "But then there was always Sunday dinner, wasn't there?"

"Well, yeah, there was," he admitted. She could just imagine Sunday dinner at Sissy Eastman's house. A dozen kids running and laughing, women measuring waistlines, men fixing things. She always imagined farmers fixing something, perhaps because the men she knew couldn't fix a bent spoon without calling in someone who would charge to do the job.

"So when your sister married Mr. Eastman," Uncle Oliver continued, "you must have been pretty happy to get her baking on an everyday basis again."

"I guess," Ethan answered. He shifted his weight, examining the way the ceiling met the wall in the far corner of the room.

"You sure settled down well for a boy who hungered for all the excitement the West had to offer." Uncle Oliver poured a brandy from the decanter he kept by the side of the bed and offered it to Ethan, who naturally declined. What was it knights drank, anyway? Mead? Hers seemed to have a penchant for lemonade.

"I'm just patient, is all," Ethan said quietly.

So then he was still planning to go. And well he should. If he didn't deserve to see his dreams come true, she didn't know who did.

It sure made her happy to think he'd be leaving. To be honest, he'd actually begun to be a nuisance, there for every meal, taking over Worth's changing, taking him on his lap while she changed the sheets. Always underfoot like that.

Of course, poor Worth would be devastated to see the man go and take with him all his cowboy stories, his confidence and good looks and easy ways. Worth would miss the way his soft voice filled a room and the way he hummed when he worked without even realizing it. He'd miss waking up to the thought that Ethan Morrow was coming over soon, and he'd miss going to sleep safe in the knowledge that tomorrow would bring the man back into their lives.

She, of course, couldn't wait for him to leave. If he didn't get going, they'd never return the order to their lives and get down to life the way it would be from now on. In fact the sooner he was gone, the better for them all. There'd be one less thing for Benjamin to be irritated about.

"I think I hear the buckaroo," Ethan said, and she felt that enormous hand at the small of her back gently guiding her toward the door.

"A hat?" Aunt Imogene called out after him.

Over his shoulder he answered, "When he's sitting up on his own, Mrs. Harrington. Incentive, no?"

"Oh. Genie, to you," her aunt corrected.

No one outside of the family called her aunt Imogene "Genie." Sterling's own father hadn't even called her Genie. It wasn't until after they'd traipsed all over Europe waiting for Worth to be born, not until her aunt had agreed that she couldn't, shouldn't give her baby away, that Sterling had finally begun to call her Genie.

"Genie, then," he said with a polite nod.

No one outside the family called her Genie except, of course, Ethan Morrow.

"Tuesday?" Aunt Imogene asked as they stepped over the threshold.

"Tuesday. And maybe we'll look for a hat while we're there," Ethan promised.

"Here comes Cobb," Uncle Oliver said, looking out the window. "He's got more of those damn flowers. Probably what's setting off your asthma."

"I'd better be going," Ethan said. "You want me to use the back door?"

"Oh, my Lord!" Uncle Oliver pulled the curtains closed and turned to Aunt Imogene. "You stay in bed, now, dear. We'll let you rest."

He shooed them out of the room in front of him and then stood in the hallway, wringing his hands.

"What is it, Mr. Harrington?" Ethan asked, and then followed his line of vision down the steps to the front hall.

With a big red bow on it, as if it was something to celebrate, Benjamin Cobb pushed a tiny invalid chair across the marble foyer.

* * *

Ethan lugged his last sack of flour back into Hanson's and put it away on the shelf where it belonged. It had been hard work, but it was what he needed. Facts were facts, and wishing didn't change them. A man who wasn't going anywhere really didn't need much in the way of supplies to get there.

He leaned against the counter and he and Charlie and Risa all sighed.

"I don't know which of us is the tiredest," Risa laughed. "And I didn't even do any of the carrying."

Ethan studied his sister-in-law's very rounded belly. "You're always carrying!" he said. He wondered if a woman's belly was soft, like a man carrying around extra weight, or hard, the way it looked. When Risa hugged him to her, it felt like there was a huge hard ball under her skirts.

Risa stretched and Charlie rubbed her lower back, producing a smile on the woman that could melt the ice of winter. Old Charlie knew just how to ease Risa's pains, and apparently Risa knew just how to scratch Charlie's itches.

And Ethan? No one was scratching his itches these days. And Lord, being around Sterling Phillips, he was getting pretty damn itchy.

"You all right, Eth?" Risa asked him, that sweet little face of hers puckered with concern. "I mean about not going and all?"

"Temporary setback," he said with a nonchalance he didn't feel. "Something else'll come along."

"Yeah. Probably a tornado, with your luck," Charlie said. "It's as if the good Lord doesn't want you to leave us, the way something always gets in your way." He grabbed hold of his daughter Miranda's braids as she scooted by, and asked her where she thought she was going. Then he lifted her up and set her on the counter to tie a bootlace that had come undone.

"Just shows that by now I should've been watching for it, don't you think?" It wouldn't have been quite so awful if he'd been able to keep his bad luck to himself instead of involving the poor little buckaroo in his destiny. *Think fast and act slow.* No matter how many times he told himself that—nearly every day since that morning in New York when he hadn't thought at all—he always seemed to get it backward, and once again someone else was paying for his mistakes.

"Well, you got a little money now, anyways," Charlie said, doubling the bow on his daughter's lace and pulling it tight. "What are you going to do with it?"

Ethan opened his fist. Thirty-four dollars and forty-seven cents. Without free land, it sure didn't amount to much of a future. "Owe Cornuto Cobb two dollars," he said, separating the bills on the counter.

"You could buy a ticket to New York," Risa said. "I'm sure that Francie and Graham would help you out until you could—"

Graham Trent had been a prince about the whole incident in New York, had blamed himself really, but there was no chance that Ethan would go running to him for help now. He'd just as soon take a job digging graves with his bare hands. Hadn't it been hard enough to tell Graham what had happened and ask him to find a doctor? At least he wasn't asking them to help him— just the boy.

"He's a farmer, Risa," Charlie said. "What's he going to do in a city like New York? At least here he's got some land, he's got a home."

Not really, he thought. The land he lived on belonged to Noah. The land he was raising his grapes on belonged to John Gibbs, Peter's brother, who had moved to town a decade ago and let the land go fallow. And the home that Charlie referred to? He slept in Noah's barn when it wasn't too cold, and on his sofa when it was.

"Maybe you should put it in the bank," Risa said. "And add to it when you can."

It was what he ought to do. He'd talked Morris Ellman into new fencing and stood to make a good six dollars putting it in. At that rate he'd have a bed of his own only a year or two after he was too old to do much in it besides sleep.

When he said nothing, Risa continued. "That way when you're ready to go, you'll have the means to."

"How's the boy doing?" Charlie asked, letting Miranda crawl into his arms and settling her on his hip.

"Not as good as I'd like," Ethan admitted. "According to the Cobber there's not much hope. His guess is the cord's severed, but I'm still praying. Doesn't cost anything."

"Except maybe sleep," Risa said, her mouth twisted to one side. "When was the last time you had any?"

He stretched out his muscles and realized he was as tired as his sister-in-law was guessing he was. "The little guy can't move his legs at all. His sister or I have to carry him everywhere."

Charlie set Miranda down and began to straighten Ethan's money for him, hitting the edges against the counter to even the bills up. Miranda put her arms around her father's leg as if it was some kind of tree she wanted to climb.

"Up!" she insisted when she couldn't manage it herself. When Charlie shook his head, she turned her attention to Risa, pulling on her mother's apron.

"You're too heavy for your mama, Randy," Ethan said, lifting her easily and setting her on his shoulders. His nieces and nephews always liked the view from up there.

"Here's a honey stick," Risa said, holding it out to Miranda. "You can have it if you go back on upstairs and check on Krista."

"You go!" Miranda directed Ethan, kicking his chest and tapping on his head.

"No," Risa said. "Uncle Ethan will put you down and you go yourself, or no honey stick." She folded her arms across what had grown to become a more than ample bosom, and stared at her middle daughter.

"Put me down," Miranda demanded in the same tone that she demanded everything else. She reached for the honey stick on her way down from Ethan's shoulders.

"You still got that bike here?" Ethan asked. "The red one?"

"The three-wheeler?" his brother asked.

"How many red bikes you got here, Charlie?" he said over his shoulder as he headed for the north side of the store where he'd first seen the shiny new velocipede. And the little boy who might never ride it.

There it stood, looking freshly dusted, glinting in the late-afternoon sun. A tag hung from the handlebar with its price. Ethan Morrow tried to remember the last time he'd bought something brand-new that wasn't meant to be eaten or used in a field. Something whose sole purpose was enjoyment.

"Eth, listen . . . If the boy can't even move his legs,

how the heck is he gonna ride a bicycle?" Good old Charlie, the voice of reason.

"That's the point," Ethan said, ripping off the tag and carrying the bicycle back to the counter. "Guess he's just gonna have to use those legs of his. Got a ribbon or something?"

Charlie put his hand on Ethan's shoulder and adopted his big-brother voice. "Ethan. The kid can't. And all your wishing and praying isn't gonna change that. And buying the kid a bike isn't gonna make the miracle happen."

"Maybe. Maybe not." Ethan didn't want to argue. He wanted to pay for the bike and take what was left of his money and hightail it over to the Harrington Manor.

He wanted to see the look on the buckaroo's face when he brought that shiny red three-wheeler into his room.

"You got a pink ribbon, Risa?" he asked.

"Pink? You don't put pink on a present for a boy," Charlie said, shaking his head at Ethan's ignorance.

But Risa just smiled and nodded. "Yeah, Eth. I got pink."

* * *

"A parade!" Aunt Imogene said, clapping her hands as she stood by the window. "Look, Sterling. It's a parade!"

Sterling sighed. Her dear aunt thought that if the milkman and the iceman showed up within ten minutes of each other, it was a party. Heaven knew what it had taken to make a parade.

She looked out the window herself. Up the walkway came Ethan Morrow, his nephew James, and that black mop of a dog. And the parade even had a float. One shiny red velocipede that Ethan and James were pulling along between them.

She excused herself and stormed out the front door, blocking the parade route with her body.

"A bike?" she demanded. "You've brought him a bike?"

Benjamin had been clear as crystal this afternoon. *He will not get well. Your son is a cripple.*

"He's already gotten a gift with wheels today. One he can make use of." How had she ever thought this man was her knight in shining armor? Here she was needing someone who could help her deal with her son, and this man wanted to lie to him. She needed someone to help her face the truth, and this man wanted her to hide from it. "Take this back to the mercantile. Take yourself back to the mercantile. It's time to give up."

"Yeah?"

If he gripped the bicycle any harder, she thought, he'd bend the metal bars.

"Yeah."

He smirked.

"This isn't funny, Mr. Morrow. At least not to me."

He sobered immediately. "*Yeah* sounded funny coming out of your mouth." The smirk was back. He tried to wipe it off his face. "Sorry."

"Yes, well I don't think you'll think it's so funny when I tell you I forbid you to give him the bike. It's too cruel."

"Oh, the bike is cruel? Let me ask you this. What does an invalid's chair tell the buckaroo about his chances of recovery?" He stared at her, the bike dangling from one strong arm, and gave her more than enough time to answer. "And what does this brand-new shiny red velocipede tell him?"

She was about to say something about wishes and hopes and facing the truth when James spoke up. "I think he's right, ma'am," the boy said quietly, his hand slipping into Ethan's. "Saying something's gonna get better doesn't always mean it will, but then saying it won't doesn't give a body much to hope with." He kicked a tuft of grass at the edge of the walkway. She could hardly tell off the boy's uncle in front of him.

"It's nice to see you, James," she said, her tone as soft and welcoming as she could make it. "I think there's some lemonade inside. Would you like some?"

The boy looked at his uncle, waited for the nod, and then admitted he would. "It's powerful hot out here. For June, that is."

He sounded just like his uncle, and it was Sterling's turn to stifle a grin. "Mmm," she agreed. "Powerful hot."

"I think there might be a few madeleines too," Sterling said, taking a step or two backward toward the door. "Do you like cookies?"

The boy nodded. "My aunt Sissy makes the best cookies in Pleasant Township," he said with pride. "Maybe even all of Ohio."

Why stop there? she thought, but put on her best smile. There was no point in being jealous of Sissy Eastman. So what if James loved her? And Ethan? It wasn't as if she wanted them to love her instead. "I'm sure she does. Your aunt is just about perfect, from what I hear."

"Not *just about*," the boy said, and yanked on his uncle's arm. "Right, Uncle Eth? Ain't Aunt Sissy perfect?"

"*Isn't*," he corrected, and Sterling was glad she'd bitten her tongue. "And I think you'd better go around back and wash those hands before you try one of Miss Sterling's—what'd you call them? Madeleines? That what the princess was helping the cook bake in your story?"

She nodded. Sissy might make good Boys with Broken Legs, or whatever she called them, but Sterling made the best madeleines east of the Mississippi.

The queen herself had told her so after the cook had taught her when she was just a little girl. The recipe was a part of her—something her father couldn't stop her from taking with her when he'd thrown her out. He couldn't stop the memories, and she couldn't stop the pain.

"There's a pump out back," she told James, pointing the way.

"Guess I could use a bit of that water myself. Had to settle for a lick and a promise out at the old Gibbs farm." Ethan studied his free hand, then put down the velocipede and jammed his fists into his pockets. "There's no water out there, to speak of."

"I didn't know James's family had a farm. Don't they live in that blue house down the street from the bank? Next to the one that new couple from Pennsylvania bought from Etta Dow?"

"It belonged to James's grandmother. It's abandoned now, but it still belongs to John Gibbs legally. It was just lying fallow for years, and I . . ."

He shuffled his feet. He shifted his weight. He looked over the top of her head and down at the ground.

"What do you do out there?" she prodded. She couldn't remember ever seeing him embarrassed before. Such a giant of a man, and he was kicking at the dirt with his boot and looking tongue-tied.

"My brother-in-law in New York sent me some seed-lings from Italy. Noah needs every inch of his land for wheat and corn, so I asked John if he'd mind if I put them in over there." He pulled his hands out from his pockets, looked at them, and shoved them back in. "I'll just go check on James."

"What is it you're growing there?" she called after his retreating back.

He threw the word over his shoulder. She heard him all right, but she just didn't want to believe what she'd heard. It couldn't be. If she'd doubted it before, she knew that now it was time to get him out of her life, before it was too late for both of them.

Ethan Morrow was growing grapes. And wouldn't Aunt Imogene just have a field day with that?

* * *

Ethan and James were as clean as two new milk pails when they came back to the front of the house where Sterling Phillips stood waiting by the new bicycle. At the sound of their voices she dropped the ends of the pink ribbon she was fingering and shined a dazzling smile at James. Oh, if only Ethan could be eight years old and the recipient of one of those!

"I'll have Abigail bring up some of those cookies and a nice cold drink and we can give Worth the bicycle," Sterling said, leading the way into the house.

"Want me to wait on the porch?" Ethan asked her, picking up the bike and carrying it toward the door.

She seemed to be considering her answer. Finally she shook her head and held the door open for him.

"Think he'll like it?" she asked James, taking him by the hand as they headed across the marble foyer.

"Who wouldn't?" James asked in return.

Maybe a little crippled boy who might never be able to use it, Ethan thought. *That's who.*

"Wait!" Imogene called out after them just as they'd passed the open parlor doors. "Just a moment, young man."

James halted in his tracks, his shoulders falling, and waited. Ethan put a hand against his back, urging him to turn around and face the woman who was quickly crossing the floor with her hand outstretched.

"Aren't you that sad little twinless twin everyone calls One Shoe?" She tilted her head this way and that, examining him. "Yes, I'm sure you are. Well, I'm that rich old lady everyone calls crazy. It's about time we met, don't you agree?"

Poor James. He surely didn't know how to react to the small woman with the shaking head whose finger was only inches from his nose. It was hard enough when the kids made fun of him—but could a nine-year-old stick out his tongue at Imogene Harrington in front of his uncle?

"So you and I are supposed to take it all to heart, cry in our hot milk, and such . . ."

Imogene's finger finally connected with the boy's chin and lifted his face until their eyes met.

"Well, the joke's on them, isn't it?"

"Ma'am?" James fixated on the small mole on Imogene's left cheek. Just when Ethan began to wonder about his powers of observation—he could have sworn it was on her right cheek the other day—she pulled at it, removed it, and placed it right between her eyebrows!

"There's a lesson there, if you're clever enough to find it," she said, straightening up and looking at Sterling first and then at Ethan.

"I'm sure Worth's waiting," Sterling said, reaching for James's hand.

"The lesson is," Imogene said, placing her foot on top of Sterling's so that she couldn't leave, "it's still me, isn't it?"

"It certainly is," Sterling said, somewhere between annoyance and amusement.

"Here's the thing, One Shoe," she said.

"His name is James." Ethan placed a proprietary hand on the boy's shoulder. While he knew Imogene never meant any harm, he thought it was asking a lot to expect James to make allowances for an old lady's eccentricities.

"He knows who he is," Imogene said, all her attention once again focused on the boy. "It's the others that are mistaken. And it doesn't matter how others view you as long as you know who you are—isn't that right, James One-Shoe Gibbs?"

He shrugged, apparently not sure how to answer her. Ethan didn't blame him.

"Go ahead and say it," Imogene told the child. "You can call me Crazy Old Lady Harrington. Won't change a thing. I'll still be me. And you'll still be you. And Sterling here, no matter what anyone might think of her, what conclusion they draw, will still be whoever she is."

"Aunt Imogene, Worth's waiting. Can I have my foot, please?" Sterling's chest rose and fell sharply and she kept her eyes glued to the floor while she waited for her aunt to release her. Ethan had to admire her patience. Or maybe, then again, he was just admiring the rise and fall of her chest.

"And your uncle here—would it matter what they said about him? What they thought?"

"Nobody thinks bad of Uncle Eth," James said, his small fist balled. "And they better not."

Ethan knew full well what the whole town thought of him. He was Sissy's youngest brother and nothing more. He was the baby of the family, with Francie gone and married and making a life for herself. There wasn't one of them that thought of him as a full-grown man responsible for himself or for anyone else. And they never would. It was why he had been so set on Oklahoma, where he wouldn't be anybody's baby brother.

"Want it?" Imogene asked James, pulling off the mole from her forehead and offering it to him.

A smile played at the edges of James's mouth, growing wider until it reached his eyes. It was a wise smile, a smile that spoke of understanding and decision. "Yeah," he said, reaching out and taking it from her. He plopped it on the center of his own forehead.

"It might take more glue," she said as James tipped his head back to keep it on. "And I think I've got a pirate patch around somewhere. Should I put it aside for you if I find it?"

"You're not crazy, are you?" James stood on his toes trying to see himself in the small gilt-framed mirror that hung on the wall.

"It's a matter of opinion," she said, glancing over her shoulder at Oliver, who had borne silent witness to the whole exchange with James. "Are you half a pair?"

James's smile faded. "Yes ma'am,"

"Well," she said, her little head wobbling more than usual to indicate that she disagreed, "I guess then I am crazy. I just see one little boy here, with two of every-thing a little boy is supposed to come with."

James looked down at his feet, then seemed to take stock of himself, as if for the very first time.

"Yes indeed. Two arms, two legs, two ears, two eyes, two noses." Imogene laughed at her own joke, easing the tension in the room. "You don't seem to me to be missing anything. Except perhaps a smile."

The boy stood a little straighter, and his eyes were bright. "No, ma'am, I think I got that too." His lips were trembling just a bit, but the smile was something to behold.

So much so that Imogene clapped her hands together. "Let's go make Worth smile," she said, taking James's hand in her own.

"Not you, Genie," Oliver Harrington's voice said qui-etly. "The children can do it themselves. You ought to lie down and rest. Your asthma—"

Ethan wasn't sure he'd ever heard nothing sound so deafening. No one said a word. Footsteps echoed from the stairway so loudly, they sounded like a one-man barn raising.

Abigail appeared at the door and curtsied politely. "Excuse me," she said cautiously, sensing the tension in the room and then directing her remarks to Sterling. "He's awake and wondering where you are."

"Tell him I'm coming," Imogene Harrington said more evenly than Ethan had ever heard her say any-thing. "And tell him I'm bringing a new friend."

Chapter Eight

"You doing that on purpose?" Ethan asked as he followed Sterling up the stairs.

"What?" she asked over her shoulder.

He shrugged. "Guess it's just natural. Sure does make a fellow think."

"What are you talking about?"

"You'd have to be behind you to understand. And you'd have to be a fellow. In which case you wouldn't be doing what you're doing to me."

Sterling felt herself blush. She had no right to be doing anything to Ethan Morrow, on purpose or otherwise. Fate had been cruel enough to him, and she had no intention of adding to his troubles by leading him on. Not when she knew how it would have to end.

"Are you sure this is a good idea?" she asked, pointing at the red velocipede. Benjamin Cobb was not going to like this, not one little bit. "Ethan Morrow presumes too much," he'd said just the night before, and now here he was with a bicycle of all things.

"Come on! Come on!" Imogene said, waving at them from Worth's open door.

For a knight, Ethan looked a little less than sure himself, but when he said, "It'll be fine," she let herself believe it.

When they reached her honey lamb's door Aunt Imogene was busily introducing James to Worth, who was apparently confused by the relationship. Worth's only experience with an aunt or uncle was Imogene and

Oliver. That his cowboy could be someone's uncle seemed to surprise him.

"One of your uncles?" he was asking. "You got more than one?"

"Oh, yeah," James explained. "I got five, but one of 'em lives in New York and I never met him. And I got four aunts too."

"Not five?"

"Well, not yet," James said. "When Uncle Eth grows up and gets married, I'll get another aunt." Beside her, big and tall and carrying a velocipede with just one finger, her knight blushed. "And more cousins. I got eleven now, and another one on the way. A dozen's a good lot of cousins. We got birthday parties all the time."

"I don't got any," her son said.

"I guess you can't get any, with your folks dead and all," James said.

Before Worth could respond, Sterling flew into the room, pulling Ethan with her by the shirtsleeve. "Look, honey lamb. Your cowboy's here. And he's brought you something special."

If Ethan was surprised by her sudden enthusiasm, or by the fact that she'd referred to him as a cowboy, he hid it well. He took a step into the room, the velocipede only partly hidden behind his back.

"How're you feeling, buckaroo?" It was clearly an effort for him to keep the smile off his face.

"What's that?" Worth asked, leaning to peer around Ethan's body.

"Show him!" Imogene shouted. "Wait till you see what the cowboy did, Worthie! Wait till you see!"

In all the years that Sterling and Worth had lived here with her aunt, Sterling could only remember her aunt touching the baby once. She had run one finger against Worth's cheek when he was a few months old. The look that had come over her was the softest, saddest, holiest thing Sterling had ever witnessed.

But Uncle Oliver had come in and pulled her gently away. It was as if he believed that they weren't meant to have babies to love and that no good could come of it. Sterling wasn't sure whether he was afraid for her son's sake, or his wife's sanity, or maybe his own broken heart, but she'd let him keep the distance with a heavy heart.

And Aunt Imogene had never touched the baby again. Until now. Now she squeezed his arm and then jumped away, afraid she might have hurt him. Sterling took her aunt's hand and replaced it on Worth's arm. Maybe she couldn't give Worth a dozen cousins and a bunch of aunts and uncles, but she'd brought him to Imogene, and maybe, through some magic, that could be enough.

"This?" Ethan said, gesturing over his shoulder. "You think he wants this?"

"Yes!" Imogene cried.

"Yeah!" James seconded.

"I do," Worth said. "Gimme!"

"You don't even know what it is," Ethan said with a laugh.

"It's my velo'pede," Worth said, pushing against the bed with his free hand to lift himself higher. "To ride."

"Velocipede," Sterling corrected, seeing how very right Ethan had been. But then, she'd never really doubted Sir Glad-I-am. Just because she couldn't be his fair lady didn't make him the villain in her melodrama. It was mean, short, Dr. Cobb, the troll, who had forbidden Worth from hoping. Had taken the light from his eyes that was shining there now, brighter than ever.

"This," Sir Glad-I-am said, pulling the bicycle from behind his back and placing it right up on the bed along with Worth, "is what's called temptation." He looked up, and his eyes locked with hers.

"That the brand?" James asked, looking for the label on the bars.

"That's what you call it when no matter what way

your good sense tells you it's going to end, there's nothing in the world that can stop you."

"You just gotta put your feet down on the ground," James said. "That'll stop it."

"Sometimes keeping your feet on the ground is the hardest part," Aunt Imogene said quietly. "You know how to ride one of these, James?"

"I sure do," James said proudly.

Keep your feet on the ground, Silver, she told herself. *No temptation for you.*

Sucking in her bottom lip, she backed her way toward the door. "If you'll excuse me, I've got to get changed."

"Changed? Looks to me like you're pretty perfect," Ethan said, looking her over from the messy hair that had only been given a lick and a promise because Worth was calling for her, right on down to the slippers that made climbing on and off his bed a little easier. "I wouldn't change a thing."

Glory-laury, but his eyes reminded her of the two polished tigereye stones one of Uncle Oliver's customers had given to Worth. Beautiful, but like the stones, they really couldn't see anything, could they? Certainly not the truth. "I wish you wouldn't say things like that," she said. "I'm hardly perfect."

"Sure you are. Right, Bucky? Could there be a better sister?" He looked at her intently. "I really do admire you, you know."

Oh yes, she knew. He admired the woman he thought she was, and the truth was that she enjoyed almost every moment of it—the respect, the affection. Sometimes she even got carried away on the heady scent of his attraction and imagined a future for them with passion and joy and warmth.

And then he'd go and say something about how she reminded him of his sister, or that he admired her. And she'd crash to the depths of reality, where she was a fallen woman with a crippled son and no hope for the future.

"You aren't seeing Dr. Gloom again, are you?" Imogene asked. "I don't like you stringing a man along. It's not like you."

"I am not stringing Dr. Cobb along," she said defensively. She wished that she was.

Ah, wishes! If they were flowers, the world would be spotted with gardens.

"Well, I can't really go out to dinner like this. I've been seeing to Worth." She pulled the neck of the pale blue seersucker shirtwaist away from her body.

Her blushing knight's face fell, the smile melting away. "So then it's true? You're keeping company with Cobb?"

Set him free, Silver. Let him go. Let him find a woman good enough for him and move away. Far away. So far that the only placed he'd be was in every dream.

She nodded.

Ethan took the bicycle down from the bed and set it on the floor. "James, you show the buckaroo here how it's done. And don't go letting Miss Imogene here get herself hurt. I'm just gonna step out with the buckaroo's big sister for a minute."

Taking her arm, he pushed her out the door and closed it behind them. A quick look up and down the hall proved they were quite alone.

"I really should be going," she said, taking a step toward her bedroom door before he blocked her way. "Benjamin doesn't like to be kept waiting."

"So it's Benjamin now, is it?" he asked, his hand inches from her face and just frozen there. "Guess, then, it's just me alone, getting these feelings, huh?"

"Feelings?" The word was out of her mouth before she had a chance to censor it.

"There's nothing, then?" he asked, searching her eyes with his own, and moving closer still so that she could feel his breath against her forehead. "Nothing on your side, keeping you up nights, warming your cheeks and teasing your belly as well?"

"Nights?" Suddenly she'd become a parrot, repeating phrases as though she didn't understand their meaning.

And all the while those amber eyes of his bore into her, seeing what she was trying desperately to hide. Even sleep didn't rid her of his face, his hands, his warmth. He was there in each of her dreams, tempting her body, calling to her soul, and stoking her heart. The nights were the worst, when her fantasies were set free.

They were the worst until he asked, his voice scratchy and all male, "Is it that you're just better at fighting it than I am? Is that it? Or am I just kidding myself here and the torture's mine alone?"

He'd been good to her, kind, caring. She owed him his release. "You've imagined something that doesn't exist," she said, taking tiny breaths to keep some distance between their bodies, her gaze on the old gilt-framed painting of Mary Magdalene that hung on the wall across from her own bedroom. "Benjamin and I are—"

"Don't do this," he said softly, his breath brushing her eyelids, his thumb stroking her temple, slipping lower and causing her jaw to slacken. "Don't make me think of you sitting next to him in his fancy little surrey, his arm rubbing up against yours."

"No one is rubbing up against me," she said, pushing against him, "except you. Now, if you'll just let me go—"

"Let you run? Let you run away to that heartless troll who brings invalid chairs with ribbons on them?"

"Benjamin is doing everything he can for Worth and me, professionally and socially. He's been extremely generous and kind," she said, breathing in the smell she was coming to know so well, soil and sweat and a splash of bay rum.

He laughed a short, gentle laugh. "I figured that was it. You don't have to be so subtle with your messages, Miss Phillips. If you're trying to tell me that you can have any man you want, I already know that. I already know that I don't belong on your list. . . ."

He tipped her head back and lowered his lips until they were brushing her eyelids, her temples, and, damn him, someplace deeper she had planned on keeping safe.

"But I'm there, aren't I? On your list and under your skin just as surely as you are under mine. You've fallen just as arsy-varsy for me as I have for you, no matter what you say. And the thought of Benjamin Cobb touching you, running his finger down your cheek like this—" He stroked her cheek and she knew that had he not been pressed up against her so tightly, her knees would have buckled and she would have slid to the floor.

"The thought of him playing with your hair . . ." He did that, too, winding a strand around his finger until he was tied to her cheek by a silken cord. "The thought of him pressing his lips here," he whispered, kissing her temple. "Or here." He pressed a kiss just under her jawbone, and his moan drowned out her own. "I've got nothing to offer you." His words danced in her ear. "But this need. This damn need. And that's not enough."

"Then let me go." Her voice was a whisper.

His was tight with pain. "I can't."

"Of course you can," she said, straightening her back against the wall. "You have to."

"He's going to want to kiss you, Silver." His lips were a hairbreadth from hers as he bent forward, lowering his head toward hers. "He'll bring you flowers and candy and he'll think it entitles him."

She supposed he was right. It was the way of the world, after all. Man chased woman, woman stumbled, man was triumphant.

And just as she thought she had figured out the way things worked between the sexes, her handsome knight's lips caught hers, came down, and demanded that she admit with her touch what she would never admit with her words. His hands were lost in her hair, holding her head tightly to his. He smelled warm and sharp, and his body was firm against hers, supporting her when she wasn't sure her own legs would.

When he pulled back and righted her, he stood shaking his head as if he couldn't believe what he had done.

"I'm sorry," he said. "I had no right to do that."

She sniffed and fussed at the hair that had come loose from her bun, her head down so that he couldn't see the want she was sure was so blatantly obvious.

"I'm glad I was first, though," he said, trying to help her capture her wayward hair.

She batted at his hands and pulled away, turning her face to the wall. "Is that what this was about?" she asked as coolly as she could, trying to keep her breathing under control despite her racing heart, her threatening tears.

"Of course not," he said, having stepped back a respectable distance. "Though I'm not sorry you'll have some basis of comparison."

She let her forehead rest on the silk-papered wall and clutched at her sides trying not to laugh at the irony of it all. Beyond the wall there were sounds of mirth and squeals of delight.

"At least you'll know what it feels like to be kissed by someone who loves you."

And what it feels like finally to kiss someone I love. It had been hot and heady and melted her to the wanton core her father had assured her was at the heart of her black soul. And if only she wouldn't have to watch the love die out of his eyes when he took her for his own, she'd have given herself to Ethan Morrow then and there with no thought for tomorrow.

He flew down the stairwell two steps at a time. In the marble hall the front door opened and slammed shut.

"Bye, Ethan," her aunt yelled out the window.

"Bye, Ethan," Sterling whispered quietly, wiping the tears from her cheeks and pasting on a smile.

"So," she said, taking a deep breath and entering Worth's room. "How's the bicycle?"

* * *

Ethan stood by the window in Hanson's Mercantile, his face hidden by the sign that told people the store was closed for the night. He tapped the letter from Francie against his palm as he watched Benjamin Cobb's shiny black carriage come to a stop in front of the Cottage Restaurant.

"They slumming tonight?" Risa asked him as she pulled the curtain closed. "Don't want these things to fade," she explained.

"Moon likely to do that?"

She stopped what she was doing. "You want to torture yourself? Fine. Or maybe you're thinking about doing something?"

"Risa, honey, don't I hear your family calling you?" If they weren't now, they would be soon. The moon and the earth revolved around Risa Morrow for them, as it should. It was the way it would be for him if there were a woman in his life. If there were some center to his life, instead of everything around him spinning out of control.

"What'd Francie have to say?" she asked, ignoring his comment about her family, knowing they'd wait for her.

He looked down at the letter as if it had just appeared in his hands. Outside, Corny was helping Silver down from his carriage, his hands on her waist.

"Ethan? You even open it?"

Corny held out his arm, and Sterling took it, resting a gloved hand in the crook of his elbow and then lifting her hem slightly as she stepped up onto the sidewalk. Corny pointed at her shoes, and she shrugged in response.

"What are you laughing at?" Risa asked.

"Was I?" He hadn't realized he'd let it escape. "I think Corny doesn't like being shorter than Miss Phillips." He pointed across the street where Corny was touching the top of his head and the top of Sterling's and pointing again at her boots.

Risa laughed and patted him on the back. "Well, you've got that on him, don't you?" she said.

"In spades," he agreed, bending his knees to kiss the top of his sister-in-law's head.

"You want to stay for supper?" Risa wiped her hands on her apron and untied the strings. "I've got plenty."

"Yeah," he said, knowing the view from the dining-room window upstairs would be the front table at the Cottage. And he had no doubt that Corny would have the window seat reserved. That way everyone in Van Wert would know that Sterling Phillips didn't find him too short. "If you're sure you don't mind."

"With you looking out the window," Risa said with a laugh, "we'll hardly know you're there. And somehow, I don't think you're gonna eat too much."

He didn't want to discuss what Sterling Phillips had done to his appetites. All of them.

"I'll be up in a minute. Think I'll just see what Francie has to say first."

Risa's sweet mouth pouted. "Be sure to tell me the good stuff."

He opened the letter and skimmed it, making sure that there was nothing he wanted to keep from Risa, and then read it aloud:

Dearest Ethan:

Just a quick note in case you couldn't hear me too well on the telephone. I know I could hardly hear you. We are leaving for Europe tonight (can you believe it?) and I am so very excited.

I'm sorry about the accident with the Phillips boy. To tell you the truth, Graham and I didn't even remember him. I suppose we were too busy falling in love around the time of Amelia Phillips's death.

Dr. Steinway says that there is always hope and that you can call him at any time with questions you might have. (It helps that Graham has endowed a wing at the medical college in his honor because of how he helped save Gregory's life.)

Did you say that Benjamin Cobb was treating the boy? Corny? I can't believe that man is a doctor! Just look at how far we've all come! (Though the truth is, Ethan, I never liked that boy. He was always bumping into me "accidentally." I mentioned that to Graham, and now he hates him too!)

Oh, Ethan! How I miss you. I don't know why you refuse to come back to New York. Stubborn! (Graham insists it runs in the family. What do you suppose he means by that? He also cautions you against taking all the responsibility on yourself and reminds you that accidents happen. He's terribly worried about you, though when I press him on why, he insists it's just because you are my brother. I do get the feeling there's more to it than that, and fully intend to spend some of our time aboard ship wheedling it out of the man, who sends you his deepest affection.)

Well, I must finish packing up the twins, and then we are off!

All my love,
Francie

Risa said nothing when he was finished. Ethan knew she was well aware of what he was thinking, and he appreciated the fact that for once she didn't try to buck up his spirits.

Look at how far we've all come!

Risa scratched at her belly discreetly. Baby number four was probably just weeks away.

The waiter in the restaurant across the street was seating Sterling and the doctor.

Look at how far we've all come!

"I think I'll head on home," he said softly. "I'm not really all that hungry."

Chapter Nine

"Listen to me carefully," Sterling said when she came down to the parlor where Carl had told him to wait. "I didn't want to let you see him at all, after what happened in the hall yesterday, but he's crying for you and I don't see how I can punish him for your actions."

Well, if he'd any doubts about the foolishness of that kiss, they were gone now. "It won't happen again."

"No," she agreed. "It won't. I will stay out of your way, and you will stay out of mine. I told Benjamin that you would not be seeing Worth anymore, and now I'm breaking my word to him."

"Well, I imagine you wouldn't want to lie to a man you're on a first-name basis with."

"In that case, Mr. Morrow, I won't worry about what I say to you."

"That kiss sure did rattle your branches, didn't it?" Lord, if there were droppings to be stepped in, he'd step in them. "I mean, it was only a kiss. It wasn't like we . . . like I compromised you."

They could have used her spine for a flagpole, she was so stiff, standing there with her jaw slightly open and her mind completely closed.

"Mr. Morrow, Worth's lunch is getting cold."

"I can see to him," he said. "I've been doing it every damn day. I don't see that one little kiss should change that."

She touched her lips and then quickly put her hand down. So it hadn't been just a little kiss for her either.

Might even have been her first, the way she reacted. And it had been quite a baptism.

"And no more funny business," he promised. "Nothing about how good you smell this morning, or that there's just a dot of breakfast jam on the corner of your mouth and I'd sure like—"

"I've got to see to Worth." She pointed toward the doorway, and when he didn't make a move, she stormed on in front of him and called over her shoulder. "Coming?"

Halfway up the stairs she seemed to remember his comment about her bottom, and he tried not to laugh as she obviously made an effort not to let her behind sway. Two steps later she glued herself to the wall and motioned for him to pass her.

"Jelly's still there," he said, pointing at her lip as he passed. "You want me to help you—"

"I want you to help me get some jam into my"—her hand flew to her mouth and she wiped at the jelly that wasn't even there.—"Worth. And Dr. Cobb says there is to be no exercise, no testing, and no lies. You can set him in the invalid chair when you're done."

Outside the boy's room, the red velocipede stood close to the wall, dusted and shined and out of the boy's sight. Ethan swallowed hard and kept his mouth shut.

The little buckaroo wiped the tears from his cheeks as they entered his room. Enormous blue eyes met his and then darted away toward the window. A faint smell of urine hung in the air.

"What's the matter, buckaroo?" he asked. "Don't you feel good?"

Worth shook his head as Sterling sailed toward the bed and reached for the covers, which the boy clung to with all the strength a three-year-old could muster.

"No!" the boy yelled, refusing to release the covers, his eyes fastened on Ethan.

"Honey lamb," Sterling said sweetly. "You're wet and I just want to get you changed. Then you and Mr. Morrow can have a little visit. Okay?" She pulled at the covers again without success.

"I'm not wet," the boy said, following it with an enormous sniff and wiping his nose on his pajama sleeve.

"Well, we'll just see about that," Sterling said, waiting for him to release the covers.

"No!" The boy's face was a mess of tears and runny nose.

"Let him be," Ethan finally said, staying her hand and easing the comforter out from her fingers. "He doesn't want to be changed right now."

"But—"

Ethan twirled her gently so that she was facing the door, and then made little hand motions at the boy, pointing first to himself and nodding, then to Sterling and walking his fingers out the door. The boy, lost in the pillows and quilts and bedding, nodded solemnly.

"I sure could go for a nice cool drink, and so could my pardner here. What do you say to going down to the kitchen and rustling us up some lemonade?"

"I'll get Abigail," Sterling said, looking out toward the hallway.

"You get it," Ethan said, nudging her toward the door and wondering where the woman's brains were, as he'd like to give her a gentle kick in them. Couldn't she see her brother's embarrassment? Didn't she sense that the buckaroo and he needed some time to set things right?

"It's okay, son," Ethan said over his shoulder. "Nothing to fret over."

He was pressed right up against her as he pushed her softly from the room, his thigh against the back of her leg, which he felt despite the layers of skirting she wore, his chest against her back. Her white-blond hair tickled his chin. The sweet lemony scent of it teased his nose.

Beneath his thumbs the tensest muscles he had ever felt knotted even more tightly. He made little circles with his thumbs. "He's all right," Ethan murmured, each word setting her hair to waving like a field of ripe wheat rippling in the breeze.

"But he's crying and I don't even know what it is that hurts him. Maybe it's his—" She tried to turn, but he held tight, pinning her to the wall, an arm on either side of her head. Tears were flooding her eyes and he wiped them away with his thumb, finding her silkier even than he remembered.

"It's just his pride that's hurting," Ethan said, staring at the wetness her tears had left on his thumb.

Eyebrows lowered over the bluest eyes God had ever seen fit to give a living, breathing person. Eyes bluer than the sky, than the lake, than a jay in winter. . . .

"His pride? You mean because he—"

"—watered the sheets," Ethan finished for her, making sure his voice was too low for Worth to hear and then licking the wetness off his thumb pad.

She looked at the floor rather than at him. "That's ridiculous. He's been back in diapers for weeks now. You've been changing him day and night. You've probably changed him a hundred times . . . more. Now suddenly he's ashamed to be in diapers?"

"You said it yourself. *I've* changed him."

"Yes, but at the beginning . . . and when he was a baby . . . For heaven's sake, I'm the one that got him out of diapers! I've wiped his bottom a million times! Now suddenly I'm not supposed to see to him? That's ridiculous," she said, obviously aiming to go right back into the little boy's room and tell him so. And had Ethan not reached out and grabbed her around the waist, he supposed that was exactly what she would have done, shaming him unmercifully in the process.

"I'll take care of it," he said. *I'll take care of everything.* His arm encircled her waist easily. Didn't anyone ever feed the woman? She was barely bigger than some of his nieces. Two pieces of hay took up more room than her arm. A handful was bigger than the woman's waist.

"He's not a baby anymore, Silver. And while you've changed him, it's never been in front of me. Don't you see the difference?"

"But he's mine," she said, and he could feel the injustice of it all stiffening her spine and shaking her shoulders. "You should be the one to go away."

"We can save him a little embarrassment. That's all I'm asking," he said, feeling two ribs with his fingers and realizing that the slight bulge just above his thumb was someplace he certainly shouldn't wander.

Shit.

He expected her to thrust her elbow back into his gut. He was ready for her to stomp with the heel of her boot on his instep. He wished she'd spin around and give him the slap he deserved.

Instead she stood stock-still.

So still he wasn't sure she was breathing. As for himself, he hadn't taken a breath since he'd felt his own body begin to react to the fact that the silver princess, despite their promises to the contrary, was back in his arms.

He could have stayed like that all day, or for a lifetime.

"All right," she said. He waited for her to demand he release her. And waited still.

Just breathing moved her breast against his thumb. For Ethan, swallowing became an effort; not cupping the tiny treasure, a test of his will.

"So then you'll go downstairs while I change him?" he asked, stalling for time to keep her in his arms.

She nodded, but still she didn't pull away. Didn't she have any idea what she was doing to him? Didn't she know the dangers of being so close to a man?

"And you'll knock before you come in?"

Again she nodded, that fine, soft hair of hers catching on the stubble of his chin and pulling at the strings of his heart.

He knew better. He had some experience, enough to

know that with some women one thing led quickly to another. Chemistry, his brother-in-law Noah called it. Combustion was more like it.

Damn it all!

He had no business cozying up to this woman. Especially when she'd asked him not to. It wasn't like he had anything to offer her, what with his dirty fingernails and his farm-boy education. Christ, he lived in a barn, worked his brother-in-law's farm, and still owed Cornucopia Cobb two dollars and fifty cents for her brother's care. Not only didn't he have a pot to pee in, he didn't have a place to stow it if he had had the good fortune to stumble across one.

She knew it as well as he did, so why didn't she pull away, slap his cheek, wag a threatening finger in his face? Why did she have to torture him with the soft body she planned on giving to Benjamin Cobb along with Ethan's hard-earned money?

"Cowboy?" Worth's tiny voice was filled with tears. Lord, if only he'd watched where he was going. He'd be building some lean-to or cabin in Oklahoma right this minute instead of standing in Harrington Manor, his arms wrapped around a slip of a girl who ought to have the good sense to be repulsed by everything about him. A girl whose brother he'd crippled and whose dreams he'd shattered along with his own.

"I'm coming," he called to the boy as he released the princess and took a respectful step away, nearly laughing at himself for doing so after mauling her. "Sorry," he mumbled in her general direction. "I won't let it happen again."

*   *   *

Sterling's hands shook so badly that she was lucky any of the lemonade made it into the glasses. There was no controlling her breathing, which was heavy and ragged and all out of proportion to the incident outside

Worth's room. He'd touched her. That was all. He'd needed to tell her about her son.

"Oh, lemonade! How nice," Aunt Imogene said, breezing through the kitchen on her way out to the garden, a flower basket looped over her arm. "Do you think the dog will like it?"

Sterling followed the line of her aunt's vision to the puddle of lemonade near her feet. "I'm sure he will," she said as brightly as she could while she busied herself with the cheesecloth that covered the pitcher. "Well, I've got to bring this upstairs."

Aunt Imogene crossed her arms over her chest and strummed her fingers. "You should tell him," she warned Sterling. "Before he gets too attached."

Sterling's stomach, already in knots, threatened to come up her throat and strangle her.

"Unless, of course, you'll let him." Her aunt looked out the window of the back door and tapped on it until that mangy black dog that followed Ethan everywhere got up on his hind legs and started fogging the glass with his breath.

She wished her aunt made any sense at all.

"You know I can't, Aunt Genie." Sterling forced the words out around the lump in her throat.

"Well, then, what about the boy, for pity's sake," her aunt said, pushing up against the pane so that the dog could lick at her face. Sterling wasn't sure whether her aunt was teasing the dog or not, nor whether the dog minded at all.

"Worth is the reason I can't," she reminded her aunt, who really ought to have known better.

"But the cowboy could carry him," Aunt Imogene said, opening the door and pointing the animal in the direction of Sterling's feet.

"Forever?" Sterling asked, trying to resist the dog's big eyes as he looked up at her, drooling, and cocked his head as if he couldn't understand why she wouldn't just give him a gentle pat.

Why, she wondered, would a man with all the freedom in the world tie himself to a dog that needed his chin wiped every time someone looked at him?

"Better than you. And it would just be until they got to the meadow," her aunt said, shaking her head even more than it shook naturally. "Then he could put the child in that blasted chair or on a blanket and prop him up with pillows or a basket or . . ."

The dog let out a small bark and sat with his tail banging between the cupboard and the floor as if he simply wanted to be noticed.

"Yes," her aunt said. "The dog could sit behind him and . . ."

Sterling's thoughts were spinning. She put her hands on her head and talked to herself with her eyes closed. "There is some kernel of sense here somewhere, and if I just stay calm, I'll discover it. I just have to stay calm."

"For heaven's sake," Aunt Imogene said. She pulled a piece of Leona's fried chicken off the counter and slipped it to the dog behind her back as if Sterling had any right to stop her, or perhaps Leona might come into her kitchen and tell her mistress what she could do with her chicken. "If you don't want to go on a picnic, then don't go. Lord knows, you might have some fun and we wouldn't want that."

"A picnic?"

"But I don't see why Worth and I can't go. If the whole town is invited, then that means me, doesn't it? And the boy." Her aunt pulled out a chair from the table and sat on it, patting her lap for the dog, who came and put his head in it, burrowing against her legs.

Vaguely Sterling remembered something being mentioned several weeks ago in church about a picnic, but the details evaded her. She was probably too busy watching Sir Glad-I-am's hair fall into his eyes, or the way he took one child or another onto his lap, or the way he stood and sang the hymns like they really meant something to him. But Sir Glad-I-am was just a dream.

And upstairs, Ethan Morrow, the farmer seeing to her son, was reality. Or maybe they were both dreams, and reality was a nightmare.

"You know," Aunt Imogene said, raising one eyebrow at the cost of shutting the other eye, "I could give that man up there permission to take Worth to the picnic without you having any say in it."

Sterling merely swallowed. It was as much as she could control under the circumstances. Her aunt and uncle had never challenged her role in Worth's life, letting her make the decisions, letting her be the one to comfort him, letting her be the one into whose arms he came running, despite the longing her aunt must have felt to have a child, to hold him, to love him.

"Maybe I can't make you find the joy in life," her aunt conceded, "but I can't let you hide it from him."

"I am not hiding anything from him," she said through gritted teeth. Sometimes she preferred her aunt's odd moments to those where she was blindingly, uncompromisingly lucid. "I am merely sheltering him from pain, from loss. Can you blame me for that?"

"We could pin his toys to his clothes," her aunt said, then explained the plan to the dog. "With pretty ribbons."

Aunt Genie was gone again, free within the grounds where bad things were not allowed to happen and hurt was made to stand outside the gates. Sterling came and petted her aunt's head, much as her aunt was petting the dog's. "Why would we do that?" she asked her softly.

"What else could he lose at the picnic?" her aunt asked, then looked up at her with clear violet eyes. "And what should we pin to you?"

* * *

"You're sure?" Ethan asked again, unable to make any sense of it. He pricked Worth's foot one more time, but it was clear the boy felt nothing.

"Could you open it, please," Sterling called from beyond the door. "I've got my hands full."

"Put it on the floor and get in here," Ethan shouted, not about to stop his testing for anything. "What about here?" he asked, running the pin up Worth's shin.

He could hear the rattling of glasses and the low swearing that accompanied a crash. "I said get in here," he shouted at the door again.

With a bang the door flew open and Sterling stood in the doorway, her skirt full of lemonade. "What's wrong?" she asked, her hands behind her back. "What's happened?"

"He felt the piss," Ethan said, then, realizing how crude he must have sounded, tried to find a way to say it better. "The wetness on his leg," he said, "from relieving himself. It was uncomfortable."

"Oh, honey lamb, I'm so sorry," she started, then stopped and stared at him and then at Worth. "You felt it?" She swayed, and Ethan reached out to steady her.

Her whole body shuddered against him, shoulders and elbows digging into his ribs while she grasped his shirt for dear life in one fist. She sucked at the air and swallowed as if she was drowning at sea, and she heaved great, blubbery sobs he didn't think she had in her, soaking his shirt with her tears.

He could feel her head shaking against his chest, back and forth. "He really is going to be all right, isn't he?" she finally asked against his shirt, tickling his wet skin with her breath and sending shivers up his arms.

"He still doesn't feel the pin," he admitted, hoping to ground her just a little. "At least not in his feet, but he felt something, Silver. He felt something!"

She put her hands up to her face, trying to hide the tears that still fell with wild abandon.

"Ster!" Worth screamed, pointing at her and yelling. "Blood! She's bleeding!"

Ethan pulled her away from his chest and saw the blood on her hand and face. "What the heck . . . ?" he asked, wiping her face with his shirttail and then checking her hand.

"It's nothing. Just the glasses," she said, pointing back toward the doorway, where a mess of crystal littered the floor and behind which her aunt and uncle stood gawking.

"There's nothing wrong," her aunt Imogene kept repeating, shaking her head back and forth. "There's no dead baby. No dead mama. She's all right. The baby's all right. Seven and no more. There's nothing wrong. There's no jinx, Oliver. Nobody's taking another baby."

"Let me look at it," Ethan said, grabbing at her hand while she held it away from him, her excitement about the buckaroo much too important to let a bleeding palm interfere. "At least put this around it," he said, handing her a clean towel from the dresser and wrapping her hand in it. She sat down on the edge of the bed, staring at her honey lamb as though he had just gotten up and trotted around the room.

No, ridden around it on a brand-new red velocipede.

"They're both fine," he told Imogene Harrington and her husband quietly in the hall. "The princess just cut herself on some glassware I never should have sent her to get, and the boy, the Buckaroo . . . well, he didn't like the feel of the piss on his leg!" Now he didn't care how it sounded. In fact he couldn't remember anything ever sounding more wonderful, so he said it again. "He didn't like the piss on his leg, imagine that!"

"What does it mean?" Imogene asked him in a whisper, her eyes wide as he reached around her and picked up the bicycle triumphantly.

"It means the spinal cord isn't severed," Oliver told her, taking Ethan by surprise. It hadn't seemed to him that Oliver Harrington was even aware his nephew had been injured. "It means that maybe . . . maybe, everything will be all right."

Imogene took a ragged breath. One, and then another.

"Come away now, dearest," Oliver said as Ethan watched the emotions war on his face. There was concern for the boy, concern for his wife. Mostly there was out-and-out fear.

"He's gonna be fine," Ethan said, putting his hand on the man's shoulder.

Oliver Harrington studied him, reminding Ethan that he was in dire need of a shave, a haircut, a good soak in a hot tub. He got the feeling, though, that Oliver was looking past all that for something deeper. A soft, sad smile touched the man's lips. "I don't believe you'll settle for anything less, will you?"

"No, sir," Ethan replied. "I'd better see to Miss Sterling's hand, if you'll excuse me."

"You see," he heard Imogene Harrington tell her husband as the two of them walked down the hall, Oliver's arm around his wife's waist. "I told you that boy would make everything all right, just the way *you* promised *me* so long ago."

"Shhh, now, Genie," Oliver said. "Don't we know better than to tempt fate?"

Though they were, without a doubt, the oddest two people Ethan had ever met, he found that he genuinely liked them more each day. There was just something so dear, so helpless about them, as if they'd been asked to pay too great a price for their wealth and would gladly exchange what they had for something far simpler if only they knew the way.

Or maybe it was just that he felt sorry for anyone who was foolish enough to put their trust in him. He was surely no one's savior. Not even his own.

* * *

Sterling was cradling her hand by the side of the bed, so happy with the promise of Worth's recovery that she felt no pain.

"When the prince is growed up, will he be a knight?" the Buckaroo was asking.

"Maybe," Silver answered, allowing Ethan to remove the towel from her injured hand. "More than likely, he'll be a knight."

"No," Worth said. "He's gonna be a cowboy."

"He is not!" Sterling said. She might have been telling the story for Worth's sake, but it was her story, and she was not about to let a bunch of cowboys and Indians take over where fair ladies and their knights had always presided.

"If he wants to be a cowboy, there'll be no stopping him," Ethan said, as if it was any of his business. "Now, let me see your hand."

He waited patiently, his hand extended, until she offered her own.

"It doesn't look too bad," he said. "But we'd better make sure there's no glass left in there."

"I'm sure it's fine," she said, leaving her open hand resting in his palm. "I want you to test him again. See if there's anything . . ."

But her baby's little eyes were barely able to stay open, and she couldn't argue when Ethan suggested they let him rest. Gently he guided her up from her seat and over toward the window, where she supposed the sunlight would help him see any shard of glass her hand might still harbor.

While he examined her injuries, she studied the top of his head. Every strand of his hair seemed a different shade of honey and wheat, each one glistening in the sunlight as if they were competing for her attention. Toward the back of his head, several hairs stuck upward like the shadow of a cowlick, which had no doubt been the bane of his existence as a boy.

With a damp cloth he cleared away the blood and tilted and pressed her hand this way and that. Finally he dipped his head and planted a kiss in the center of her palm. "Sissy always used to say a kiss would make it better," he explained, letting his gaze meet hers.

His hair was a hundred different colors, but his eyes

were solid amber, deep and rich and lit with a fire from within. And his gaze was soft, tender, questioning. She remembered quite clearly the last time someone had kissed her to make the pain go away. But she had been only a girl then, and naive enough to believe in the power of love.

Still, she didn't pull her hand away.

Instead she curled her fingers around the kiss that slept in her palm, and hoped that, alone in her bed some night, she might find it and remember the soft lips that had tenderly put it there.

"I understand you want to take Worth to a picnic," she said, studying a small scar that marred the perfection of his jawbone. How foolish to want to touch the spot and ask him what had happened there, where the stubble that darkened his chin refused to grow.

He cleared his throat, and she wished she could clear her head as easily. "I thought it was time the buckaroo got some fresh air, got out of that bed. I suppose you and the Cornshucker think it's a bad idea."

The poor little thing couldn't walk, couldn't even sit up without resting against something. How could he enjoy watching other children run and jump and play? And he was right about Benjamin. *Inappropriate activity,* she could just hear him say.

But when Sissy Eastman had finally managed to find the time to make Worth those awful boys-with-broken-legs cookies, he'd been delighted, not saddened. "Just imagine how he'll feel when she makes him Boys on Bicycles," Ethan had said.

"He can go," she said, hoping she was doing this for her son and not for the man with the amber eyes and the earnest look, whose surprise was growing into a smile.

"I think you'd better come along with him," he said, and she could feel the heat rising off his body and enveloping her. "Just in case he needs anything."

"All right. For Worth," she agreed, not wanting him

to get the wrong impression. Worth's feeling something was wonderful, incredible news. But it didn't change anything between the two of them. "But if it turns out that he's unhappy or uncomfortable, you'll take us right home?"

"If either of you are unhappy or uncomfortable," he agreed, brushing a curl off her face and letting his hand linger a moment in her hair.

"I'm already uncomfortable," she said, shaking her head and rubbing at a spot on the back of her neck.

"Maybe I just take a little getting used to." He backed away as if that would give her time and space to do just that. But all the time and space in the world wasn't going to change her feelings about the man whose fingertips were idly touching the blue ribbon that hung limply from her dress.

"If you're thinking that there can be something between us, Ethan Morrow, let me assure you, there can't." She pulled at the ribbon he held between his fingers, watching as he only slowly let it slip through his hand. The women in town said he was so handsome they ought to hang a danger sign around his neck. She didn't need the sign to read the signals. "I'm not the girl for you. Don't ever forget that."

"After I leave this mansion you call home sweet home, I stick these dirty boots under a rickety cot in a barn so flimsy that a good gust of wind could turn it into a memory. And you think you gotta remind me that I've got nothing to offer you? I shovel muck and patch roofs and count my pennies to pay off your doctor friend and you think I don't know that I'm not your dream man?"

"It's not the money, Ethan," she said. "We just weren't meant to be together, you and I."

"I don't know about that, princess," he said as if he just couldn't resist. "I just might be the one you've been saving yourself for."

Now, what was a woman supposed to say to something like that? Especially a woman who hadn't saved herself? She dusted imaginary crumbs from her skirt and finally looked up at her shining knight. "I think we saw a miracle today. Worth might be going to get well, and I can't tell you how grateful I am. How grateful I will always be. But that doesn't change things between us, Mr. Morrow. I am never going to be the woman for you."

"Hey," he said, all casual, all calm, while her heart raced and her breath was ragged. "If we get one miracle—and we will—who's to say we won't get two?" Then he simply shrugged his shoulders and let the last of the ribbon escape his grasp.

Chapter Ten

He waited, holding Worth in his arms, while Sterling spread out the blanket just so, making sure the ends were even, removing a cherry blossom that fell onto the fine brown wool, smoothing once again the surface as it yielded to the tufts of grass and weeds below it.

"This was a mistake," she said for perhaps the twentieth time since he'd come for them, delaying them over and over while Sissy's lunch and Honesty both melted in the wagon.

"It's just a picnic," he said with a sigh.

"I should have mentioned to Dr. Cobb that I was bringing Worth here." She pulled on a corner of the blanket, dragging it half an inch to the west.

"He gonna be here?" he asked, shifting the boy in his arms and blowing in his ear like a little bug. The child swatted at his ear twice before catching him, and then blew hard back in Ethan's face with that wonderful child's breath his nieces and nephews all had.

"No. He's got office hours until two."

And everyone knew that if Dr. Cobb had office hours, he was in that office. Blizzards, droughts, plagues, and fires. Weddings, funerals, births, and deaths. . . . Well, births and deaths he did attend to, but he preferred they happened either in the office or outside of office hours.

"You ever gonna let me set the boy down?" he asked after she had rearranged the pillows for the third time. He thought it probably took the woman an hour to get into bed at night, and then felt his cheeks warm at the thought. He shifted his weight in an effort to keep the buckaroo comfortable and reminded himself that Sterling Phillips's bedtime routine was no concern of his.

"Maybe we'd be better off over there," she suggested, pointing toward a clearing on the rise. For as long as Ethan could recall, the children had always flown their kites on the grassy hill because there were no trees for the strings to get caught up in. The rise was empty at the moment only due to the fact that it was early and most families preferred to eat first and fly later. He supposed Sterling didn't know that, since he couldn't recall her ever coming to the town picnics or the socials, nor, when he thought about it, had he seen her anywhere but at church or in Hanson's.

"Here's fine," he said, watching the sun glint off hair the color of wheat ready to be harvested. "I hope your sister brought a nice big bonnet," he told the boy in his arms, because he sure as heck didn't want to look at that hair of hers all afternoon while he kept his hands in his pockets.

"All right," she said as she smoothed the blanket one last time and picked at a tiny feather. "You can put him down now."

"You do have some kind of hat, don't you?" he asked as he got down on one knee and gently placed Worth so that he was very nearly sitting up, facing the rise where kites would soon dot the sky.

He watched her search the crowd without answering and busied himself with the buckaroo.

"Can Honesty come now?" the boy asked. "Can I call him?"

"Mrs. Eastman isn't wearing a bonnet," Sterling said, dropping to her knees and digging in the basket she'd carried from the wagon herself. After removing two sweaters for Worth and a small blue blanket, she unearthed a navy-blue hat for the buckaroo that could only be called jaunty—unless one wanted to be nasty, in which case it could have been called useless.

"This is the hat you brought to keep the sun off the

Ghost Rider?" he asked, making Worth laugh as he set the hat sailing in the air and called to Honesty to catch it. "Jeez. Go ahead and call him, Bucky."

"Come, boy," Worth yelled, and Honesty, a very wet blue hat dripping from his mouth, came bounding over to the blanket, the closest thing to a smile that a dog could manage on his stupid face.

Sterling, however, wasn't smiling.

"He can wear my hat," Ethan said, placing his genuine imitation cowboy's sombrero on the boy's head and tilting it back far enough so that the boy could not only see but breathe. "But you," he said to the girl, whose face had never even been licked by the sun, never mind out-and-out roasted, "are another matter."

"Is that not your sister," Sterling asked, pointing with her chin toward Sissy and Noah's blanket, where the children were already gathering for kites made of flour and sugar and love, "with the invisible hat on her head?"

"I'd be real careful about comparing myself with Sissy if I was you," Ethan said softly. Sissy was as close to perfect as Ethan had ever known a woman to be. And he didn't like the way this new baby that was growing inside her was taking its toll. There were dark circles under her eyes, and she was having more trouble keeping down her meals than he remembered from the last time.

But Jeez, he hadn't meant to give offense. There wasn't any call for the tears that were threatening in Silver's eyes.

"I only meant that she's been in the sun all her life and it's not gonna burn her the way it would you." The woman put her nose in the air. Maybe that was just so that he couldn't miss the fact that it was out of joint.

Ten o'clock in the morning and already the day was going to woe in a wheelbarrow.

First off there was the fact that although Worth had finally begun to respond on his own to the steady diet of licorice, Earling's Fig Tonic, and Sissy's dynamite—and it was Ethan's feeling that it was just another sign that the child's body was coming back—the boy had felt nothing this morning when Ethan had tested him.

Then poor Genie'd gotten so excited about coming along on a picnic that she'd had another asthma attack and wound up in bed with her bottom lip sticking out so far he thought it was an extra blanket.

And all Worth wanted to know was how that damn Princess Sugarlips was going to get over the moat now that she'd been unflowered.

Not to mention that Sissy'd packed caution in with every morsel of food she'd put into the hamper, insisting he was making a big mistake getting involved with Sterling Phillips and her brother. And he had warned her right back that if the circles under her eyes got any darker, she'd look like Noah had taken to beating her to keep her in line.

Ah, yes! A fine day for a picnic, if one discounted the haze that sat over the tops of the oak trees, the scowl on Silver's face, the sight of Noah helping Sissy off to the copse of trees, no doubt to lose another of her wonderful meals, and Honesty's nose in the basket he'd brought.

And contrary to the weather, to the circumstances, to the warnings and the futility, just the scent of Sterling Phillips was making his insides flip. It was nothing she did on purpose—he was sure of that. The last thing she could have been trying to do was attract this particular bee to her honey, but it took every last bit of strength he had to keep himself from buzzing around her. And he was so all-out tired of fighting it, the effort proved too great to resist.

So he went ahead and let himself reach over her to swat at the dog. "Get outta the basket there, Honesty," he said, his shoulder blazing at the contact with her breast. "Come on now," he shouted at the dog—all the while praying the mutt would never stop his nosing so that the feminine thigh that was nestled in the pit of Ethan's arm could warm his insides indefinitely.

"Mr. Morrow," she whined at him, trying to push him off her lap. "What do you think people will suppose if they look over this way?"

"You sure you don't have a hat?" The sun could sure eat up those pale cheeks, and that pert nose too.

"Same one your sister's got on," she said, spreading her skirts out around her like a fan and touching Worth's cheeks to check his temperature.

"You all right, buckaroo?" he asked, tweaking the boy's foot a moment before realizing that the boy couldn't feel it. There was something about getting him outside, down on the ground, that made him seem healthier; something about Honesty tugging at the hat he'd placed on the boy's head that made him seem happier.

"He knows it's yours," the boy said, awkwardly pulling off the hat that was ten sizes too big for his head and trying to hold it out to Ethan.

"He'll get over it," Ethan said, gesturing for the boy to keep the hat on. Not a lick darker than his sister, the two of them were gonna be roasted marshmallows come the afternoon.

"You want me to see if I can borrow a hat from one of my brothers for you?" he offered, sorry he hadn't thought to bring an extra, though a girl that pale ought to have thought of it herself.

"Oh, really. You're making too much of this. It isn't even sunny out. And I've never burned," she said as if the whole subject bored her.

"Okay, but don't blame me when you're burned to a crisp and someone mistakes you for the Indian in front of the smoke shop."

He pressed her nose slightly with one finger. The skin was even whiter when he took his hand away. He hoped she wasn't already starting to fry.

"So, I was thinking that maybe if there was a bird big

enough, he could take Princess Sugarlips on his back and fly her over the moat," Sterling suggested, pointing to a robin that was pecking at the ground only a few feet from the blanket.

"But how could the bird get big enough?" Worth asked, rubbing at first one arm and then the other.

"She could feed him magic seeds. Are you warm, honey lamb?" She set about pushing up his sleeves while Ethan saw to removing the boy's cotton hose. She lifted a few stray hairs off her own neck and blew at her forehead, sending curls flying. "It sure is warm out here."

"We could start on your clothes next," Ethan suggested, and got a preview of what she'd look like sunburned when her cheeks flamed. "You really are too easy a target," he teased as he dusted the fuzz off the bottom of Worth's feet.

The boy, who had been busy playing with Honesty while he and Sterling fussed over him, turned abruptly at his touch. "Stop it!" he whined. "It feels funny."

The smile that spread across Ethan's face took longer than the one on Silver's. Hers was instantaneous, and fleeting, as she covered her face with her hands and her shoulders trembled.

Maybe she didn't want to share the moment with him, all turned in on herself like that. But it was too wondrous to keep to himself, so he rose to his knees and crawled over to where she wept silently. They were on the edge of the meadow, and all it took was half a turn to wedge his body between hers and any onlookers who might have been interested in what was going on over at the Phillipses' blanket. "Give in," he said as he put his arms around her and pulled her hands away from her lovely face, contorted now from trying not to cry. "Let it go."

He felt the shaking of her head against his ribs, but all her resolve couldn't will the tiny sobs away nor stem the flow of tears that wet his shirt. Over and over she told him that Worth was going to be fine, as if he was the one needing reassurance.

"She's just happy," he assured a worried Worth, whose chin quivered at the sight of his sister falling to pieces in Ethan's arms. "She's so happy inside, it just has to come out somewhere," Ethan explained, rubbing her back and hoping it would take a long, long time for her to settle down, because nothing and no one had ever felt so right in his life.

There was something hitting his shoulder, tapping on him like some small woodpecker, but he paid it no mind. Stroking the white-blond hair that tickled his nose and inhaling the lemon verbena scent that rose from her head, he crooned softly to the woman in his arms. "Didn't I promise you he'd be all right?"

"You gonna fly it with me?" The voice was young, small, and came from just over his left shoulder.

"James?"

Sterling stiffened in his arms and jerked away, sniffing and pulling herself up prim all at once.

"My pa said to ask you to fly it with me." James tilted his head as he stared at Worth, who had begun to slant to the side and was unable to right himself.

"Let me help you there, buckaroo," Ethan said, pulling the boy up and then transferring him to his lap. "How's that?"

"The kite," James repeated. "Are you gonna fly it with me? You can't fly a kite by yourself, you know."

"No, I suppose you can't," Ethan said, his eyes on Worth as he tried to arrange the boy so that he'd be comfortable. Finally he settled for placing him between his legs, where his thighs made two good armrests for the child. "Why doesn't your father help you?"

"*He* can't fly one," James said, gesturing with his chin at Worth. "Can't even walk, never mind run."

"He's gonna be just fine," Ethan said, not sure that Worth had any idea just how seriously he'd been hurt, nor how permanent it could be.

Not that it mattered, now that he was beginning to get the feeling back in his legs. It had to mean that the worst was over, no matter how cautious the Corn Cockle had been when they'd told him about Worth's discomfort the other day. Even though he continued to counsel them that the boy's recovery was far from guaranteed, he'd been forced, however reluctantly, to admit it was a good sign.

James kicked at the dirt beside the blanket, and the tick next to his eye that had started after his brother died seemed to go crazy. "Guess it was my fault," he said, a tuft of grass flying from his boot toe up into the air and landing inches from Sterling's clean white skirt.

"It was not your fault," she told him adamantly, ignoring the dirt as she reached out and took his hand. "You just wanted to say good-bye to your uncle. There's nothing wrong in that."

"But he turned around to see me," James whined.

"And he shouldn't have," she said quietly, moving herself away on the blanket and tugging James with her. "But I should have been watching Worth myself. It wasn't you who's to blame."

Shit. Just when he'd gotten her to let go of some of that guilt, for both their sakes. It was all off the back of the buckboard now. To prove it, she leaned over and took the baby from where he was nestled comfortably against Ethan and settled him on her own lap as if that was where he belonged.

"Go on back to your blanket now," he told James, fighting the grimace that was trying to claim his mouth. "Aunt Sissy's probably got some cookies for you."

"They're not for me," James said quietly, still kicking at the ground. "I saw them. They're for him." His chin jutted in Worth's direction again.

"I should have thought to make you some more madeleines," Silver said to James. "You seemed to like them."

"Aunt Risa said I shouldn't come over here. She said to leave the lovebirds alone."

Oh, that was great. Ethan rolled his eyes and sighed. Just what the day needed—rumors running rampant, and his own family starting them.

"Your aunt's a real kidder, James. Well, buckaroo, what do you say we saunter over there and get ourselves a couple of Sissy's cookies? She was still decorating 'em when I took off to get you." Ethan stood up and stretched.

Every muscle in his body was objecting to his labors. It was the ice hauling that was the worst, cutting his hands until they were raw, taxing his back and his spirit as he picked at the block in the dark cellar and then raced it to his deliveries before too much of it became an inviting puddle to drown himself in right there in the back of Mr. Hertel's truck.

"We'll wait here," Sterling said when he reached down for the baby. "Then, I think, considering the way things look even to your own family, it's time for us to go."

"My father left a kite for me," James told a tuft of grass.

"That's nice," Ethan said, putting a hand around James's shoulder. "Isn't your dad here?"

James shook his head sullenly. "He's never here."

He'd have accused the kid of exaggerating, but he couldn't remember the last time he'd seen Peter Gibbs. The day of the accident, he supposed. Just what James needed, a father who was always at the bank and a mother who sat by the window watching for his dead brother to come home. Why was it that the nasty, mean people of the world never got the short end of the stick, and sweet, decent boys like James and Worth were left orphaned and hurting? And why was it that he couldn't do a damn thing about it?

With a sigh he put his arm around James. "Let's go get some cookies before they're all gone."

"And then?" Sterling asked him.

"I told you I'd take you home whenever you asked," he said as pleasantly as he could muster. "But it's a shame for the buckaroo to miss the kite flying, don't you think?"

"You and I could fly it," James said, slipping his hand into Ethan's.

He saw the look on Sterling's face. *I knew I couldn't trust you*, it said. "Sorry, James. It looks like I've got to go."

"Next year?" James asked a dandelion.

"I don't know where I'll be next year," he said as they walked away from the blanket. Judging the way the wind was blowing, he guessed she heard him just fine.

*   *   *

"Ready, then?" he asked, apparently not pleased that while he was off saying good-bye to the entire population of Van Wert, all of whom he seemed to be related to, she had managed to pack up everything, fold up the blanket, and was standing ready to leave.

"All set," she said as pleasantly as she could. "Sure you said good-bye to everyone? I stopped counting at a hundred and twelve."

"Jealous that I've got so many relatives and friends?" he asked. She supposed her face showed that she was, because he was quick to tell her he was only kidding. "Want to know the latest gossip?"

"No!" The word was out of her mouth so quick and hard that Ethan nearly lost his balance backing away from her. "I don't like gossip. It's hurtful and destructive."

He looked at her as if she'd grown a third ear. One side of his lip came up. "Fine. I won't tell you who's expecting if you don't want to know."

"That's just what I mean," she said, her hands on her hips now that he'd taken Worth from her arms. "Rumor and innuendo, hints of scandal. It's nobody's business, I tell you."

He blinked at her twice. "Heck, it's just Tessie Winestock, honey. And you ought to see the reverend, picking her chicken off the bone for her like it's too great an effort for someone in her condition."

"Oh." She felt like a fool. A jealous fool.

"I guess we'd better go," he said, gathering up what he could in addition to Worth. "Must be the sun or something," he muttered to the boy as they started across the meadow toward the wagon.

"Wait, Uncle Ethan!" a voice called, and for just a moment, a second, her heart stopped cold in her chest and she couldn't stop herself from gasping and grabbing at Worth, as though it wasn't weeks too late. The words had caught him too. There was wild fear in his amber eyes. His Adam's apple bobbed furiously.

"What's the matter, Hannah?" he asked, handing the baby over to Sterling and wiping his palms on his jeans.

"One Shoe's up a tree," she said, her gaze darting between Ethan and Sterling. "I mean James. He says he's gonna jump, and Daddy said to get you fast."

"Me?" Ethan asked. Sterling supposed that in addition to all his other talents, Ethan Morrow was the best tree climber in Ohio. It didn't surprise her that her knight in shining armor might be someone else's too. He gave her an apologetic shrug and gestured to Hannah to lead the way. Sterling followed along like a faithful squire, her baby in her arms.

There was a good crowd gathered beneath the spreading limbs of an old white oak, all with their heads craned upward, many wringing their hands in despair. It felt as if she'd fallen into her own fairy tale, which seemed overly dramatic until she tilted her own head back and realized how high the boy had climbed and how precariously he was perched.

"Get on that branch good and secure," Ethan yelled

at his nephew. "I don't want to shake you loose with my climbing."

"Think I'll die if I jump?" the boy asked, swinging his leg and looking down over the crowd until he found his uncle.

"That what you had in mind?" Ethan asked him. He sounded cool as a spring breeze, but his face had lost its color and the vein by his temple was throbbing visibly.

"Or will I just be a cripple, do you think?"

"If you don't hold on to that branch a damn sight better than you're doing . . . ," Ethan muttered. Then he cleared his throat and called up the tree, "What's this all about, James?"

Around her Sterling heard the children whispering to each other.

"One Shoe's crazy."

"One Shoe's gonna jump!"

"Don't jump, One Shoe! We'll let you use our kite if you don't jump!"

"I don't want your stupid kite," he called down, his leg still waving with studied carelessness. "I got my own kite. But Uncle Ethan won't fly it with me."

"That what's bothering you?" Ethan called up to him. He looked around at the crowd and whispered to Noah Eastman. "Where the heck is Peter? The bank's not open today. Why isn't he here?"

Noah Eastman's usually open face slammed closed. "James came along with Charlie and Risa and the kids."

Charlie, coming up behind them, added, "And it was like getting molasses off the cat to get him to come at all. The only thing that got him here at all was when Risa told him you'd be coming."

"You blackmailing me, James Gibbs?" Ethan hollered up to him. "This how I taught you to get what you want in life?"

"James," Sterling called up to the boy, who looked mighty small from so far away. "Your uncle wanted to fly that kite with you, but I asked him to take me home, so he couldn't. It wasn't his fault he disappointed you, it was mine."

Glory-laury, but the crowd quieted down in a hurry. Ethan, his upper lip wet with perspiration, gave her a smile that could leave the town a swimming hole where the ice cellar used to be. And there wasn't a woman or a man under that tree that missed it.

"Nobody makes Uncle Eth do anything he doesn't want to," James called down to her.

"James, sit in the crook of that branch and I'll come up and get you," Ethan said, rolling down his sleeves to protect his arms.

"I'll go," Bart Morrow said, stepping out of the crowd and looking for a leg up. "Eth's still my baby brother," he explained to his wife, Willa, who had pulled away from the crowd of women to lay a possessive hand upon his arm.

"Jeez, Bart," Ethan said, "you'll pull down the whole tree." He poked at his brother's belly, and it struck Sterling that this family touched each other all the time, as though they had a right to each other's arms and bellies and hearts. "I climbed a tree like this a few years ago," he said when Bart refused to get out of his way. "When was the last time you climbed one?"

"He went up to get you down when you were about six," Charlie said, ruffling his younger brother's hair. "Guess it's your turn to rescue someone."

"Don't want to be rescued," James said loudly. "So you can all go away and fly your kites and all. I got a good view from up here, anyways."

"You don't want to be rescued?" the boy's aunt Sissy yelled up. "You gonna live up there?"

"Maybe."

"Well, let's see," she said too loudly for anyone to believe she was just thinking. "I suppose we could rig up some sort of pulley to get your food up there . . . or I could just give that cookie with your name on it to some other little boy. . . ."

"Why don't you give it to the Phillips kid?" James said, and a handful of leaves came showering down on them. "He already has my uncle Eth. Might as well have my kite cookie, too."

The boy was jealous. Jealous of a toddler who might never walk, whose greatest joy for the week was feeling himself pee. Sterling didn't know who to feel sorriest for, until she looked at Ethan Morrow's glistening eyes.

"I'm still your uncle Eth," he said with a sigh as he rested against the tree. "And there's nobody I care about more than you, James. You know that. I'm willing to climb this stupid tree to help you down, aren't I?"

"You'd climb it for any of us," one of his other nephews said.

"And you'd swim the ocean if I was drowning," one of his nieces added.

"And you'd fly if I was stuck on a cloud, right, Uncle Eth?" a little one who was clinging to Risa's skirts asked.

"Maybe he could get Princess Sugarlips across the bridge," Worth said. It didn't seem to Sterling, thank goodness, that anyone heard him.

"You said you had to go to Oklahoma." James's voice drifted down from the tree along with a leaf or two. "You said it was your dream and your destiny, remember?"

Ethan Morrow, still leaning against the tree, closed his eyes and swallowed.

"Then you stayed for *him,* but you wouldn't stay for me."

A good two dozen people stood under the tree listening to the sound of one young boy ripping leaves off branches. Another few dozen watched from the distance.

"Well, James," Noah Eastman said finally. "It's time to come down. I think you've tortured your uncle Ethan sufficiently."

"Sit tight, son," Ethan said, taking a deep breath and signaling his brother Bart to set his knee so that Ethan could use it for a step up. "I'm coming." How James had managed to get himself up, Ethan couldn't imagine.

"You mad, Uncle Eth?" There was a slight quaver to James's voice. " 'Cause if you're mad, maybe I'll stay up a while longer."

"I'm not mad," Ethan said.

Most of the people around Sterling seemed to relax at the sight of Ethan Morrow climbing an enormous oak tree in pursuit of his nephew. Of course, they were sure that the golden boy could do it with ease. Probably with one hand tied behind his back. Apparently Sterling Phillips wasn't the only person in Van Wert who had mistaken Ethan Morrow for Sir Glad-I-am. Maybe, in fact, they weren't mistaken.

But Sterling wasn't quite as relieved as the rest of the onlookers, and only managed to take a breath when her knight's foot was securely set on a fresh branch that didn't crack beneath his weight or slip out from beneath his footing.

Annie Eastman held Risa Morrow's hand, various children clinging to their skirts. All the while the men in his family watched the daring man's ascent, straining with him as he reached, setting their feet on the ground while his searched for something firm in the air.

In her arms Worth struggled to catch a glimpse of his hero, squirming and trying to turn himself around as Sterling clutched him to her. She shifted him so that they could both watch, and rubbed his back reassuringly as Ethan Morrow moved farther and farther away from the safety below him.

"He's a good climber," Risa Morrow told her, throwing one arm around her shoulder and running a sun-tanned finger down Worth's pale nose. "You'd better keep that hat on him. The sun's mighty strong today."

The branches got smaller and smaller the higher he went. One cracked beneath his boot, and Sterling's gasp was lost among those of the rest of them.

"And the crowd roared," he called down to them, "as

the daredevil high-wire artist skillfully made his way higher and—"

"Yea for the cowboy!" Worth shouted up to him.

Sterling thought she heard a faint chuckle before a second branch cracked. Looking more like a bear than a man, Ethan hugged the trunk of the tree and slid slowly down several feet. Sterling thought of his palms, already raw from all the work he did when she and her son weren't imposing on him, and wondered how he managed to hold on.

"Listen to me carefully," he told the boy. "I'm too heavy to get all the way to you. You have to do exactly what I tell you to, James. Will you do that?"

"I'll get some blankets," Noah told his wife. "Just in case."

"Hold on, Eth," Bart yelled up. "We're gonna get ready just in case."

"Listen. Be ready for James. But if I come down, just get the hell out of the way. And move all the kids. And the women," Ethan called down. Then quietly, as if they'd just sat down to a picnic supper the way they were supposed to, Ethan said, "So, James, what's new?"

There was no response from the boy, who was no longer swinging his leg but instead was clinging to the branch on which he sat.

"Is it a good kite, at least?" she heard Ethan ask.

"It's okay."

"What kind is it?" He was inching his way up the trunk, depending on the strength of his arms and legs to keep him in place, since nothing was beneath his feet.

On the ground the men were holding blankets taut, ready to catch James should it come to that.

"A fish."

"A fish?" Ethan asked. "I climbed this whole tree for a puny fish kite? Next week we'll make a dragon kite. What do you say to that?" He was even now with the boy, but they were still several feet apart.

"Aren't you leaving?"

"Okay. Now, when I tell you, I want you to lean down and get your belly on the branch. Can you do that? Don't let go, just get down and hug it like it was that pretty Sarah Jane Firk I saw you eyeballing in church."

"Uncle Ethan!"

"You ready down there?" he shouted.

The men snapped their blankets. "Ready."

"Lean down now, son."

Sterling had moved away with the crowd of women and children, but she was close enough to see the dark patches of sweat on Ethan's shirt. Worth's body was heavy and warm against hers.

"Now take your left hand and just put it in front of the right one, like you're shortening up on a bat. Slow, James. We've got all day. One fist touching the other."

Sweat seeped down Sterling's sides, collected beneath her breasts. If the boy was moving on the branch, it was imperceptible. The distance between James and his uncle seemed to grow instead of shrink. She shifted Worth to her other hip and kissed his forehead.

"Here's his hat," Miranda Morrow said, handing up Ethan's ridiculous cowboy hat to Sterling. "Uncle Eth'll be sad if he gets burned."

For all his cocky talk, it seemed to her that "Uncle Eth" spent an awful lot of time being sad, or brave, or worrying about someone else.

"Okay. Pull up your knees just a little. That's good, that's good. You're practically in my arms already."

And what good would that do? Sterling wondered. How in the world was he going to get down that tree with the boy in his arms?

"Don't worry," Miranda said matter-of-factly. "Uncle Eth won't let anything happen to One Shoe. If he likes you, he'll make sure you're always okay. And he likes One Shoe a lot."

Ethan's voice floated down. "I'd say a half a dozen

more fists and I'll be able to reach you. You know how many half a dozen is?"

"And if he doesn't like you?" Sterling asked the child.

"Oh, Uncle Eth likes everybody. Except if they lie or do something bad."

"Two more, maybe, James. One . . ." Ethan's hand closed around James's wrist, dragging the boy toward him, grabbing him around the back and under one armpit. In one fluid motion the boy was on his back, his arms around his uncle's neck, his legs fighting their way around Ethan's waist.

"You're pulling me off the tree," he told the boy, not a touch of panic in his voice. "Rest your feet on my hips, okay?"

James made the adjustment.

"We're coming down," Ethan shouted to a cheering crowd.

With infinite care, arm over arm, he lowered himself and James until he could once again depend on the branches for support. Then he made it look like he'd climbed the tree for sport, and quickly he and James were within the reach of waiting arms. Someone plucked the boy from his back and then offered him a hand down.

"Where's my big brother?" Ethan demanded, and Bart, sniffing loudly, put out his arms and caught Ethan like he was still his baby brother.

"Ya did good," Bart said, setting him on his feet and patting him so soundly on his back that it was hard for Ethan to keep his footing. "But you've smelled better."

"It was a stupid fool thing to do," Noah said to James while he hugged and kissed the boy soundly. James seemed to agree, and couldn't stop shaking in his uncle's arms.

Annie kissed her brother Ethan, pulling him against her and stroking the back of his hair. She only released him when Risa demanded a turn.

Well, Annie was standing next to Risa, and Risa was

standing next to Sterling, and everyone was kissing and hugging everyone else, and before she knew it, she was standing face-to-face with Ethan Morrow, each of them out of breath.

They were all hugging, men with men, women with men, husbands and wives and brothers and sisters, and Ethan reached out and took her around, pulling her and the baby against his chest. His head rode her shoulder and she could feel the weight of it, feel him sag against her slightly, and knew that the fear exhausted him far more than the effort.

He had been magnificent. Unable to stop herself, she planted a small kiss on the temple that throbbed just inches from her lips. "Bart was right. You did good."

He turned his head, and his lips found hers. It was a chaste kiss, soft, brief, passionless. Nothing that anyone should have taken notice of. But that didn't stop her heart from pounding against his chest. It didn't stop her breath from coming in little gasps.

And it didn't stop the whole darn town from uttering a collective "oooh," which, she bet, Benjamin Cobb could hear all the way in his office.

"That," he said, stepping back, taking the baby from her, and settling him on his hip, "made it worth it."

Chapter Eleven

"Oh, my word!" Aunt Imogene said when she flitted into Worth's room the next day and saw Sterling's face. "Aren't you a sore sight for eyes!"

"It's sight for sore eyes," she corrected her aunt, looking in the mirror again as if five minutes could have changed her condition. It had. She looked even worse.

"Are your eyes sore, too?" her aunt asked sympathetically. "You know, I've seen strawberries less red than you are. Are those blisters on your eyelids?"

"Excuse me," Abigail said, dipping her head into the room. "Carl says that Mr. Ethan is downstairs and can he come up?"

"Yes," Aunt Imogene answered.

"No!" Sterling said, looking again in the mirror and wincing.

"Why, dear, whatever is the matter?" Aunt Imogene asked. "I'd think this was a simply perfect time for you to see him."

"I don't want to see him, and I certainly don't want him to see me." He'd warned her she wouldn't turn all honey golden like his sister. He'd told her she was going to fry.

He'd left out the part about the blisters. Had he mentioned them, she might have been convinced.

"But don't you want him to see what he's done? You were so right about the picnic, after all. You were uncomfortable and you didn't belong there, just as you said." Aunt Imogene turned to Abigail. "Tell him to come up."

"No!" Sterling said again.

"You don't want him to see you, do you?" her aunt asked, clapping her hands together. "I knew it, I knew it!"

"I wouldn't want anyone to see me like this."

"Is that Dr. Cobb's carriage?" Aunt Imogene asked, looking out the window. "Can they send him up?"

Sterling looked in the mirror again. Maybe it wasn't as bad as she was making it out. And Benjamin was a doctor, after all. She supposed he'd seen worse. "Yes, send Dr. Cobb straight up."

"Don't you mind if he sees you?" Aunt Imogene came and tipped her chin to get a better look, then clucked and tsked. "What an amazing shade of pink. I think I'll call it Sweet William pink!"

"I'm hoping to call it a memory, since I've pinched myself and I can't call it a dream. Maybe Dr. Cobb can help calm it down a little."

"You'll have to ask him when he comes," her aunt said. "But I'm sure Ethan'll know what to do."

"But Dr. Cobb is coming up and Ethan isn't," she reminded her aunt.

Aunt Imogene looked at her blankly. "Oh. That was just a test. Cobb couldn't be here now. He's got hours, and you know that you could bleed to death before he'd leave that office in the morning. But the test proved it and I'm glad."

"That's nice," Sterling said, too uncomfortable to bite.

"Now you'll have to admit it, at least to yourself, honey."

"Admit what?" She checked her nose in the mirror. It had swelled, she was sure, to twice the size it had been when she'd woken up. Abigail made sympathetic faces at her in the mirror and then caught Worth's eye there and waved.

"Well, I was having a hard time with it myself." Aunt Imogene waved back at Worth, too, then at Abigail, and then looked at her hand in the air as if she wondered how it got there. "I wanted Ethan because he was a farmer. But then Cobby being a doctor, with Worthie needing him . . . I couldn't really decide if Ethan hit him to come into our lives or to bring the doctor in. And then I thought the doctor had his chance years ago. And I couldn't choose which one to root for. Well, I really liked Ethan tons and tons more, but I thought I was being selfish. . . ."

"Aunt Imogene, there's nothing to root for. There's no contest going on here, and I'm certainly not a prize." She frowned, but it hurt, so she just stared at her aunt, hoping to get an answer of which she could make sense.

"Fine," Imogene agreed. "Have it your way. But I'm glad that Ethan Morrow won, just the same."

"Abigail, send him away, please," Sterling said, wishing Worth would suck his lip back in. Her honey lamb could see Mr. Morrow another day. A day when she didn't look like an apple that had exploded from the heat. A day when the man's kiss wasn't so fresh in her memory. And her lips didn't appear seared by it.

"Send him up," Imogene countered. "I want him to see the harm he's done. Guilt is a powerful weapon to wield."

Ethan Morrow's voice rang loud and clear. "Don't you go teaching that innocent girl your tricks. I'm disappointed in you, Miss Imogene."

Oh, the look on that man's face when he got all the way through the doorway and saw her!

"Holy Hannah!" A two-headed rat running across the floor couldn't have shocked him more.

"Excuse me," Sterling said, her hands covering her face as best she could as she tried to pass him in the doorway.

Naturally he grabbed her arm, because Ethan Morrow couldn't leave anything alone and just let a woman get by and go to her own room. She should have made him stand by the window so that she'd have had enough room to get by. Then if he'd grabbed at her, she could simply have pushed him out.

"Holy Hannah!" he said again, pushing her hair away from her temple and then sucking in his breath. "Wow!"

"Why don't you just say 'I told you so,' and let me pass?" she demanded.

"You don't really think I'd say that, do you?" He looked hurt. "Think it, maybe, but never say it. What have you put on it?"

"I know how to take care of a burn," she said. It sounded better than *Huh? Put on it?* "And Dr. Cobb can see to it later."

"She doesn't care if Cobby sees her," Aunt Imogene informed him, nodding as though that proved some point.

"You don't know how to take care of a—" He stopped himself short, looking over at her honey lamb. "Sorry. You shouldn't wait for Corn Fritters to show up. By the time he gets his . . . wagon over here, it'll be even worse."

"I was just about to put some cream on it," she said. "If you'll let me pass, that is."

"Cream!" Aunt Imogene said. "That reminds me, young man."

"I haven't forgotten," he said, planting a kiss on her aunt's cheek and causing her to squeal. "But I've been awfully busy."

"What do cowboys use for burns?" Worth asked him.

"You mean besides a hat?" he said with obvious irritation. "Because a milk-faced cowboy—or -girl— wouldn't ever go to a picnic without a hat in the first place."

"What if she was in the desert and didn't have no hat?" Worth asked. "And she got rescued by a real cowboy who knowed better?"

"Kickapoo salve. Sissy's been using it ever since we were kids. Or buckaroos. That's what us cowboys do."

"Ster don't want me to be a cowboy. She thinks I'm a prince." He looked thoroughly disgusted.

Ethan appeared to sympathize with him, as if he thought she had him pegged wrong too. "I know what you mean," he said, throwing the boy a quick nod of understanding before returning his attention to her fried face.

Gently he pulled one of her hands away and winced at the sight. "Jeez, blisters. I should have taken you home as soon as I got James down from the tree. Does it hurt much?"

"I'm all right," she lied, hopping that eventually she would be.

"Yeah," he agreed. "I can see that. And I'm the king of France."

"No," Aunt Imogene said, "you're a vintner and can bring forth wine from the earth!"

"Yeah, well, tell my grapes," he said a little too sadly for Sterling's liking. "And then tell my sister to keep her jelly-making hands off them."

"You've grown grapes?" Aunt Imogene asked, eyes all wide, head shaking like a dandelion in a strong wind. There'd be no stopping her now. Sterling threw up her hands in disgust.

"Jeez," Ethan said, staring at her face. "That old sun ought to be ashamed of itself, messing with God's work like that. You got something to put on it?"

"I told her," Abigail said, "but does she listen to me? No, she wants some cream from the pharmacy, when everyone knows there ain't nothing better for a burn than some grated potato and slippery elm."

"That sometimes works," Ethan agreed, "but I'd go with carbolic acid and glycerine myself. Those blisters are gonna open and it'd kill me to see them get infected. Oh, gosh! Even your lips!"

"You know a good cure for that too?" Aunt Imogene asked.

"Well, my sister says—"

"Oh, no," Sterling said, backing away. She remembered quite clearly that Annie Eastman's remedy was to "kiss it and make it better." And kissing Ethan Morrow was not going to make anything better. Not in the long run.

He smiled, no doubt reading her mind. "Why, Miss Phillips, whatever are you thinking?" He moved a step closer to her, not caring that her aunt was there, her maid was there, her honey lamb was there. "Everyone knows what an expert my sister is. Don't you think Sissy knows how to make things better?"

"It's not Sissy I'm worried about," she said, putting her hands up against his chest and bracing her elbows.

"How can you still be so beautiful?" he asked softly, as if they were the only two people in the room. "You're pink to your hairline, got more freckles than I can count and three . . . no, four good blisters going there. So how can you still make a man's insides—"

"Oklahoma," she said abruptly, so anxious to change the subject that she groped for anything rather than allow herself even a moment to bask in the glow of the light he kept shining on her.

"I beg your pardon?" The teasing went out of his eyes. His shoulders fell. The smile faded from his lips.

"I know you wanted to go sooner, but now that Worth is getting better, surely you must have to be going. It was Oklahoma, wasn't it? Isn't that where you're supposed to be headed?"

"Oh, but he can't go to Oklahoma," Aunt Imogene said matter-of-factly. "He's got vineyards waiting. He's a farmer, not an Indian wrestler, for heaven's sake!"

Sterling could see the sadness in his face and knew the answer without his admitting it. It was too late.

"I'm sorry," she said, brushing a fly away from his ear and wishing she could touch his hair, just this once, for a moment. "I didn't realize . . . I should have known. I'm truly sorry."

"Yeah," he said, taking her hand in his and examining

the back, which was sunburned, and the palm, which still bore traces of the glass cuts she'd suffered. "So am I."

"Oh," Imogene said. "Everyone's sorry! Now you two can kiss and make up."

Sterling could feel him studying her, that little smile she was coming to expect, playing at his lips.

"No, Aunt Imogene—" Sterling began.

"Well, wait a second," he said. "Not so fast." He lifted the hair off her neck, looking, she supposed, for a spot of skin that wasn't burned, and then bent his knees slightly and placed his lips just beneath her ear. The kiss was so gentle, so soft, that there seemed no reason to object. Afterward she heard the tenderest of sighs just as he pulled away.

"I wouldn't want to disappoint your aunt." His face was nearly as red as her own as he licked his lips nervously.

He'd better get used to disappointing Aunt Imogene, Sterling thought. Or they'd wind up married.

"Then we're going for ice cream," her aunt said. "And we'll bring you back something special, young man," she said to Worth, who had, it turned out, fallen fast asleep during what Sterling supposed a young boy might call "the mushy stuff."

"I'll take you for ice cream, Aunt Imogene," Sterling offered, hoping to spare Ethan the chore. The man did enough for everyone in his own family. It didn't seem right that he was now required to take care of hers as well.

"You?" Aunt Imogene said, pointing at her face. "Have you had a good look at yourself today? You really shouldn't let anyone see you, you know."

Ethan had said she was beautiful and had made her forget for a moment that she looked like she'd had a fight with a smashed tomato and it had won.

"I believe, Mrs. Harrington, that we have a date," he

said, extending his elbow to her and bowing slightly. "And I always keep my word."

"I suppose you never lie, cheat, or steal either," Aunt Imogene said.

He shook his head. "I sure try real hard not to. My sister deserves better than that from me, and I'd give an arm before I'd disappoint her. I suppose everyone feels that way about their family."

Oh yes, Sterling thought. Everyone felt that way. That was why there were no evil people in the world.

"No wonder you're such a good farmer," Aunt Imogene said. "You sure are knee-deep in horse droppings! Don't they ever let you off the farm?"

"You'll need your hat," Sterling said, guiding her aunt off in the direction of her room and then coming back for a moment alone with Ethan.

"Keep her away from any children," she whispered. "She gets too upset and it sets off her asthma. And make sure she leaves the silverware on the table."

His eyes widened.

"And don't go anywhere but the Marsh Hotel dining room. They know her and we can always bring them back whatever she might—" She stopped when she saw her aunt coming toward them down the hall. On her arm was her travel valise.

"I don't think you'll need that," Sterling said, trying to ease it from her aunt's grasp.

"Aren't we going to the Marsh?" she asked Ethan, who, to his credit, wasn't making a mad dash out the front door.

"That we are," he agreed. "Unless there's somewhere else you'd like to go."

"They don't have those wafer cones there," her aunt said. "Like the ones from the Chicago Exposition. I liked those. The Exposition was wonderful."

"Until she got thrown out," Sterling said under her breath. "It has to be the Marsh, Aunt Imogene. You like it there, remember?"

"She means well," Aunt Imogene said, taking Ethan's arm and heading for the stairway. "It's just that she's so confused. If only she could see things clearly, she'd be as fine as I am."

* * *

The Marsh. Why didn't he just take Imogene Harrington to Bellefontaine and buy her a fur coat? He knew the princess had him confused with someone else, but surely she didn't think he had a golden goose somewheres and was just living in a barn for the fun of it, did she? Did she think he had some sack of gold somewheres, sending him to the Marsh, where a puny dish of ice cream cost a quarter?

Well, he did have a couple of quarters now that he wasn't going to Oklahoma.

"Was that a sigh I felt?" Imogene Harrington asked him.

"No, ma'am, I don't think so," he said, fairly certain he'd kept his disappointment to himself.

"Not you," she said, slapping at his arm. "Me. I do believe I sighed."

"It's not much farther. Are you tired?" There was a smooching bench just around the corner he was familiar with, but he felt a little funny taking Imogene Harrington into the bushes with him. He thought that if she wasn't too tired, he might take her to Herndon's instead of the hotel. Herndon's gave two scoops for a dime.

"There!" she said, smiling at him in amazement. "I did it again. Didn't you hear it?"

He had, in fact. Everyone on Washington Street probably had too. "Aren't you feeling well? Should I take you back?"

"Clams sigh, you know," she said, hugging his arm more tightly as they walked. "And that's when they open and give up their pearls."

That decided it. He'd best take her to the hotel where

they knew her. Clearly this was not going to be one of Imogene Harrington's better days.

"Sterling won't give up her pearls again, you know. Do you suppose that clams make a new pearl after the old one is taken from them?"

"It's oysters that make the pearls," Ethan corrected her gently. "And I think they destroy the oyster to get the pearl out."

"Then why do they say 'happy as a clam,' young man?" She stopped walking and waited for his answer.

"I suppose they're happy they don't have pearls, since they'd be destroyed for them." The hotel was just across the street. Ethan gestured toward it. "Shall we?"

"Oh yes!" she said, her eyes alight like a little girl's. "So then it's clams that sigh?"

Ethan nodded as he helped the older woman down from the sidewalk into the street. He'd never read anything that specifically said clams didn't sigh.

"Sterling should have been a clam instead of an oyster, don't you think?"

Ethan had trouble imagining Sterling Phillips as a clam or an oyster. With milky white skin that glowed in the moonlight, was there any doubt that she was the precious pearl? Too precious for the likes of him.

On the other side of the street they approached the hotel and he held open the door. "I try not to think about your niece, to be honest, Miss Imogene."

"Genie," she reminded him. "We're practically family."

He kept her arm firmly looped through his by continuously patting her hand as he steered her through the lobby to the dining room.

"Two, please," he told the man in the fine black suit who stood waiting for them at the entrance.

"How nice to see you, Mrs. Harrington," the man said, eyeing the valise Ethan was carrying for her and reaching for it. "Why don't I take care of that for you, sir?"

"That seems highly extraordinary to me," Imogene said, that head of hers shaking rapidly.

"I meant no offense," the man said, releasing his hold on the bag.

"It is kind of heavy," Ethan said quietly to Imogene, letting his arm sag.

"But it's nearly empty," she replied, pushing the side of the bag suspiciously.

"Didn't I see you putting dreams in it before we left?" Ethan asked her.

She smiled and swatted at imaginary flies.

"And hopes?"

"Young man," she said, waving at the maître d' to take them to their seats, "I am too old for dreams and hopes. I have *plans*."

He couldn't help but smile back at her, even as his own dreams had gone to seed.

"You think I'm a crazy old lady, I suppose," Imogene said, pulling off her gloves and setting them on top of the silverware that sat beside her plate.

"Perhaps I'd better put those in my pocket so that we don't forget them," he said, reaching for the gloves and, having no pockets big enough or clean enough for a pair of women's lacy gloves, placing them on his thigh.

"I take things that aren't mine," Imogene whispered, leaning over the table to confide in him. "I tried to take children, but they can be so unpredictable. I'm afraid of horses, and they'd probably find their way home anyway."

"Should I worry about you stealing Honesty?" he asked her, trying to look wholly serious.

"I really wouldn't know what to do with the truth anymore. Unless you mean my sweet little doggie."

"*Your* doggie?" He had few enough possessions to be quite sure what was his.

"All right, all right," she said, patting his hand gently. "Our doggie. And don't lecture me about counting chickens, for heaven's sake. I've my jailers for that."

"Your jailers?"

Before Imogene could answer, a waiter came and took up residence beside their table. He smiled at them, pencil paused over pad, but said nothing.

"Three scoops of their best ice cream," she told Ethan. "I've a lot of time to make up for, and who knows when they'll let me out again."

"Three?" Ethan asked. Three scoops of ice cream at the Marsh would cost him a good couple of hours at the icehouse. *Three?* "Are you sure you can eat that much ice cream? I wouldn't want you to get sick."

"Oh, I think so," Imogene said. "I've certainly had more than my share of sour in this life, and nobody ever said it was too much and made it stop, did they?"

"Do you think any amount of ice cream will change that? 'Cause if it will, I'll sell my horse and you can eat until next week."

"Oh, we don't have to pay for it, cowboy," she said, looking to the waiter for confirmation. "I just say, 'Charge it to my account'!"

"I invited you for ice cream, ma'am, and I intend to pay for it."

She looked crestfallen, as if he'd taken away her magic toys, but he didn't see what else he could do. A man didn't ask a woman out for a treat and then let someone else pay for it. Where was the pleasure and satisfaction in that?

"Do you think I might have one small scoop of chocolate, then?" she asked Ethan.

"Mrs. Harrington will have three scoops of chocolate ice cream. With a cherry on top," he added.

"And you, sir?" the waiter asked.

Imogene wiggled in her chair, unable to keep still. Her gaze roamed the restaurant happily, and she sighed what Ethan took to be her happy sigh.

"I think I'll just watch," he told the waiter, leaning back.

"I'll bring you an extra spoon," the man said with a

wink, and pointed to Ethan's place setting. "In case that one disappears." He rolled his eyes toward Imogene, then winked again.

"No Oklahoma, I gather," Imogene said, fingering the spoon by her plate and then placing it in front of Ethan. "I could have told you that you weren't going, but nobody asks me anything."

"Yeah, well, I suppose I should have known it myself," Ethan said, running his finger around the edge of one of the finest water goblets he'd ever seen. Almost as nice as the ones they used to toast his sister Francie's marriage to Graham Trent.

He pushed the glass away, not willing to remember New York.

The waiter returned with an elegant crystal dish heaped with chocolate ice cream. Imogene waved first one spoon and then the other at him proudly. She took a spoonful and savored it with her eyes closed, and Ethan didn't need to taste it to get the full enjoyment and know he was surely getting his money's worth.

Digging in for a second spoonful, she asked, "Well, how could you run my vineyard from Oklahoma?"

"This the California vineyard?" he asked, remembering her conversation with Corny after the buckaroo had been accidentally . . . well, after he'd mowed the child down in the street.

"Open that valise," she directed him, pointing with her spoon. "Make yourself useful."

"We taking out your plans?" he teased, pulling the valise onto his lap and opening it. "Sure they can stand up to the light of day?"

To his surprise, in the bottom of the suitcase was a small stack of papers tied with a red ribbon.

"Genie?" The papers looked official, with seals and stamps at the bottom. "Where did you get these?"

"It's the vineyard," she whispered reverently. "It was a gift from my mother for Amelia and me. She never wanted it; so I'd always planned to give it to my babies, you know."

"But I thought your babies . . ." Lord, what an idiot he was. Only the fact that he already stuck out enough in his well-worn jeans and chambray shirt in the most elegant restaurant in town stopped him from getting up and kicking himself in the buttocks.

"You can say it," Imogene said, nodding at him encouragingly with her shaky head. "I know they're dead. Everyone acts like they think I don't know. Where do they suppose I think they are, then?"

Ethan flipped over the stack of papers in his hands. "So then, these . . . ?"

"Are mine. Amelia's gone to watch my babies and I plan to take care of hers best I can. Seems like this is the way to do it."

"What does your husband think?" Ethan asked, playing with the ribbon but unwilling to untie it.

"Oliver thinks I'm crazy. He's right, of course. Oliver is right about everything. Just ask him. He knows I can't have babies around me because of what losing another one will do to me."

"But the buckaroo . . ." Ethan thought about how little Imogene and Oliver saw the child, how they watched from doorways and across rooms.

Imogene sighed, but she was hardly clam-happy anymore. "Isn't he the most wonderful, the most beautiful little boy in the world? I felt his skin once. It was the softest silk I've ever touched."

"He's quite a boy," Ethan agreed. He'd only felt one cheek softer in his life, and the woman it belonged to was well out of his reach.

"I have it all worked out," she told him, pointing again at the valise. "See? In there?"

He looked in the suitcase. "I'm afraid it's empty."

"So put your dreams in," she said, pushing the ice-cream dish toward him. "Here. You'll need something sweet."

"I'll need more than ice cream, Genie," he said, pushing the dish away. "You enjoy."

"You have to help me," she said, once again pushing the dish toward him, "and I'll help you."

"I'm afraid that I'm beyond help now," he said, ashamed of himself for admitting defeat.

"I know. Isn't it amazing? Who'd have thought you'd have to hurt a little boy to get what you want? Not that I think you meant it, of course."

He wished she'd just finish the dish of ice cream so that he could take her home. Trying to understand her tired him. Life tired him. "Done?"

She shook her head. "I don't give up. Do you?"

"Maybe there's a difference between giving up and just giving in. Some things aren't meant to be, and knocking your head against the wall isn't going to change that."

"You're telling *me* that?" Imogene said with her eyes wide. "Close the bag. Go ahead. Close it."

He replaced the papers and snapped the suitcase shut.

"Shake it. Shake it hard, Cowboy."

He did as she directed, and his heart broke for this woman whose dreams had died a bloody death so many years ago.

"Open it! Open it!"

"Genie, I think it's time we headed home. Sterling and Worth'll be worried about you if we stay out much longer." He stood, but she waved him back into his seat and pointed again at the damn satchel. He opened it and showed her that the only thing inside was the packet of papers.

"*Voilà!*" she exclaimed, and he wondered what in the heck that was supposed to mean. The Lord only knew with Imogene Harrington. "New dreams! See? Different ones. Ones we can have."

"I can't make your dreams come true, Genie, any more than you can make mine. I'm not a fool, ma'am, and I know you're wishing something could happen be-

tween your niece and me. So let me set you straight. I
live in a barn. One I don't even own. All I know is
farming, and I don't own two feet of land. And if all
that's not enough, I bashed up your nephew. Much as I
hate to admit it, Dr. Cobb is the man for her. He's rich,
good-looking, and he can see to fixing what I've gone
and broken."

"Humph!" She poked him in the shoulder, a long
reach for her across the table, and mumbled something
about being short. Then she asked him, "Anything
wrong with your back? Or your heart?"

He was trying to reason with someone who had lost
hers. He was matching wits with someone who didn't
have any. And somehow she still made him feel like he
was losing.

"No, but—"

"Now the important question. Anything wrong with
your grapes?"

Chapter Twelve

Sterling watched Ethan Morrow and Aunt Imogene come down Washington Street, arm in arm, her aunt chattering away, her knight nodding as if he agreed with every crazy thing her aunt was saying. She saw them take note of the milkman's wagon, Aunt Genie stopping as they passed the cream-colored horse, no doubt to ask him how he was enjoying the warm weather. Beside her aunt, Ethan Morrow said something Sterling couldn't hear and then reached into his shirt pocket, pulled something out, and put it in Aunt Imogene's hand. Guiding hers with his own, they offered their gift to the horse, who seemed to appreciate it.

Maybe not quite as much as her aunt, whose squeal of delight along with Ethan's hearty laugh carried up to Worth's open window. The slight breeze cooled Sterling's burning cheeks, but they still hurt when she smiled. What was she thinking going to a picnic without a hat?

She was thinking that Ethan Morrow worshiped his sister and the woman wore the sun on her cheeks like two badges of honor. Sterling's cheeks looked more like purple hearts.

"More!" her aunt shouted, and patted Ethan's broad chest looking for another treat for the horse.

He shook his head firmly but sympathetically and, taking her aunt's elbow, led her toward the front door. Sterling lost sight of them under the porch roof.

She heard them come in the front door, heard him

tell Imogene he was coming upstairs and ask if she wanted him to see her to her door for a rest.

The man had just lost any chance of going to Oklahoma. He'd had to take her aunt out, and he was coming back to entertain a three-year-old before he went to work on who-knew-what. A roof? A field? Yet he was concerned about her aunt.

Benjamin was wrong about Ethan Morrow. He wasn't a dreamer who never grew up and who never would. He was a man who cared so much about others that he never got around to taking care of himself. And she wasn't about to add to his troubles. She had just decided to ask him not to come anymore when he sauntered into the room twirling a miniature of his own hat on one or two of his fingers.

"My hat!" her son shouted, reaching for it with one hand.

"Like it?" Ethan asked him before turning to her. "Would you mind leaving us alone for a while?"

"Alone? Why?" she asked, not wanting to miss seeing her son in his new hat.

"Can I have it?" Worth asked, reaching out for it while Ethan just stood looking at her, waiting, his jaw twitching wildly.

"Fine," Ethan said through gritted teeth. "Then can I see you in the hall?"

Something terrible had happened. She could feel it. It left her arms heavy and her stomach down around her knees.

"Of course," she said, worried that he was going to tell her that he'd given up on Worth, or that someone he loved had died.

But that was ridiculous. He'd seemed perfectly fine outside with Imogene.

And apparently he wasn't in any rush to tell her, because he tossed the little felt hat in the air and caught it on a finger. "Mine!" Worth cried out.

"Think you can reach it?" he asked the little boy, holding it out temptingly.

"Don't tease him," Sterling said as she grabbed the hat and tried to hand it to her son. "Or me. What's wrong?"

Ethan's fingers caught her wrist and plucked the little Stetson from her hand.

"There's a difference between teasing and tempting. I should think you'd know that. And that's what's wrong." He looked her up and down as though he was trying to decide whether she was a tease or a temptress—even though she'd tried so hard to be neither. He kept the hat out of Worth's reach.

Well, she was not about to allow her son to be the battlefield if he planned on declaring war on her.

"I've done neither." She reached again for the hat, but he held it above his head. She certainly had no intention of playing that game with him. "You're the one who's teasing."

"No, I'm tempting. He'll get what he wants in the end. But you, Miss Phillips, are teasing, aren't you? Or is it toying?"

Miss Phillips? What had happened to *Sterling?* Or better still, *Silver?* "What are you so angry about?"

"Those from Corny?" He gestured toward the roses on Worth's dresser. He was jealous!

"Yes, but they're for Worth."

His look told her he didn't like to be taken for stupid. "Some guy at the Marsh told your aunt your gloves'll be ready tomorrow. They were real sorry about the stains. They hope that Dr. Cobb won't hold it against them."

"My hat!" Worth reminded them.

Ethan put the miniature Stetson at the foot of the bed, far enough away so that she couldn't easily reach it herself. "I'll just leave it here."

"And I'll just—" Her fingers touched the brim at the same moment as Worth's, and she pulled her hand back so that he could claim the hat.

"I got it!" Worth's shout was pure victory. Somehow he had managed to turn himself around and now he was flat on his belly, his head raised and his face covered with the ridiculous black felt cowboy hat.

"Did it hurt you anywheres?" Ethan asked him, gently scooping up her honey lamb and righting him against the pillows.

Worth was all smiles as he shook his head, the hat scooting from side to side loosely.

"Was there a point to that?" she asked when she could claim her voice. Oh, there was nothing wrong with a toddler rolling around on his belly. A few months ago she'd have taken no notice. Now the thought that he might still be doing it at ten, or twenty, or forever, twisted her insides and wrung her heart dry.

Ethan was smiling away like a fool who couldn't see the forest for the trees. "You can look at that face and still need to ask? I guess maybe you just haven't known enough adversity in your cushy little life to recognize the thrill of triumphing over it."

So that was how he saw her. So be it. He could presume what he wanted. And so could she.

"Oh, and do you triumph often enough to be familiar with the satisfaction?"

He took a step back, stunned as surely as if she'd slapped his face. Worth stared at them both, his little mouth open while Sterling dug her nails into her palms and kept her own mouth clamped shut.

Another man would have yelled back, maybe stomped away and slammed a door. But not this man, this man she was trying so hard to keep her distance from. Oh no. With his thumb and forefinger working nervously around each other, he spoke quietly. "I had no right to say that. Losing your ma, and all . . . taking care of the buckaroo . . . I'm sure you've had your share of being kicked in the ribs, and you picked yourself up and dusted yourself off real good."

"I'm the one who should be sorry. It was just that I

couldn't stand watching him struggle. Still, I shouldn't have said that."

He shook his head and leaned up against the wall, tipping his head back as if the answers were written on the ceiling. "We're quite a pair, aren't we? All we've got in common is that we're both polite on occasion."

He studied his two big hands before shoving them into pockets that were too small for such strength. "But you're right about my lack of success. I'm so desperate, I take my triumphs wherever I can find them—convincing some dusty old patch of dirt to let a cluster of grapes grow in it, getting a smile from a kid with scarlet fever, taking my hands off the back of a bicycle some kid's trying to learn to ride."

Pushing off the wall, he added, "Now, seeing that *honey lamb* of yours get up out of that bed and take a stroll around this room—that'd be quite a triumph for me."

She had always measured her life by her mistakes and her failings. And by her losses. He seemed to measure his by the tiniest of conquests. Maybe the difference came from where they had started. Once, she had had everything. Ethan Morrow had begun with nothing at all.

"I think those are the worthiest of successes. What a triumph Oklahoma would have been for you."

One triumph in a lifetime of putting his own dreams on hold, and he had lost it because he was simply too nice to walk away. It didn't seem fair. Another man would have been gone by now. But Ethan Morrow had vowed he'd stay until Worth walked again. And the truth was, his staying somehow made her believe it would happen.

"Something else will come along," he said, and shrugged. "Or it won't. It doesn't really matter."

He was a very good man, but a very poor liar. Maybe it was true what they said about opposites attracting. "Somehow," she said, staring at the floor because she couldn't bear to look at his sad face, "I think it makes all the difference in the world."

He lifted her chin with one strong finger. "Yeah, well it doesn't leave me with much to offer a woman, does it?"

"The right woman would think what you have is more than enough."

He shook his head and touched just the tip of her nose. "The right woman deserves more than I can give her."

She thought about the truth of his words. A woman good enough for Ethan Morrow would deserve the world on a platter, but just getting to be held in his arms would be more than enough.

It was clear that he took her silence for agreement, and she let him, let him think she wanted more than he could give. Better for him to be disappointed in her for what he thought she wasn't than hate her for what she really was.

"Maybe it's time you went after that dream of yours," she said finally. "And someone to share it."

"What about your dreams?" he asked. "What does a woman who has everything wish for?"

She handed Worth the rope she'd found out in the gardening shed. "Maybe the cowboy can make you a lasso," she said, then looked up at Ethan. "What do I wish for? The strength to face reality."

"Reality can be pretty ugly," he warned her, taking the rope and making a few quick knots. "I wouldn't toss away my dreams so fast if I were you."

"You could catch 'em," Worth said as Ethan twirled the rope over her little boy's bed. "Right?"

"Mr. Morrow's dreams are far away," she said softly. *And they don't include us.* "And he's got to get going before they're too far out of his reach."

"As soon as the buckaroo's better," he said, letting the rope come down gently on the bed. "I was brought up to believe that obligations come first."

" 'Obligations.' " That had a charming ring to it. "Well, Dr. Cobb is certainly qualified to see to Worth. We've both kept you long enough. Too long, really. Benjamin will see to us."

"Benjamin." Ethan took Worth's hand in his own and wrapped it around the rope. He glanced up quickly and then bent to his task. "I see. I get the feeling you're asking me to go."

She nodded, not able to force the words from her throat, and kept her hands at her sides, balled into fists to keep from pushing the honey-blond hair out of his eyes as he worked at showing Worth how to move his wrist.

Ethan didn't see her, but her honey lamb did. "No!" he cried. "If the cowboy goes away, I'm gonna go with him."

"I'm not going anywheres," he reassured her son as if what she said carried no weight at all. And then he brushed the honey hair out of his eyes himself. "Except out into the hall with your sister for a little grown-up talk." He winked at the lilliputian cowboy in the bed and gave her a wide berth out of the room.

"Wait!" Worth called. "What's that?"

"What, honey?" she asked, trying to follow where his finger was pointing. It looked to her like the same old window with the same old tree outside it. "Do you see a bird?"

"The magic seed!" her son said, waving his arms. "It's the magic seed!"

Sterling squinted her eyes. What in the world was that thing hanging in the tree? She pulled back the curtains for a better look. Hanging from a thin rope, shining in the sun, was a ball of something gooey with seeds stuck all over it. A pair of cardinals sat on the branch above it, chattering to each other as if they found the ball quite as miraculous as did her son.

"Why, magic seeds!" Ethan said innocently. "I wonder where they came from. They're just the kind a bird would need to grow big and strong so that he could carry Princess Sugarlips over the moat."

"So that old troll, Mr. Rutabaga, can't get her," Worth agreed.

"Mr. Rutabaga?" Ethan asked, his eyebrow getting lost behind that darn lock of honey hair that kept tempting her.

"Yeah, the one that unflowered the princess. He hates flowers 'cause they're prettier than him. He's ugly." Worth pointed at the window again. "They're eating it! They're eating it!"

The two cardinals were balanced precariously on the string, picking at the suet ball.

"All trolls are ugly," Ethan said, and looked at Sterling. "Aren't they?"

"And short," Worth told him. "And they have hair coming out of their noses that people think are mustaches, but they're not."

"And they have big ears," Sterling added. "And mean dispositions."

"We hate the evil Mr. Rutabaga," Ethan said. "He doesn't even taste good."

"We hate rutabagas!" Worth chanted. "We hate rutabagas."

"That's right," Ethan said to her son as he steered her out into the hall to wait for him while he took an extra moment to compliment her honey lamb's new hat.

A cowboy hat and a suet ball. As if that was all it would take to make their dreams come true. She'd been very careful to keep her imaginary world separate and apart from her real one. And here he was crossing lines and confusing things. Confusing her.

Sir Glad-I-am was riding out of the pages of her fairy book. And if he knew what was good for him, he'd keep right on riding.

* * *

"Like a real cowboy," Ethan said from the doorway, winking at the tiny little boy in the bed. Lord, he could have gotten a doll's hat to fit that head. Probably saved money too.

She was waiting in the hall for him, that foot of hers tapping away. He wondered if her face hurt much, but decided it wouldn't be real tactful of him to remind her how awful she looked. Not that she could really look less than sighing-beautiful, even with a sunburn.

He'd never put much stock in great wealth. Never needed it, never really wanted it. Now he'd sell his soul to the devil for enough money to have the right to court this woman and offer a future to the buckaroo.

"How do you feel about the library?" he asked without any explanation. "Or doing some shopping or taking a walk?"

She looked at him as though she thought he'd lost his mind. Well, she and her little brother weren't shackled to each other, as far as he could see. She could leave the house without him.

"There must be someplace you can go when I come to visit the buckaroo." He looked up and down the hall. "What about staying in your room?"

"What?"

"I won't stop seeing the buckaroo. I told you I wasn't walking out of here until he could chase me down the block to say good-bye to Honesty, and I meant it. But I don't have to be under your feet. I can stay out of your way, if you can stay out of mine."

"I'd appreciate that."

"I was pretty sure you would. It's the only thing I have to offer you, Miss Phillips. But I'd be a liar if I didn't tell you I wish it could be otherwise."

"And you'd never lie, would you?" she asked him. Asked? It was more like an accusation.

"No, I wouldn't. Would you?"

She was staring at his left earlobe. Staring so hard, it

made him itch, but he stood there waiting for her answer without flinching.

"As you said, reality can be pretty ugly. So can the truth sometimes."

Lord, he thought there wasn't a prettier or sadder face in the whole world than the one he was looking at now. It was like Mother Nature wanted to even the scales. The way she made a blue jay handsome and then gave it the ugliest of voices. She'd given Sterling Phillips the most beautiful smile and then made her think there was nothing to smile about.

"Are you admitting to being a liar, then?" he asked, trying to make it sound like a joke, adding a laugh at the end, raising his eyebrows in mock surprise.

"Isn't that like asking *are you asleep?* The right answer has to make a liar out of you. If I say no, I could be telling the truth, or I could be lying about telling the truth." Unconsciously she fiddled with the dark blue ribbon cinched around her tiny waist.

"Are you?"

"Cowboy?" Worth's voice called to him from the other room, saving her.

"He's coming," she called back, then lowered her voice. "Well, then. I guess this is good-bye." She extended her hand for him to shake it.

"I usually say good-bye with a kiss." He took a step closer to her and tilted up her chin. "Mind?"

"Yes," she said, but her face remained raised, and her lips twitched nervously.

This was something he shouldn't do. There wasn't a piece of him that didn't know it, wasn't shouting at him to restrain himself. Voices in his head were yelling *No!* but his damn heart was beating so loudly, slamming against the confines of his chest with such determination, that he could hardly hear the warnings over all the commotion.

He tilted his head down toward hers, until their breaths mingled. *Run!* his brain was telling his legs. But it wasn't his brain that was calling the shots anymore. It was his heart and his soul, and if he had to give up yet another dream, it wasn't going to be without kissing it good-bye.

"Yes, I mind," she said, and the words brushed against his lips. "Not yes you can."

He was as gentle as he could possibly be. Hell, even her lips were burned. And even burned, they were soft and oh so sweet. He ran his tongue along the seam, tasting, testing. Either she meant what she said, or she was too innocent to know what he wanted. Her lips finally parted slightly, and his tongue slipped tentatively between them.

Lord, this woman smelled so good, so fresh, tasted so clean and pure.

"Cowboy?" Worth's plaintive call broke the spell, and he backed up slightly, steadying her with one hand in case she felt half as dizzy as he did.

"You're one heckuva liar, Sterling Silver Phillips," he said, licking his lips to savor the last drops of her sweetness.

He couldn't tell if she was blushing, but she sure had trouble meeting his gaze.

"Good-bye, Mr. Morrow."

"Good-bye, Miss Phillips."

She waited for him to go back into the boy's room, and he waited for her to walk down the hall. So neither of them moved at all. Except to shift their weight. And he licked his lips again. And she touched hers with one graceful finger. And his heart flipped over.

Maybe he should have listened to Sissy and asked Graham for a loan. Francie's husband had plenty to spare and he seemed to like Ethan well enough, despite what he knew about him. Maybe if he had a little piece of land, a house . . .

"Something funny?" Sterling asked.

He supposed he'd laughed at the thought. Asking Sterling Phillips to move out of this mansion, leave her frilly dresses and parasols and fine things behind her and share some shack with him. It wasn't funny at all. It was pathetic.

"No."

He had nothing but his self-respect. His ideals. And now that he'd returned his provisions to Charlie and Risa and paid off the doctor, he didn't owe anyone a dime. He dealt with enough shame when it came to Graham Trent. He wasn't about to go begging to him, and with nothing to his name, he knew better than to borrow.

"Cowboy!"

"I'd better go see to the buckaroo," he said, trying to keep the frustration out of his voice.

"Good-bye, then."

"Take care of that burn," he said, pointing toward the small blister under her eyebrow.

She nodded.

"I finished the Wellers' roof. I'll be looking for another pickup in the morning. I don't know when I'll be over to see him, but it would be best if you weren't here."

"Another pickup?" She lifted the blue ribbon and idly ran the end over her lip. Ethan tried to concentrate.

"Work. You know, pick up some work here, some work there. . . ." No, she didn't know. What would she know about pickups or work or busting his ass for fifty cents?

"Oh."

What she was doing with that ribbon was making him crazy. "I've got to go," he said, having difficulty swallowing.

"Yes. Good-bye." She let go of the ribbon and extended her hand.

"Are we doing good-bye again?" he asked. "Because another kiss might kill me."

Her eyes widened and her cute little mouth dropped open. "Oh! No, I . . ." She began backing down the hall. "Worth wants . . ." She pointed toward the door. "I . . . uh . . ." She turned on her heel and fairly ran the rest of the way to the staircase. Ethan was relieved to see her slow down for the steps.

She minded if he kissed her. The woman was a world-class liar.

* * *

"It's a bad burn," Benjamin told her when he arrived that evening. "But then, you know that."

"I should have worn a hat. I don't know what I was thinking."

"I had no idea you would be going to that little picnic," he said, digging in his black medical bag. "It seems so provincial for a city girl."

"It was," she admitted. She kept to herself that it's provinciality was what she liked best about it.

"A lot of farmers and laborers with their children running amok. And every year one of them wanders off or gets hurt or picks a fight." He found the jar he was evidently looking for, and set out a clean towel, moved a chair, and beckoned her over.

"Don't you like children?" she asked as he adjusted the lamp so that it shone in her eyes and she had to close them.

"Very much," he said, and she felt a cooling sensation on her forehead. "Like to have at least half a dozen of my own. Three and three, two years apart. After that I might want to reassess."

His finger ran down her nose, leaving relief in its wake.

"Triplets?" The thought was horrifying.

Benjamin laughed. "No. Three each—boys and girls. Two years apart each. Oldest a girl. Youngest a boy. Of course I'd take them in any order."

"I'm relieved to hear it."

"Are you?"

She left the question hanging in the air and asked one of her own.

"Did you go to the picnics when you were a child?"

"This hurt?" He pressed on her eyelid gently.

"No," she lied.

"Mmm. You just like to raise your shoulders and squeeze your eyes even when they're closed. Kind of a habit, is it?"

"What did you ask for, if you already knew the answer?" she asked while he switched to the other lid, which hurt just as much.

"I don't rely on patients to tell me the truth. Nobody does." He stopped his ministrations as if to make his point. "But then, I'd say that truth is an overrated commodity. I never rely on it."

He continued to smooth cream on her cheeks while he spoke. "When it comes to diagnosing, I hardly have to ask my patients anything. Know from just looking, or touching. Sometimes a smell will tell me everything I need to know." He put his hand against her neck, pressing lightly. "Tired?"

"No," she lied again.

"Funny, I'd think you were," he said knowingly.

She shifted in her seat and sniffed as daintily as she could. Did he know she was having her monthly? At least with her cheeks so red and covered with cream, he wouldn't be able to tell she was blushing.

"No need to be embarrassed. I'm a doctor, after all. A woman's body is no mystery to me. And then, I notice things. What you do, and things like that. You were very hungry last night, for example. Uncharacteristically. And you're sitting . . . well, the point is you have no secrets from me." He picked up one of her sunburned hands from her lap while she shifted uncomfortably in her chair and he gave her a look as if to say he'd told her so. "You sure did a job on yourself. I don't suppose the picnic was worth it."

"That feels a lot better," she said, trying out a smile and finding that it didn't hurt at all.

"Of course it does. So which kid was it this time? One of the Morrows? When I was very little, I once caught Jack and Zena in the woods. Didn't know until I was a lot older what it was they were doing. It was no wonder their kids were always getting lost or into fights."

"No one got lost or into a fight. Were Jack and Zena Ethan's parents?" He pulled back her hair and applied ointment to the tips of her ears. She hadn't even realized she'd burned them.

"Yes. Zena died when Francie was born. It's no wonder Ethan didn't amount to much, with just his sister to raise him."

"You don't think he's turned out well?" She squinted open her eyes and found that he'd moved the lamp and was cleaning up after himself.

"Not bad for that family, I suppose. They've got a twinless twin, a farmless farmer . . . I guess Sissy was a childless mother for years."

"That's a bit uncharitable, don't you think?"

"I think if I'd been with you at that outing, I'd have noticed that you were getting a burn. I think if I'd been driving that wagon, your son wouldn't be upstairs confined to his bed. I think I have a fine house, a thriving practice, and a good future. I don't know what more a woman like you is looking for." He snapped his bag shut loudly.

"A woman like me?" she asked. "I'm looking for the same thing every woman is looking for. And just because I don't deserve to be put up on that pedestal and worshiped doesn't mean I'm not wishing it all the same."

Dr. Benjamin Cobb breathed deeply and put his hands behind his back. He took several steps away from her, then several back. He chewed on the inside of his cheek.

And Sterling twirled her pink satin ribbon and felt foolish.

He stopped pacing. "All right."

She dropped the end of the ribbon, but it clung to her finger. "What?"

He threw up his hands. "You're up there. On that pedestal."

"But I'm not. You know I'm not."

"Have I brought you flowers?"

"Yes, but—"

"Have I taken you to the finest restaurants?"

"Yes, but—"

"Have I ever not treated you like a lady?" He helped himself to the scotch in the decanter on the sideboard.

"No, but—"

"And that despite the fact that I know the truth about you?"

"Yes."

"What, no *but* this time? I'm glad to see you're being reasonable." He took a careful swig of the scotch, measured out some more into the glass, and replaced the stopper.

"I hope you aren't asking me to marry you, because I don't know what I'd answer."

"I didn't hear an offer, Miss Phillips. But before you let that farm boy, Morrow, kiss you again, you'd be wise to think twice."

Her hands flew to her lips and he laughed.

"Just a good guess, knowing Morrow. And knowing you, I expect one of his cheeks is as red as yours."

If Benjamin Cobb didn't value the truth, and he'd said as much, then she didn't see any need at the moment to straighten him out.

"There's a chance that I'd be willing to take care of your son. I'm in a position to offer you a life of ease. I've agreed to respect and trust you, which, considering your past, is no small matter. There's no one else who can offer you what I can, because there's no one else who knows what I know. I am the one person, the only person, who you need have no fear of learning the truth about you and your son. And you tell me you don't know what you'd answer?"

"You haven't mentioned love. Not you for me nor me for you. All you've mentioned is my past. Twice in fact."

"Love is a luxury I'm not sure either of us can afford. After all, I assume you had love the first time," he said, looking up at the ceiling toward Worth's room. "How far did that get you?"

"It got me my son," she said, looking at the backs of her hands, shiny from the ointment he had administered.

"My point exactly," he said, saluting her and then draining the remains of his scotch.

Chapter Thirteen

"Thought you were coming home at lunchtime," Noah said when Ethan dragged himself into Sissy's parlor that night.

"Ground was just right," he answered, studying the splinters in his palm by the lamp.

"You been putting in fenceposts all this time?" Sissy asked, coming over and pulling his hand into her own. After a few grimaces and tsks, she told him to get her tweezers and then called after him. "There's another letter from Francie and Graham for you on the kitchen table, Eth."

He went straight for the letter, figuring that the splinters weren't going anywhere. It was addressed in Francie's fancy hand, and he opened it while still standing, anxious to see if they might have been able to find out anything more for him from the doctors in New York.

Dear Ethan,

You must be wondering about the postmark on this letter. [He hadn't even looked at it.] *We were all set to leave for Europe when Matthew came down with the measles. Not a day later so did Michael. Dr. Steinway says that in another few days it's likely that Gregory will be wearing the same spots as his little brothers.*

Graham is just beside himself. He runs between the house and the medical college comparing pictures

*in books to the boys' rashes, and reading them stories
to keep their minds off their discomfort.*

Ethan reached into the icebox and poured himself a
tall glass of milk. Sitting at the table with it, he reached
for the usual pile of Sissy's cookies and was disappointed to find none there. There was nothing like
Sissy's cookies and milk before bed. Except maybe those
madeleines and lemonade.

*I really think my poor husband feels worse than
the children. And he's driving the doctor to drink, no
doubt, checking out his credentials and comparing
them to every other doctor who ever graduated to
make sure our boys are getting the best care.*

*It's lucky that Dr. Steinway doesn't take offense.
While he was here, I asked him again about little
Worth Phillips and he advises that you should apply
hot compresses to his legs several times a day. What
you are to look for (and hope for) is a tingling in his
legs. Once this starts, the boy is well on the road to
recovery.*

Every time he worked with the buckaroo, he could
tell that the boy was feeling more. A pinched face here, a
squirm there—it was hard to prove it, but Ethan just
knew, even if the boy hadn't *prickled* yet.

On the other hand, Ethan's whole body prickled every time he was in that house on Washington Street.
He'd kissed her. Really kissed her. Lord, but it was everything he'd imagined it would be. And she'd kissed
him back. She might be spending her evenings with
Cornuto Cobb, but he had no doubt that her nights,
once she was alone, were all his own.

*And fat lot of good that'll do you, Ethan old boy. Maybe
you could put a couple extra cots in the barn and offer her
a home.*

He took another swig of milk and wondered if Hannah was old enough to start making the cookies instead of Sissy. Maybe she could learn to make those madeleines. He'd never tasted anything so light. They were little bits of heaven.

But (and this is the bad part) no one knows when or if that tingling will occur. The doctor did feel that the more active you keep the boy, the better the chances that the body will respond. In other words, if you let the legs sleep, they might not wake up. He likened it to a concussion to the head and said that just as you would continually wake up (or try to) a person's head, so should you try with his body.

Well, he had woken up one body at the Harrington house. He was sure of that. Only it had been the wrong body.

We hope this helps.
Love,
Francie and Graham and the boys (Sorry about the sticky finger marks—Matthew is on my lap.)
P.S. Graham contacted Cyril Phillips to offer his sympathies. (Remember meeting him at the wedding? He was that stuffy man who didn't take off his hat because he wasn't staying.) Lord, but he is a cold fish—acted as if he hadn't even heard about the accident. We recommended Dr. Steinway, but don't know what'll come of it. I think anyone would be better than Corny. I keep telling Graham I just can't believe that man ever became a doctor!

The dour man in the coat. He remembered him with the same stark detail as he remembered every bit of his trip to New York. There wasn't a moment in New York that he'd forgotten, no matter how hard he'd tried.

But the truth was that he had never connected the stern man in the ballroom of the Trent mansion with the incredibly soft, delicate woman he was fighting so hard not to fall in love with. Not that it mattered. New York was behind him.

Hadn't Graham assured him that even though the papers reported on the melee outside Graham's office, no notice had been taken of Graham Trent's new brother-in-law and the part he'd played in the whole mess? Despite the injuries suffered on both sides, there had been no charges filed. Strikes and protests, Graham had said as he'd put Ethan on the train back to Van Wert, were everyday occurrences in a city like New York.

New York. Even the words were hard, guttural. *York.* A person couldn't say it softly, pleasantly.

He'd spent his visit there in a kind of shock. Between the trolleys and elevated trains, the electricity and the plumbing, and the tenements and the mansions, he'd found his sister in love with a very wealthy man one moment and had witnessed their marriage the next. And all of that had been nothing compared with the day he'd spent with Graham and his brother Perry at their offices.

Heck, everyone was remarking that he was still dazed a month after he was back in Van Wert.

When the pretty, young Sterling Phillips had shown up at her crazy aunt Imogene's all in black, her little brother bundled in her arms, only to go into seclusion for weeks, he'd just supposed that her father was dead, if he'd given it any thought at all. Oliver Harrington had said they were in mourning, hadn't he? Ethan shrugged. Recalling his encounter with Cyril Phillips, Ethan supposed that having lost their mother would have been heartbreak enough.

"Eth? Where's that tweezers?" Sissy called. He rose and found the tweezers in just the same place she had kept it in the house they grew up in—the cabinet closest to the sink, along with all the salves and ointments and bandages that life on a farm required. Nothing ever changed around him. Nothing ever would. Sissy had dreamed of a life of ease in town. He'd dreamed about wide-open spaces. And the two of them were still on a dirt farm well outside of a small town that was never going to grow enough to be called a city.

Nowhere's where they'd gotten, but his sister didn't mind it one little bit. He slammed the cabinet shut and put the tweezers down on the chopping board beside the sink, where two enormous rutabagas sat waiting to be prepared for dinner.

We hate rutabagas!

He could hear the buckaroo's voice, loud and clear. Rutabagas whose nose hair was masquerading as a mustache. He fingered the little roots that stuck out from the point of the bulbous yellow overgrown turnip.

We hate rutabagas!

Lousy trolls that wanted to unflower innocent princesses. He picked up the cleaver and came down hard on the bigger of the two rutabagas, severing it in half.

We hate rutabagas!

Creepy short things that asked for favors to which they weren't entitled, who made poor sufferers fork over their tolls and then acted the swell with the blood money they'd stolen. He turned the cleaver over and smashed the rutabaga with the dull side, mashing its middle.

He pounded it again, pieces of it flying up and hitting the wall, landing in the sink. He went after the second vegetable, cutting it in a half-dozen pieces and then laying the cleaver on its side and pounding it with his fist.

He smacked it again and again, until bits of it clung to the cabinet and spotted the front of his clothes.

"Ethan?" Sissy's voice was soft, her eyes wide with surprise as she stood in the kitchen doorway. "What in the world are you doing?"

"We hate rutabagas!"

"What's going on in here?" Noah asked, coming up behind Sissy and staring at the mess he'd made.

"Uncle Ethan! What did you do?" Hannah asked, peering around her father.

"Your uncle was just helping your mama get dinner going," Noah said, his eyes on the ceiling where a string of pale yellow rutabaga hung tremulously over his head.

"What are we having?" Julia asked, pushing her father over slightly so that she could see what all the commotion was about.

"Rutabaga," her father said, fighting the urge to laugh.

Sissy's giggle filled the kitchen. "Creamed."

* * *

Ethan couldn't remember when he'd enjoyed a meal more. He'd finished every last scrap of the creamed vegetable, all the while telling his nieces about birds that were big enough to carry fairy princesses over rivers and away to castles in the air. Despite her admonitions to take care of his splinters first, he did the dishes and cleaned the kitchen—it was the least he could do after he'd blasted the evil Mr. Rutabaga to kingdom come— and came out into the parlor gingerly wiping his hands.

Isabella, Noah and Sissy's youngest, sat on her father's lap in the easy chair. Her sister Julia was perched on the chair's arm, a book in her hand, which she was reading to the baby with her father's help. Gracie, third in line, but the first child of the wonderful union of Noah and Sissy, was in her big stepsister's lap, Hannah trying to teach her to lace her boots.

Sissy sat at the end of the sofa closest to the lamp in order to be able to help him with his splinters. Her eyes were closed, her hands resting on the slight mound that would soon be too noticeable not to mention to the rest of the family. There was a faint smile on her lips, and Ethan couldn't blame her. It might not be where he wanted to go, but she was getting somewhere in this life, which was more than he could say for himself.

He stood by the light picking at his splinters, not

wanting to disturb her rest. In silent agreement, one after another, they put a finger to their lips and pointed to the center of their lives, who was snoring ever so gently, her head tipped back against the sofa.

"Hard day?" Noah asked softly.

"Aren't they all?"

"She's worried about you," Noah said, gesturing at his wife with a nod of his head.

"Just because I attack defenseless vegetables?" he asked, trying to lighten the mood.

"You're working too hard. She doesn't like the way you look."

"I'm worried about her too," Ethan countered, pointing to the fact that she was snoring well before bedtime in the middle of a crowded room. "Makes us even."

"Charlie came by earlier."

Which of course was enough. It meant that Sissy knew about the bicycle.

"He's worried about you too."

He sighed, picking at yet another splinter that was embedded deeply in the heel of his hand. He'd probably impaled himself when he'd attacked the rutabaga. "I'm getting tired of being worried about," he said.

"Mama says you got all the responsibilities of being a family man with none of the benefits," Hannah said matter-of-factly.

"Oh, did she?" Ethan said, stopping a moment to ruffle the girl's hair. "I can see we'll have to be careful talking around you now that you're growing up."

Hannah beamed up at him. "And she said you better *not* be getting any benefits."

Noah began to cough, nearly knocking Julia off the chair. Ethan steadied her, and they tried to quiet everyone back down.

With her eyes still closed, Sissy said evenly, "She's as good as one of those phonographs."

"I was thinking she might grow up to be a mynah bird," Noah said, raising an eyebrow at his daughter.

"I didn't know it was supposed to be a secret," she said, scratching her forehead as if she could erase the information stored there.

"Darling, it's not a secret," Sissy said, stirring herself and stretching. "There isn't a person in Van Wert who hasn't noticed that in between three other jobs your uncle seems to be seeing to the whole family over at Harrington Manor."

"Not like you to exaggerate, Sissy," Ethan said, then went after the splinter mercilessly.

"Then you didn't take that dear old woman out for ice cream? That wasn't you at the Marsh Hotel shaking some valise over the table like you were doing voodoo?" Sissy peered up at him and held her hand out for the tweezers.

"I can do it," he said, jabbing his hand and trying not to wince. "And what if I took Imogene Harrington out for ice cream? What of it?"

"Don't raise your voice to your sister," Noah warned him as if he was another one of the kids. "She's tired."

"And carrying again. Were you two ever gonna tell me?"

Hannah's eyes widened. Julia's mouth dropped open. Gracie stared at her mother's belly in disbelief.

Shit.

"Thanks, Ethan," Sissy said as all the kids gathered around her solicitously, stroking her stomach, asking if they could get her anything, pulling over a stool for her feet. "That was just how I imagined telling them."

To all their questions Noah answered "With God's help," and "If all goes well," and "Let Mama rest some."

"I'm sorry," Ethan said, and realized that those words were feeling all too familiar on his tongue lately.

"Don't go worrying about that too," Sissy said, extending her hand to him so that he could help her up. "It would have come out soon enough. You want some dessert? I meant to make a pie, but time keeps getting away from me these days."

"I can take something myself," he said. "I'm not your little boy anymore, Sissy."

"No, you're a man, and a man needs looking after," she said as she peeled children from her legs and headed for the kitchen. "Women are different. They can take care of themselves and they can take care of others."

"Are you saying a man can't take care of his family?" Noah said, trailing after them with a child on one arm and one clinging to his leg.

"Never!" Sissy said, turning that gorgeous smile of hers on her husband. "A man'll do anything for his family. He'll move a mountain. He'll walk through the fires of hell. But he'll forget to eat and sleep while he's doing it. A man just can't take care of himself."

Noah seemed to think about it for a minute and then cozied up behind his wife, wrapping his arms around her belly. "Long as I can take care of you, I'm taken care of."

"Think I'll bake some cookies," Ethan said. "Anybody want to help?"

"You'll what?" Sissy asked, her hands on her hips.

"I'm gonna bake some cookies," he repeated. The way he saw it, he could take care of himself and anyone else he wanted to. "I'm gonna bake a lot of cookies."

"I thought I heard she was a good cook," Sissy said, pulling out flour from here and sugar from there.

"Who?" he asked, setting his nieces into chairs around the table.

"*Who?* You an owl now?" She looked pointedly at Hannah. "Every stalk of corn's got ears."

"Are we celebrating because of the new baby?" Julia asked, rolling up her sleeves.

"She bakes good. Real good," he answered Sissy, while Noah nodded at Julia.

"Never mind her baking skills," Noah said. "I'm more worried about her lighting a fire."

"Who's lighting a fire?" Gracie asked, taking the spoon from Isabella, who was banging on the table.

"Don't be ridiculous," Ethan said, slamming the bowl on the table. "I said I'd make the cookies. What's everyone doing in here?"

"I'd say he's hot under the collar," Noah said.

If he could manage to keep his heat there, he'd be fine. It was when it headed south that he was in trouble.

"Probably because his brains are draining down his neck to other places," Sissy said, giving him a long, hard stare. "Ethan Morrow, you're red as a beet!"

"She's a beautiful woman," Noah said, addressing Sissy. "Not as pretty as the one I've got, but not a bad second place. And she's good to that brother of hers, just the way you are to Ethan. . . . Can't you see her someday, standing in that grand parlor of theirs and telling that boy his brains are leaking into his pants because he's looking on the wrong side of town?"

"She would, too. That nose of hers is so far in the air, I bet Ethan doesn't even know what color her eyes are!" Sissy measured out a cup of flour and dumped it into the bowl.

He knew what color they were at every hour of the day, how dark they seemed when he was up close, how bright they could get when Worth showed the slightest sign of progress, how much more like cornflowers they looked in the morning, how like a June sky they were at dusk.

"They're blue," he said dully.

"You're doing it yourself," Noah told his wife. "That girl's not supposed to notice that she's got more than us, but it's okay for us to dwell on it and make your brother's life miserable."

"Is Uncle Eth miserable?" Hannah asked.

"Not yet," Sissy said, waving her spoon at Noah. "And I don't want to see him get hurt."

"Then you'd better close your eyes, my love," he said tenderly. " 'Cause here it comes."

"You're making the cookies yourself," Ethan said as she poured the sugar into the bowl and began mixing as if she was digging to China right through the table.

"You can cut the shapes after I roll it out," she snapped at him.

"Sissy," he said at the doorway, "I'm not one of the kids." He left her with her mouth open and four little girls chattering around her and made his way out to the barn.

He'd been born in Van Wert and lived there all his life. He'd wanted to leave for years. But he'd stayed. Stayed and watched as each of his brothers and sisters made a life for themselves. Stayed while they'd raised corn and chickens and kids. Helped them reap, helped them sow.

And what did he have to show for it all? Ten dollars and a field of grapes he didn't even own. He kicked the leg of his cot. Once the buckaroo was well, he'd have no excuse for hanging around the Harrington house, and there'd be no reason for Sterling Phillips to tolerate the likes of him. He touched his lips and cursed himself for daring to kiss her. Who did he think he was, kissing a woman like that?

And worse. Who did he think he was that he would dare to do it again?

Chapter Fourteen

"I think they're probably cold already," Ethan said, reaching for the wet towels she had wrapped around Worth's legs.

"Benjamin says there's a real danger we could burn his legs," she said, defending herself. If he couldn't feel anything, they could scald him without even knowing it.

"Yeah, well, I guess we'll just have to be careful, 'cause I don't see *Benjamin* doing anything to get him well, do you?"

"Dr. Cobb says—" she started.

"*Dr.* Cobb? Are we on the outs with Benny today?" Glory, but he was irritating. It didn't matter what she called the doctor. It was clear she'd get an argument from Ethan.

"Where's the pin?" he asked, sticking out his hand as if she was his nurse or something.

"The birds are still puny," Worth said, watching out the window while Ethan dried off his legs. "Ster, how we gonna get the princess over the moat?"

She hated it when Worth brought up Princess Sugarlips in front of Ethan. It was their private story and she didn't want him butting into it with his suet balls and troll tolls.

"Ster?"

His lip trembled.

"Well, let's see. Since Princess Sugarlips is a flesh-and-blood princess, I guess she can't float on butterfly wings like Princess Amelia."

"Melia's an angel," Worth explained to Ethan, whose

business it wasn't. "So she can fly. But her spirit's broken, so she—"

It was like standing in front of Ethan Morrow stark naked. Only instead of seeing her body, he was seeing her soul.

"A turtle," she suggested, pulling the idea from thin air.

Ethan looked at her as if she'd grown another head.

"Yeah," Worth said. "She could sit on his back and he could fairy her 'cross the moat."

"*Ferry.* He could *ferry* her across the moat."

"And the prince and his friend could just run 'cross the bridge."

"Doesn't the evil Rutabaga stop the prince?" Ethan asked.

Sterling just gritted her teeth. She was willing to bet that the prince's friend was a cowboy.

"No, the Rutabaga doesn't see the prince," Worth said.

"Why not?"

Worth raised his shoulders. "I think he just sees the princess."

"Oh. He's only got eyes for her."

"Aren't you going to test him?" Sterling asked, looking in the drawer by Worth's bed for the damn pin.

"What about the prince's friend?" Ethan asked. He was working on Worth's legs with a fury, rubbing the calves until Ethan's upper lip was coated with a thin sheen of sweat.

"He lives in the treetops," Worth said, taking Sterling by surprise.

"Is he a monkey?" she asked.

"No. A boy." Worth reached down and pulled a pin from the side of his mattress and handed it to Ethan. "But he doesn't go near the water 'cause he can't see himself."

Ethan looked to her for an explanation, but she had

none. Glory-laury, she hadn't even known where the pin was!

She stationed herself by the window, looking out at the suet ball, which was melting in the rain and losing all its magic seed. It was still preferable to watching Sir Glad-I-am wield his mighty sword since each time yielded no new results.

Instead she watched out the window, wishing on stars that refused to come out to play, but which she knew were there, somewhere, waiting for her prayers.

"Ow!"

It was the sweetest word she'd ever heard. She spun around in time to see a grin split Ethan's face, and suddenly the room was brighter, despite the rain that knocked at the windows and sent rivulets down the panes.

"What about here?" he asked, pricking Worth's other foot gently. The baby shook his head. "Here?" Ethan skimmed his little leg up toward his knee, but there was no reaction.

"His toe!" Sterling cried out when she saw it twitch. "He moved his toe!"

Ethan raced around to the other side of the bed, lifting Worth's foot and twisting it this way and that while Sterling turned on the lamps despite the early hour. "Try again," he said, and they both stared at five tiny little toes that looked like they belonged on an ear of corn.

"I can't," her honey lamb whined, squirming in the bed and batting at the sheets.

"You gonna at least try?" Ethan asked the pouty child whose arms were now crossed over his chest and whose bottom lip was stuck out far enough to serve breakfast on.

"Honey lamb?" she tried to cajole, but he just turned his head and studied the wall. "The prince would try."

He glared at her over his shoulder.

"For the princess? For his new friend the monkey?"

"He isn't a monkey. He's a boy with no face in the water."

"A reflection?"

"That." He turned back to the wall.

The oak tree outside rustled in the wind, and the ends of a branch brushed at the window, its leaves sticking to the glass for a moment, then pulling away. Wind-driven rain smacked against the house, and Sterling rubbed her arms searching for warmth.

Finally Ethan spoke, addressing no one in particular. "James sure did like that new bicycle. What a beauty!"

Sterling knew just what he was doing, and tried to help him along. "I wonder what it feels like to ride one."

"Depends on how fast you go," Ethan answered, pretending that he wasn't saying any of this for Worth's benefit. "At first it feels a little like a carousel, the wind playing with your hair, the world going by in a blur. . . ."

The child's gaze shifted to the shiny red velocipede. She and Ethan exchanged a look that said, *It's working!* Despite her resolve not to, she smiled at the handsome man who caused her heart to lurch at the sight of him, encouraging him to go on even though he needed no prodding from her.

"Then," he continued, "when you build up speed, it's like nothing you've ever felt before. Like flying on a bird's wings—like Princess Sugarlips—you soar! And it's scary and wonderful all at the same time."

Now Worth's eyes were aimed at the foot that rested once again in Ethan's hand.

"Of course, you gotta be able to push the pedals," Ethan said, holding his palm against the bottom of Worth's foot. "You gotta push," he encouraged. "Harder! Come on, Bucky. Harder!"

She was clutching the front of her dress, gathering more and more of it into her fist, holding her breath. The strain showed on the child's face, as it did on

Ethan's. She thought she'd die before they told her anything.

Gently Ethan put Worth's foot down and covered it carefully with the comforter. She swallowed hard, but couldn't find her voice.

"Guess I'd better keep those wheels greased, Buckaroo," he said, and all the air seemed to rush out of her at once. "Won't be long before we're telling you to get off that bicycle and wash up for supper!"

Oh, didn't he paint a pretty picture! She could see it now. She'd be wiping her hands on her apron, and Ethan would be standing in the doorway, toweling off his bare chest and telling her about his day in the field. And then he'd call to Worth, and the boy would come running in on two good legs. Ethan would scoop him up under his arm and carry him off, laughing and squirming, to get him cleaned up for supper.

And they'd all sit down at the table to say grace. And glory would she have a lot to be thankful for.

"I pushed you good, huh?" Worth asked, and turned to her without waiting for an answer. "Can I go ride with James like he said?"

Before she could answer, Ethan asked, "James said he'd take you riding?" He sounded very skeptical.

Worth nodded convincingly. "And he likes to climb the trees."

Stretching out his lanky body, Ethan made his way to the window. With a suntanned hand he pulled back the curtains and stared out at the storm. "Does he? James doesn't play with other children much," he said softly, tracing the path of a raindrop down the pane. "I don't think he's been to the park since . . . well, since he was the buckaroo's age."

Sterling knew better than to believe anything could come of her imaginings. She knew her dreams about Ethan Morrow would never come true. But the envy she felt of the woman who would share his life and bear his children, and of the children who would come to call him Daddy, cut so deeply into her soul that she had to close her eyes to stop the tears.

"You all right?" he asked her, the same gentle hand that had coaxed movement from Worth's foot now stroking her upper arm. "You're trembling."

"He moved, didn't he?" she asked, sure that was why she felt so close to tears.

He nodded, then called over to Worth. "We sure got our work cut out for us, huh?"

"I could do it," the boy said, his gaze intent on the lump under the comforter where his feet lay waiting.

"I never doubted it," Ethan said, and Sterling noticed that the man's eyes were as bright as her own. "You're gonna be chasing after Honesty before we know it."

And then Ethan and that mangy dog would climb up in that buckboard and drive out of their lives. This time for good.

"Lousy weather," he said. "Gonna be a late summer, I think. Spring just doesn't want to quite give up."

"Must be related to you," she said with a smile as she fussed over Worth's supper tray.

"Born in May," he admitted. "I've got renewal in my blood."

"Spring's got its share of snow and rain and destruction. Isn't it tornado season too?"

"You accusing me of something?" he asked, taking mock offense. "Now even the weather's my fault? When's your birthday, anyways?"

She hadn't had a casual conversation with anyone in years. It was too hard to think about what the smallest bits of information might reveal. *So, when did your mother die?* for example. The answer to that would surely lead to a problem or two. Would knowing her birthday give anything away?

Amber eyes studied her. "It wasn't a trick question," he said. "Unless . . . it isn't today, is it?"

She shook her head. "Early July." It was always best to be as vague as possible in her circumstances. And

Independence Day hadn't been auspicious for her anyway.

"Thunderstorm season yourself, there," he said as if he'd discovered some weakness in her. He looked out the window again as the rain lashed against it. "And it looks like the wind just blew some company your way."

Sterling joined him at the window and peered down, not particularly curious. Men came to see her uncle Oliver fairly often. No doubt the man being helped from the coach was just another business associate in a fine top hat and handsome cloak. He had the walk of authority, waving away the driver and stalking toward the house, his head bent against the rain as if it had no business getting in his way.

* * *

Cyril Phillips hated his brother-in-law's house. Only a fool built a staircase without some sort of awning to keep the rain off the steps. He hated the street it was built on, which suffered from poor drainage, and the fact that it was a good fifteen minutes from the train. Or rather, a bad fifteen. He hated the entire town. After Amelia's death he thought he was through with Van Wert, Ohio. He hadn't been able to deny her the visits to her sister, especially once Imogene's mind had snapped, but he'd expected the cord to be severed with her death.

He supposed Carl would answer the door, if the man was still alive. Oliver never got rid of anyone, no matter how far from their usefulness they may have strayed. *Strayed.* It was a poor choice of words, even in thought, for it brought him to the reason for his visit.

Sterling. Why was it everything to do with the girl took place in the foulest of weather?

He rapped at the door loudly, assuming by now Carl was completely deaf instead of just merely hard of hearing.

She'd been born in a thunderstorm, his fair-haired

daughter, complete with streaks of blinding lightning and crashes of deafening thunder. He'd lost his finest maple in that storm. And the replacement was a puny substitute for such majesty.

The rain crawled down his neck and he kicked at the door with a soggy shoe. Robbins had sent him off without his umbrella and Cyril made a mental note to dock his pay, filing it with the many other notes he'd made since Amelia had passed on. He'd had such high hopes when he'd married her—a dynasty of sons would carry on his business into the next century and beyond. But she'd presented him with a girl, and nothing more. And then she'd up and died without even making sure he had good household help.

He'd sent the girl away from the house in heavy rain, her cries muted by the constant smack, smack, smack of rain against the windows that not even the heavy velvet drapes could muffle.

And he'd thought himself done with it all.

"Mr. Phillips!" Carl's eyes were comically large, as though a ghost stood on the top step of Harrington Manor grimacing at him.

"Move, man!" he shouted, pushing his way into the house and out of the driving rain. It had been a long time since he'd seen the servant, but apparently the man had learned nothing about butlerage in the interim. "You take the hat. You take the coat. You show me to the drawing room and have me announced. Dammit, man, you wouldn't last five minutes in my employ."

"Yessir," the man said feebly, reaching for Cyril's hat and trying to assist him with the removal of a very soggy cloak. "Thank you and thank God!"

"Incompetent and oversecure. Oliver Harrington is an idiot." He shook his head, and droplets of water flew into the butler's face. It made him think there was some small modicum of justice left in the world after all.

"So the mountain has come to Muhammad," Oliver said, coming out into the hallway. "I've been dreading this day for more than three years and wishing there was a damn thing I could do about it."

"Not the warmest welcome I've ever received, but then again, not the worst." He nodded politely, sending water droplets to the hardwood floor. "I'd like an awning and a drink. But since the awning's too late, I'll settle for a double."

"Scotch?" Oliver asked, leading the way to the drawing room.

They'd known each other since the first time he'd traveled to Van Wert to formally ask Amelia Weldridge's father for her hand. She'd been the first woman who hadn't just rolled over onto her back for him, and he'd been determined to have her. And had her did. Once, twice, sometimes three times a night.

But it hadn't filled the void for either of them, and while she kept searching for love in his arms, he was reduced to seeking an heir between her legs. And instead she'd given him a daughter with the morals of an alley cat, loved the girl instead of him, and then succumbed to pneumonia and left them both to mourn in their own ways.

"Cyril? Scotch?" Oliver repeated.

"Over twenty years and you still have to ask?" He looked around the room. There were flowers everywhere. The thought that he might be too late stopped him in his tracks. "Has someone died?"

"Oh, my babies in heaven! Arabelle, Clarabelle, Jeezebel! What are *you* doing here?" Imogene Harrington floated into the room and clung to the back of a chair as though she might just lift off at any moment if she didn't keep hold of something solid. She'd gone gray since the last time Cyril had seen her, but her eyes still sparkled and her skin still shone. Insanity apparently agreed with her.

"See she isn't any better," Cyril said to Oliver. There had to be something to that Weldridge blood. The resemblance was uncanny. There was no mistaking that

Imogene was Amelia's sister, just as there was no mistaking that Sterling was Amelia's daughter. He wondered about the boy, as he had nearly constantly since Graham Trent had told him of the accident. "The boy hasn't . . . ?"

"God, no!" Oliver said, turning a ghastly green. "He's better every day. Why the sudden interest?"

"He's my flesh and blood," Cyril answered. Even in his own mind he hadn't ever thought of the boy as that before. Perhaps because he'd never been that certain about the fidelity of the boy's grandmother. Still, an heir was an heir, and he wasn't about to go find a new wife at this point in his life. The odds were fifty-fifty that he'd get another daughter, and what good would the bother of it all do him then?

And there'd be no guarantees with a second child, women being the creatures they were. He wasn't even sure his father's blood ran in his own veins. Boys and men held no blame, as far as he could see. They spilled their seed and took their chances.

Fool me once, shame on you. Fool me twice, shame on me. He'd carved it into a board when he was young, and into his heart as he grew. He was not about to be cuckolded twice.

"They've been your flesh and blood since the beginning," Oliver said. "You threw your flesh and blood out. You left her to the mercy of the world."

"She made her bed," he said, deliberately using the allusion. "And she can lie in it. The boy's done nothing to earn my wrath."

"I never did know how my sister could stand you," Imogene said. "But she thought you were God. Now I see who gave her the idea."

"I'd like to see the boy," Cyril said, ignoring her comment. It'd be a cold day in hell when he worried about the opinion of a certifiable lunatic. In fact, it'd be a veritable blizzard before he worried about the opinion of anyone at all.

* * *

"Psst."

It had been a wonderful dream, full of the soft passion that he felt for Silver all the time now. But Imogene Harrington's *psst* didn't fit into it. In the soft yellow chair where he'd fallen asleep, he opened one eye and watched Silver tiptoe toward the door.

Unfortunately Imogene had mastered, much to his surprise, the art of whispering, so he only caught a word here and there. But Silver's reaction was impossible to miss. Even with the traces of her sunburn still coloring her cheeks, she had clearly gone white. She gripped the edge of the doorway and swayed before turning to look in his direction.

Closing his eyes quickly, he pretended to be asleep. It was a dirty trick, but since he was already trespassing in her life, this was like giving her privacy without having to get up and excuse himself. And, he rationalized, he could hardly hear them. Not to mention that if he waited for them to tell him the truth, he'd be tripping over a long gray beard.

"I don't know what he wants," Imogene said, flapping her hands. ". . . my fault. I never should have touched him. No, never."

From beneath nearly closed lids he saw Imogene shake her head in Worth's direction and mutter about losing yet another one.

"No one's losing anyone," Silver said, but her knuckles were white as she gripped the edge of the door. "Why would he come now?"

"He knows about the accident."

They argued about how he, whoever *he* was, could know.

"Are you going to come down?" Imogene asked finally.

"I don't suppose he'd just go away if we asked him,"

she said. Her shoulders clearly said she didn't have a prayer that he would.

He wished there was something he could do to help. Pretending to have just woken up, he asked, "Who's *he*?"

He'd have sworn Silver couldn't get any paler. But he'd have been wrong.

"I don't suppose if I asked you to stay up here, you'd do it," she said.

He was tempted to agree to her request, if only to take the frightened look from her face. But what good could he do her hidden in her brother's room? "No more than *he'd* leave if you asked *him* to go."

She swallowed hard, took a last look at Imogene, and then faced him, shoulders squared, head high. "My father is downstairs."

He didn't think this was quite the moment to tell her that it was probably due to him that the man had come. Hell, if she'd told him it was a secret, he'd never have written to Graham. If he'd known how the blood would drain from her face, he'd have done whatever it took to keep the man away.

"You're not surprised," she said, examining his face.

It was his turn to swallow. "Not really," he admitted when he could.

"You knew my father was alive?" Her head cocked. Her lip rose slightly. He nearly expected her to say, "Huh?"

"Actually yes," he admitted. "Though I wasn't reminded of it until the other day."

"The other day?" He could see the wheels in her mind turning, trying to remember what had happened that had given her away.

"My brother-in-law mentioned him." Well, in for a penny, in for a pound, as the saying went. "Remember I told you that I wrote to my sister and her husband in New York?"

She stared at him blankly.

"Well, Graham knows your father and mentioned to him that he was sorry to hear about his son."

Sterling's jaw dropped. Her eyes widened. It didn't seem to Ethan that she could breathe. "His son?" she asked as if she didn't even imagine them related. Doing his best not to startle her, he eased himself out of the chair and slowly walked toward her. Extending a hand to steady her, he led her to the small yellow sofa near the door.

"Oh, my!" Imogene said. "The cat's out now and Honesty's caught it!"

Chapter Fifteen

Cyril took stock of the parlor. Oliver was standing by the doorway, looking like a rooster left to defend the henhouse from a fox. His feathers might have been shouting, "I'm king of the walk," but they didn't cover his knocking knees. There were other men, Cyril knew plenty of them, who would have enjoyed being the fox, but none as much as he was enjoying it himself.

Oliver Harrington had earned every shake those knobby knees were causing him. It had been a simple plan for a simple girl. A week or two on the street and his tarnished Sterling would have had to come crawling back to him with the name of her lover on her tongue. If the man had been suitable, he'd have forced the marriage, and he'd be bouncing a grandson on his knee a few months later. If not, these things could be taken care of. Money cut a wide path around the law, and from what he'd heard, it didn't take much.

But Oliver had subverted his plan when he'd come to the girl's rescue, offering her a way to save face by agreeing to accept the baby as his and Imogene's. Then, when she'd been unable to part with the bastard, he'd compounded his error by allowing her to stay with the child and pretend he was her brother, knowing that Cyril would never drag his own name through the mud by bringing up technicalities such as the fact that Amelia had been dead long before the child was conceived, never mind born.

Oliver's plan had been stupid, silly—but he knew his neighbors well. Apparently not one of them had asked *when* the boy's mother had died. Well, they'd cooked their own goose, and now he was glad to take it out of the oven and serve it up to them all.

An heir was an heir, he told himself again. Provided of course that he was made of the right stuff, despite his parentage. Provided of course that the boy was quick-witted and capable of being taught by the right teacher. Provided of course that he wasn't crippled or disfigured by the accident.

An heir was an heir.

Provided of course that the boy's mother wasn't part of the deal. The less people remembered about his darling daughter, the less likely they were to put births and deaths and dates together. The girl had had her options—marriage or a simple procedure to rid them of the problem. Either would have been acceptable to him and the people that mattered, few that there were.

She'd chosen neither and imagined impunity. Her mother was right of course. Their daughter was a dreamer.

The girl came into the room, trembling like a leaf on a tree that was already feeling the quiver of the logger's ax, and he smiled amiably. How many deals had he closed by hiding the dagger behind the grin, coming in for the kill after the niceties had cleared the path and laid bare the enemy?

"Sterling." He nodded at her as cordially as he could. She looked like hell, not that he'd expected otherwise, but the rumpled dress, the red cheeks, the lip she gnawed on—sixteen years of lessons and manners, the best of schools and tutors and friends, and it had all been for naught. "You look well."

Behind her was a good-looking man, young, healthy, at home here in the Harrington house.

"Ethan," Oliver said, a slight quaver to his voice. "I didn't realize you were here."

Before he could answer, Sterling turned to him, and while Cyril couldn't see her face, he couldn't help notice the familiarity with which she touched his sleeve. "He was just leaving." Her head was tilted up toward his, and while Cyril couldn't read the girls eyes, he couldn't miss the man's as he studied the girl's face. "Please?"

The man grimaced, but nodded. "Oliver. Genie. I'll see you all tomorrow." He turned to leave.

"Just a moment," Cyril said, "I didn't catch your name."

"Ethan Morrow," he said, extending his hand, and Cyril had one of those feelings as if he'd stood in some other parlor, somewhere else, and shaken hands with the same man.

"Ethan has been helping with Worth," the girl said, encouraging him to leave. "But he's quite busy with his own chores. A farmer's work, you know."

She prattled on, something about plowing or sowing, while he savored the boy's name. *Worth.* It was a good name. At least she'd done something right.

"It's raining," he finally said, hoping to end the litany of a farmer's chores.

Ethan Morrow nodded. "Which makes it a good day to take care of the barn and help out my sister and do all the things that a body can't make time for when the sun is shining."

Another prattler. Cyril was ready for him to go before he'd turned and headed for the door.

Just before he left, he turned and looked hard at Cyril. "I'll need to talk to you, sir, after you're settled in."

Cyril nodded at the man, let his gaze drift toward his daughter, and sighed. She'd gotten herself involved with a farmer. What was next? The help?

"We have nothing to discuss," he said, and turned abruptly, dismissing the man who would come calling on a woman in his work pants.

"I wish that were so," the man said softly, but was gone by the time Cyril turned back around for a second look.

His relatives stood motionless, apparently waiting to hear the door close, and then observed another minute's silence for good measure.

When those around him finally resumed breathing, he asked, "How's the boy?"

They all exchanged looks as if they needed to decide which version of the truth to give him. All Weldridges, all right. There was the truth according to Amelia, the truth according to Imogene, and there was certainly, that morning in September when the doctor had said that his daughter's influenza would run another seven months and produce a child, the truth according to Sterling.

"I think I've a right to know how my *son* is," he said, relishing the surprised looks on all their faces. All except Imogene, who had probably forgotten the boy wasn't his to begin with. He shook his head at all of them, then crossed the room and shut the doors behind Sterling. "Did you think I'd come to disgrace you? Is that why you think I'm here?"

"Why are you here?" the girl asked. Her chin was sharper than her mother's. A bit more like his own, he noted with a certain satisfaction. Wouldn't it be something if this brush with tragedy (and he hoped that was what it was) were to reveal to him the very thing he longed to know, and deliver him up the fruits of loins as well? "I thought you wanted nothing to do with me."

"You?" This had nothing to do with her, except as the bridge that connected him to the boy. A bridge that, once crossed, could easily be burned. "We've all made mistakes," he said graciously, quite convincingly, he thought. "Yours wasn't the first unwise choice."

He'd even chosen unwisely himself, and for numerous reasons, not the least of which was that he'd never gotten in writing from Amelia's father the promises of business or land in California. And then there was the matter of only the one child, and that one not a son.

Defiantly spitting into the cyclone, she said, "I wouldn't take it back now, even if I could."

"You wouldn't take it back then, either, as I recall," he said as he sat down in one of the Windsor chairs.

After she'd refused to reveal the father's name, he'd offered her a second option. He could have it taken care of, in the same way that he supposed that other fathers of unwed, pregnant young women did. Surely his daughter hadn't been the first. And then he could marry her off to some unsuspecting fool who would be so happy to have him for a father-in-law that he'd overlook the clean sheets on his wedding night. But she'd refused.

And left him no choice but to wash his hands of the entire matter. There'd been a merger pending, and her situation was an unwanted and unwarranted distraction. The merger had gone according to plan. The business with his daughter had not.

Was it any wonder that he always preferred business to family? He could not only predict the outcome in business, he could control it. There was a crossover now, though, if he could finesse it right. An heir.

"He's really beautiful," she said, getting that look on her face that women used when they wanted to get their way and the only weapon they had was their femininity. So, her mother had taught her something after all. Unless it was just instinct, like an animal. "He's smart, and funny, and he's got a smile for everyone."

The boy could smile. That was certainly worth dragging the family name through the mud. "And the father," he asked, "is he smiling too? He ought to be, having gotten off scot-free."

"I hope he is," she said softly, as if the memory of him still boiled her blood.

Not exacting revenge, not tasting satisfaction, still galled him. He was known up and down Wall Street as a vengeful son of a bitch, and the epithet was as well earned as it was enjoyed.

And his daughter knew it. She shouldn't have been so

surprised when he'd shown her the door and booted her out of it. And he hadn't had a moment's remorse over it either.

Not until recently, when he'd had the good fortune to buy up large chunks of businesses that had been left for the pickings by the deaths of several of his contemporaries. His own business was too fine, too successful, to be left for his competitors to scramble over and tear to shreds once he was gone. He'd rather dismantle it himself than see J. P. Morgan get a piece of it.

And a male heir was a true heir.

So he asked once more, this time without any intention of being stalled again, "How is the boy?"

"Have you been keeping tabs on him all this time?" Imogene asked, flitting behind one chair and then another. "Do you know what he looks like? When his first tooth came in? Christmas '93. Do you know when he learned to walk?"

"I understand he isn't able to do that right now," he said, trying in his mind to pin the woman to the chair like some specimen of butterfly under glass. "Is my information correct?"

"Why does it matter to you?" Oliver asked, helping himself to another glass of scotch. "We're doing everything that can be done for him."

"He might need more than you can do," Cyril said. He didn't want a cripple, especially one that couldn't even control his bowels. If that was the case, he'd happily leave him to the boy's mother, who would only get what she richly deserved.

"He gets better every day," the girl said. "Some of the feeling is returning now. Dr. Cobb feels there's reason to hope, and we work with him, getting him to try a little harder, push a little more. And while it's only in tiny increments that he improves, he is improving."

Yes, a real dreamer, just as Amelia had called her as a child, as though to dream was an accomplishment worthy of praise and adulation. His wife had told him each of the girl's lackluster achievements until he'd patiently explained to her that the reason he saw the child only on Sundays was that the girl held little interest for him. After that the only way he could get Amelia's affections in their bed was to ask after the girl. He'd suckled breasts to a recital of Sterling's marks on tests. He'd discovered numerous positions that made it hard for a woman to talk, and even a few that made it impossible. But no son had planted himself in Amelia's womb, and while he endeavored, he learned more about the little blond girl than he could possibly want to know.

The minute the doctor had announced that his wife had borne him a daughter and not a son, he'd known more than he wanted to know.

But now there was a son. *His* son, as far as everyone in Ohio knew.

"I'd like to see him," he said, rising to his feet.

Sterling looked just the way he remembered her. Guilty, nervous, unsure. "He doesn't know about you," she said in a whisper. "Nobody does."

"And you're afraid." He couldn't keep the contempt out of his voice. She'd been so high and mighty with her ideals that last night in the house, protecting her lover. Well, the years had taught her a lesson he felt she should have been born knowing—that Cyril Phillips was someone of whom she should be afraid.

"No one points a finger at him. No one calls him a name."

"And naturally you're afraid I'll end all that."

"You could," she said. "I'm praying that you won't."

"Your prayers have been answered," he said, smiling broadly at her and then showing his teeth to Oliver and Imogene as well. "As far as everyone in this town is concerned, I'm the boy's father. Let's leave it at that."

Only Imogene squinted at him, as if she was trying to see just what he had up his sleeve.

*   *   *

Ethan had finished every chore Sissy could think of for him long before Hannah and Julia had come waltzing in the door from school. They'd dragged everyone out to see a rainbow, and then settled down with their homework. Only after Sissy had agreed to lie down for a while had Hannah remembered that James had asked about Ethan. He'd been wondering if Ethan had mentioned the kite-flying he'd promised to do with him.

So with guilt pushing his boots, he'd trudged over to James's in the mud and muck and suggested the boy might like to fly the fish kite out at the old Gibbs place while Ethan saw to the vines.

Now the kite lay in the mud, and James was up to his elbows in clippings as he helped Ethan prune the vines.

And with all the busy work he'd done, he still couldn't get the feel of Silver's trembling back out of his hand, the look of pure fear in her eyes as Genie told her that her father was downstairs waiting for her.

He'd taken the coward's way out, agreeing to leave before telling the man that here stood before him the lunatic who had mowed down his son. He'd left the silver princess to face him alone rather than muddy the waters with his presence, and he was ashamed of himself for doing it. No matter that he had made it clear that he would tell him, and soon.

Hiding the truth, or running from it, could take a lifetime.

"Do I cut this here?" James asked, pulling back some leaves to show Ethan where he meant. "I don't wanna hurt it none."

"Just right," Ethan said. "You sure do have a knack for this, James."

"How come you call the Phillips kid *Buckaroo*?" James asked.

"You asking about the kid or about why I don't call you nothing but James?" he asked in return. He'd been tempted to call the boy a few good names (and on occasion, a few bad ones), but with half the town calling him One Shoe, he thought maybe the boy needed to be reminded who he really was.

James busied himself with cutting, tweaked a tendril and let it spring, and then finally answered, "James is kinda formal, don't you think, Uncle Eth?"

"Got anything in mind?"

He studied the boy and knew that he did, but that he was reluctant to admit it. And much as he cared, Ethan was having a hard time concentrating on anything but what was going on back at Harrington Manor.

"James? You gonna tell me?"

The boy's narrow shoulders rose again. Ethan remembered when James was just a baby. He and Samuel were two little terrors, all right. The things they got into! Bugs and dirt and . . . he looked around. Maybe James hadn't changed so much. Maybe everyone around him had. Maybe he acted the way he did because everyone treated him carefully, as if a piece of him was missing, and so it was.

Ethan dug until he found a nice fat earthworm. Then, on his hands and knees, he crept over to James and pulled the boy's shirt away from his chest, letting go of the worm so that it fell down toward the boy's belly.

"Hey!"

"What's the matter, Jimbo?" Ethan teased, the name coming out just like it had all those years ago when he'd nicknamed the boys Jimbo and Sambo. "Don't you like worms anymore?"

He was getting damn tired of looking at eyes that were brimming with tears and trying to decide if they were happy or sad. James's lip trembled. He plowed into Ethan's chest and burrowed against it.

"I love you, Uncle Ethan," he said softly.

"Then I guess that worm'll forgive you," Ethan said. Wouldn't Della be surprised when she went to wash the boy's clothes?

The carriage startled them, coming down the lane toward the farmhouse. No one ever came out that way.

It was a fact that Ethan had relied on, once or twice, when he'd been courting Velma Webb. They'd done some pretty heavy petting right there on Mrs. Gibbs's old bed. If that rat hadn't run clear across the mattress, he might be a more experienced man by now. And Velma might be married to him instead of Hiram Marsh.

Rats, he decided, weren't necessarily a bad thing. He was sure Velma would agree.

He recognized the carriage and rose quickly, his only thought that something must be wrong to bring Oliver Harrington out there to find him. He knew he never should have left that house. Silver had been scared to death and he'd simply walked out.

"What's wrong?" he asked, trying to dust himself off and realizing that he was one big mudball. He stripped off his shirt. "What is it?"

Oliver tied the reins, set the brake, and climbed down out of the buggy. "Had a need to get out of the house," he admitted. "Nothing more than that. She's all right. So's the boy."

He nodded. Well, he supposed that he wasn't doing the best job of hiding his feelings for Sterling and her brother. Not that they could come to anything.

"Those the grapevines?" Oliver asked. He ruffled James's hair as they walked. "Nice to see you, young man."

"You can call me Jimbo," James said. "That's what Uncle Eth does."

"Jimbo? It has a nice ring to it. Tell me, Jimbo, you think you could find me a glass of water?" He unbuttoned his top button and then shrugged off his suit jacket.

"Might take me a while," James said. "Want me to put that back in the carriage?"

Oliver handed him the jacket. "Thank you, son. And you take your time. There's something I want to talk to your uncle about." He reached into his pocket and produced a nickel. "Think that'd be enough for a glass of water?"

"I can get lost for a while," James said, plucking the nickel from the man's fingers. "I'll cough loud when I'm coming back. My papa does that when I'm supposed to be asleep and I've been reading. I hear him in the hall and pretend I'm asleep. Works pretty good."

"How's your mama?" Oliver asked. "She doing all right?"

The smile left James's face. "I think she'd do a lot better if I wasn't around. Going west, you know, when I'm old enough. I'll get you that water now."

He took off running, the mud sucking at his feet and splashing as he went.

"His mama's not gonna be too happy with those clothes," Ethan said, worried about what it was that Oliver could want with him. *Stay away from my niece? Don't take Imogene out? Don't come visiting while Mr. Phillips is around?*

"Guess he takes after you," Oliver said, watching the boy until he was out of sight. "Wanted a boy more than anything, you know. Not that we wouldn't have loved a girl just as much. Think we might have done all right with a monkey, even."

"Well, nice that you've got your niece and nephew with you," Ethan said. His hands were too dirty to put into his pockets. He let them hang limp by his sides.

"If I could have let myself enjoy them," Oliver said. "Held them at arm's length. I knew he'd show up here sooner or later. Could *you* stay away from her?"

Ethan coughed and Oliver put up his hand.

"I take that back. Didn't mean it the way it sounded."

They strolled as they talked, Oliver obviously trying to ignore the mud that fought with him for his hand-sewn Russian calf boots as best he could, Ethan too nervous to worry about the ooze that left him on slippery ground.

"You wanted to tell me something?" Ethan prompted after they'd covered two rows in silence.

"It's not so easy," Oliver said, staring at the vines. "Look! There's a grape!"

"Yes," Ethan said, crouching to pull away the leaves and show the older man a cluster of new grapes.

"I tried to buy you," the man blurted out. He stared off at the horizon.

"Pardon?"

"Imogene had lost our last baby. I couldn't let her try anymore. I couldn't bear to lose another one, even if she could stand it. And I didn't think she could." He shrugged and slid his hands into his pockets as if he were finished with his admission.

"And?" Ethan demanded.

"And your mama had four fine children and was expecting her fifth. Your pa didn't have two spare nickels to rub together, and your mama was canning up fruit and selling it door to door. I remember she was so big, she could hardly walk. Sissy was passing out the jars, and Bart—he was big even then—was pulling a wagon with the jellies and the rest of the family in it."

The man looked wistful—jealous of a memory that didn't belong to him.

"And you tried to buy one of the children instead of the jelly?"

"I went to your father and offered to make sure he always had enough money. Jack Morrow wasn't an extravagant man. He didn't live the high life, your father. I told him he'd have whatever he and Zena needed if they would let me and Genie adopt the baby she was carrying." Tears rolled down the man's face, but he pinched his lips and fought the sob.

"What did he say?" Ethan asked, not able to imagine any of it. This man had tried to buy him from his family. Had offered money for a man's son.

Oliver laughed. "He punched me out cold. Said I didn't know the value of a human life. Seven babies I buried, a piece of my heart along with each one, and he told me I didn't know the value of a human life." He sniffed and looked at Ethan.

"I've watched you from the day you were born, imagining what it would have been like if Jack Morrow had had one ounce of greed in his body. I admired him, while he hated me. I even admired him *for* hating me.

"And I loved you as if you were my own. As if you were some part of me. My heart broke for your every failure. But I could never help you leave. And now I'm sorry."

"Why are you telling me all this?" Ethan asked. He felt as if that worm he'd put down James's shirt was crawling on him. As if a hundred bugs were crawling all over him, giving him the creeps as he thought of this man, this stranger clear across town, watching him and wishing he were his.

"It's all going to come apart. I know it. And when it does, I want you to know there was nothing I could do. There was never anything I could do. I finally see that Imogene is right. There's a plan, and it isn't ours."

"I don't know what you're telling me. I don't know what you're asking me," Ethan said, running his hands down his jeans before wiping his brow.

"You watch out for Cyril, Ethan. He's a mean and spiteful man. He doesn't care whom he hurts. Not even his own. I don't know what he—"

There was a loud cough.

"Here comes my water," Oliver said. "So how are the grapes doing?"

Ethan watched as Oliver took the glass of water from James. "He's a good man, your uncle Eth," he said, drinking the water and returning the empty glass to the boy. "I've no doubt he understands the value of things."

*   *   *

"Of course I will be responsible for the boy's bills," Cyril told the doctor as they sat in the parlor awkwardly. It was wise of the man not to have gone into business. A formidable adversary had to be able to look an opponent in the eye, not the Adam's apple.

"They've been taken care of," the doctor said. He flexed his fingers, concentrating on his left hand. "And there will be no further charges."

"I'll see to it that you're reimbursed," he said to Oliver. There was no reason for him to incur expenses on Cyril's heir's behalf. He didn't wish to owe Oliver anything but retribution.

"Oh, we didn't pay them," Imogene said, tying a purple ribbon around her neck that Cyril would gladly have tightened for her. He noticed that his daughter had the same inclination. "The man who hit him took care of it."

"Hit him? You mean Graham Trent's brother-in-law?"

Oliver patted Imogene's hand. "That's Francie's husband," he explained to her before answering. "Yes, that would be the man."

"I've been waiting to meet him again," Cyril said, trying to keep the menace out of his voice. "What does the man do, besides make a habit of running down people in the street?"

"But you—" the doctor began, only to be interrupted by Sterling, whose manners hadn't improved with age or distance.

"Actually he was leaving town," Sterling said between bites of her lip. "There was land being given away in Oklahoma."

There was of course more to it than that. He could see that in the looks his daughter gave the doctor and that his relatives gave each other, and he doubted he'd get much out of them, with the possible exception of the doctor, who couldn't seem to hide his confusion.

"So you've been well taken care of?" he asked the man with the plaid suit and the immaculate white shirt.

"By small-town standards," the man replied.

"Are you from around here?" Despite the suit, which was hideous and out of date, the man had a polish to him that put Cyril in mind of a bigger city. Boston, he thought, or Chicago.

The man nodded. "But I earned my diploma back east, and did my training in New York."

"Got bigger things in mind than Ohio?" Cyril asked him, sizing the man up and storing the information away for future reference.

"Much bigger," the doctor said.

Cyril smiled. It appeared he had one ally in Van Wert, Ohio. And his name was ambition.

"I'll see the boy now," he said, rising from the butter-soft leather chair that Oliver had paid for with money from the business Amelia's father had promised Cyril.

"I'll let you have some time with him alone," the doctor said, rising as well and bowing very slightly. He checked his watch and addressed Sterling. "This took longer than I thought. I've hours, you know. I'll be back tonight. I can check your . . ." He hesitated and looked at Cyril, things coming clear to each of them.

"—brother," Cyril said with great emphasis.

"Yes," the doctor agreed. "Her brother."

The girl just chewed her lip. It was lucky the doctor was interested in her. That lip was bound to need medical attention before too long.

Chapter Sixteen

Sterling trudged up the stairs as though they were steps to the gallows. And behind her the executioner's feet followed steadily, making certain that she didn't turn and bolt, but saw her fate through.

"He might be asleep," she said when they reached the door. "He's been working very hard and it makes him tired."

"I won't wake him," her father agreed, reaching for the doorknob. "But I'll have a look at him. Unless there's a reason I shouldn't?"

She fidgeted, despite the effort she made not to. She knew he hated it when she touched her hair, or bit at her lip, or . . . the list was endless. It had grown every time he'd set eyes on her from the time she could remember. *Don't slouch. Don't put your fingers near your mouth. Don't scratch. Do you think I care that it itches? I said don't scratch. Don't bolt your food. Don't dawdle. Don't speak until you're spoken to. Don't you have anything to say?*

There was often a trick to it. If she followed one rule, she found herself breaking another. She remembered a childhood filled with banishments from the room, which only ended when she was banished from the house.

"Is there a reason I shouldn't even see the boy?" her father asked. His face was a mask without emotion. No lines radiated from his eyes, the way they did Ethan's. No smile hinted at his lips. There were no signs of sun or wind or joy or sorrow that wrote their tales upon his brow.

And though he wouldn't like what she had to say, there'd be no evidence of it on his face. "It's just that he won't know who you are, and I don't know how to introduce you."

"How about a distant relative?" he suggested. "It's accurate enough for the time being."

"Just how long do you think you'll be staying?" she asked quietly. Her father didn't like to be questioned, but Worth would need to call him something, and if he were to be overheard by someone . . .

"You're trembling like some silly schoolgirl." He shook her by the shoulders and grimaced. "Just what is it you're so afraid of? I told you I won't reveal your secret. What have I to gain by doing that?"

She had no idea what he had to gain by exposing her or by keeping her secret, but she didn't doubt that he'd thought it all out and would be sure not to lose either way. He was much cleverer than she was, and had so much less to lose.

"I don't know," she admitted. "Perhaps you think that we might have to turn to you again, and then you'd get what you want."

"And just what is it you think I want?" he asked, those cold gray eyes of his so piercing she could almost feel them prick at her skin.

"Again, I don't know," she said. "To see me ruined? Begging for your forgiveness?"

"I've already seen you ruined, haven't I? Begging for forgiveness?" The idea seemed to appeal to him, but instead he said, as if that both surprised and wounded him, "You have a very poor opinion of me." He'd thrown her out without so much as a second set of underthings. For half the night she'd stood on the mansion steps to stay out of the rain, clutching a cigar box full of photographs under her umbrella and waiting for him to change his mind. And then she'd wired her aunt

and uncle, who'd sent her enough money for her to eat
and take a room until they could get there and take her
under their wing.

"That surprises you?"

"What if I told you I'd made a mistake. Been foolish
and hasty?"

They were the words she'd been waiting for for almost four years. But hearing them wasn't all she'd expected it to be. In fact his overture was more frightening
than welcoming. There was a reason that she'd never
allowed him into her fantasies, not as the wrathful king
or as the evil sorcerer or as the black knight. The minute she let him in, she was sure he would take control of
the fantasy and Princess Sugarlips would be doomed.

"I'm getting old, not that it shows. The house is big,
empty."

"Are you asking me to come home? Me and Worth?"
She couldn't do that, could she? Henry would still be
there, seeing to her father's carriages, only now the rest
of his family would be there too—his wife and little
girls, who had arrived from Ireland that first morning
she was sure that a life was growing inside her.

"I had hoped that motherhood would have instilled a
little patience into you, but I should have known better.
Because I've asked to see the boy hardly means that I
want you back under my roof."

She would never learn. Every time he dangled that
olive branch in front of her, she made a lunge for it.
And each time, he yanked it away and let her fall on her
face. Rats in laboratories were smarter than she was.
Puppies were trained more easily.

"And if I say you can't see him?" she asked, throwing
back her shoulders as if she could fool him, knowing
there wasn't a chance.

"On what grounds?" he asked, picking a piece of lint
off her blouse and then dusting the shoulder as if there
was dirt there. "After all, I'm his father, aren't I?" Her
father's hand returned to the doorknob and he turned it

ever so slowly. "Or would you prefer to tell people otherwise?"

He'd used her own lie against her, and she was trapped. It had been hard enough to run before, when Worth was safe within her womb, whole and protected by her love. "What would you have him call you?"

"What about 'Papa'?" he asked. "I've known fathers and grandfathers, and even just older men called that. It'll suit for now and it'll suit for later."

"Later?" She gnawed at her lip and then stopped herself. She couldn't afford to irritate him now.

"No one knows the future, Sterling. The truth might come out for one reason or another. The boy, others, may find out who I really am."

"But—" she started. It was too late. He'd already opened the door and entered her son's world.

"Cowboy?" Worth called out hopefully. Sterling shuddered. Her father wasn't going to like playing second fiddle.

* * *

"I think it's a mistake," Sissy was saying as Ethan came into the house, spanking clean and smelling like Grandpa's Witch Hazel soap, Honesty trying to undo all the good work he'd done at the pump.

"Those hot compresses seem to be helping the boy," he said as he plucked a peach from a bowl on the table, rubbed it on his jeans, and sank his teeth into it. All he could think of was Oliver Harrington's strange confession. Would Sissy have known about it? She'd never keep something like that from him. She didn't have any more deceitful bones in her body than he did. The whole Morrow family was so honest that other people found it nearly a failing.

"Didn't hear you come in," Noah said, coming to his feet and taking an envelope from the mantel. "This is for you. Some lawyer dropped it off this morning on his way out of town."

"A lawyer?" Ethan didn't much care for the sound of that. He'd yet to meet a lawyer who had good news for him. He signaled for Noah to put it down on the table and took another bite of his peach, eyeing the letter suspiciously.

"Go on and open it," Noah said, and Sissy put down the mending she was doing and took Isabella onto her lap. They both watched him intently as if they knew just how important the contents were.

"So, you know what this is?" Ethan asked, giving the peach to Honesty to polish off and drying his hands on his pants. "Mind the pit, stupid," he told the dog as he searched his family's faces for clues.

Noah shrugged noncommittally. Sissy fussed with the baby, her head down.

"Come on, come on. You know, don't you?" Lord, was there anyone he wasn't suspicious of?

His sister and her husband exchanged a look, and Noah put up his hands as though he hadn't even wondered about the contents of the envelope. "The lawyer just said you'd be happy to get it. Something about the Widow Garvey, he said."

"The Widow Garvey? She's been dead for months. What could it have to do with her?" Ethan lifted the envelope to the light, trying to see through it. It had a soft feel to it, padded, as if there were several papers in it.

"Open it, Eth." Sissy put the baby on the floor in front of her and leaned forward. "Could be good news."

"Okay," he said with a heavy sigh and a big intake of breath. "Here goes."

The glue gave way easily, and he slipped out the letter. As he unfolded it, a wad of money thudded to the table.

"What the . . . ?" He lifted up the cash and hefted it. Even in singles, there was a good amount there. Flipping the wad over proved it wasn't only singles.

"Oh, my!" Sissy said. "Imagine that!"

Clearly she'd known just what was in the envelope. And equally clear, should the farm ever fail, they'd better not have to live off her acting skills.

"What did the lawyer tell you?" he asked them, opening the letter. "Is the money mine?"

"How should we know?" Noah said. "Read the letter."

" '*Dear Ethan,*' " he said. "Well, it is to me, anyways."

> *If you receive this letter, I will have passed on. You will never know what a help you were to me when my poor Ben predeceased me. All the wood you cut, all the water you hauled, all the fixing up you did around the place—and I never even offered to pay you. See, I was afraid that with Ben gone, I'd find myself in a fix one day. But I put the money I owed you aside and I'm instructing my lawyer to see that you get this if I die. I'm sorry I didn't give it to you before I died. I sure should have.*

"Fancy that!" Sissy said.

Getting money sure did make her strange.

Ethan continued. "There's more."

> *Oh, as to the writing, I had my friend from Cleveland write this out for me since I think you know that I can't write so good myself. Good luck to you, Ethan. I'm sure you'll put this money to good use, 'cause it wasn't easy to come by.*

Noah made a face at Sissy. "Of course he'll put it to good use. He's nobody's fool. He knows what he should do with it."

"I sure do," Ethan said, fingering the stack of bills, too nervous to count it. "I think I'll go to Chicago, find me some fast women and good booze, and just enjoy myself till it all runs out. How would that be?"

"Ethan!" Sissy's little mouth was wide open in horror.

"You're right," he said, trying to get a straight face to stay in place. "Better to invest it in something that'll last longer—like a set of new clothes and a fancy wagon with one of those awnings on it so my pretty clothes'll stay dry!"

"Ethan Morrow!" Sissy's hands were pressed to her flaming cheeks.

"Don't worry," he said. "You can ride in it too. Everybody but Honesty. I'll get you one of those silk dresses and—" He couldn't keep it up any longer. Old Lady Garvey had left him a fortune and it had come at just the right moment in time. Two months ago he'd have used it to leave Van Wert. A month ago he'd have used it to pay off his bills and still go.

But now? Now he could afford to put a payment down on the future. Maybe he could even afford to pay the troll toll and get Princess Sugarlips out of the castle and across the moat, though the troll seemed like only a small mouse with the hawk circling overhead.

"Ethan Morrow—if you think for a moment that you can take that money and just fritter it away, willynilly—well, I've better use for the money than that!" Sissy was so cute when she was mad. He remembered how he used to frustrate her when he was a boy, just to see her put those hands on her hips and sputter at him.

"Hey," he reminded her. "It's my money. I can do what I want with it."

Noah put an arm around Sissy and tried to calm her. "So what *are* you going to do with it? A hundred and sixty-seven dollars is a lot of money."

"That how much there is?" he asked, fanning back the bills. "Good old Mrs. Garvey. See how wrong you were about her, Sissy?"

Sissy rolled her eyes and looked to Noah to intervene. "So, what are your plans?"

"Think the bank would give me a mortgage with that

as a down payment?" he asked. He'd never had more than forty-eight dollars to his name.

"You'd have to talk to Peter about it," Noah said. "But I'd think that between the money and being Peter's brother-in-law, you'd be in pretty good shoes."

"You gonna try to buy the Gibbs place, then?" Sissy asked. Her color was returning now, and Ethan realized she was in no shape to be kidded.

"Would it make you happy?" he asked. "I mean, you wouldn't mind having me just a few miles away, now, would you?"

"A farm of your own is a big undertaking," Noah reminded him. "Hard to run a farm all by yourself."

"I don't plan on being all by myself," he admitted. "Not by a damn sight."

"Ethan!"

"Oh, let the man alone. How often does a man get left a fortune?" Noah rose and shook his hand. "Congratulations, Ethan. I don't know a man more deserving of a break in life. I hope this is everything you want."

Not quite everything, but the means to it. Now he'd have not only that pot to pee in, he'd have a place to store it and enough room to put a few pots next to it. A finer one, a smaller one, and maybe someday a few more than that.

"You seen my fiddle?" he asked, checking behind the chair in the corner, Honesty's tail thumping against his leg as he looked. "I feel like doing some celebrating!"

* * *

She was still practicing breathing like a normal person when through the parlor window she saw Ethan Morrow come walking down the street toward Harrington House. She'd gotten one man who frightened her— her father—out of the house, only to have another one come waltzing along. And waltzing he was, that dog at his heels, playing a violin as he danced down the street, filling the night air with a sprightly tune and setting her nerves on edge.

At the door he kicked gently with his foot, not losing a note as he did so. She'd told him she played the violin, but she didn't remember him sharing the fact that he also played, and more than competently at that.

"I'll get it," she yelled to Carl, and pulled open the door reluctantly, grateful at least that her father was out. Though dinner at the DePuy couldn't last forever—he'd reluctantly gone there with Aunt Imogene and Uncle Oliver after complaining about Leona's cooking until they couldn't stand it anymore.

"Come on out," Ethan tempted her. "The air is full of roses and music and I want to share it."

"I can't," she said. "My aunt and uncle are out and I've got to stay where I can hear Worth." She'd almost said "my son." Just having her father in the same town had made her jumpy, possessive, and careless.

"His window's open. We'll hear him. Won't we, Buckaroo?" He shouted over his own music, which he hadn't had to stop in order to talk. When she played, she needed total silence to concentrate. But not Ethan. He could probably hoe—or whatever it was farmers did—with his toes while he fiddled with his hands.

"Cowboy? That you?" Worth's little voice carried down on the wind, competing with the violin to be heard.

"Close your eyes, Bucky, and see if you can't pretend you're out on the moors somewhere." He changed the tune to a softer one, more mournful, and called up again, "The troll's asleep, and all around you there are fireflies lighting up the dark like diamonds in a mine. You there, son?"

"What about the moon and the stars?" Worth asked.

"The moon's just a sliver, and up above, there are a million stars," he called up, his eyes fixed on her. "Just ripe for wishing on. Wanna make a wish?"

A wish? She didn't dare.

He lowered his voice and spoke only to her. "I'm wishing you'd come on out here and talk to me." He backed up and eased his bottom against the railing of the side porch. "I'm wishing you'd tell me why your father scares you so much and I'm wishing I knew how to tell you what I'm wishing most."

He didn't have to tell her. It was written all over that honest face that hid nothing because he had nothing to hide. Just being around him made her feel ashamed.

"You play very nicely," she said. "I'll listen from Worth's room." Glory-laury, but she was a chicken. She couldn't even sit on the porch with him, enjoying a nice cool evening.

Well, it was best not to encourage him. It would be awful to let him think, even for a minute, that something could actually exist between them. That they could ever be even so much as friends. That they could make each other happy.

"Please don't go," he said softly, letting the violin fall from his chin to hang silently by his side. "Or let me come with you. Something wonderful's happened and I need to share it with you."

"I shouldn't stay," she said. "And you certainly can't come in."

"But don't you want to know what's happened?" he asked. He was fairly bursting to tell her, and it was too hard to deny him just that one small question.

"All right," she said, still inside the house, her back against the open front door. "What wonderful thing happened?" She prayed it was something that would take him to the other side of the earth, right then.

At least she tried to pray that it was.

"I've come into some money," he said. He drew a line with the tip of his shoe and then another. Honesty chased both imaginary marks. "Not a lot. Not by your standards. But enough, I think, to get myself some land."

She fought to swallow, leaning heavily now against

the door. "Where?" She didn't know which she feared
more, his leaving or his staying. At least if he left, she
would never have to see the look in his eyes when he
learned the truth about her. And that's what would happen if he stayed. She knew it. Was sure of it. Because
he'd want to love her. And she couldn't let him love her
unless he knew, and he couldn't love her *if* he knew.

It was another conundrum, just like pretending her
father was Worth's father. No good could come of it.
Just like revealing Worth's real father when he had a
family of his own already. No good could come of it.

And what of her father? What would he do to Ethan's
hopes and plans? Surely he had some punishment in
mind for him.

"I was thinking I could get the Gibbs place for a
song." He interrupted himself to play a couple of notes.
"And I've already got the vines producing over there.
And there's a house and a barn and a couple of out-
buildings. . . ."

She had never been sorry that she'd sought solace in
Henry's arms. She'd never been sorry that Worth had
burst into her life and into her heart to fill and then
overflow the void her mother's death had left. She
wasn't sorry now for what she'd done.

But because of it, she was very, very sorry for what
could never be.

"Well, a farm would suit you well," she said.

A brief shadow crossed his smile, and she marveled at
how open he was, how unguarded. He lifted the violin
to his chin and played a melody she had never heard. It
wound softly around them, telling of dreams and wishes
that would never come true.

"What is that? Brahms?"

"Morrow," he answered. "My father used to play
something like it before he got sick. I remembered it as
best I could, but it always sounded too sad for my taste.
It had no hope."

"I like it," she said. Naturally she did. *It had no hope.*

"Care to?" he offered, holding out the instrument to her.

It had been a long time since she'd played. She'd bowed such sad songs after her mother died that her father had instructed Clara to take her violin away. Her fingers itched to touch the strings, her chin yearned to lean into the music.

"Oh, no," she said. "I haven't played in years."

"All the more reason," he said, pulling her gently from the door and curling her fingers around the instrument's slender neck.

"I couldn't," she protested, but slipped her chin into the warm rest that held the faintest scent of him, and placed her fingertips against the finger board. She took the bow, caressing the stick where his hands had held it and feeling a thrill at the intimacy of holding what he had held.

Coming around her, he took up a position behind her back and lifted her bow hand to position it over the strings.

"I do know how," she said, shaking him away. It would be hard enough to make music alone. It would be impossible for them to make music together.

"So play," he said, and went back to lean against the railing to watch her.

Tentatively she ran the bow over the strings, feeling her way. A soft purr came from the fiddle. It had a different tone from that of her own violin—richer, lower, more masculine. It whispered at her much the way its owner did. *Play me. Don't be afraid. Play me.*

And she did. Oh, how she did! Beethoven and Mendelssohn, Tchaikovsky and scales. Her fingers burned from stopping the strings. Her neck stiffened from cradling the rest. Her back and arms ached when, spent, she finally lowered the violin and let Ethan take it from her hands.

"Never in my life have I heard playing like that," he whispered. "It was . . . holy."

"It was competent," she admitted. She played well, but then, she had been taught well. Her music came from books and teachers and practice. His came from the heart.

"You don't believe that, do you? That it was just *competent*?"

She smiled wearily at him, as tired as she could ever remember being. All she wanted was to soak in a hot tub and crawl into bed and never come out from under the covers.

"Will you come and look at the farm?" He'd laid the fiddle down on the settee and was tucking a strand of her hair behind her ear.

She closed her eyes, savoring the moment and pretending it belonged to her. *Will you come and look at the farm?* It was as good as a proposal, and it hurt like the pains of childbirth to have to decline. But the woman that he wanted wasn't her, no matter what he thought. No matter how much she wanted it to be, wished it was. *If wishes were flowers . . .*

Over his shoulder she could see Benjamin's carriage coming down the street. "I should think you'd want to show that farm to your girl, not me," she said, her eyes on the carriage so that she didn't have to look at him.

Waving as if Ben were some long-lost friend just back from the wars, she slipped beneath Ethan's arm and headed down the stairs.

"Oh, Ben's here! How wonderful." She ran to meet him as he stopped the carriage in front of the house, and was waiting to take his arm as soon as he alighted. "I'm so glad you're here."

Benjamin's chest flared and he took her arm and looped it through his own. Studying her face, he commented on how much better it was looking, and she realized she'd forgotten about her burn. When he asked after her family, she realized that she'd also forgotten about her father for just a moment. Smiling like the only lemonade vendor at the Independence Day parade, he nodded at Ethan.

She had not, not for a moment, forgotten about Ethan Morrow.

* * *

It had been a dirty trick, pushing her into saying yes just to get rid of him. But rather than discuss it further, Sterling had agreed to see the farm. Well, vaguely anyway. No mention was made specifically of anything in front of Dr. Corns and Bunions.

"Was ten too early?" he'd asked.

"No," she'd tried to say. "That is, yes." Tongue-tied in front of the doctor, she'd hemmed and hawed until the sound of her aunt's nervous laughter danced down the street and she'd quickly said, "Ten," thrust his violin at him, and run into the house with the cornball on her heels.

"You again," Cyril Phillips said as he approached the porch and found Ethan there. His sharp eyes, more gray than blue, more hawklike than human, searched Ethan's face. "I know you."

"Of course you do," Genie said with a nervous giggle. "You met him yesterday. " 'Night, Ethie." She waved and tried to push Oliver through Cyril Phillips and into the door.

Cyril Phillips would not, however, be budged.

"I met you in New York," Ethan said, wiping his hand on his pant leg before offering it to Sterling's father. "At Graham Trent's house. I'm Francine Trent's brother, Ethan Morrow."

Ethan expected it to take a moment or two for Mr. Phillips to put dirt and water together and come up with mud. But he underestimated the man, who nodded and said simply, "I'll have my pound of flesh for my son's injuries."

"I'd give it gladly if it would make him well," Ethan

said in response. "I'm giving him my days and nights and sweat, but it doesn't seem to be enough, yet."

"Time!" Cyril huffed at him. "That'll never be enough."

"It's all I've got to give him," Ethan said honestly. "I'm hoping to have more to offer him soon."

"And her?" the man asked. "You think to make her part of the equation?"

"Her? You mean Miss Phillips?" In a way Ethan was glad that her father hadn't used Sterling's name. He didn't want to hear it spoken in the man's hard voice, rolling off his angry tongue.

"When I get done with you, son—"

"He doesn't have anything you want," Oliver Harrington said quite suddenly in that way he had of surprising Ethan when it seemed he hadn't been paying attention at all. "He's been too busy being honest to acquire anything you might value."

"In general I've found that people who spend their time going around being good are either stupid or guilt-ridden," Cyril said, his beady eyes narrowing.

Before Ethan could answer, Genie's finger went up in the air to signify she had something to say. "But it doesn't work the other way around," she said, the gaslight from the porch lantern shining on the curly hair that danced around her face. "I've known many stupid people who ought to be guilt-ridden and they don't go around being good at all. In fact, I know one who just keeps doing more he ought to feel guilty about."

"It's time to go in," Oliver said, shooing Ethan gently from the porch. "Go home. Get a good night's rest. I'm sure there'll be plenty of time tomorrow for Sterling's father to make idle threats."

"Idle?" Cyril said indignantly.

"When you've got nothing," Ethan explained with a shrug that he hoped hid his embarrassment, "you got nothing to lose."

"Even I don't measure everything in dollars," Cyril

Phillips said in return. "There are other things one man possesses and another man wants. But Oliver's right, it's time to go inside. I can hear Sterling and Dr. Cobb laughing, and I do have a great deal to talk to the good doctor about."

He turned and entered the house without so much as a nod in Ethan's direction. Oliver followed him, shaking his head, and Genie stopped to blow Ethan a kiss before going in and shutting the door.

Ethan sat down on the front step for a moment to collect his thoughts. "Honesty?" he called quietly, wondering where the damn dog had gone off to. He got to his feet slowly, reluctantly, and started around the side of the house in search of the flea bag.

Lord but Sterling had acted happy to see Cobb. Not that he believed for a moment that she actually was. She was a complicated woman, this silver goddess he knew he was falling in love with. She had fears and secrets and needs he couldn't even guess at. But if she thought for a moment that Benjamin Cobb was the man who could make her happy, she had to have piss for brains. He was sorry, but there was just no way that Cobb could fill the need she had.

And Ethan knew it, because he'd created it. He'd made her want to feel everything he could make her feel. He'd made her want him. So what was she doing running off to Corny's carriage and greeting him with a peck on the cheek?

". . . and without the most up-to-date equipment it doesn't matter how much a doctor knows." Corny's voice floated out of the window above Ethan's head. Where was the damn dog? It was time they headed home. Or maybe over to the Gibbs farm for a few minutes. Just to check on things—see them through her eyes.

"Nice night," he heard Cyril Phillips say, and froze where he was in the lilacs. "Too damn many dogs in this town, though."

Honesty, now clearly visible as he chased after moths in the lamplight, stopped to bark once in his direction.

"As I was saying," Cobb continued, "a doctor's hands are tied when it comes to diagnosis if he hasn't got the latest machinery. Did you know there's a machine being developed that can see right through a patient? The inventor says it will be able to take pictures of a man's bones. Think what that will mean. We could actually see what's gone wrong in a person's body."

"You mean you could see inside Worth's back and know what's stopping him from walking?" Sterling asked, that wonder infusing her voice the way it sometimes did.

He sighed, and was glad that Corny's voice covered it. "That's exactly right," Corny said. "But it'll cost a fortune, and a small-town doctor can't hope to afford one."

"I've heard about that X ray," Mr. Phillips said. "New inventions always interest me. I suppose that if a doctor was to open a practice in one of the larger cities and he had a machine like that, his clientele could cover the investment in no time." Ethan could hear the ice hitting the glass that Cyril Phillips was sipping from, and he held his breath.

"Oh, without a doubt. Say, New York, for example," Corny said.

There was silence, and then very deliberately Cyril Phillips said, "Say, San Francisco."

"Yes," Corny answered slowly as if he was considering it. "A man could make a name for himself out west. San Francisco."

"We're going to California," Imogene piped up cheerily. Until then Ethan hadn't suspected she was in the room. "Aren't we, dear?"

"Aunt Imogene," Sterling said gently. "I think you're looking very tired. Would you like me to help you to bed?"

Genie made a noise between harrumph and raspberries. "Nah. I wanna see what's gonna happen. Don't you?"

"Go to bed, Imogene," Mr. Phillips said with resignation. "Nothing's going to happen tonight."

Ethan could hear the party breaking up, glasses being set down on tables, ladies' skirts rustling, men's bones creaking. "Well, it is getting late," Corny agreed. "I've a full load of patients tomorrow."

"Have room for one more?" It was Cyril Phillips's voice. "I haven't had a physical in a while. And then we can discuss my *son*."

The man fairly choked on the word, as if it left a bad taste in his mouth. Jeez. The man hadn't seen the boy for years, and then it sure was no happy family reunion. He understood from Genie that Sterling and Worth looked just like Amelia, Genie's sister. They surely bore no resemblance to Cyril Phillips. Maybe that was the reason he'd sent them away. He just couldn't bear being reminded of his dead wife.

"Certainly," Corny said. "I'd welcome the opportunity to get to know you better."

"I would guess there'd be something of mutual interest to discuss."

"Yes indeed," Corny agreed. "I'll take my leave, then."

"I'll see you out," Silver said without enthusiasm.

"Big day tomorrow," Corny said. "Very big day."

Silver's sigh floated out the window to hang over his head like a black cloud. "I suppose tomorrow will be a big day for all of us."

There wasn't an ounce of joy in her thin voice. Only a sad resignation. Maybe dragging her out to the Gibbs place was a mistake.

Ethan tightened his grip on the violin's neck. The way Sterling sounded, he'd have liked to wring hers as well.

Chapter Seventeen

Sterling sat next to Ethan Morrow in the wagon, a shawl wrapped around her, thinking that she was making the biggest mistake of her life. But like so much of her life, she seemed to have had no control over it. At least if she went with Ethan to see the farm he hoped to buy, she could point out to him just how unsuitable it would be, and he'd go off to lick his wounds and let her see to her own.

So now here she was, on her way to the Gibbs place, her thigh within inches of Sir Glad-I-am's, hoping that she could keep her heart in her chest when she saw the future that he wanted to offer her and that she had to refuse.

Oh, yes, Ethan dear! I'd love to live here with you. Of course, we'd have to bring Worth because he isn't really my brother but my son. Oh, didn't I mention that I gave myself to one of my father's servants? Did I forget to tell you that I am not pure, not honest, and not worthy? Did I mention that on our wedding night you'll find out that you were not my first?

Even imagining the look on his face sent waves of fear down her arms.

"You cold?" Ethan asked her, adjusting her shawl higher against her neck. "You're shivering."

"It's just the wind," she said, watching the treetops shimmer in the breeze and letting it blow her hair back behind her freely, carelessly, recklessly.

Being alone with Ethan Morrow was a dangerous, stupid thing to do.

The wind was ruffling his hair, too, and carrying the scent of fresh earth and lye soap across her path. There was the soft sound of his humming, interrupted only by the clicks and whistles with which he signaled his horse.

And there was the rub, rub, rubbing of his leg against hers as the wagon pitched and swayed on the rutted road.

Being alone with Ethan Morrow was a foolish, painful thing to do.

He stopped his humming. "You're very quiet."

How else could she keep from giving herself away? "I've other things I should be doing."

"I know. I appreciate your coming. It's a bit run-down. No one's lived in the house for a good ten years," he said, his gaze glued to the horizon, where the sky was getting dark despite the hour.

"I hope this won't take long," she said, wishing in some way that she and Ethan could spend forever at the house on the outskirts of town. "I don't want to leave Worth with my father for . . . Looks like rain, doesn't it?"

"Your father's had a son for three years and he's had to watch him for an hour. Don't worry so. Maybe he feels it's time he got to know the boy. It's taken him long enough."

"My mother's death was hard on him." Not of course as hard as it had been on her. *Oh, what a tangled web,* her mother would have said. Now ironically that web had her defending her father.

A gust of wind set her skirts flapping, and she tried to tuck them tightly under her legs and not touch Ethan's as she did so. He watched her attempts, a small smile playing at his lips as she fought the billowing waves of blue-striped fabric. As though he'd done it before, and often enough to know how, he put his hand down on the fabric to secure it and then shifted his leg to keep the skirt in place.

And keep her trapped against him.

"James was here with me the other day, helping out. Sometimes I think he's more my son than he is Peter's. I don't understand men like Peter or your father." He put his hand on his hat to keep the wind from claiming it, and gestured with his chin toward a dot in the distance.

"That's the Gibbs place," he said just as rain began to fall in fat, hard drops. "Lord, don't you ever have a hat?" he grumbled and thrust his onto her head.

"Maybe we should go back," she said. The last thing she wanted was to be trapped in an old farmhouse with Ethan Morrow, a wet shirt stuck to his chest, during a rainstorm. Well, maybe not the last thing. . . .

"We'll be fine," he said. But that didn't stop the drops from coming faster and harder, nor the thunder from rumbling in the distance. He flicked the reins and yelled at the horse to move his damn carcass faster, then colored and mumbled an apology about his language.

The sky was as dark as early evening, and seemed more green than blue. The trees that bordered the road danced wildly, rattling their leaves as if they were warning Sterling that to go any farther was a mistake.

"I want to go back," she yelled at Ethan, turning to look behind her and catching the crack of lightning that lit the sky. "Take me home!"

Worth was terrified of lightning and thunder. And she knew her father wouldn't tolerate his tears, wouldn't hold him and croon that it would be all right, wouldn't pretend it was just the sun yelling for the clouds to go away and sending bolts of sunshine to kill the darkness. Princess Sugarlips was afraid of melting in the rain.

And so was Sterling.

"Grab a blanket out of the back," Ethan ordered her, his hair plastered to his head, his face soaked with rain. "And put it around yourself."

"I'm all right." She had to shout to be heard over the wind. "Just hurry." She was shuddering uncontrollably, her voice quivering badly.

"Get the blanket or I'll stop the damn wagon," he

shouted back, the wind ripping the words from his mouth. "That roof had better be watertight," he swore under his breath.

Her hair was a wet whip, smacking her face, lashing Ethan's shoulder. She reached back for the blanket and felt his hand around her waist, steadying her. A tree branch fell behind the wagon and she jumped, then felt the band of his arm tighten and pull her against him. Sheltering her with his arm, he tucked her against his side and yelled at the horse to go faster still.

Through the driving rain the house was barely visible. It turned out to be nearer than she thought when he came to a sudden stop in front of it, threw the brake, and leaped down, all before she could even take in her surroundings. Another second and he was pulling her from the rig and carrying her to the porch.

"Go inside," he said after he'd set her on her feet. "I want to get Buckshot into the barn. I'll be right back."

She watched him jump into the wagon and head it for the barn before she turned and entered the house.

He'd cleaned it.

She noticed that right away, despite her shivering. She couldn't help but see the bouquet of wildflowers on the table, nor that the floors onto which she was dripping fat circles of water shone. When had he found the time? All week he'd put Worth through his paces, put the fence posts in for Mr. Ellman, hauled ice, and who knew what else.

And he'd taken the time to get the place ready to show her. Ready to ask her.

"You're soaking wet!" he said, coming in the door and peeling off his shirt. "Did you see if there was anything around you could change into?" He headed toward the steps and, she supposed, the bedrooms.

"I'm fine like this," she lied, so cold that even standing still, she was moving.

He smiled at her, coming back from the stairway to stand only a foot or so from her, and looked her up and down. "You sure are," he admitted, his eyes glued to her chest. "But with that dress painted on you like it is, I'm not."

She looked down to see what he meant. Two cold-stiffened nipples strained against her silk blouse, despite the camisole that hugged her skin. Around them two dark circles were clearly visible. She crossed her arms over her chest, and when that didn't suffice, she turned her back on his hungry eyes.

"Don't be afraid of me," he whispered. "Don't you know I'd never take advantage of a lady like you?"

* * *

There'd been other women. Ethan remembered each one. And while he'd never taken any of them fully, he'd kissed a lot of lips, touched his share of breasts, and even explored between a few pairs of thighs. And a lot of that had happened right in this house, in this room.

But Sterling was finer than any of those girls, who were full of giggles and squirms and knew just how to tease a man to distraction.

They weren't women he wanted to spend any more than a few stolen moments with. Sterling was the one he wanted to spend the rest of his life with, and he wasn't going to jeopardize that for a quick feel of her breast, no matter how tempting it was, no matter how his man-hood burned for it and caused his apronless overalls to cut into him.

"I'll go finish with the horse. You find something you can change into and when you're all done and present-able, you put your wet dress out on the porch." He slogged in his soaking boots to the door. "I'll be watching for you."

He closed the door behind him and leaned against it, fighting to control his breathing. Lord, she was glorious! The first night they were married, he would give her a bath and then stand her naked and wet for him to marvel at. He wondered if she'd let him. Probably not.

She was a lot shyer than the girls he was used to. If he so much as touched her, she jumped. But she was a good learner. It had taken only a second kiss to coax her lips apart and let his tongue do to her mouth what a husband had the right to do to his wife. Twice he'd kissed her, and twice she'd taken him to heaven.

The way those nipples pressed against her dress . . . pink? No, they were darker. Dusty rose? Brown? He groaned and slid a good way down the door. He was torturing himself, but what sweet, sweet, torture.

The wind was fierce, rattling the barn door as if to remind him that he'd wanted to make sure he'd actually put Buckshot in a stall. He ran down the soggy path to the barn, his pants smacking in the wind, his chest wet and cold. The wind stung his eyes and pulled at the skin on his cheeks. Jeez, this was going to be one hell of a storm.

The barn door fought him, and when he finally managed to get it open, one set of hinges gave way and the door nearly flew from his hand.

Shit.

He'd seen this kind of storm before. Green sky, bone-rattling wind, rain coming from more than one direction at once. He rushed to Buckshot and let him loose from the wagon as fast as he could manage. The horse's eyes were wide balls of panic, and Ethan just hoped that they didn't mirror his own.

"I don't know if you're gonna be safer in here or out there, boy," he told the horse. "So I'm gonna let your own instinct tell you what to do."

He left the horse in the middle of the barn, untethered, and left the door open behind him as he headed for the house. In the distance he could see the cloud of dust rising from the ground to meet the sky.

Thankfully Sterling's soggy dress lay heaped by the door, the wet blue lines crisscrossing one another like a maze. There might not be time for politeness, and he wasn't about to risk her life because she couldn't find something to wear.

"I want to go home," she all but demanded as soon as he got through the front door. Dishes left in the cabinets long ago by old Widow Gibbs rattled.

"I know," he said, trying not to frighten her. "But we can't go just now. We have to wait for the weather to pass."

"He's afraid of storms," she said, and he didn't have to ask who *he* was. The buckaroo was always on her mind, just as he was always on Ethan's.

"Pink," he said, noticing her dress. "Pretty." It hung around her like an old flour sack. The Widow Gibbs was one of those old ladies who looked like they'd stuffed big heads of cabbage into their dresses along with them. The dress still had the lumps where Mrs. Gibbs strained the seams and buttons. Sterling's thin frame was lost inside the folds.

Still, seeing her in calico instead of silk, in a wrapper instead of some fancy catalog dress, in this farmhouse instead of in her mansion—it made a man think. It made a man smile. It made a man ache.

On the roof the shingles began to flap, and there wasn't the time he wanted to stand around gawking at a pretty girl. If all went well, he could do that for the rest of his life. Now he had to open as many windows as he could, as fast as he could, in the hope of saving the house.

"Get that window," he told her, pointing toward the front of the house. "I'll get the ones in the back."

"Get it?" she asked. "I think it's already closed. Please, Ethan, just take me home."

"I will, honey, later. After." It was all he had to offer.

He got the back windows open, the last one just as a branch came crashing toward the house. He prayed he had time to make it upstairs. He had to, because he wasn't giving up this one last dream, this dream that meant more than all the rest had ever meant.

He took the steps two at a time, yelling over his shoulder as he went, telling Sterling where to find a lantern in the kitchen and where the matches were. He settled for one window in each room, and felt the bannister sway beneath his hand as he hurried back down the stairs, the treads shifting beneath his feet.

"Come on," he yelled, wind now whipping through the house. He grabbed Silver around the waist and half-pushed, half-carried her toward the door. "We've got to get to the cellar."

"Wait!" she cried, and ran back to get something from the table.

Twice she tripped on the old pink calico.

"Come on!" he said again, and then, deciding that it would be faster, lifted her in his arms and carried her out the door and into the front yard.

A piece of fencing missed them by inches. A branch smacked his leg. Buckshot's terrified whinny carried on the wind. Just at the horizon he could see the black funnel swooping down from the sky.

Setting her on her feet, he pulled out the stake that kept the old cellar closed and threw back the door. "Get in," he yelled, his voice ripped away so fast and so far that he wasn't even sure she heard him. "Go ahead!"

Even in the near blackness that surrounded them he could see the terror on her face. He wanted to tell her it would be all right, but he knew she couldn't hear him. Instead he held her tightly for a moment and then guided her down into the dark cellar and followed fast on her heels.

"The lantern!" she shouted as he closed the doors over them, pitching them into darkness. "I left it on the kitchen table! I have to go back—"

He felt her hands on him as he fought to secure the doors. Ten icicles sliding on the wetness of his warm skin, and he thought that if the storm didn't kill him, his need to take care of her might.

He'd been down in the storm cellar once, many years

ago, when Mrs. Gibbs was still alive. She'd sent him down for something.

He remembered that there was a table to the left, and he guided Silver in the darkness until he felt it with an outstretched hand. He lifted her easily and set her on the table, then found a place beside her, hugging her to his side as balls of hail rained down on the cellar door like so many fistfuls of rocks on their graves.

"They've a good storm cellar over there," he said loudly, hoping she could hear him over the crashing ice that pelted the wooden planking above them. He stroked her wet hair and lifted it off her dress. "Your uncle's been through this plenty of times before. He'll know just what to do."

"It's not just a storm, is it?" she asked. Of course, coming from New York, she'd never seen a twister. He wished he was a better liar.

"No. But we'll be just fine, and so will the buckaroo. It may not even hit town."

She burrowed deeper into his armpit, her cold face sending chills down his spine.

"What if—?" she began, but he cut her off.

"Everything'll be fine. They sound worse than they are," he lied. Surely she could hear the whistle of the wind as well as he, could feel the walls shake and the ground beneath them rumble.

"Do you suppose that a storm like this could blow Mr. Rutabaga to kingdom come?" he asked her. "And then the princess wouldn't have to worry about paying that darn troll toll?"

She made a little noise that he supposed was meant to be a laugh.

"Cold?" He ran his hand up and down her arm as he held her, shushing her fears, swallowing his own.

He didn't know when it was no longer her arm that he was stroking. Had he shifted? Had she? Beneath his palm was a soft mound of female flesh. It filled his hand with its roundness, and his fingers explored it through well-worn cotton and nothing else.

It was soft and pliant and yielding, except for a tiny pebble that grew harder as he stroked and petted and kneaded.

"We aren't going to die," he admitted reluctantly. "So if you want me to stop . . ."

Something crashed against the cellar roof, followed by a second and then a third bang. Her fingers bit into his arm, and she shuddered against him like a dandelion in a strong wind. To keep her together, he gathered her into his lap.

"What have you got there?" he asked as she fiddled with something within the confines of his arms. Every movement she made pressed her deeper against him, teased him, tortured him.

"My mama's brooch," she said, and he felt her elbow hit his neck.

"What are you doing?"

Her arm rubbed his chest, her elbow now digging deep against his belly.

"I want to be buried with it on," she said. "If we die here, I want to be sure that it doesn't get lost. It's all I have left of her."

"I told you we're not gonna die," he said, feeling in the dark and taking the brooch from her hands. "I'll do it."

He slipped one hand within the neckline to protect her skin and used the other to pierce the fabric. Her neck was warm against his hand, and he could feel the quick beating of her heart.

"I'm gonna unfasten this, if that's all right," he said, sliding the small buttons through the holes without waiting for her permission. He fastened the brooch easily, but didn't hurry to remove his hand. Instead he found her naked breast and cupped it.

So soft! If the tornado wanted him now, he was ready to die!

He wanted to ask her if it was all right for him to kiss her, but it seemed ridiculous in light of the fact that he was teasing her nipple into attention. And so he bent his head, nuzzling her until he could determine just what his lips had found. One sweet eyebrow, which he traced with his tongue to its end. An eyelid, so soft against his lips he thought he'd die. Lashes fluttering against his nose as he placed one tiny kiss after another down her cheekbone.

A peck at the tip of her upturned nose. And then his lips found hers. His moan was stronger than the wind, her sigh, louder. He eased her down gently onto the wooden tabletop, clearing it with a swipe and then making a pillow of his arm.

"It's not a bad house, is it?" he asked, tracing her features with his hand and then trailing it down her neck. "If there's anything left of it."

She didn't answer with words, but she arched her back, just enough to encourage him, and he swooped down and captured the tiny bud of her breast with his mouth.

She was small. He'd expected that, confirmed it with his hand. But no amount of looking or touching could have prepared him for how sweet she was. Intoxicating. Sweeter than wine.

"I . . . there are things you . . . Ethan, I . . ." she whispered.

He'd have listened, if only her hips hadn't begun to rock ever so gently, against her will, ever so rhythmically, against his thigh. "You should know, Ethan—"

Lifting his head reluctantly from her breast, he warned her. "Shhh. This is the kind of moment people say things they shouldn't—when the truth gets twisted like a ribbon in the wind."

"But it's still the truth." Her voice was low, raspy. "And the truth is all that matters to you."

"Not at the moment."

He returned to her breast, which quivered wet in the cold.

She moaned, and he felt it rattle her chest more than he heard it reach his ears. Felt it and took it for his own, deep within his belly.

Down her midriff his hand trailed, still inside Mrs. Gibbs's roomy dress, still finding naked skin. But beneath his fingers she warmed to his touch. And the lower his fingers crept, the warmer she became.

"I need you, Silver," he said, his hand finding curls he was sure were palest gold.

His wet jeans hugged his manhood, strangling him. If he went for his buttons, he'd have to stop what he was doing to her, let her down from the cloud he'd brought her to. If he didn't, he'd burst.

He decided to pleasure her, no matter what it cost him, and slipped his fingers against her soft folds.

She gasped, groaned, sighed. "I can't . . ."

He lifted his head. It was quiet outside. Silent as the grave. There was the eerie calm that signaled that the destruction was over.

Slowly, so, so slowly, he pulled his hand up over her tiny belly, a finger dipping slightly into her navel as he passed her waist. Careful to avoid her breasts, he followed her breastbone until he was free of Mrs. Gibbs's wrapper.

"You deserve better," he said, helping her to sit up and buttoning her buttons for her. "When our time comes, there'll be fresh clean sheets and soft down pillows and God's sanction. And I'll honor you the way you deserve, and be as gentle as I know how. I know it's supposed to hurt, but it won't. There must be a way that it won't."

Her voice scratched in her throat. "You talk like you've never . . ."

He was silent. Embarrassed.

"Oh, God." She sounded horrified.

"Would you rather I had? Even though I've never

loved anyone before? I know there are different rules for men, but I just couldn't see asking more of my wife than of myself."

Her breath was ragged, there in the dark, and he eased himself down off the table, expecting her to follow.

"Silver? You coming?"

"Is the storm over?" Her voice was tiny—frightened and unsure.

"Yes."

"We're safe?"

He felt his way to the doors, groping along the wall, and wished he had some idea what to expect when he threw them open. Was the house still standing? Did he have a future beyond the two wooden panels?

Outside, it was still and calm, a gray pallor hanging in the air. The rain had ended, and the house stood tall and proud against the sky.

He offered a hand down to Silver, but she refused it. In the dim light he saw the streaks of tears that covered her cheeks.

"Take me home," she said. "Please." She climbed the steps herself, her arms wrapped around her thin body, and stopped at the top of the stairs. "Oh, my God!"

Like a million tiny pieces of kindling, a pile of rubble sat where minutes before the barn had been.

"We can rebuild," he said, taking her elbow and helping her out of the cellar. "Bart and Charlie and I can get a new barn up in less than a week."

It had been there. A whole big wooden thing, standing there as if it had been planted and had just grown. And now it wasn't.

"And I won't have to cut firewood for years," he said, only the barest trace of disappointment in his voice. He pushed the hair from her cheek and said, "I can concentrate on other ways to keep you warm."

The house didn't look too badly damaged. One shutter still clung to the house at an angle. The rest were gone. Miraculously the chairs still sat on the porch, still rocking as though there were ghosts in them. A man and his wife could still make a home here, even after the wind had tried to decide otherwise.

They could battle the elements and wrest a living from the land. And they could raise a family in a house like this. And then they could grow old here together, after the children were grown, alone again just the way they'd started out.

Not her home, but a fine home. One Ethan could be proud of.

"I know it looks a little run-down," he said, watching her stare at the house. "But I can make it perfect. Or ready for perfection. I think that probably takes a wife. . . ."

She closed her eyes and swallowed hard. It would be so easy to say, "But, Ethan, you don't have a wife." And he would say there was only one woman in the world for him and ask would she be his wife? And she would say, "Oh yes!" And they could live happily ever after.

If only she believed in the fairy tales she wove for Worth.

"Well," she said, kicking at a piece of the barn that had come to rest within a few feet of the front steps. "I hope you can find someone that's willing to put up with this mess."

"Messes are easily fixed," he said with a shrug of a shoulder.

Not the one she'd gotten herself into. "A body would have to be willing," she said.

"Oh, the *body* is willing," he said, looking her up and down and stopping at her buttons. "It's the spirit that's lagging."

"Don't go misinterpreting what happened, Mr. Morrow. I let you take advantage of me out of fear and panic, not love and passion," she said, pulling the overfull bodice of her dress closed. "I've Worth to worry about and a good life I'm not about to give up for this!"

She gestured toward the house as if it was some hovel and not the house and life she dreamed of nightly, would dream of for the rest of her life, no doubt.

"You know, I'm getting pretty tired of hearing about the buckaroo as if he's got no one but you in the world to look after him. You're worse than Sissy was, and while I admire you for taking him on, the boy belongs to your father and you're gonna need a damn better excuse than that if you want to get rid of me."

"I don't need an excuse. I don't love you. Isn't that enough?

"But you do love the good doctor?" He grabbed her arm. Without looking at him, she yanked it away, her eyes on the horizon.

"He's got a lot to offer me," she said.

"Does he make your knees weak? Does your body open up to him the way it did to me?"

She slapped him, hard and fast, and her hand stung and turned as red as his cheek.

"Face it, Silver. You're in love with a no-account dirt farmer and you want him so bad that it hurts. Aches in your heart and your belly and lower still. And before you slap me again, I'd like to hear you deny it."

She sank to her knees on the wet ground. "I deny it."

"Liar."

She had no answer for him, so she said nothing at all, just sat there in the wet grass lost in Mrs. Gibbs's old wrapper and in her thoughts.

"I'm sorry. I had no right. I should have kept my hands and my needs to myself." He offered her a hand up, but she shook her head and got to her feet herself.

"I want to go home, Ethan."

"I know you do. I'll just . . ." His voice trailed off as his eyes searched the horizon.

"Your horse!" was all she could say. "He must have gotten out of the barn. He must have gotten away. Ethan?"

"I suppose after what he did to Worth, you wouldn't waste any tears over him."

"For God's sake, Ethan. I don't wish your horse dead."

"Well, one for two, anyways. You see any sign of him?" From a distance he studied the rubble that had been the barn.

"No," she admitted. "But I've got to get home."

"It's a long way," he told her, looking down the road toward town.

She knew that well enough, because for four years home had been someplace she could never reach.

Chapter Eighteen

Ethan headed her in the right direction, taking a moment to glance over his shoulder at what was left of the Gibbs place. It hadn't been a palace before the storm, he knew that. The shutters had been held on by threads. Beneath the swing, the porch floor had a hole right through it. There were several broken windows where no doubt kids had practiced their aim with slingshots or rocks.

Now who knew where the shutters were? They could be in another county.

Christ Almighty, *Buckshot* could be in another county.

This run-down, tattered home was what he was offering a woman who had grown up in a house where even footprints knew better than to mar the floors. What did he think she could do? Eat his love? Wear his need? He really did have his nerve.

"Ethan?"

Her voice quavered. She was probably scared to death that something awful had happened to her poor little brother while he was pawing at her under the ground.

Lord, wasn't he just the answer to a woman's prayers?

"I'd like to get back as fast as we can," she said. Still, she stared at the house along with him, shaking her head as if she just couldn't believe that he'd had the nerve to offer it up as though there was even a chance she'd ever live there.

"Sorry," he said, bidding good-bye to the house and the dream with just a nod of his head and turning toward town. He supposed it wouldn't make matters any worse to give a whistle for Buckshot. Figuring the horse was dead wasn't a whole lot better than knowing it for sure.

"Just a second," he said, letting loose a call for the horse as loudly as he could and listening for hooves.

"There!" Sterling said, pointing off in the distance, one small hand shielding her eyes from a sun that seemed oblivious to the destruction it was shining down upon.

The horse galloped toward them, evidently as happy to see they had survived as Ethan was to see his old friend had made it. From her smile he gathered Silver hadn't really wished the old horse dead, though whether it was because he'd get her to town faster or because she'd forgiven him, Ethan wasn't sure.

"All right, boy," he said as the horse nearly shoved him over, smacking his face against Ethan's shoulder, his head, and the center of his back. "You're all right," he reassured the horse. At least something he treasured had survived the storm intact.

The wagon, like the house, had suffered damage, but was still sound. Planks could be replaced. A harness could be repaired.

"I'd like to check on Sissy," he said as he led the horse to the wagon to see if there wasn't some way he could hitch him up and save them the long walk. "It's on the way back to town."

"Ethan, I . . ." She stumbled on a piece of the barn, thrown in the pathway by a wind that was now just a memory.

He caught her around the waist, preventing a fall, but it was a mistake. He'd have been better off letting her go, for a scraped knee couldn't hurt nearly as much as a bruised heart. He had no doubt that she was in as much pain as he was. His touching her only made matters worse. He could see it in her bright eyes, her pursed lips, her rounded shoulders. Could feel it in the way she held her body away from him yet couldn't seem to let go of his arm.

"It's no better than a shack." He spoke to the ground as he improvised a harness that would hold well enough if they took their time in the wagon. "And you've been counting on a castle, Princess."

For a princess she heaved a mighty unladylike sob. If it had been anyone else, at any other time in his life, he'd probably have made a joke about how much it sounded like a pig snorting. Instead he just shook his head and tried to work faster, fighting the urge to take her in his arms.

Because holding her one more time was going to push him right over that edge. And he was beginning to think that if she couldn't be his wife in one way, he'd settle for another.

She was standing too close.

She was breathing too fast.

Her hair, blowing in the breeze, shone too brightly. And her face was too sad and life was too unfair.

"Worth is probably terrified," she said. Mrs. Gibbs's oversized skirts twitched beside his cheek as he bent to his task. "Maybe I should start walking."

"I've got it," he said, testing the leather and praying it was sounder than it looked. "We'll just go by Sissy's. If things look fine, we won't even stop. All right?"

She nodded reluctantly. Anything, he supposed, to be on her way. To put out of her head the memory of his groping. "I've got to get back to Worth." Did she think he wasn't worried about the buckaroo as well? But the boy was a trooper—brave and cheerful despite everything that had happened to him. In some ways the Gibbs place had been as much for Worth as it had been for himself and Sterling. The kid would have loved it.

And Ethan had played the doting uncle long enough. He'd thought himself ready to be a father to the boy.

But the boy already had a father, he reminded himself. A rich one at that. One who could give him everything a boy could need or want.

He gave the tumbledown house one last look, seeing it through the eyes of a Phillips, and nickered for Buckshot to move along.

There was nothing to keep them there.

* * *

He'd seen worse damage than that which had been done to Noah's farm, but that didn't lessen the burden it would be on an already strained budget—and Noah not what one would call handy with a hammer either. It had always been Noah's brains and Ethan's brawn, and they made quite a team.

"Is that your sister?" Sterling asked, her brows furrowed and her eyes squinting toward the horizon. "Ethan! Hurry, she's sick!"

With a "Ha!" to Buckshot he covered the distance as fast as his makeshift harness would allow. Before he'd come to a full stop, Sterling leaped from the wagon and, tripping over her long skirts, ran to his sister's side.

"You're all right," she crooned, leaning over Sissy as she retched, holding back her hair for her, shouting over her shoulder to Ethan to fetch some water. "You're gonna be fine."

"Wait!" Sissy screamed after him, just as he was turning Buckshot toward the house. "It's Gracie! Have you seen Gracie?"

Ethan felt the world slow down. Clawing through air as thick as mud, he reached for the brake and forced himself down from the wagon. "Gracie?" was all he could manage to get out. His voice croaked as he said his little niece's name.

Sissy looked up at him with frantic eyes. Gripping Sterling's arm, she tried to take a deep breath, but it was ragged. She needed five or six half breaths to get enough air to talk.

"I can't remember where she said she was going."

Sissy shook her head, her eyes closed as if she was trying to conjure up some picture of her little girl and what the child had said. "Isabella was fussing, and I was so tired. She said something about Honesty and ducks and a friend and . . . I don't know," she admitted, dissolving into tears. "I don't know where my baby is!"

"I'm sure your baby's just fine," Silver said soothingly, making big circles on Sissy's back with her fine hands. "Ethan will find her and bring her home before we've gotten the house back to rights."

He took his sister's free arm, and he and Silver supported her as they made their way back to the house, Sissy explaining that Noah had gone off to look for Gracie and that the big girls, Hannah and Julia, were seeing to Isabella.

"You go ahead," Silver said, her eyes connecting with his over the top of Sissy's bowed head. "I'll stay with your sister. Only, Ethan—check on Worth for me, will you?"

It was one of those moments he knew would stay with him always. The twinkle in time that would mark forever what he'd had to give up. Never again could he pretend that she was some spoiled little rich girl who hadn't been worth the love he'd wasted on her.

She was too good for the likes of him, and it wasn't fair to fault her for recognizing it before he had. The best had been her birthright, hers and Worth's, just as his was hard work and sweat and little more.

"No," Sissy argued. "Go look for Gracie. I won't be all right until she's found." Her hand clutched at her belly, and Ethan worried for the new life that depended on her for its existence.

"Are you all right?" he asked, his own hand covering hers as if he could help bear the burden. "Is something wrong?"

He could see the understanding in Sterling's eyes, sense the sudden proprietary air that was all woman, all

female, as her arm went around Sissy's back and she
slowed the pace to a mere crawl.

"Do you feel anything?" he heard Silver whisper. He
leaned away, keeping his eyes on the horizon to give
them what privacy he could offer. "You aren't . . ."

"No," Sissy said. "But wouldn't it serve me right if I
was? Too sleepy to listen to my own daughter. Too busy
to know where she was when a twister . . . She could
be under some pile of rubble somewhere, crying for me.
She could be lying out there, unconscious, hit by some
tree, or a rock, or a—"

"Don't do this to yourself," Silver said, helping her
up the steps and shooing Ethan away. Next to the steps
stood a raw stump of wood where only that morning a
handrail had been. "I'll help you get settled and then
Ethan and I will find Gracie. I promise."

"Hannah!" Ethan yelled toward the front door. "You
in there?"

His niece came to the door with a broom in one hand
and a rag in the other. It was so like his oldest niece to
try to make order out of chaos. Sissy's influence on
Noah's girls was showing more every day.

"Help your mama in," he ordered. "Miss Phillips and
I are going to look for your sister."

"Give me a minute with her," Sterling said, curving
her arm around Sissy's back and leading her toward the
rear of the house, while Sissy wanly pointed out the
direction of her bedroom.

* * *

"You're sure you're not bleeding?" Sterling asked her,
kneeling by the woman and unlacing her shoes. Sissy's
ankles were so swollen that she'd had to tie the laces
several hooks below the top. "We could get Dr. Cobb if
you need him."

Sissy Morrow shook her head. "I'm not . . . I'm
fine, Miss Phillips. I'd think the doc's got a lot more to
worry about than a lady in my condition." She leaned

back against the pillows, closing her eyes and throwing an arm across them.

"I'm just gonna put this pillow here," Sterling said, lifting Sissy's feet and sliding the pillow beneath them. "I don't want you getting up for anything. No matter how much you need to." She poked under the bed. "Good. You use this pot if you have to. No getting out of bed."

Sissy lowered her forearm from her face and squinted at Sterling. "Was that brother of yours a hard birth?" she asked.

Sterling's heart seemed to stop, her chest clogged with fear. The breath caught in her throat. She could feel the color drain from her cheeks, leaving her cold and shaken in its wake.

"I'm sorry," Sissy said. "Of course it was difficult. Guess I'm not thinking straight. And I can see it's still hard for you to talk about your mama." She clutched Sterling's hand. "Please find my little girl."

And then her hand flew to her belly again, and Sterling knew she was having twinges that could mean she was losing the baby, or they could mean nothing at all.

"Safe to come in?" Ethan called from beyond the doorway.

"You don't need to check about . . . ?" Silver gestured toward Sissy's femininity.

"Come on in, Eth," Sissy said, struggling to sit upright on the bed.

"Brought you a little water to rinse your mouth." He carried a glassful of water and a bowl into which she could spit out the remains. And Glory-laury, but he didn't just hand it to her and turn his back. He helped her sit up fully, supporting her back with one hand while he held the bowl in front of her chest with the other.

Apparently it wasn't enough for Sterling to know that she was giving up a darling little house with a swing and two rockers on the front porch and checkered curtains in the windows—a house that she could imagine with a wreath on the door at Christmas and roses along the rails in June. It wasn't enough that she would never again feel the warmth of Ethan's breath on her skin, or the strength in his hands as he pulled her against him.

No, it was as if God was making sure that she knew she was losing the best of his creations. A man who was thoughtful, caring, loving. A man who couldn't bear to watch suffering without doing whatever he could to ease it. A man who, when he married, would give his heart and soul and body without limits.

"Please, Ethan, find Gracie and bring her home."

A man who could be counted on to do the impossible. A man Sterling Phillips had already learned could do just that.

He eased his sister back down and called his nieces in from where they stood in the doorway.

"Your mama needs anything, you're to get it for her." He ruffled both their heads. "Don't worry so. Mama will be fine.

"And don't you touch that glass," he said, gesturing over his shoulder at the shards of the window that now covered the floor. "I'll take care of it when I get back."

"I want to go with you to help find Gracie," Hannah said softly. "Julia could see to Mama." She exchanged a look with her sister, who nodded solemnly.

"Your mama doesn't need anything more to worry about," Sterling said, cupping the girl's chin. "Before you know it, your father or your uncle will be back with Gracie and then your mama will have to be worried about you."

"If I'd been worrying about them in the first place, none of this would've happened," Sissy said, more to herself than to anyone else.

"Tornado your fault now?" Ethan asked her, grimacing and shaking his head. "Anything else you want to take the blame for while you're at it? Hear there was a railroad crash over by Cleveland a week or so ago. . . ."

"I'll allow for the rain and the wind just as soon as you do, little brother, and not a moment before. A mother should know where her children are." A tear trailed toward her pillow and she sniffed and swallowed hard.

"A mama's human, same as everybody else," Ethan said gently, wiping the tear with the back of his hand. "And you're better than most. In fact I'd say you're about as close to perfect as a mama could come."

Sterling struggled to swallow. She fingered the brooch at her throat. For some women perfection seemed to come so easily. And for others, like herself, it seemed always out of reach.

"Well, it ain't perfect enough," Sissy said with a sniff. "Not if something's happened to my little Gracie."

"Life ain't perfect," Ethan said, his voice soft and warm. "If it was, I'd be J. P. Morgan and you'd be the queen of England."

It was apparently an old joke, as each of them smiled tight little smiles of recognition. Maybe under other circumstances they'd have laughed. Right now not a one of them, and Sterling included herself in the lot, looked like they would ever laugh again.

"I owe you an apology, Miss Phillips." She winced, and gathered a handful of the blanket into a tight fist.

Sterling was about to ask her what she meant, but decided that it really didn't matter. No one owed her an apology for anything.

Ethan took her arm and they backed away from the bed just as Sissy closed her eyes against another pain.

"Get some rest," he said. "We'll be back with Gracie before you know it."

* * *

He couldn't remember ever feeling so torn. He loved his niece. Wanted to be sure she was safe and well.

Wanted also to reassure Sissy, especially in her condition, that Gracie was all right.

But the buckaroo had carved his own place in Ethan's heart. And since he couldn't look for Gracie and check on Worth at the same time, he had to choose whether to head for town or out toward the neighboring farms where it was likeliest Gracie had gone.

A man took care of his own family first in an emergency. Sterling had made it clear that she and Worth didn't belong to him. But damn it all, he was worried about Worth, and Imogene and Oliver.

They'd become his family, without Sterling's blessing. Without his own. Noah would turn Pleasant Township upside down to find Gracie, and Ethan would help him. Just as soon as he knew his own family was safe.

He headed for town, letting Buckshot go as fast as possible, considering he hadn't changed his harness. The closer they got to the heart of town, the whiter Silver's knuckles became as she clutched at the seat.

Two houses on the outskirts of town stood with their roofs next to them, as if some giant had been playing with a set of wooden blocks and had been distracted before finishing his game. The Lutefoots and the Webbs signaled they were all right, and Ethan urged Buckshot on, his pace slower, as they followed the path of the tornado through town.

If Sterling was breathing at all, it was so shallowly that Ethan couldn't hear or see it. Aside from the occasional swallow, she looked more like some life-size doll than a real live woman.

"Make a difference to you which street we go down?" he asked, just to make sure she was still capable of speech.

He'd seen half a dozen or so twisters touch down in his life. She'd seen none. From the pale face and the gnawed lip he didn't think she'd care ever to see another.

She shook her head. "Whichever is fastest."

"It's hard to know," he said, eyeing Elm and seeing a few downed electrical wires. "Depends on what's blocking the road. I'd like to try Chestnut just to see that Charlie and Risa's place is okay."

"I can walk from there," she said, her jaw dropping and her neck craning as they passed the Marcuses' porch, now settled on the Whelans' front lawn, then John Gibbs's place, the top floor sheared away.

"I'll keep going," he said. "I just want to know if I need to come back."

She nodded, and her little hands were lost in the immense folds of Mrs. Gibbs's skirts.

The mercantile appeared untouched. On the steps out front sat Cara, Miranda, and Krista. They waved to the wagon, and Ethan came to a stop. Even with the noise of wood being cleared and debris being hauled, Ethan could hear a woman's moan come from inside the house.

"Somebody hurt?" he asked, ready to let Sterling go on alone.

"Mama's havin' her baby," Cara said in a loud whisper. "Go sit down now," she directed her younger sisters. "Aunt Della's with her, and—"

There was a groan that turned Sterling's face white, and then a moment's silence, as if all the work of setting the town to rights had come to a halt.

"Where's the wail?" he heard himself demand. "Where's the goddamn wail?"

Nearly as loud as Risa's groan, a baby's cry pierced the quiet.

"Zachariah Floyd Morrow," Charlie shouted out the window. "And a big one he is!"

"Zachariah Floyd?" Ethan said, tasting the name and wishing he could spit it out. "Risa all right?" he yelled up.

"Mother and son and store all doing remarkably well under the circumstances," Charlie yelled back. What a grin! Ethan supposed that having a son about made a man's life complete. Not that a daughter wasn't just as precious a gift.

Suddenly he couldn't wait to check on the buckaroo a moment longer.

"Tell Risa," he shouted up as he shooed the children away from the street, "to give the name a few days before she makes any hasty decisions!"

"You didn't tell them about Gracie," Silver said.

"There'll be nothing to tell," he said in answer. "Sissy said she went off with Honesty somewhere. That dog'll see to it that she's safe and sound somewheres. He won't let harm come to anyone he loves."

He turned the corner and stopped the wagon. Every window at 204 Washington Street was broken. The white curtains blew in the breeze like flags of surrender. The front door stood open, and the front gate was embedded in the porch steps. A flower box hung precariously from the buckaroo's window.

And Sterling stood and silently got down from the wagon by herself, stiff and brittle. He let her go, jumping from the wagon to walk beside her, not touching, not speaking, barely allowing himself the luxury of a breath.

The front steps were blocked by pretty white pickets that stood merrily out of place, their points forbidding anyone from passing.

"Let's go around the back," he suggested, not sure where or even whether a storm cellar existed. Wouldn't it be just like Oliver Harrington to think that a twister wouldn't dare touch down in his part of town?

The nasty thought took him quite by surprise. It ambushed him just when he thought that he'd gotten beyond Sterling's family money and had convinced himself that the problem was hers alone.

After all, he liked Oliver. He adored Imogene. And Sterling and the buckaroo . . .

"Bucky!" he yelled toward the open windows. "Bucky? You hear me?"

Chapter Nineteen

"Cowboy?"

"Ethan?"

"You up there?"

"Is it safe to come out?"

Cyril Phillips got to his feet in the dank cellar and waited for the doors to be opened. He could hear his daughter's frantic voice and the scraping of metal upon wood as someone worked on the hatch.

Leave it to his idiot brother-in-law to have a storm cellar built with only a way in and no way out. No doubt one of Imogene's brainstorms that had made sense to her at the time. And Oliver, fool that he most certainly was, had no doubt indulged her.

"Oh, thank God!" Sterling said when the doors were thrown back and Cyril and the others stood blinking at the sudden light. "Oh, my baby!"

It was a wonder to him how such a careless ninny had pulled off the little charade for so long. He handed the child up to her and refused Morrow's hand as he climbed out of the abyss.

"How bad is it?" Oliver asked before venturing up the steps.

Cyril tilted his head back. Miraculously the building appeared sound, save the windows and a gewgaw missing here or there which, in his opinion, a house was better off without.

"Brick, man," Cyril said, wondering what his dolt of a brother-in-law could have been thinking to build with anything else. His own manse in New York was brick and marble. Kept out the cold in the winter, the heat in the summer. Here, it would have withstood the wind a damn sight better than some clapboard and timber.

"Like the Three Little Pigs," Worth said, obviously able to grasp the moral of a story more readily than the adults by whom he was surrounded. "I heard the huffing and puffing," he told everyone within the sound of his voice.

"Were you very frightened?" Sterling asked, pandering to the child's fears as she cuddled him in her arms.

One pair of bright blue eyes looked into another, and for the shortest of moments Cyril thought of Amelia and actually missed her, but the moment passed quickly and was gone.

"I worried about the princess," the boy said, and looked up into the trees. "And the turtle and the birds. Do you think the magic ball is gone?"

In the meantime Morrow was reaching down into the cellar. "Let me give you a hand," he said to Imogene, who probably still had her eyes closed, as if that would stop the rain and calm the wind. And now that the storm was over, the woman probably credited her actions with its demise.

Oliver brought up his wife's rear, in the literal as well as the figurative sense, coming up with his hand against her bustle. Cyril witnessed the warm embrace between Imogene and Morrow, the somewhat cooler handshake between the men. Leave it to his relatives to embrace the man who'd mowed down his "son."

"Well, cowboy, have you heard from that lawyer friend of yours yet?" Imogene demanded. Cyril had difficulty imagining that the farmer had a lawyer for a friend, and thought it appropriate that Imogene would place her faith in either of them. "I swear, God'll just blow me there if I don't get myself on a train!"

"He's checking with the land office," Ethan assured her. "But I don't want you holding out too much hope."

"It's in the valise, cowboy, right along with yours," his batty sister-in-law said, bringing a gentle smile to the man's mouth. Where did his family find these people? All of them spineless and sickeningly sweet. Except the doctor, who seemed sharp enough and savvy enough to grasp the subtleties of a delicate negotiation and whose feigned concern for Sterling's welfare added a nice touch to the business at hand. His malleability seemed to increase in direct proportion to the figures Cyril threw around. But then, most men had their price. It was all a matter of finding which pocket was closest to a man's heart. That was where his wallet, and his soul, resided.

In truth Cyril had been prepared to go higher if it had become necessary. They'd been interrupted by the ludicrous dash to the storm cellar as if their very lives were in jeopardy, and Cyril couldn't be completely certain where the man stood.

"Benjamin?" Sterling interrupted herself, which was just as well, as she was talking nonsense to the boy about some prince and a troll. "I didn't know you were here," she said as Cobb came up from the cellar, the last of them—if one didn't count the servants, which Cyril made it a point never to do. It didn't appear she'd given a thought to the good doctor, but she clumsily erased the impression as quickly as she could.

"I'm so glad you're all right," she said, peering down into the cellar as if she was anxious to see for herself that he was still in one piece.

He should have apprenticed the girl to the theater. The outcome couldn't have been any worse, and she'd have been assured of making a living until her breasts fell and the wrinkles set in.

"Do you think the evil Rutabaga got blowed away?" the boy asked.

"Doesn't look like it," Morrow answered as if the boy's question had made any sense.

"Do you think my velo'pede's okay?" Worth asked as

Cobb climbed slowly from the cellar, blinking like some nocturnal animal let loose in the day.

Had he read the doctor right? Had the man gotten the drift of his offer, or was he one of those mudbrains who would need it spelled out in one-syllable words?

The short man in the plaid suit took in his bearings and then pulled Sterling to his side. Plucking Worth from her arms and handing him to Cyril, he hugged the slip of a girl to his chest. "Thank the Lord I haven't lost you. I was afraid that everything I was hoping for could be gone. All I could think down there was that if both of us survived, it was time to make plans."

Cyril stopped wondering about just how clever Cobb was as Sterling's cheeks reddened and she feigned innocence, shyly studying the tips of her boots.

Cyril took in a deep breath of fresh air. All in all, it had been a good day. A very good day.

His grandson had been resourceful, needing little from those with whom he'd sought shelter. His grip on Cyril's neck had been firm and sure, without clutching or clawing in fear. On the contrary, he'd been brave— none of that whining-for-his-mother business to which Sterling had so often resorted.

But then, that was the intrinsic difference between girls and boys: Girls were weak, useless, needy beings who required a watchful eye and could lose their value in just the wink of one; boys were but men in training, the scions of business, rulers of nations, commanders of armies.

There was no question in Cyril's mind that the boy would walk again. He'd felt the awkward movements of the boy's foot against him before he'd handed him off to the tall Irishwoman—whatever her name was.

It was all coming together nicely. He'd discussed the costs and merits of a San Francisco practice with Cobb, and what it was that Cyril expected in exchange for his rather generous investment. And just as Cobb had assured him she would, Sterling showed every indication of accepting his attentions, which would wound Morrow to the quick, a happy little additional benefit to enjoy.

If one was to believe Cobb, and the doctors with whom Cyril had spoken in New York, his grandson was on the verge of recovery.

And most importantly, as he'd predicted, the price of gold was doubling by the day.

The Morrow boy looked around, obviously less pleased with the turn of events than Cyril himself was. But then it wasn't likely that he had much invested in any market beyond the one that carried fruit. "I've got to search for Gracie," he said to Sterling, grimacing at the fact that she remained in Cobb's embrace. "You coming?" he asked Sterling. It seemed more a challenge than an invitation.

"She can't," Cyril told him. "She has to get my boy settled." He passed the child to her, straightened his jacket, and told her, for Morrow's benefit, that maybe she and *her man*—he gestured toward Cobb—could catch up with him later. "When you've changed into something suitable and explained how you came to be wearing someone's bedsack."

He lifted one eyebrow accusingly. How she could have been raised in his household, with the advantages he'd provided, and still not understand the importance of appearances being kept up, he'd never understand. But there she stood, clutching the neckline of a dress that even the Harringtons' cook wouldn't strain the seams of, with her cheeks as pink as the yards of faded calico that hung from her shoulders. She'd damn well better have a good explanation, or Cobb would be left looking like a fool and a cuckold. And while no details had been offered, and none asked, from what he understood, the man wouldn't tolerate being put in that position. Again.

"Of course there is a logical explanation," Cyril said, his hands folded across his chest and his foot tapping.

"The rain—" she started.

"We were—" Morrow began.

"I'm sure there's nothing to explain," Cobb said, knowing exactly on which side his bread was buttered. Cyril wondered how much that little bit of understanding was going to cost him. Well, promises were cheap enough.

"We all know that Sterling's reputation is impeccable. And Morrow's no cad. It's an insult to them both to think otherwise. A reputation is the most important thing a woman brings to a relationship. I'll not sully it with groundless suppositions."

"Miss Sterling's reputation remains untarnished," Morrow said with a slight bow.

"There's always a good rubbing with pot ash," Imogene said, touching a mole that seemed to have sprouted on her chin overnight. "Or is that tar and feathers?"

Sterling stood quietly throughout the conversation, clutching the oversized sack to her chest, her pale lips pursed. She seemed to sense that she had a lot more to lose than any of them.

Well, perhaps she had some of his blood after all, and wasn't as stupid as he'd always thought.

Not that it would matter in the long run.

* * *

On the way back out to Noah and Sissy's, Ethan had stopped back at the mercantile, just to check on Risa and see if any news of Gracie had turned up. He'd found James, who'd assured him that Risa had changed the baby's name three times since he'd been there.

He'd casually asked after Gracie, and James, smart as a whip and practicing to be Ethan's shadow anyway, offered to help look. With the tick by his eye jumping like a flea in heat, he told Ethan that his father was busy making sure the bank was sound and his mother was crooning to Risa's new baby as if it were her own. His uncle Bart, James told him, had been by to check on them all and was out with several other men trying to make sure no one was trapped under the debris that littered the town as if a war had been fought down its main streets.

By the time they got to the farm, Ethan's heart had begun to beat normally again.

Seeing that big house on Washington Street—all the windows blown out, the eerie silence of the open door—his heart had stopped. And just when he'd gotten it beating again, Cyril Phillips had taken great pleasure ripping it from his chest and stomping on it. *Sterling's man?* He'd called Benjamin Cobb *Sterling's man.*

And she hadn't corrected the old coot. She'd taken Corny's plaid-covered arm and walked to the back door without so much as a look over her shoulder at him. And all the while he was still tasting her on his lips.

She needed security for her brother, she'd said. *I've Worth to worry about.* The Gibbs place was a tumble-down shack with some grapes growing behind it. There was no cash crop, no milking cow, no chickens laying eggs in a coup.

It was a damn good life he'd asked her to give up for a word she claimed meant nothing to her. *Love.*

His hand had traced her belly, cupped her breast. His lips had tasted the rain on her neck, coaxed the buds on her chest. And his heart had touched hers, no matter what she said.

She hadn't fooled him, and he didn't really think she was having much luck fooling herself. Maybe a body just needed what they'd been raised to value. He needed love, she needed security. But could she really have one without the other?

"Any word?" James asked Hannah, who came out on the porch as they pulled up in front of Noah and Sissy's place.

"Papa's covered all the houses to the south," she said, wringing her hands nervously. "And the Millers and the

Johnstones. But Uncle Eth—my mama's belly's hurting her something bad, and I don't know what to do."

Ethan jumped from the wagon, throwing the reins at James. "You head north. Try the Morrises and the Fosters. I'll see to your aunt Sissy."

"Yes sir," James said, easing Buckshot around. "And I'll mind the broken harness," he added before Ethan could even remind him.

Oh, James! Could he never think of the boy without that damned itching in his throat?

But he couldn't dwell on it now. Now Sissy needed him, and he charged into the house only to find her in a heap on the living-room floor.

"What are you doing out here?" he yelled at her, scooping her into his arms and carrying her back to her bed. "Weren't you told to stay off your feet?"

"But Gracie," she said, then drew in a sharp breath.

Women! It seemed to him they didn't have a lick of self-preservation in them. Always thinking about one little one or another instead of themselves.

"Dear God, Sissy! Leave Gracie to me and Noah, and you take care of the one we can't!"

He took a deep breath as she gripped his neck tightly enough to strangle him. *What if it were Silver in his arms? What if it was his child that might be lost?*

"All right," he said, laying her down on the coverlet and putting all the pillows he could find beneath her feet. "Are you bleeding?"

"Ethan!"

"Look, I'm all you got for now. I could go for Dr. Randall, but judging from the looks of town, it could take me hours to find her. I need to know what we're dealing with here, Sissy."

She studied her own toes. Quietly she admitted, "A little."

"What's *a little,* honey? Just a trickle?"

"Ethan!" She gave his name a few extra syllables. "You're too young to know about such things."

Was there a point to telling her that he was older than Charlie when Cara was born? Older than Della when she'd had the twins? Older even than she was when one of those twins died? To Sissy he would always be the baby.

"I'm getting older by the minute today, it seems. And I'm what you've got. I can't even go and fetch you Risa, 'cause she just delivered your nephew—"

"Risa's had her baby?" She tried to rise up on her elbows, and he rolled his eyes and pressed her down against the bed. "It's too soon. I've got to go—"

"She's fine. The baby's fine. Charlie's dancin' on the ceiling, and they're lucky enough to have one. Della's with them. I'd get Willa, but Bart's out somewhere, and I've never known Willa to be of use yet. So for now, all you got is me. Tell me what you'd do if it was Risa lyin' here, and I'll do it."

She smiled at him sweetly, her eyelids looking heavy. "I'd get her legs up, like you've done. You're doing just right. When did you get to be so grown up?"

"I did it behind your back, just like I did everything else." He circled the bed to the far side and folded the coverlet over her. "You cold?"

"I'm scared, Eth."

He grasped her hand tightly. "I know you are, honey. But don't be. I'm here. I won't let anything happen to you."

She gripped his hand harder. "I'm not scared for me. If something's happened to Gracie—"

"It's them!" Julia yelled. "I can hear Honesty!"

Sissy rose to her elbows. He pinned her by her shoulders to the bed.

"Any farther and I'll put a brick on your chest," he warned. "Promise you won't as much as sit up, and I'll go see what's going on."

Sissy promised, and he went to the front porch and gazed toward the setting sun. On the horizon he could just make out a man, a dog, and one little girl skipping beside them. Well, Noah had his family, safe and sound. And even if Sissy lost this baby she was carrying, he'd still have his wife and four daughters, a roof over his head (even if only barely), and a plot of land to work.

Ethan refused to make comparisons.

"I see one big mangy black dog and one little honey-haired creature bobbing along next to a tall man who's a heck of a lot grayer than he was this morning," he called over his shoulder before asking Hannah why her father hadn't taken the wagon.

Hannah pointed over to a pile of rubble near the barn. Around it flies buzzed noisily.

"He looked just like a unicorn," Julia said as she balanced Isabella on her hip. "Like a unicorn that fell asleep on the ground. Papa and I threw some boards over him so Izzy wouldn't see. Lucky she's too little to understand."

Jeez, he didn't know where Noah and Sissy would ever find the money to fix up the house and buy a new horse and wagon. Even the windwheel was gone. And the last thing it looked like Sissy ought to be doing was getting her water from a pump again and making trips to the outhouse.

* * *

Well, the furniture had danced around the house a bit, but Sterling thought that, considering what she'd seen, they were a mighty lucky bunch.

That was, if furniture and houses were what counted.

As for her, sitting by what until a repair could be made was a permanently open window, she thanked her lucky stars that the people she loved were all right. Without Worth, without Aunt Imogene and Uncle Oliver, she'd have chased that tornado and thrown herself right in its path.

If something had happened to Ethan . . .

All right, so she did love him. Her heart had known it for weeks and her head hadn't been far behind, no matter how strong a fight it had put up. Not that it would do her any good, and not that admitting it made her anything but miserable.

Just because she loved Ethan more than life didn't mean he'd love her in return once he knew the truth about her.

How would he feel if she were to tell him how she'd snuck down to the servants' quarters not once, not twice, but night after night, seeking comfort. And that she had allowed what had started out as a willing shoulder to become something more? That she had continued to come to Henry knowing the risks, and offering herself to him in hopes of stopping the pain, stopping the loneliness? What if she told him how Henry had begged her not to come, warned her that one night he wouldn't be able to resist the final act that could bind them forever with a child?

And how would he feel to know that she wanted that baby, wanted that sweet someone to love?

For just that moment in the cellar when she was sure that they would die and she would otherwise never know the taste of love at his hands, she'd been willing to give herself again. More than willing. More than wanting. But they hadn't made love, and they hadn't died.

And now that she knew that life wasn't going to end, she wished in a way that it would.

She picked up a pen and scribbled on the paper that rested on the desk in front of her. *Mrs. Benjamin Cobb. Sterling Cobb.* Almost without thought she put a box around the names, leaving one corner open, and trailed a line away from it.

As a child, her favorite pastime had been mazes. Her mother would draw them out for her on the inside of parcel wrappers, some of them as big as the table in their library. With a different color chalk for each attempt Sterling would try to find the path that would allow her to claim the prize that waited at the end.

Over and over, she would make the wrong choices,

learning in the end that the easiest way to win was to work backward, from the prize to the starting gate. *Know where you want to wind up in the end, Silver,* her mother used to tell her, *and then do whatever it takes to get there.*

She suspected that what her mother wanted was to live well, and her father's money had certainly allowed Amelia that. But it had never seemed a happy life, and Sterling had no wish to follow the path her mother had taken.

She scribbled over the paper, obliterating the words, and replaced Benjamin's name with Ethan Morrow's, allowing herself one real wish. It was a big wish, full to bursting with her and Ethan and Worth in the Gibbses' farmhouse. Worth was running on two good legs, and Ethan was watching, his arms around her rounding belly.

And all she had to do was reach out and take it—tell him she loved him. Tell him the truth.

But there was no way she could have him without telling him the truth, and such a tiny chance that she could tell the truth and still have him.

He thought it was the money that was stopping her, but she wasn't the spoiled little girl he imagined. Instead she was the spoiled woman he never even suspected.

Mrs. Benjamin Cobb. She couldn't get the words to pass her lips. Not lips that had been pressed against Ethan Morrow's. She ran a finger over her bottom lip, dreaming, wishing.

"Thinking about what happened between us?" Ethan's voice made her jump from her chair so quickly that it clattered noisily to the floor behind her. "Remembering what it felt like?"

"You shouldn't be here," she said, righting the chair and keeping it between them. *It felt like heaven. I wish you could touch me again.*

"I thought you'd want to know that Gracie is all

right." He gave her a lazy smile, a smile that swore he knew what she was thinking.

"And Sissy?" *I am not thinking about your hands, and your lips, and the way you smell. I am not thinking about how hard it is to breathe around you.*

He shook his head, grimacing. "They're not sure."

She closed her eyes against the truth. "She lost the baby?"

He lifted one shoulder. "We don't know yet. We got Mrs. Webb over there, and she says only time'll tell."

"Your sister must be devastated," she said softly. "She loves that baby already." Sterling remembered the moment she knew for certain that she was carrying. How she didn't have to feel a kick or a roll to love the tiny being inside her and be willing to face the wrath of God or Cyril Phillips to keep her baby safe.

"She's blaming herself. I've never known her to be so pigheaded. So stupid! You'd think she'd know better than to get so all fired upset in her condition. It's only making things worse."

"And I suppose you told her that. Heaped a little more blame on her head, as if she didn't have enough."

"Actually," he said, "I told her that she's never done a thing wrong in her life, which has made it damn hard for the rest of us, living with such perfection. And that she could blame the twister, blame me for leaving her there and taking you home, blame God or anyone else she chose, but to leave my Sissy out of it, because she doesn't deserve any blame."

She should have known he'd say the right thing, do the right thing. "Women spend a lot of time feeling guilty," she said, fingering her mother's brooch. "They don't want to disappoint anyone. And it's so easy to make a mistake. So easy."

"So she didn't know where Gracie was. Is that supposed to make it her fault if this baby . . . So what if she had made a mistake? Is she supposed to be perfect?"

"But she didn't really make a mistake," Sterling said. "There's nothing to forgive."

"In her eyes she did. She let her child go off some-wheres with the weather bad, and it was only luck that kept her from harm. I think she thinks she might have to pay with this new life."

Sterling knew there was no arguing with a woman's fears, her guilt, her shame. Still, she persisted as if Ethan was the one who needed convincing. "It's not her fault, and she's done nothing to be ashamed of."

"Ashamed? There's never anything to be ashamed of if you've owned up to it. There's only shame when you hide from responsibility. Sissy seem like someone who hides from responsibility? She made a mistake, that's all. Everyone makes 'em and most everyone deserves to loosen their own reins. She's been damn near perfect, if you'll forgive my language, but for her it ain't near enough."

"Do you really believe that?" Sterling asked. Did Ethan Morrow, unlike her father, believe that everyone made mistakes? And could he forgive them?

"That Sissy's perfect? I don't believe anyone's per-fect." He touched the tip of her nose with his pointer finger. "Except maybe you, Sterling Silver Phillips."

"I'm not, Ethan," she said, brushing his finger from her face. "I've made big mistakes. I've sinned and I've lied and I've—"

He wiped away her words with a sweep of his hand. "Tell me one thing," he said, so close she could almost taste the salty drops of summer on his tan skin. "Were you lying in the cellar? When you sighed against me? When you let me touch you where no other man has ever been?"

She shook her head. Her swallow was deafening in her ears, crackling like lightning. Her lips were dry.

"Are you in love with me?" He tipped her chin up so that she had to look at him. Amber eyes seemed to search her soul. "Are you?"

"Love isn't always enough, Ethan," she said in answer.

"It's more than you'll ever have with Cobb. I don't see you wallowing in guilt over leading him on. You want to talk about lying, there's your lie, Silver, and I don't like it at all."

"Benjamin knows the truth about me, Ethan. He accepts it. And I can accept what he has to offer me."

"Money? You'd sell our chance at happiness for a nice apartment above his office and a few good dresses? Will a few baubles and some meals at the Marsh be payment enough for accepting his seed and carrying his child in your womb?"

She sat down at the desk once again, folding her hands over the paper on which she'd been scribbling. "That was a hurtful thing to say. Is it so awful to take a man's ability to provide for a wife into account when considering a proposal? Are you calling me a harlot because I want to marry a man who can feed and clothe me and my—"

"No! But dammit, do you think I'd make you live on love? I've got the money from Old Lady Garvey. I can get the Gibbs place for next to nothing, fix it up. . . ." He gripped her by the shoulders, his earnest love so hot around them that she was dizzy from it. "I'd work myself to death before I made you do without. I swear I'll give you everything Cobb can, and love too. Can he promise you that?"

"Ethan, there are things you know nothing about. . . . When I lived in New York—"

"I know, I know. You think I don't know how rich you were? What you must be used to? I admit I can't promise you that kind of luxury, Silver, but neither can Cobb. And I swear that you and the buckaroo will never go hungry and I'll—"

"It's not the money," she said. "Your life and mine are so different. While you were being raised with all those brothers and sisters, I was all alone. I didn't have any love around me. I needed someone to hold, Ethan."

"And you poured all that love into your brother. Don't you think I know that? It's what makes you so wonderful—like Sissy."

"No, Ethan," she said, shaking her head to stop him. *Don't bring up Sissy. Not now when I'm ready to tell you the truth.* "I'm not wonderful. I'm not Sissy. I'm not—"

His fist hit the desk and then he pointed up at the room above their heads. "You're more a mother to that boy than the old man is a father, aren't you?"

I am his mother.

She tried to say the words, push them past lips that refused to open, but they wouldn't come. Instead she asked, "You love him, don't you? It's not just guilt, is it? And nothing could change it, could it?"

"The buckaroo?" Ethan asked, a note of shock tinging his voice. "He's a part of you. Do you really need to ask?"

If any piece of her had considered lying to this man, it was conquered in that moment. He deserved to hear the truth, and he deserved it from her.

"Ethan, there's something you need to know." Oh, but even that much was a relief. Her shoulders eased, she licked her lips, ready to begin.

"Oh, when you do that!" he said, running his finger against her moist lip.

"Wait until I'm done," she begged him, coming out from behind the desk and reaching for his hand.

"First there are things I've got to get taken care of," he said, backing toward the door. "Bart says everything's okay at the farm, but nobody's gone out and checked whether he's just trying not to worry us all, and Charlie's gonna need some help at the store. I'd really better go, but I'll be back tonight."

"But, Ethan—"

"Just after supper."

She nodded, watching as the sunlight lit him from behind like her own personal savior.

"And we'll talk."

She nodded again. It would feel good to have the truth out in the open.

"And I'll make you trust in me."

The wind ruffled his hair, and the sleeves of his shirt billowed in the doorway.

"In us."

Us.

It had been a forbidden word for as long as she could remember. A word that never included her.

"And no going to dinner with Corny."

She shook her head. "No going to dinner with Dr. Cobb."

"So then you'll think about it, Silver? Will you at least consider marrying me?"

It was there for the taking—everything she'd ever wanted.

She gave him a tight little nod, too afraid to let herself believe the possibilities. His smile was brighter than the sunshine, and she could hear his whistle all the way down the walk.

Maybe, just maybe, through some miracle, she'd make it through the maze this time and claim the prize.

Chapter Twenty

"What's in the box?" the buckaroo asked him for the tenth time since he'd gotten there.

"I told you," Ethan said, having difficulty keeping on top of his temper. "Not until you've done your exercises. Now, come on, Bucky. You can do better than that." He pushed gently against the boy's heel and felt the resistance. "Better."

"Could it push a pedal?" Worth asked, watching Honesty roll on the grass outside so that every flea and tick in Ohio could find a home in his hair.

"You're gonna have to work a lot harder than that," Ethan said. It wasn't fair of him to be taking his anger out on the buckaroo. Just because life wasn't going his way didn't justify giving the kid a hard time.

"Try this one," Worth said, lifting his other foot off the bed and pointing it toward Ethan.

They both stared at the foot as though it wasn't attached to the buckaroo.

Worth wiggled it in the air.

Ethan grabbed at it and ran his finger up the bottom.

Worth squealed.

Ethan squealed too.

"How long you been doing that?" Ethan asked him as if the kid had actually been holding out on him.

Worth's big eyes were full of surprise. "It's moving!"

"Kick me," Ethan said, moving so that he was within the boy's reach. "Kick me as hard as you can!"

It was feeble, weak, misdirected. But it was the most

glorious kick Ethan had ever received, hitting its mark—his heart.

The door opened a crack. Sterling's pretty head peeked in, obviously surprised to see him there. He hadn't come back the night after the tornado, nor all the following day.

"Ethan?" She slipped in and closed the door behind her. "I didn't know you were here."

"Look what he can do," Ethan said. Surely Worth's progress would erase the hurt that lowered her gaze from his own. "Show her, Bucky. Give us a kick."

One foot wiggled in the air, dropped to the bed.

"And this one," Ethan urged, tickling the bottom of the other foot.

Worth giggled, the perfect giggle of a child who was finally feeling what every other child felt.

Sterling hugged the boy, lifting him from the bed and dancing him around the room with joy, singing and cooing and dipping him in her arms.

"Do it again, honey lamb," she said, returning him to the bed and waiving his foot for him. "Do it again!" One leg made an awkward circle in the air, and Sterling hugged herself and laughed.

She wanted to hug Ethan. He could see it all over her face, but she kept her distance.

"I guess I should have sent word," he said, kicking himself for being so thoughtless. It wasn't like she wasn't on his mind. It was just that there was so much else there as well.

"I guess the break in your visits was good for Worth," she said in response. "Maybe it was good for all of us. Before things got out of hand."

Did she think he'd changed his mind? Had she? Life did go on outside this house, though it seemed to him, what with the windows already replaced and the front gate back where it belonged, that the people who lived here had no idea there was a world outside of 204 Washington Street.

"Sissy lost the baby." He could have couched it, but it wouldn't have changed the truth any.

She sat down next to Worth, all the joy gone from her face. "How awful. Is she doing all right?"

He shrugged. The tornado had taken its toll, in lives, in property. If he didn't fight it, it would take his dreams.

"They want my money," he said as abruptly as he'd said everything else. "The money from Widow Garvey. Noah's horse, his wagon, a portion of the house—all gone, and they've no other way to replace them."

"That money is yours!" she said, her hands on her hips. "They have no right to it."

"I promised you a lot, and it's gonna take every cent I've got to come through. And they come along and say they need the money." He picked up Worth's left leg and massaged the calf, feeling the boy fighting him. "That's it, Bucky. Kick me if you can."

Sterling watched him, a hand on her son's arm. "What about the rest of your family? Charlie and Risa? Maybe they could help."

"Oh, they're all doing swell." He switched to the buckaroo's other leg. "I spent half of yesterday helping Charlie salvage the goods at the mercantile and couldn't even ask him for payment, what with the new baby. And then I helped Bart repair what he could of the barn roof before the rain started and half his hay got soaked."

He put down the boy's leg and covered him up. "He's gonna need hot compresses tonight. Legs'll be sore."

"All right," she said. She laid a gentle kiss on her son's temple. "You rest a bit. It's been an exciting day. Ethan and I will be just outside your door." She handed him his sack, which bulged with candy and gifts that the neighbors kept sending.

"But what about the box?" Worth said.

Ethan hit his forehead with the heel of his hand. He'd forgotten entirely about it. Actually he hadn't had in mind to bring the boy anything. And certainly not what was in the box. But when it crawled out right into his path, what else could he do but find a carton and bring him along?

"Well," Ethan started, sitting down heavily in the chair by Worth's bed and playing with the boy's foot just because he couldn't resist. "You know how you were so worried about that Princess Sweetlips not being able to—"

"Sugarlips," Worth corrected. "And she can't get over the bridge 'cause of Mr. Rutabaga. And the magic seeds are gone." He pointed to the window where the string hung naked on the tree.

"Yeah, well, she isn't going to need the magic seeds, because of what's in the box." He lifted it and put it on the bed. "Go ahead. Open it."

Worth's eyes grew into giant saucers. Almost as big as his sister's big blue peepers.

"A turtle! For the princess to ride!" Worth lifted the ugly box turtle out of the box. It filled both his hands and he put it down on the comforter, where it pulled into its shell and sat there looking dead. "Can I keep him?"

"Guess you'd better ask your sister," he said, looking up at Sterling, who was doing her best not to appear horrified.

"I think the princess is probably too big to ride on him," she said somewhat hopefully.

"He'll grow, won't he?" Worth asked Ethan.

Truth was, Ethan had never had a turtle long enough to see it grow. Sissy didn't like confining wild things. She always said it was cruel, though Ethan thought that the fact that she was stretching food to feed all of her brothers and sisters probably had something to do with her belief that wild things ought to fend for themselves.

"Doesn't the princess have any friends?" Ethan asked, trying to change the subject.

"Oh, the coachman's nice," Worth said.

Sterling got up and pulled back the shades to look

out the window. Ethan noticed that all the drawings he had done for Worth were tacked once again to the wall. He nearly popped his buttons when he saw the little captions she'd written beneath them. *Worth beats Honesty in race! Worth's kite touches the clouds.*

"Why doesn't she just leave with the coachman?" Ethan asked.

"The coach is already full," Sterling said, her back to him.

"Oh, yeah," Worth said as if he'd just remembered that part of the story. "The coachman's family takes up all the space and there's no room for Princess Sugarlips. She needs a coach of her own. But then little Prince Perfect comes to live with the princess and she doesn't have to be alone. She could take care of him."

The turtle stuck out his head tentatively and looked around. "Hey, look!" Worth said.

"Maybe we'd better put him back in his box," Ethan suggested. A suet ball was one thing. So was a turtle. But he didn't think he could deliver up a royal coach. "One of these days we'll take him outside, whaddya say to that?"

"Yeah," Worth said. "And I can race him. And win!"

"You get some rest now," Sterling said softly. "Ethan and I are going to go out in the hall so that you can sleep, all right?"

"I'm not tired," the boy said, rubbing his eyes and yawning. "You just want to be alone."

"And you're too smart!" Sterling said, pulling the covers up to his chin and placing a kiss on his forehead. "Now, you just think about Princess Sugarlips riding on that pretty turtle's back, across the moat and away from the troll."

The boy's eyes drifted shut, and she and Ethan tiptoed out into the hall.

"Ethan, can't anyone else help Sissy and Noah? What about Bart?"

"Bart's hardly got a roof over his head. And then

there's Peter! There's a great story. Went to see him about how much I'd have to put down on the Gibbs place, and what does he tell me?"

He certainly couldn't tell her what Peter had told him. Not while those innocent blue eyes stared up at him.

"Of course—Peter Gibbs! He must have some money put away."

He had money put away all right. Only he'd put it into the house next door. Seemed he owed his neighbor a roof over her head in exchange for certain services she'd been providing. Services Peter claimed that Della had ceased to provide after their son died. And then Etta'd up and sold the house and turned all the money over to Clyde Dow. And only right, too, since Clyde'd be raising Peter's baby for him.

"Other obligations," Ethan answered, putting it as gently as he could. Peter had been keeping two households, and he expected Ethan to bear the brunt of the family's financial needs as a result. And keep his secret as well, because what would become of Della if she found out? She was doing poorly enough trying to face reality the way she thought it was.

"You know, Ethan," Sterling said, the corners of that sweet little mouth of hers turning down. "It seems like everything always falls on your shoulders. One brother needs you for this. One sister needs you for that. What about your needs?"

Before Sterling, he'd never had any real needs to speak of. Oh, he'd wanted to get himself a place, a woman, some land. But the needs of his brothers and sisters were always more pressing, more urgent. So he'd helped each and every one of them when he should have been helping himself instead so that when he found her, his Sterling, he'd have something worthy to offer her.

Instead he was doing half the farmwork at Noah's, and watching the children, and taking care of Sissy's chores too, when she was carrying, which seemed like always. And where were his children to show for it? Where was his farm?

For the discount Charlie gave him at the store, Ethan shelved, carried, delivered, and stacked. Had it gotten him a roof over his head?

And what had Bart ever done to earn the farm he called his own? Get born before Ethan?

Why, he was nearly raising James. Considering what he now knew about Peter, that was enough to get his heart pumping oil. It wasn't like *he'd* gotten any from some woman next door. It wasn't like he'd gotten any, period.

"I guess I can't really fault your family, Ethan, when we cost you Oklahoma. It seems like every time you get something going, somebody needs something from you. When's it going to be your turn, if not now?"

Downstairs the door knocker sounded, and a moment later Abigail came trudging up the steps muttering, "And he's got another one of those suits, he does, that could blind a mole. And the way I see it, if that awful man likes him, it's just one more strike against him."

"Abby? Did you want something?" Sterling asked, trying to keep a straight face. "Or did you just come up here to mumble?"

"He's wanting to see you," she said, running her tongue around her teeth as though she was still working on her dinner. "First that father of yours, with his orders and his complaints, like I never waited on a gentleman before—he's got to tell me what to do and what not to do, and where I went wrong. He's a fine one for that, I'll tell you."

"Mistakes have always been a favorite dwelling place for my father," Sterling agreed. "Where is he, the study?"

"It's not him that's wanting to see you. It's the other one." She rolled her eyes in Ethan's direction as if he wasn't supposed to know who it was that was waiting for Sterling. Which meant that it could only be one person.

"Cobb?" he asked.

"In the plaid," Abigail said, still looking like she could use a toothpick to get the taste of Corny Cobb out from between her teeth.

"I need to talk to you," Sterling said, looking at his left arm bashfully. "If you still want to talk to me. I know a lot's happened since—"

"Circumstances have changed, but my feelings haven't. I'll wait," he said, stepping closer to her. "As long as it takes. I'm kind of hoping you will too."

"Doesn't he want to come up?" Sterling asked Abigail. "Wait until he sees what the buckaroo can do!"

Ethan laughed out loud at the sound of the name on her lips. With all his troubles he'd nearly forgotten about how spectacular a day it had been for the boy. His recovery would be by leaps and bounds now.

"In the parlor," Abigail said. "He said he'll see the boy at eight o'clock. 'As usual,' he says."

Sterling started to head for the stairway, but he grabbed hold of her wrist and pulled her back against him.

"Just remember this while you're talking to him," he said, then cupped his hands around her ear. But instead of whispering anything at all, he traced her ear with his tongue.

He couldn't help laughing as she ran toward the steps, scarlet-faced. He followed and, standing at the top of the staircase, called softly, "Don't you go telling him what I said!"

* * *

Cyril could hear her on the stairwell and coughed to cover the sound of his daughter hurrying down the steps like a hoyden. Though clearly it wouldn't have mattered to Benjamin Cobb, who was already arranging his new, ultramodern medical office in his head.

Sterling fairly burst into the room, then slowed down when she noticed he was there.

"How's the boy?" Cyril asked her as he cut the tip of a Havana cigar.

"He kicked his foot!" she said. "Really. And his other leg too." Her hands flew to her cheeks. "He's going to be fine!"

"Don't fool yourself," Cobb said. "He'll need a great deal more care before he's well."

"Well, Ethan is—"

Cobb cut her off. "Morrow's up there? Again? Doesn't the man have anything else to do? I meant a *doctor's* care."

"Do you want to see him?" she asked.

"Of course I do. I need to check his progress myself. Your father surely doesn't want some farmer's opinion of his *son's* progress. And Sterling, dear, I know you've been busy, but I thought we discussed that I'd prefer you wore shoes with a lower heel on them. Safer, you know. And they don't destroy the back." He stood next to her, trying not to be obvious about comparing shoulders and chins. "Yes. Flat soles would do. They'll make me taller."

"My shoes won't change your height in any way," Sterling said, as if she didn't know what the man meant.

"I will *appear* taller," Cobb said, allowing for the truth of her statement. "And appearances account for a great deal. Wouldn't you agree? Appearances and perceptions?"

"I suppose," she agreed, and Cyril cleared his throat. "Yes, of course they do," she amended. *Better*, he thought.

"In line with that sentiment, I would like to request that you refrain from being seen with Mr. Morrow anymore." Cobb took the cigar that Cyril offered him and pulled out his own silver clipper.

"I'm afraid that's impossible," she said, her eyes on the ceiling. Cyril didn't know what was going on up there, but his daughter seemed unable to concentrate on anything else. "He's helped him so much and—"

"Helped?" Cyril said. "The man is responsible for the condition that child is in, which, even if you have, I haven't forgotten. The fact that I have to see him only reminds me that while the child is suffering, *he* seems to be doing rather well. I trust I've made myself clear." He could see from Sterling's face that she'd gotten his point. While he had her there, there were a few other points worth making.

"You know that your aunt Fruitcake and uncle Useless have had a reversal of fortune," he said. "You know also that they annoy me no end and it was only for your mother's sake that I ever tolerated them."

He stood and poured himself a scotch. "With your mother gone, there's very little that disposes me in their favor." He saluted Cobb with his glass and opened the door. "Pleasure talking to you, Benjamin. I do believe you have the power to bring out the best in our girl."

Benjamin nodded at him while Sterling sat with her mouth open, inhaling dust motes he hoped she'd choke on.

"Have you given any more thought to what I have to offer?" Benjamin asked Sterling after her father had closed the door behind him.

Despite the warm June night she was rubbing her hands up and down her arms searching for warmth. "What?"

"I've asked your father for your hand," he said. He crossed his arms over his chest.

"You what?"

"I'll be happy to check for wax in your ears, Sterling, if you're having difficulty hearing."

"Benjamin, you've been very nice to me, and to Worth. I appreciate all you've done—"

"I wouldn't rush to put the *but* on that, Sterling, if I were you. Your father and I had a long talk. He carries a lot of anger within him. I know I wouldn't want it directed at me."

"I'm sure it's not," she said as someone knocked at the door. "I'll just get that," she said, coming to her feet.

Benjamin's arm reached out and encircled hers. "That's what Carl is for. Sit down. I don't think you really understand what's going on here, so let me explain it to you."

It sounded like Noah Eastman's voice, and Sterling heard a man's footfalls on the stairs.

"What?"

"Damn it, Sterling," Cobb shouted at her. "Listen to me! Your father can ruin lives. Lives of people you obviously care about. He's given me your hand in marriage, and I've accepted it, despite all I know and what I suspect."

"Suspect?" There were little gobs of wax on his mustache, and two on the lapel of his god-awful plaid suit.

"It's obvious that the farmer has some appeal for you. Maybe because he's so like your father."

Maybe she *should* let him clean the wax from her ears. "Like my father?"

"They both see things in terms of right and wrong, good and evil. Look at how your father views what you did. I guarantee you Ethan Morrow would think the same thoughts, call you the same names."

Upstairs there was shouting.

"If he knew."

A piece of furniture scraped along the floor.

"They're the kind of men who don't forgive, Sterling."

The voices above them escalated.

"I'd better go see what's wrong," she said, vaguely waving at the ceiling.

"Tempers," he said, shaking his head as if she just didn't get it. "Go ahead."

*   *   *

"Your sister said you'd react like this, but I didn't believe her. Not for a second," Noah Eastman was saying. " 'Not our Ethan. Not the Ethan we all know and love. He's not that naive. He'll understand,' I told her."

"Well, you sure were wrong, weren't you?" Ethan said. His thumb and forefinger whirled frantically around each other, each finger rubbing the nail on the other.

"The whole house can hear you two," Sterling warned them. "My father. Benjamin Cobb. Not to mention—" She pointed at Worth, whose big eyes were glistening with tears in his pale face.

"I've got nothing more to say," Ethan said, waving off his brother-in-law with his hand. "Tell my sister she'll have the money in the morning and that I'm moving out."

"You're not moving out," Noah said. "Not now anyway. She isn't even up and about yet, and you're not gonna give her a new heartbreak before she gets over this one."

"Yeah, Noah, I am. I'm sorry for your loss. But if you think you can lie to me, all of you, and that I'll just forget it, you're dead wrong."

Sterling grabbed hold of the bedpost to steady herself. When it gave her no support, she sank down onto the bed and watched anger contort the face of the man she thought would understand anything.

"It was for your own good," Noah said, trying to lay a hand on Ethan's shoulder but giving up the attempt at Ethan's brush. "You wouldn't have taken the money if we'd told you the truth, would you?"

"I guess we'll never know, will we?"

"I just don't see the great harm here," Noah said. "We tried to provide you with a little nest egg, but nature broke it right in your pocket. Three days ago you were telling her not to blame herself, and now you want to hold your sister responsible for I don't even know what."

Ethan was shaking his head. His anger had begun to melt into hurt, and Sterling stared out at the dark sky rather than into those warm amber eyes that held such pain, such betrayal. "She lied to me. You lied to me. My whole family was in on your little joke. Let's make a fool of Ethan. Well, you did a good job of it, I'll give you that. Never for a moment did I think you'd all do something like that."

"Well, aren't we awful, giving you all the cash everyone who loves you could scrape up so that you could make something of your life? Just get out the crosses and the nails, why don't you?" Noah stalked across the room and opened the door. Before he left, he said, "I'll tell your sister you'll be home late. I don't want her worrying about you on top of everything else."

"She all right?" They were the first soft words to cross Ethan's lips.

"She lost a baby, Ethan. How do you think she is? You coming home?"

"It doesn't change things," Ethan said, turning to the wall and pressing his head against it.

Noah's steps were heavy on the stairs, and the door slammed behind him.

"I hope they find him," her honey lamb said in the silence.

"Find who?" Sterling asked him, her voice thin and dry.

"The baby that's lost," he said sleepily, cuddling up next to Honesty, who had somehow, in all the excitement, managed to worm his way into the house and onto Worth's bed, where he'd staked out a corner for himself.

"Go to sleep now. Everything will be all right in the morning." She raised her eyes and studied Ethan's back. His shoulders rose and fell raggedly. "Won't it, Ethan?"

He shook his head slowly. "If they'd used a knife, they couldn't have cut me deeper," he whispered.

"Do you want to tell me what happened?" she asked him, trying to put the puzzle together herself and coming up several pieces short.

"I should have known that Old Lady Garvey wouldn't be any more generous dead than she was when she was alive." He turned and sat down in the little chair beside the bed, petting Worth's head as he slept.

"So the money was really your sister's?"

"Sissy and Noah's. And Charlie and Risa's. And even old Bart kicked in a few bucks, according to Noah."

"And you don't think it was a wonderful thing that they did? All of them sacrificing for you, because they love you? And maybe because all of them owe you too?" She held her breath, waiting for the answer.

"Yeah, it was a good thing. Or it could have been. But the way they did it—they lied to me. Don't you see? Lying took the choice out of my hands. It was like saying they didn't trust me to understand what they wanted to do, so they tricked me into it. Doesn't say much for what they thought of me, does it?"

Clutching at straws, she asked, "But the fact that they told you . . . doesn't that change things now?"

"The time for telling me was at the beginning. Before they made a fool of me. Before all the love I've showed them over the years, all the stuff I did for them, the time I gave them, all seems like it was somehow dishonest." His pointer traced around and around his thumb, the only indication that he was nervous.

"I've got to give them back the money, Silver," he said and raised his gaze to meet hers. "It's not mine to keep. The dreams are all gone."

"You aren't really going to stay angry at your sister, are you? Not now with the baby and all."

Please, Ethan, say you won't stay angry. Say "Of course not." Please!

He sighed heavily. "Sissy's been good to me my whole life, and I wouldn't make her troubles worse. But I'll be moving out tomorrow, just like I said. I'll tell her that it's 'cause the barn's in no shape to stay in and they don't have room for me in the house. No use hurting her just because she's hurt me."

"So you'll forgive her," she said, reaching out to take his hand.

"I didn't say that," he said, tracing the lines on her palm. "I just don't see how I can tell her what I'm feeling now. But keeping it to myself isn't gonna make it go away."

"What is it you feel, Ethan?" she asked in a whisper, afraid she already had her answer, had always had her answer, but let her hope blind her to the facts.

"Betrayed," he said, squeezing her hand so tightly that she winced. "I feel betrayed by the people who were supposed to love me, and I don't expect I'll ever forget how much that hurts."

"I'm so sorry," she said, watching his face blur as tears ran down her cheeks.

There was of course no hope for them. There had never been, but just as Ethan had let his dreams carry him away, so had she. And they were both the sorrier for it.

"You're sorry?" he said with a sad little laugh. "I'm the one who's sorry. I've got nothing to offer you, Sterling Silver Phillips. Not a stick of furniture or a rundown room to put it in."

He wiped at the tears on her cheeks and she backed away and brushed them off herself. "Maybe after Sissy's better, you should consider moving on. I hear that land out in the Dakotas is affordable. I really think that if you stay here, your time is never going to come."

"I don't think you'd like life out there all that much,

princess. If you thought the Gibbs place was a mess, you'd sure have a hard time adjusting to a soddy."

The dreaming was over, and Sterling knew it. It didn't make it any easier to break it to Ethan.

"I wouldn't be going," she said softly, rising from the bed and making sure that Worth was well covered. "Benjamin Cobb asked me to marry him tonight."

"You don't love Cobb."

"Noah is right about you, Ethan. You're very naive. Benjamin has a good job and a good future."

"You don't love him," he repeated.

"Love isn't everything," she said, wishing it were otherwise.

"You're the one who's naive if you think that's so," he said, still sitting in the chair as she turned down the lamp and opened the window a crack to give her son some fresh night air. The only light came streaming in from the hallway, silhouetting his profile as he studied the ceiling.

"I'm not the girl for you, Ethan. I never was. I like the easy life. I like fine things."

He tapped his knees with his fingers. "And I'm not fine enough, huh?"

Try as she might, she couldn't force those words from her throat. She settled for the truth. "I've lived without love my whole life. I don't think I'll miss something I never had."

"Don't kid yourself, Silver. You think the price tag's too high on love? It's nothing compared with the cost of regret."

"Luckily I'll be able to afford it," she said, sweeping from the room and leaving him in the dark.

Chapter Twenty-one

"It's all arranged," Ethan told Sissy as she sat crossways on the sofa with her feet up. "It'll give me a chance to spend some more time with James, and I think it won't hurt Della any to have me there either."

"How does Peter feel about it?" Noah asked. Things between the two of them were strained, but civil.

"I don't much care," he admitted. He hoped it put a real crimp in Peter's style. In fact it was a good part of the reason he'd decided on Peter's place rather than Bart's. That and the fact that he'd sampled Willa's cooking more than once and wanted to live a few more good years before he gave up the grave.

Not that he had anything left to live for.

"You know we don't need *all* the money," Sissy told him for the hundredth time. "Just enough to replace the horse and wagon. Then you could help Noah with the rest of the repairs and—"

"I got my own life to think about," he said more sharply than he meant to. "I mean, I already built that windwheel once, and put in that bathing room too. I do any more building, I'd like to be on my own land."

"Maybe if you wrote to Graham," Sissy started in again.

Even if she didn't know the whole truth, surely she could see the shame in asking for a handout, couldn't she? He didn't see Noah asking Graham for money to repair the house. He didn't see Charlie or Bart running to somebody for help. Unless of course you counted him. Everyone ran to him for help quick enough.

"I'll get up your windwheel and patch the roof," he said through gritted teeth. "But that's gotta be it, Sissy. I've got my own life to start, and if I keep waiting for the right time, it looks like it's never gonna happen."

"You're still mad, aren't you?" she asked. She twisted with nervous hands the thin blanket that was draped over her and watched him.

"I'm not mad," he said. It was a half-truth; he was more hurt than angry.

"You taking Honesty?" Noah asked, running a napkin under the dog's chin.

"I don't suppose he'd fit in well here," Ethan said, unable to resist the little dig.

"You know, Ethan," Sissy said with her arms crossed and her lips a thin line of disgust, "it's not the lie that's got you so angry. If the storm hadn't come along, and you'd been able to buy the Gibbs place, like we all planned, and ten years down the road we said, 'Oh by the way, we gave you that money, not old lady Garvey,' you wouldn't be mad at us for lying. You'd say we shouldn't have, but you'd be grateful as the flowers are for rain, and you know it."

"Of course she's right," Noah said. "And you know you aren't any worse off than you were before all this happened. We've got a broken windwheel, a dead horse, a demolished wagon. We've—"

"Not any worse off?" Ethan asked, feeling the anger swell from his chest until he thought he would choke on it. "I'd learned to live with my circumstances—like a blind man I found my way in the darkness and made do. But there was this light suddenly, at the end of the long dark tunnel of my soul, and it was glorious! And then you snuffed it out, simple as that, and left me in the darkness.

"And you say it's the same darkness, so why complain?" He rubbed at his nose with the back of his hand, fighting the onslaught of tears that threatened to make a boy out of the man he had become. "Do you know what I saw in that moment of light? There was a family in that light, a future. There was everything I wanted, or near enough, and I could see it with my heart, taste it on my tongue, feel it in my bones. . . ." He couldn't continue. And what was the point anyway? It was all gone now.

"And now you know what you're missing." Sissy wiped at tears of her own, and searched up her sleeve for a hanky. "Oh, Ethan. Of all of you, you were the one I always worried the most about. The one I was so afraid would be hurt somehow. And I'm the one that went and hurt you."

He took a deep breath, and a deep swallow followed it. "It wasn't your fault," he admitted, coming to the couch and placing his own hand over hers as she cradled her empty belly. "I'll find some way to make up my losses. I wish there was a way to make up yours."

"Remember, Eth, when you were a kid? You made mistakes and I fixed 'em. I made mistakes and you fixed 'em. It was so easy once upon a time. But then you all grew up, and the bad things that happened couldn't be fixed with a kiss and a cookie anymore. Saying I'm sorry didn't mend Francie's heart when Noah fell in love with me instead of her.

"Look at Della . . . all she ever cared about was how she looked and things like that. Now days'll go by and I swear she never even takes a brush to that hair of hers. What I wouldn't give to be able to yell at her for looking in the mirror too long again. But with Samuel gone she's not the same."

She blew her nose daintily and pushed the hanky back up her sleeve.

"I'm sorry, Eth. You didn't deserve to have the rug pulled out from under you after you've worked so hard to weave it."

If it was a matter of deserving, maybe he was getting just what he'd earned. Sissy'd always told him that there would be a price to pay for his wildness, his penchant for acting first and thinking later. And New York had proved it. The man in the crowd in front of Graham's office had thrown a brick at Perry Trent's head. Had called him a stinking plutocrat and a faggot to boot and had picked up a second brick between insults.

Graham had told Ethan he'd had just cause when he'd picked up one of the many bricks that had been thrown and taken aim for the man's head. But, jeez, he'd been pitching rocks at tin cans forever, just the way the gunslingers he read about did with their guns. And he knew when he cocked his arm that he'd get the guy. He just hadn't realized there'd be so much blood, or that a man could lie so still with a crowd of men screaming all around him.

Graham had said it was Carnegie's fault, not Ethan's. Carnegie and the strikers themselves, who'd gone about it all wrong, according to Graham, and wouldn't accept the fact that the fight had ended in November. Carnegie Steel would never hire the strikers back. And just because Graham and Carnegie had some investments in common didn't mean that Graham could do a damn thing for the Amalgamated Association of Iron and Steel Workers.

But Ethan knew it wasn't Carnegie throwing that brick, and in a daze he'd let Graham hustle him out the back and send him back to Ohio, assuring him all the while that the man would be fine and that the police would have no interest in Ethan's confession when the crowd had been at fault to begin with.

But Graham had been wrong. Ethan would have been able to live with himself, to get on with his life.

Instead for three years it had weighed on his shoulders and his soul. A conscience was the roughest of taskmasters, the harshest of tyrants.

"Maybe it's just what I deserve," he said, squeezing Sissy's hand and rising. "Anyways it is what it is, and I've got to get going. I'd like to beat James home from school."

"I put a couple jars of your sister's grape jelly in there," Noah said, pointing to his secondhand valise. "Thought you might want to savor the fruits of your labors."

Damn. He'd been intending to make wine from those grapes, or at least try. He'd read the directions in Sissy's *Mrs. Hale's,* and it seemed a simple enough thing. Just some soaking and some sugar and the wine would be good for ten years. But then, Sissy didn't like wine in the house—hadn't even before their nephew had choked on a wine cork and died, and certainly didn't afterward—so she'd turned his dreams into a couple jars of jam.

"Great," he said. "Thanks."

"I'll see you out," Noah said, directing Sissy to stay where she was, slipping out from beneath her feet, and walking him to the door. "You know, this is still your home," he said quietly, standing awkwardly next to Ethan, his arms hanging limply at his sides.

"Yeah, well," Ethan said with a shrug. He'd always looked forward to the day he'd leave Sissy and Noah's house. He'd expected it to be a triumphant exit, arms raised, face creased with a smile. He never thought he'd leave this house in anger or in hurt, but here he was, wrapped in both, walking out the door with a couple of changes of clothes, his violin, and two damn jars of grape jelly.

"Maybe we were wrong, Ethan. 'To err is human,' as they say—'to forgive, divine.'"

Well, he sure as heck wasn't God. Their little deception had cost him all his plans. And with his dreams gone and the woman he loved now thinking about marrying some other man, the forgiving wasn't going to come easy, if it ever came at all.

Just as Noah's hand reached for the doorknob, they heard a knock. Some stupid, silly part of him thought that it would be Sterling, come to say she'd changed her mind, but it was the Reverend Miller Winestock who stood on the porch when the door was opened.

"Miller," Noah said, extending his hand and shaking the reverend's. It was hard to believe that these two men were ever rivals for Sissy's affection, but then, Mr. Winestock was no longer the cold, dispassionate man who had been prepared to marry Sissy because it was what the town expected.

"How is she?" the reverend asked in hushed tones. It was easy to see that this was no routine call for him as he stood shaking his head sorrowfully. "I came as soon as I could. There's been so much tragedy in town, so much loss with the storm. And I didn't want Tessie to know—"

"Then what I heard at the picnic wasn't just a rumor?" Ethan asked. He couldn't wipe the ridiculous grin from his face. The reverend apparently couldn't either.

"The good Lord willing," Miller Winestock said, his smile trembling slightly. "Considering her illness. When I heard about Mrs. Eastman, I had to come tell her how very sorry I am for her loss. And yours of course. Is she seeing anyone?"

"I'm sure she'll see you," Noah said, backing out of the doorway and inviting the older man in.

The reverend removed his hat as he came into the house and went directly to the couch. "Ah, Sissy!" He pulled up a chair and clasped her hand. "For you to have to suffer a loss like this . . ."

Sissy looked up at Ethan. "The storm took its share from everyone," she said softly, more to him than to the reverend. "It was nice of you to come, Miller. How is Tessie doing?"

Lord but time changed things. Ethan remembered when Tessie's health was the last thing Sissy would have asked after. But that was before they all knew about her having that multiple sclerosis that accounted for everyone mistaking her for a drunk all those years.

"The doctor says she's doing better than he expected. He tried to talk her out of this baby, you know." He reddened and corrected the impression he was afraid he might have made. "Before the fact of course. But she was so set on it. I have to admit that I was against it. Dead set against the whole idea."

"I take it you've changed your mind," Noah said, coming to sit near Sissy's feet again. "You don't look like a man who is sorry he's about to become a father."

A glow came over the reverend, as bright as some Madonna's halo, but it came from inside him, showed in the sparkle of his eyes and the red roundness of his cheek. "Nothing I ever did in my life compares to this," he said in a reverential whisper. "To create a life, to be responsible for it. Tessie said she was willing to give her life to see this child born, though thank the Lord the doctor says it shouldn't be that dire. Pray God it doesn't happen! He does admit she could have a flare-up. . . . I want to blame her for taking the risk, but I can't, because I know I would give my own life, if I could, to see this baby safely into this world."

Noah reached out and squeezed Sissy's hand, and the reverend shook his head in embarrassment.

"I am so sorry. Here I am talking about our baby when you've just lost yours. And my sole purpose in coming was to offer my condolences, to give you comfort, and I've made things worse with my ramblings."

Ethan watched his sister do what she always did—make everyone else feel better. "Don't be silly. Hearing you talk about your good fortune puts a smile back on my face, and seeing you sitting there so happy makes me happy for you. I'll look forward to *your* baby for a while instead of to my own. How's that?"

"It's very generous of you," Mr. Winestock said. "I hope you won't mind if Tessie and I come to you with our questions and worries. You've done such a fine job, over the years, with all your various charges."

"I don't know that everyone would agree with that," she said, looking pointedly at Ethan again.

"Oh, yes they would," Noah defended.

"Sissy's great with the little ones," Ethan agreed. It was just that she didn't know when her little ones had grown up. She didn't know when they were adults, and when protection crossed the line and became deceit.

"I never appreciated any of it before," Miller said, almost to himself. "The *tender age*, the *mother's love*, the *father's pride*. It's all a miracle to be treasured and defended at any cost, isn't it?"

At any cost. Ethan didn't know about that. Everything came at some cost, didn't it?

"Well, I've got to get going. See you in church," Ethan said, pushing off on his knees and rising. He walked to the door, feeling Sissy's eyes on his back. "You take care now."

"You take care of yourself, Ethan Morrow," she said, wiping her red nose with the old hanky that had been up and down her sleeve more often than her arm. "I'll expect you for dinner on Sunday."

"Sorry," he said, gripping his fiddle case tightly. "I don't think I'm gonna be able to make it on Sunday."

"I'm making apple pie," she said, trying to tempt him. "And a honey-roasted ham, and I think I've got a couple of those nice yellow yams you like so much."

"Sounds divine," the reverend said. "I remember a time you couldn't resist that, Ethan."

"Times change, Mr. Winestock. Sissy's got a lot of resting to get done. And enough mouths to feed," he said as he heard Isabella begin to fuss. "Noah, you tell Hannah and Julia and Gracie I was sorry to miss them."

He was becoming a pretty good liar himself. The last thing he'd wanted to do was look into the faces of those three little girls and tell them he was moving out. He'd stayed in the barn until they'd left for school, only then coming into the house to say his good-byes.

"Ethan?"

He was already on the porch when he heard Sissy calling after him. He came back to stand in the doorway.

"I love you."

"I love you too," he admitted with the hint of a smile. Some things, he supposed, would never change.

* * *

"He bites his nails," Sterling's father said when she sat down to breakfast. She was glad that Worth was upstairs with Abigail having his breakfast in peace.

"Yes," she agreed. "He does. But he's just a baby, Father, and with all that's happened to him . . ."

"Bad habits start early," her father answered brusquely, moving the jam out of her reach. Too many sweets, he had always contended, made for a weak mind. "I should think you'd be all too well aware of that."

"All habits start early," Aunt Imogene said. "Except mustache twirling, I suppose," she added, spreading several layers of jam on a small slice of toast. "And cigar smoking. And stroking one's beard. Of course that falls in the mustache category, doesn't it?"

"I suppose it does," Uncle Oliver agreed. He pulled out his watch and checked the time, as he had been doing every few minutes.

"That's another," Aunt Imogene said. "Watch-watching. Can't do that before you learn to tell time. Now nose picking—that starts early."

"Imo-gene—we're eating." Sterling's father refused to pronounce her name the way she preferred it, so her aunt had taken to ignoring all comments addressed to her by him.

"Oh, please," Imogene said, rolling her eyes. "We all do it. We just get more careful about where and with whom as we get older. What *are* you waiting for?" she asked Uncle Oliver when he took out his watch yet again.

"I'm expecting my accountant." He pursed his lips, relaxed them, pursed them again. "He's been going over the books."

"Having difficulties?" her father asked. He examined his fingernails, buffed to a high gloss, and then moved his gaze from her uncle to Sterling. "I did see what was left of the Harrington's Wines and Spirits this morning when I took my constitutional. You didn't have much stock in there, did you? I mean the bulk of your inventory was in the cellar of course. Wasn't it?"

Uncle Oliver shook his head, and Sterling felt breakfast rise in her throat. A slight twitch—an imperfection she'd never seen before—played at the corner of her father's mouth. It brought to mind the slight shimmy of a cat just before he leaped to the kill.

"Oh, that's too bad," her father said with no sincerity at all. "Too bad. You know, I was considering investing in the import business."

He looked not at her uncle Oliver but at Sterling, and tapped his fingertips one after the other on the table, leaning forward slightly. "If I didn't have Sterling here to worry about, I might just be able to advance you enough cash to get you out of your difficulties."

"Leave Sterling out of it," her uncle said, balling up his damask napkin and throwing it into his plate of eggs.

"That Dr. Cobb is a very interesting young man. Ambitious. Intelligent. In some ways he could be the answer to everyone's unfortunate situation, don't you think?"

Her father was losing his touch. There was no subtlety in his veiled threats. But then, he had no need. After all, fate had put everyone just where he wanted them.

She toyed with the eggs on her plate, then, realizing that her father was watching, took a bite of them, laid her fork at just the right angle, and chewed while she counted in her head to twenty before swallowing. With his eyes assessing her eating skills as if she were still ten years old, she took a small second bite.

"Have you options of which I am unaware?" he asked her, leaving her the choice of either swallowing too soon, answering with her mouth full, or signaling for him to wait. Each was unacceptable, as always. Since she had nothing to say to her father in any event, she decided to shake her head.

"I've a land option," her aunt said. "Will that help her?"

"Dear God! It's your own silverware," her father said with disgust as her aunt slid her sticky jam knife up her sleeve.

"It's her knife, Phillips, and she can do with it what she pleases," Oliver said, patting his wife's hand and pushing his own knife toward her. "Have another, dear."

"It may be all you're left with," Cyril Phillips said. "Unless, of course, you listen to reason. But then, I suppose there's little hope of that with the lot of you." He stood abruptly and threw his napkin down onto the table. "You!" he yelled at Carl as the old butler came into the room with a heavy silver carafe of hot coffee.

"Lord!" Carl answered, not quite respectfully, not quite a curse.

"I want a tincture of quassia prepared immediately. If you've no quassia in the house"—he looked at Aunt Imogene and closed his eyes briefly—"then one of iodine, cayenne, and soap. And I want it brought to the boy's room in a bowl the appropriate size in which he may soak his fingers."

"No!" Sterling's throat closed at the memory, bile pooling in her mouth. She remembered his instructions to her nanny: *Soaked for five minutes and in her mouth for ten. From now until dinner.* She'd thrown up three times before her mother had found her and put a stop to it. "I'll see he stops."

"Promises can't be trusted, Sterling."

She didn't know whether he meant that she shouldn't trust Worth's or that her father didn't trust hers. It didn't matter.

"I promise you this," she said, rising from the table and gripping the back of her chair. "He will not have that mixture put on his fingers. Ever. And you can count on it."

"As long as I am his father," he said, nodding at Benjamin, who had appeared in the doorway from nowhere, "*I'll* make those decisions."

* * *

"Arrogant, awful, arbitrary, abhorrent," Sterling shouted as she dug behind the clutter of her baby's memorabilia in the back of her closet.

"Do you think we can move on from the *a*s?" Aunt Imogene yelled back at her from the bedroom. "I've some wonderful ones with *b*s."

"Asinine, antediluvian . . ." she moved the last box of baby clothes and reached in the dark for the cigar box.

"And there's one with an *s* that involves his parentage. Oh, lots of *s* ones."

Sterling backed out of the closet, hugging the box against her chest, while her aunt continued to mutter.

"Slimy, sneaky, sedentary—"

"Sedentary?" Sterling asked her as she sat down on the lacy bedspread next to her aunt.

"Well, he just sits there, doesn't he? Like he's king of the world."

Sterling had to agree that he did.

"I just have one question," her aunt said, rolling onto her stomach, her feet up in the air behind her, her head propped on her hands like a schoolgirl. "How did he arrange for that tornado?"

Sterling lifted the lid of the old wooden cigar box she had decorated at her mother's side when she was a small girl. Her mama had handed her each piece of lace, each snippet of paper, each little pearl, and had praised the result lavishly, swearing it was the loveliest keepsake box she had ever seen.

Sterling also remembered the disgust on her father's face when her mother had somehow forced him to agree with her assessment. She'd been sent her off to bed immediately, and just before she'd fallen off to sleep, her mother had slipped into her room.

"Asleep?" she'd asked.

Sterling had shaken her head and moved over on the bed to make room for her mother.

"I've only time for a quick story," her mother had said. *"Your father is having a cigar downstairs and expects me to . . . well, just a quick story, sweetheart."*

"About Princess Sugarlips?"

Her mother had laughed lightly, that wonderful musical laugh that Aunt Imogene still had. She'd touched the tip of Sterling's nose and said, *"Who else, Silver, but the lonely little princess?"*

Sterling had nestled under the covers, curving her body around her mother's form.

"Once upon a time, there was a little princess, and her name was Sugarlips. That, of course, was because she was so sweet. From the moment her mother first laid eyes on her, she knew that the princess was destined for great things. Happiness beyond measure. Love beyond bounds. But it was a long, hard road, and her mama, the queen, warned her that she would meet people along the road who—"

"You in here?" her father's voice had thundered as he'd cracked open her door. The light from the hallway had streamed into her room, blinding her.

"I was just saying good night to Sterling."

He'd stood there, waiting.

"I've got to go, princess," her mother had whispered, rising from the bed and leaving Princess Sugarlips in peril without finishing her warning.

In the dark, cold without her mother's warm body to

cuddle against, Sterling had lain awake in her bed hearing her parents argue in the hall.

"You were having your damn cigar, Cyril. I can't do it by myself. You act as if I'm doing it on purpose," her mother had said. *"I want another child as much as you do, though I do love the one we have, which is more than I can say for you."*

"A boy!" her father had shouted. *"An heir. What goddamn use is a girl? She can't be someone else's problem soon enough for me. Now, come to bed, Amelia."*

"Tonight isn't . . ."

"I played your little game, Amelia, didn't I? Told the child that piece of crap was beautiful, didn't I?"

She heard the light thud of her mother being pressed up against the wall, the derisive laugh that always sent his anger flaring. *"You weren't all that convincing Cyril, dear."*

"You needn't be either. . . . Now, come to bed before I decide what else your little darling has done wrong."

"Let her be, Cyril."

"Do you suppose she wants a glass of water?"

"Let her be, Cyril."

"How much do you think that little bladder of hers can hold?"

"Cyril . . ."

"Just a moment, dearest. I think I hear our darling calling for water."

"Aren't you going to open it?" Aunt Imogene asked.

"Come to bed, Cyril."

"Shouldn't I get her that water?"

"Come, Cyril. We'll work on your son."

Sterling struggled to swallow. She had been the battlefield on which her parents had staged their war. And now her father was hoping to use her to do the same thing to her son.

"Do you think that Benjamin Cobb really plans to move to San Francisco?" she asked her aunt as she lifted the lid of her precious box and took out her mother's favorite handkerchief.

"Didn't you just love the look on your father's face when Cornuto-boy told him that he hardly knew the child and should defer to you in matters of his upbringing?" Aunt Imogene picked up the top photograph and turned it over, reading the writing on the back as if she hadn't memorized every one of Sterling's photographs.

Benjamin had stood up to her father impressively. She'd actually felt a moment of relief when her father had agreed with him until he'd added that he needed to get to know Worth better. A continent between them might be just what was called for. Out to the *Wild West*.

But she couldn't think of the Wild West without thinking of Ethan. Ethan, with his big strong hands, his muscles straining his clean white shirt, the tiny lines that radiated from the corners of his eyes and spoke of a man who smiled when he worked, even if that work was just following a horse up and down a row of dirt.

"Look," Aunt Imogene squealed. "Your mama and me when we were girls!"

Sterling looked at the photograph. Imogene and Amelia had had each other. Ethan had had a horde of sisters and brothers. Sterling had known what it was like to grow up alone, and if she didn't make a life for herself soon, Worth would know the same loneliness she lived with every day.

The next picture was one of her mother with Sterling on her lap. Beside them was a dog they never owned, there just to give the impression of a fuller family. She tried to imagine herself married to Benjamin Cobb, sharing a bed and a life and her child.

There was a knock at the door and Carl stuck his head into Sterling's room.

"Abigail tired of playing checkers with Worth?" Sterling asked.

Carl shook his white head. "No, ma'am. Mr. Morrow is here."

"Tell him he is free to see Worth, but I don't want to see him. Tell him I—"

"He's here to see Mrs. Harrington," Carl corrected. "He's waiting down in the study with Mr. Harrington."

"Oh." She brushed the hair away from her face and got up from the bed, gathering the photographs and gently laying them into their little wooden coffin, where all her memories rested.

"You're making a mistake," her aunt said softly, busily wringing her hands behind her back.

Perhaps she was, but only for herself. It was the right thing to do for Ethan, setting him free to find happiness with someone as wonderful as he was. It was right for Uncle Oliver and Aunt Imogene, who would need her father's financial support and to whom she owed everything. And it was right for her son. Giving him a father who would stand up to her own, taking him to San Francisco, as far as she could get from Cyril, and providing him with the medical care he needed. And all of it came in one wrapped-in-plaid package—a man from whom she had no secrets.

She wiped the tears from her cheeks and threw back her shoulders. A girl couldn't ask for more than Benjamin Cobb.

Not a girl like her anyway.

* * *

Genie Harrington floated into her husband's study on the same butterfly wings with which she seemed to go everywhere. She flitted first to one chair, in which Ethan knew she'd never alight, and then to another.

"She won't come down," she said with a heavy sigh, and then looked accusingly at Oliver. "I'd swear she was from your side of the family. She just seems to go seeking misery like some sort of mouse after cheese in a trap."

Oliver sucked in a big breath of air, held it within his cheeks, and let it out only slowly. When he was done, he refilled the glass of scotch he'd been working on when Ethan arrived and took another gulp.

"Is she all right?" Ethan asked. Not that he wanted to know. Not that he wanted to care. He wasn't here to talk about Sterling Phillips. Not today anyway.

"Yes, she's—" Genie began.

Yes was enough, and he cut her off. "I got some mail," he started, pulling an envelope out of his pocket. "From the lawyer in California. It seems that there is indeed a large parcel of land in the names of Amelia Phillips and Imogene Harrington in the Napa Valley."

He waited for the news to sink in, watching Oliver's eyes widen and Genie's smile turn smug.

"The lawyer says it's suitable for planting and that grapes have been successful all around the area."

"I'll be damned," Oliver said, shaking his head as if that could clear the whiskey haze and then grabbing at his temples when the effort backfired.

"I told you," Genie said, squirming in her chair. "Didn't I tell you?"

"Is it worth much?" Oliver asked. "Does he say?"

Ethan handed the letter to Oliver. "You can see for yourself, but it appears to be worth over a thousand if you wanted to sell it."

"Sell it!" Imogene screeched. "Sell it? Over my dead body—"

"Genie!" Oliver chastised. "Get hold of yourself. What are we going to do with land in California but sell it?"

"I'm going to farm it," she said, rising and coming over to link her arm within Ethan's. "Or rather, the cowboy is. Won't you, Eth?"

Oh, but he could taste it! When he'd read the letter from the lawyer, all he could think about was which of his grapes might do best out in the West with more sun, less cold, better soil—that *terroir* he kept reading about—the special combination of climate and soil that told the grapes it was all right to grow there.

"I've got to sell it, Genie," Oliver insisted, staring at the letter and running his fingers over the words. "I've got no choice. I've got to do it for Sterling as well as for us."

Genie took a shallow breath next to him. One, and then another. Then one more, shallower, louder than the one before. The grasp on his arm tightened, and Ethan felt his own breath catch in his throat.

"Easy, Genie," he murmured, guiding her to a large leather chair while Oliver hurried over, his hand searching for the precious vial he kept in his pocket.

"Damn it, I must have left it on the dresser." He ran to the doorway and yelled to anyone who could hear him above the horrible squeal that accompanied Genie's attempts to take in a breath. "Get the bromide of ammonium, quick—she's having an attack!"

Ethan was kneeling in front of Genie when Oliver came and crouched by his side. Panic molded Genie's features, enlarging her violet eyes, hollowing her cheeks, bluing her lips. From a dry mouth, spread wide as if the air could rush in by itself, came sounds Ethan didn't realize a human could make—timbers shifting, rafters bending, metal train wheels grinding to a halt—all of it punctuated by Genie's hands closing around Ethan's arm tighter and tighter and tighter until the tiny bit of a thing was actually causing him pain.

"Dear God, Genie, breathe!" Oliver shouted. He grasped her arms, loosening them from Ethan's forearms, and shaking them until her head wobbled uncontrollably. "Oh my God!"

She ran in, his Sterling, tipping the small glass jar against a fine lace handkerchief as she came, and leaned over Ethan, her breast so close to his face that the silk that covered it brushed his cheek. He jumped up, finding breathing difficult himself, and gave her room as he backed farther and farther away from the chair until he finally hit the wall.

Silver put the cloth to her aunt's mouth and nose.

"Look at me, Aunt Genie," she ordered. "Watch me." She breathed in deeply through her nose, her back filling out and shrinking as she released her breath.

"That's it," Oliver said, stroking his wife's curly gray hair off her forehead. "Again. In slowly. Again."

After what seemed like forever, Genie finally sank back against the chair. Her eyes were glazed, her arms were hanging limply at her sides.

"You're all right," Sterling told her, easing herself down until she was sitting on the floor at her aunt's feet.

"I won't be all right," Genie said softly, letting her eyes close, "until we're all out west where we belong."

Sterling looked from her aunt to her uncle, and then to Ethan. "Out west?"

Across the room Oliver stared at him, closed his eyes, took a deep breath, and nodded.

It was as close as Ethan expected to get to a blessing.

"Maybe someday," she reassured her aunt, looking at the blue that still tinged the ends of her fingers. "For now I think I'd better go get Dr. Cobb."

Cobb. Well, old Cobb could give her medicine, but Ethan could give the dear woman California . . . which might even cure her.

"California's gonna be as crowded as Van Wert," Imogene said with her eyes closed as Sterling rose, her taffeta skirts rustling noisily.

"Not quite," Sterling said, throwing a glance Ethan's way. He smiled, twiddling his thumbs innocently as she made her way out the door.

After Sterling was gone, Genie began to shift this way and that on the chair, then pulled something out from beneath her skirts. "What have you got there?" Oliver asked his wife.

With a shaky hand she held a photograph out to Ethan. "My sister, a few months before she died. Could you make a drawing for Sterling of her mother?"

Ethan took the picture. Sterling's big light eyes stared

out at him from the photograph. Her pale hair was bundled on top of someone else's head. Even Sterling's straight back and fine bearing were there, as this woman leaned out of a fancy carriage. A footman held the door open as she waved at the camera. He turned the picture over. In a fancy hand was written, *Henry holding door for Amelia, June 1891.*

Amelia was lovely, her features as captivating as her daughter's. It was no wonder that Cyril had sent Sterling away after Amelia died. To look at one was to see the other. But it was Henry who caught his attention. Deep dimples gouged his cheeks. A cleft split his chin. He'd seen the man before, he'd stake his life on it.

Chapter Twenty-two

Sterling found Benjamin standing with his back toward the door of his waiting room, shaking his head. "Good Lord, Etta! What did he hit you with? The pump?"

"No I-told-you-sos, Ben, please."

"Put your hand down so that I can at least see it," he said. "Whoa! That's some gash."

"Can you just make it stop bleeding, Ben? I've got to get back before Clyde notices I'm gone."

Sterling froze in the open doorway as Benjamin shifted his body, and the woman who stood before him came into view. Blood ran down her chin, covering the bib of her apron. One eye was nearly swollen shut, the cheek below it showing signs of discoloration.

"I'm going to have to stitch it," Benjamin said as Etta's other eye widened. "Etta?"

Etta pointed at Sterling. "I'd better go," she said, lifting up the corner of her apron to hide her face.

"You can't go," Benjamin said as he held her arm. "It's got to be stitched. It's not going to stop bleeding on its own."

"I can't," Etta said, her eyes still fixed on Sterling. "Clyde'll know I was here if you sew it."

"Well, he'll be a widower if I don't. And I don't think he'd like everyone to know how his new wife died. Miss Phillips'll help us. We'll lay you down on the table and snip-snip, it'll be fixed. And no one will know besides the three of us." He motioned for Sterling to come forward, and cautiously she took several small steps in his direction. If Etta wasn't happy to see her there, it was only a fraction of how unhappy Sterling was to be there herself.

"I came at lunchtime so that nobody else would be here," Etta mumbled, her hand pressed against the side of her mouth. "Clyde's a good man, Ben, don't think otherwise. Better than me, that's for sure."

"Your husband did this?" Sterling asked as they made their way to the examining table, Benjamin trying to signal her over Etta's head not to ask questions as she helped the injured woman keep her balance.

"A good man? Well, undoubtedly he's got a good arm," Benjamin said, looping a clean white apron over his head.

"He had his reasons," Etta said through clenched teeth as she steadied herself on the step-up and then sat on the leather table. "Good ones."

"Well, he didn't knock any sense into you, that's for sure," Benjamin said, dabbing at the cut with some cotton and causing Etta to wince. "There's no good reason for this, no matter what you might have done."

"You know what I've done, Ben. I'm carrying." She said it as if the two of them were alone, and Sterling wished they were.

"I'll just . . ." she said, backing away from the table. "My aunt had another attack, and I just wanted . . . I can wait outside."

"I'll need your help," Benjamin said. "Stay."

Dragging her feet, dreading each step, she came back to the table. "What do you want me to do?"

"I need you to hold her still," he answered, helping Etta lie down and placing Sterling's hands on either side of the woman's head.

"Clyde'll kill me if he knows I came here," Etta said. "He thinks the baby's yours."

"Of course he does. So would everyone else. Isn't that what you had in mind, Etta? Until I found out?"

"Maybe I should just—" Sterling started again. Ben glared at her, warning her to stay put.

"And what did *you* have in mind but owning one of the nicest houses on Chestnut Street?" she said in return. "You knew where that house came from . . . that I wasn't some unplowed field—"

"I thought that was way in your past, Etta. I didn't know you were dishing out devil's food cake down the block while all I was getting was beggar's pockets."

"Well, it all came out this morning," Etta said, coughing as the blood trickled down her throat. "Damn it, Ben, can't you fix this?"

"What happened this morning?" Sterling asked when Benjamin didn't. He rolled his eyes at her but said nothing.

"Who knew a farmer could count? He demanded the truth, so I told him. Ever since our wedding night he's been suspicious. . . ."

"I warned you, Etta, didn't I?" Benjamin asked her. He was threading a needle with heavy black thread. "This is going to hurt, but then I guess you heard that before. Did you tell him whose it was?"

"The man has enough troubles with his crazy wife and that poor kid dragging around."

Sterling shut her eyes. She'd seen Etta with Peter Gibbs on several occasions. Each time, Etta had made a production about how the check for her mortgage was late in arriving and how she was just discussing her inheritance with Peter. "All business," she'd say. Funny business! Monkey business! No wonder Peter didn't have any money for Ethan.

Benjamin handed Sterling a wad of clean cloth. "Open your mouth," he told Etta, then directed Sterling to hold the cloth against the inside corner of Etta's mouth. "I'm gonna sew it from the inside so that maybe Clyde won't notice. You let him think it's mine, didn't you?" He inserted the needle into the inside corner of

Etta's lip. The woman groaned and gripped the sides of the table.

"Good thing Clyde's not all that strong. He could have done a lot more damage if he was big and strong." Benjamin took his eyes off his work and looked at Sterling. "Farmers. No sophistication. You don't need a diploma to know the difference between a wife and a heifer."

Sterling held Etta's head tightly as Benjamin inserted the needle again and pulled the gash closed.

"Hold on, honey," he said, and Sterling didn't know which of them he was addressing. "I warned you, Etta, didn't I? I told you a farmer isn't the type to just forgive and forget."

Etta's head jerked against the pull of the thread. Blood gushed wildly from her mouth.

"Damn. I suppose I should've started from the back," Benjamin said, pressing more cotton gauze at Sterling as he pierced the inside of Etta's cheek.

The room began to spin slightly, and Sterling leaned her hips against the leather, watching the window multiply until the wall was full of windows, all of them letting in an odd yellow light.

"That's better," Benjamin said, pulling the thread through the inside of Etta's cheek and checking the tension. "It's not in a man's nature to forgive. Love can turn to hate in the blink of an eye if a man finds out his woman's not what he thinks she is. Clyde's no different from a hundred other farmers around here. If any one of them was to find out the truth about the woman they'd put up on a pedestal . . ."

He tugged at the thread. Etta cried out in pain, and the room spun wildly out of control for Sterling. Her fingers slipped from Etta's face, pawed the table feebly, and then there was nothing at all.

* * *

"She'll be all right." Benjamin's voice came from a deep well. Or maybe she was in the well, way at the bottom, his voice echoing around her. "You go on, Etta, before Clyde comes after me."

"I'm sorry I ever cheated on you, Ben," she said, the words coming out sounding like her mouth was still full of gauze. "I didn't know a good thing when I had it."

"It's all for the best," he said softly.

"You don't suppose this one'll run out on you too?" Etta asked.

"No. I don't suppose she will." He raised her wrist and pressed against it.

"He makes me face the pillows, Ben. He says he can't look at my face."

"I'm sorry for you, Etta. I really am."

"You warned me, Ben. I should have listened."

He pulled at Sterling's eyelid. "Come on, now, Sterling. Time to wake up. Life's waiting for us, sugar plum. I got a practice to start."

She tried to rouse herself, but her eyelids were heavy. Her head was heavy. So was her heart.

"I've been thinking how awful it would be if Morrow was to learn the truth about you. . . . What a shame it would be to see this face all bashed in like Etta's. . . . And the boy . . . *Bastard* is a cold— There you are!" he said when she opened her eyes. "I thought that might get you up. Let me help you."

He put his arm under her shoulders and helped her to a sitting position.

"Are you all right?" He waved something under her nose and she felt the bile rise up and coat her tongue. She covered her mouth just in time to hide her retch. "Fine help you were! You were supposed to be helping me, and you wound up a patient!"

She blinked a few times and fought to get her bearings, but her head still swam. Where was Etta? What had she heard?

"Your father's due here in a few minutes, Sterling,

and I don't think you want to be here when he comes. Not like this anyway. You need all your wits around him."

She nodded, still not able to get her thoughts from her head to her mouth. Had he mentioned her son in front of Etta? He couldn't have. Had he really threatened her? He couldn't have.

"He's got his dander up about the accident. If I were Morrow, I'd finally hightail it out of Van Wert. He's thinking about bringing some kind of charges against him."

"What kind of charges?"

"Sure. For Morrow you've got your tongue back from the cat." He helped her up from the floor, an arm looped around her back. She felt his fingers exploring the side of her breast.

"Are you afraid of my father?" she asked. "Does he terrify you the way he does me?"

"You've got a lot to be frightened of," Benjamin said, twisting her in his arms. "But no, I'm not afraid of your father. Or anyone else."

"What about Clyde? What if he comes after you?" She could feel his hands tentatively touching the outside curve of her breasts as he held her.

"I'll tell him it's not mine," he said simply. "Let him figure out whose it really is. The way I see it, a woman's entitled to certain secrets."

"I'd better go. Aunt Genie had a bad attack. Will you be over later?"

He nodded, then reached for something on his counter. "Wait. I had to loosen a few of your buttons after you fainted. Here."

He handed her the brooch that belonged to her mother. She fastened the two little buttons at her collar and then tried to put the brooch in place. As she did so, her father opened the examining-room door. She clutched the pin tightly in her hand.

"It's one o'clock," he said, pretending he didn't even see her there. "Time for my appointment, is it not?"

"Sorry, Cyril. I'm running a little late. I'm with a patient." Benjamin tried to hide her with his body, but there was no doubt that her father knew she was there. "Please have a seat in the waiting room."

One of her father's eyebrows rose, but he turned on his heel and left the room.

"There's nothing to worry about, Sterling," he said once the door was closed again. "As you can see, you're safe with me. I have taken care of everything."

* * *

"Can we sit outside with Honesty?" the buckaroo begged him when Ethan was finally able to come up and see him. First he'd had to settle Imogene into bed, join Oliver for a drink, and read the letter from the attorney three more times.

"I don't see why not," he said, scooping up the boy in his arms and carefully setting him on his shoulders. "You'd better hold on tight," he warned, one hand locking the boy's legs together against his chest, the other steadying the boy's back.

In California, big enough for a good-size vineyard and owned by Imogene Harrington, there really was a plot of land just waiting for him to sink his roots into. He wondered if a man could see the ocean from Napa Valley. He'd tried to find it on a map in one of the books in Oliver's study, where the man and his accountant were now holed up, but couldn't locate it.

"Could I try to ride the bike?" Worth asked when Ethan finally set him down and Honesty was done slobbering over him.

"Bucky, you can't stand up yet," Ethan told him as gently as he could. "You gotta stand before you can walk, and you gotta walk before you can ride."

Honesty nudged the boy's bottom as if he understood every word of their conversation. There was no question the boy was getting better. Still, he wasn't exactly running down the road to say good-bye. But then again, Ethan wasn't going anywhere just yet.

"Okay," Ethan said, remembering the millions of ways his nieces and nephews got from place to place when they were toddlers. "Let's try this."

He lifted Worth and put him on his feet next to the short brick wall that surrounded Sterling's prize peonies. He put the boy's arms over the edge of the wall so that they could help support his weight.

"You all right?"

The buckaroo nodded.

"I'm gonna let go, okay?"

The buckaroo nodded more vehemently.

"Now."

He took one hand away and then the other. Worth tottered on wobbly legs, trying desperately to stay upright, thoughts of the damn red bike spurring him on before his tiny legs buckled and he came down hard, his chin, his nose, and even his forehead scraping along the unforgiving brick wall.

Ethan grabbed at the boy, hugging him tightly to his chest, not sure whose tears were wetting his shirt, his own or the buckaroo's. Worth held his chin, sniffing and sobbing, while Ethan crooned and comforted, petted and promised.

"Next time," Ethan told him as he wiped the boy's bloody chin and runny nose with the tail of his shirt. "Next time you'll stand and maybe even take a step."

"And then I can ride," the boy told him, rivers of tears streaking his tiny face, "like the wind."

"Like the wind," Ethan agreed, carrying the boy into the kitchen and setting him next to the sink to see to his cuts and bruises. He could just see the good doctor's face when he took a look at Worth during his evening visit. That was, if the man took his eyes off Sterling long enough to even see that the kid was battered and bumped.

"Oh my," the cook said when she saw the buckaroo's face. "I'll see to him." She handed Worth the mixing spoon she'd been using, dripping with chocolate, and asked if he'd mind cleaning the spoon while she cleaned him. When he looked at her uncomprehendingly, she winked broadly and suggested he use his tongue for his job and she'd use a cloth for hers—unless of course he wanted her to use her tongue and he could have a cloth.

"And then the cook said to the prince, 'You can help me,' right, Eth?" Worth asked him.

It took Ethan a moment to remember the story. It took him a moment to think about anything except the bloody little chin and the scraped nose of the sweetest little boy he'd ever known. With Worth's face blurring slightly in front of him, he said, "No shells in with the eggs there, Prince Perfect! And no cups with the flour."

Leona gave him a "hmmph" and waddled back to her bowl to put another spoonful of chocolate within Worth's reach. "Eggshells in my cooking! That'll be the day!"

"No teaspoons either," Ethan warned as he left them happily licking spoons and tending wounds and headed for the stairway to say good-bye to Genie. Lord, she'd scared them all to death with that attack. He checked the clock in the hall. The good doctor sure was taking his sweet time about coming over to check on the woman who he hoped was going to be like a mother-in-law to him.

Abigail answered his knock and seemed glad to see him. "She's been asking for you. If you could be keeping her in that bed, I'd say more power to you."

"Hard keeping her down?" he asked, peering past the maid at the patient, who was propped up in bed, a purple shawl thrown over her shoulders.

"Hard keeping her off the ceiling," Abigail said. "She's already got me packing, she does!" The maid shook her head at such foolishness, but not without a smile on her lips at Genie's antics.

In her bed, a pad of paper propped against her knees, a pencil over one ear, and another in her hand, sat Imogene Harrington. She waved at Ethan and signaled for him to sit on the edge of her bed.

"We've a lot to do, cowboy," she said.

"We do? Do we need your valise?"

"Don't you laugh at me," she said, looking down her nose at him. "Didn't I tell you that land was there for us? And now it's time. You ready?"

"Genie," he said with a sigh, "I haven't even got the price of a one-way ticket out to the coast."

"Bought 'em the new windwheel, didn't you?" She shook her head at him. "You gotta cut those ties that bind, cowboy. They're cutting off your air, strangling you, sure as my asthma is strangling me."

"There are things you don't know, Genie. Things I don't want to explain." Like guilt. And gratitude. And then there was the whole matter of what had happened in New York, and Ethan's fear of exposure. And more guilt. Lots more.

"There are things you don't know, too, cowboy. Everybody's got their secrets. You got skeletons in the closet, she's got ghosts in the attic, I've got bats in the belfry. It's time, Eth. It's now or never."

"You don't understand, Genie. It's gonna take a great deal of money to get this thing off the ground. Yeah, you've got the land, and I'm willing to work it for some small share, but there's equipment, supplies, the vines themselves, there's—"

"Under the bed." She pointed with a bony finger to the foot of the bed.

"I beg your pardon?"

"Under the bed. Start pulling 'em out." She shooed at him with her hands. "Go on."

He lifted the dust ruffle, feeling a bit like he was lifting a lady's skirts, and felt under the bed without looking. It was packed tight with boxes and containers and sacks. He pulled out the first one. It was a hatbox from a store called Bloomingdale Brothers. "A hat?"

She shook her head. "Smell it."

He sniffed at it and quickly pulled his face back. "Ew! What is that?"

"Oranges. Just remembered where I put 'em."

"When?"

"Christmas?"

He sighed.

"It's a yellow sack you're looking for."

"What's it got in it?"

She pointed to the foot of the bed. Obviously she wasn't going to tell him.

He found her valise. He found a boxful of shirts for Oliver she'd forgotten to give him. He found a wig and an eye patch in a yellow sack, and she decided the one they were looking for was lavender.

He found a lavender box. Two sets of purple slippers. Three place settings from the Marsh Hotel, and a coffeepot from the DePuy. He'd all but given up when he unearthed a lavender sack and knew it was the right one when Genie squealed.

"That's it! That's it! Dump it here." She spread her legs and he opened the sack and let the contents fall into her lap.

Dollar bills, some tied together, some loose, in every denomination, rained down from the sack. Ethan smacked his forehead. Taking silverware was one thing—not necessarily all right, but not quite the same, to his way of thinking, as money. Lots of money. Lots and lots of money.

"This get us started?" she asked him. She held up two twenty-dollar bills in one hand while she rooted around through the piles, then raised a fifty in front of his face.

"Where'd you get all this money?" he whispered, sitting on the edge of the bed before he plumb fell down.

"Stole it," she whispered back.

Why was it that everything good that passed under his nose was always too good to be true?

"From where?"

"You mean from whom," she corrected.

"All right. From whom?" There was over a thousand dollars on the bed between them. Could a woman who was as sick as Imogene Harrington still go to jail?

"Me."

"What?"

"I stole it from me." She looked very satisfied with herself. Ethan supposed if he'd managed to steal this much money from himself, he'd be pretty satisfied as well.

"Every morning Oliver used to leave money for me on the dresser. For whatever I needed. Hairpins. A hat. A lacy pillow slip. Soon I had everything I needed. But he kept leaving me money."

"Since . . . ?"

"Since we first got married. Nearly thirty years. At first I thought I might need it, so I put the extra money in my shoe, but it got too hard to walk with, all that stuffed in the toe. So I put it in a shoe box. Then it was in two shoe boxes."

"Why didn't you tell Oliver?"

She rolled her eyes. "Tell Oliver? Oliver loves me, cowboy, but he hasn't heard a word I've said in twenty years. Not since the babies."

"I think he's just protecting you," Ethan said, adjusting the purple shawl around her shoulders.

"And I'm protecting him. But in the meantime there was all this money. I kept saving it for a rainy day, Eth. And I think it's pouring!"

"We really could start a vineyard with this," he said aloud. "But there aren't any guarantees, Genie. We could get wiped out, and what would you and Oliver do then?"

"We'd die," Oliver said from the doorway. "But we'd

die trying, and if we stay here, Genie's never going to last another winter."

"I didn't hear you come in," Ethan said, jumping up from the bed and dropping the money.

"You always were smarter than anyone gave you credit for, lovey," Oliver said to his wife, his gaze sweeping over the money and alighting on her face.

"It could set you back up in business," Ethan said, letting dollars and dreams slip through his fingers again.

"That it could," Oliver agreed. "The grape-growing business. But I'd need a partner. Someone who knows how to coax things from the soil."

"I'm your man, sir," Ethan said, sticking out his hand.

"Someone who would look after Genie if something were to happen to me." He sat down on the edge of the bed.

"I'm your man, sir."

"Someone I can trust—whom I already love like a son. Someone who is as good as the day is long and as bright as the sun in June. Someone who knows the value of a dollar and the—"

"For heaven's sake, Ollie, shake the man's hand before he jams it in his pocket like he's trying to do."

"Fifty-fifty?" Oliver said, his hand extended.

"I couldn't do that, sir," Ethan said. A chance like this came once in a lifetime. There was no need to be greedy. Having anything at all to offer Sterling would be enough. "I'd like twenty-five percent, if that's not asking too much. And we'll need proof of Amelia's death."

"And Ollie says forty and the cowboy says thirty and you can both agree on thirty-five." Genie put up one hand, then the other, then both.

He reached out for Oliver's hand and, at a light knock on the open bedroom door, looked up to find Sterling standing there, a bundle from the mercantile in her arms.

"Oh. You're here too," she said, staring at him.

"Good. I thought you'd all want to know. I'm marrying Benjamin Cobb a week from Saturday."

"That's the stupidest thing I've ever heard," Imogene said. "The man doesn't even have a dog."

Sterling smiled gently at her aunt. "He's got everything a girl could want, Aunt Imogene. He's kind, patient, understanding, and knowing me the way he does, he still wants to marry me."

"I didn't hear you say you loved him," Ethan said, his heart on the floor where she could stomp on it.

"Can I see you in the hall?" She put her parcel down on the bench at the foot of her aunt's bed. Ethan could see the folds of ivory satin sliding out of the package.

If he parted his lips to answer her, there was no telling what might come out, so he just nodded and followed her out the door, stopping for a quick touch of the fine satin cloth. It wasn't half as smooth as her cheek.

She stood in the dim hallway waiting for him, her hands near her throat. A lock of hair clung to her eyelashes and he brushed it away, letting his hand feel the softness of her temple, the silkiness of her curl.

"I can't believe you're going to do this," he said, trailing the back of his finger down her cheek.

"He's a good man," she said, stopping his hand with her own.

"No, Silver, he's not. I've known him all his life. He's one of those men who believe that the end justifies the means."

"And I'm one of those women who agree."

He took a step closer to her so that their bodies were nearly touching. She reached up and touched his forehead, moved the hair out of his eyes, and watched with a smile as it fell back to the same place it always did.

"I've wanted to do that since the day I met you," she admitted quietly.

"Why didn't you?" He pulled her up against him, drunk with the scent of her, crazy with need. His coarse fingers twisted in her silken locks as he tipped her head back to look at the face that wouldn't go away even when he closed his eyes.

"Because it would have led to this."

"So?"

"So one thing leads to another and you find yourself on a path that takes you someplace you never intended to go." She pulled back from him and straightened her blouse, ran her hands down her skirts.

"You saying that you want to be with Cobb, and not with me?" The thought of Cobb unbuttoning those little pearl buttons at her neck sickened him. Her tight nod made him dizzy with despair.

"I know you feel responsible for Worth's accident and that you've vowed to stay until he's well." She fumbled in her little purse as she spoke. "But he's clearly on his way to recovery, and Benjamin will certainly do all that's humanly possible to see that he has everything he needs to get well."

"Good." He turned to leave. "Of course I don't go back on my word, so I'll keep coming around until he can—"

"—run after you and Honesty to say good-bye. I know. But I'm afraid that we'll be leaving before that. My father has offered to set up a practice for Benjamin in San Francisco. We'll be leaving after the wedding."

"California, huh?" Genie was right about how crowded the West Coast was going to be.

"Yes, it was my father's idea." Ethan was sure it was. Cyril had found a way to punish him for what had happened to his son. And giving Sterling to Cobb would have been enough—more than enough—but giving to Cobb Ethan's dream of California, too, would be what Noah called the coup de grâce.

His heart lay on the floor before her, waiting for her next move.

"Anyway I figured you'd be wanting to leave town, and I know that we've cost you a great deal of time and money and I'd like to repay a small portion of it." She held out her hand. In it were several bills.

His heart stopped beating, but his body didn't have the sense to fall down and die. "This the change from your wedding-dress cloth?" he asked, looking at the money in her hand. "Guess all my hard work wasn't worth much. Getting the boy to feel, to move." He laughed a bitter laugh. "Getting the same out of you."

"It's what I have," she said, holding it out to him.

"Keep it." He started down the stairs.

"Can you leave town without it?" she asked him.

He turned, holding on to the banister, and looked up at her. There was something different about her, but he couldn't place it. Maybe it was that Cobb's kiss was still on her lips. "Is it so important to you that I do?"

"Yes." There wasn't a tear in her eye. She didn't gnaw her lip. She just stood there with her hand outstretched, the money in it.

"Fine." He took the few bills and shoved them into his pocket without even looking at them. "You sold out cheap, Silver. You could have had a vineyard to keep you fed and a husband who loves you to keep you warm. But at least you'll be healthy, I guess."

"Good-bye, Ethan." She turned and walked back past her aunt's room, past the buckaroo's room, and opened the door to her own room. She never looked back.

"Good-bye, Princess," he said so quietly that only his heart could hear it.

It was time, then, to say good-bye to the whole dream, not just a piece of it. He knocked gently on the door to the buckaroo's room and stuck in his head at Abigail's greeting.

"Cowboy!" Worth sat up in bed, keeping his balance with one hand. It hurt Ethan to see the bruises on the boy's forehead, his scratched nose, his scraped chin. None of them stopped the boy from smiling at the sight of him as if Ethan was some sort of God. "I was hoping you'd come!"

"Howdy, Buckaroo," he said, tamping down his emotions as he took the chair beside Worth's bed and twirled it around so that he could straddle it backward. "How're you feeling?"

"I wanna ride the velo'pede," the boy answered. "Could I?"

"Velocipede," he corrected despite how cute the kid sounded saying it his way. Sterling always corrected him, so Ethan supposed he ought to as well. "Maybe tomorrow. But I've got to talk to you about something else."

Worth's little lip began to tremble, and knowing that this would probably be good-bye, it wasn't that easy for Ethan to keep his own from doing the same thing.

"You know," he started, "that I love you, don't you?"

Worth's eyes filled up with tears.

"And you know I'm gonna be real disappointed if you don't learn to ride that bike pretty soon."

The boy nodded solemnly.

"But I might not be here to see you win a race."

One tear rolled down the boy's cheek.

Shit.

"Okay. Never mind. You want to hear about Prince Perfect?" So he was a chicken. It wasn't as if he hadn't known that since he'd bolted from New York without looking back. And here he was, causing pain and running away again.

Worth's head bobbed up and down and he batted away a tear with the back of his hand. Ethan pushed a hanky against the boy's nose.

"Blow." He waited while the buckaroo pulled himself together and got ready for his story. With a big sigh, he began. "Well, the little prince was about as lonely as his sister, Princess Sugarlips, you know."

"Yeah. But he had a friend, remember?"

"Oh, yeah. Monkey boy. In the trees. Right?"

"Yeah. Where's Honesty?"

Ethan looked out the window over Worth's bed and

pointed. Honesty was asleep in the peony beds. He loved that dog. And he loved this boy.

"So the prince was lonely, even though he got to play with Monkey boy sometimes. He wished he had a friend all his own who could stay with him night and day."

"But the evil Rutabaga . . ." Worth began.

"The prince wasn't afraid of the evil Rutabaga, because he knew that one day a great knight would come along and cream the Rutabaga. And besides, being a troll, the Rutabaga was short, and before too long the prince would tower over him and then he wouldn't have to be afraid anymore."

"But he *was* afraid," Worth insisted.

"Ah, but he didn't have to be, because one day, on the doorstep of the castle, he found a great black dragon, with a note around his neck."

"A dragon? Did it breathe fire?"

"Well, once upon a time it did, but a brave knight fought with the dragon and poured so much water into his mouth to put out the fire that to this day water still drips out of the dragon's mouth. All the time."

Worth smiled. "Prince Perfect could wipe it for him."

" 'What are you doing here?' the prince asked the dragon when he found him on the castle's steps."

" 'I've come to protect you,' the dragon said, right?"

"Well," Ethan said, trying to keep a straight face. "I didn't know it was a talking dragon, but that was just what he was doing there, all right. 'I am a very brave dragon,' he told the prince. 'Monsters that lurk under beds, bogeymen that live behind curtains, trolls that hide under the bridges don't frighten me. And now they won't frighten you.' "

He stood and stretched out his legs. Every damn chair in the house was too small for him.

"Will you be back tomorrow, cowboy?" Worth asked him, watching Honesty swatting at a fly in the garden.

"I don't know, son," he said honestly. "But a piece of me will always be with you."

* * *

"Your heart could sound better," Benjamin Cobb told Cyril as he pulled the stethoscope out of his ears. He had not come to be examined, but the two men had become so good at their charade that a free checkup seemed just another part of the deal. If he had to withstand the doctor's insolence to convince Sterling that the greedy practitioner had her best interests at heart, he ought to get something immediate in return.

"Well, you're one of the very few who know I have a heart. Keep it to yourself, won't you?" Cyril said as he refastened his shirt. They'd been telling him for years that his heart wasn't all it should be. It was enough for him.

"I still don't understand what you're getting out of this arrangement," Cobb said, resting his plaid buttocks against his desk. "It seems to me we have the same interests here, and both of us can't get what we want."

"The same interests?" Cyril doubted it. He was counting on them being quite the opposite. "I thought we had rather little in common."

"Well, I'm interested in your daughter—"

"My point exactly." It was amusing to see the shock register on the good doctor's face. He let the message sink in before adding, "I'm interested in the boy."

Slowly a grin played at the corner of the doctor's mouth. Cyril could clearly see the wheels as they turned in the man's head. "You're right as usual," he said, letting the smile give him away. "We have nothing in common."

"I wouldn't go that far," Cyril said. He was sitting in the doctor's chair, and he leaned back and put his feet up on the desk. "There's the practice in San Francisco that interests us both."

"I still don't quite get it," Cobb said.

"It's really very simple." Cyril put down his feet and

leaned forward. "You get the girl and a practice in California. I get the boy."

"You get the boy?" Cobb's eyebrows lowered. "I don't think that your daughter will allow—"

"What's she going to do about it from three thousand miles away, Cobb? Are you going to give her the money to come to New York? Am I?"

"She'll never agree to it," he said, shaking his head. "I've no objection of course. Every time I look at the boy, I'm reminded that I won't be the first."

"But that machine that sees through patients would help you forget. . . ."

"It would go a long way toward that, yes," Cobb answered.

"Then it's settled." Cyril rose and reached for his hat.

"As far as I'm concerned," Cobb agreed. "But how am I going to get her to leave without him?"

"I think that my son will need to see some doctors in New York while you take an extended honeymoon. I think you'll recommend it."

"Yes, but—"

"They'll recommend he stay for treatment awhile." Cyril reached for the door. "A long while. It might be best if you didn't wait. The boy could always join you later."

"Much later," Cobb agreed as he opened the door and Cyril reached out his right hand.

"She won't like it," Cobb said.

"You're right." Cyril released the door and folded his arms patiently. "Perhaps we should just forget it. You could stay right here in Ohio lancing boils and stitching gashes and someone else could use that new X-ray machine I've ordered. And get a rather beautiful young woman as a bonus."

Cobb licked his lips. "If I don't marry her, Morrow'll come sweeping her off her feet, and then where will either of us be?"

"I'll be in New York with the boy. Where will *you* be?" Cyril shrugged. "I'd say you'd just better not fail."

Cobb turned a pale shade of green, which, Cyril noted on his way out, went rather well with his plaid suit.

Chapter Twenty-three

Ethan didn't like any of it. Didn't like the way Corny and Cyril were suddenly talking about Worth's lack of progress and taking him to see the doctor in New York. He didn't like the fact that he hadn't even seen the buckaroo in several days because either Corny was examining him or Cyril was in with him or there was some other feeble excuse that kept him barred from the room.

Silver, too, had refused to see him, but that didn't stop her face from swimming in front of him now as he sat at the kitchen table in Della and Peter's house. He picked up the pencil with a heavy sigh and tried again to capture Amelia's eyes on the paper. Lord, but she and Sterling and the buckaroo all shared the same huge pair of blue eyes that melted his resolve every time he looked at them.

Eyes were the hardest for him. Maybe because they could tell, or hide, so much about a person. He'd seen the shutters close in front of Sterling's eyes when last he'd looked in her face. *I can't love you*, they said with finality, despite how sure he was that she did.

He'd been so angry, he'd had to fight the urge to shake her silly, until all that armor she'd wrapped herself in came loose and that soft woman hiding inside could come out and let herself be loved.

"Aren't you finished yet?" Della asked him, coming into the kitchen in her dressing gown despite the fact that it was nearly time for James to be home from school.

"You wash Jimbo's underwear?" he asked her as she shuffled toward the sink and filled a dirty glass with water.

"I hate it when you call him that," she said, lifting the glass to her lips.

He pushed back against the table and got to her just before she actually started drinking. "For God's sake, Della! Look at yourself!" He'd been quick to censure Peter for seeking comfort outside his marriage. Maybe too quick.

He spilled out the water and washed the glass, dried it with the semi-clean edge of a towel, and refilled it for his sister, who stared out the window over the sink as if she expected to see her son Samuel at any moment.

"He isn't coming, Del. Not now, not ever. You've got to go on without him. Let him rest in peace and take care of what God left you."

He wrapped his arms around her and rested his chin on her head. Within his embrace she shook, no matter how hard she tried to stand stiff, cold.

"James needs you, Del. He's alone and scared and he feels guilty for reminding you that Sambo isn't here."

She twirled in his arms so that she was facing him, and squinted up, leaning back until she could get him in focus. Her breath smelled like whiskey and sleep when she spoke. "He needs *you*, Eth."

"Not me, honey. I'm leaving." This time there was no false bravado in his voice. This time he knew he was going and that it would be for good.

"Take him with you." Della's eyes were dry and clear. The trembling had stopped. "For his sake mostly, but for mine too. I pull myself together and he walks through that door and I—"

Out front a door opened and swung shut, slapping closed. Boots clomp, clomp, clomped across the floor.

Della stared at the door, her breath caught in her chest, her heart beating rapidly against him as she clutched at his sleeves.

"Mama?"

She swallowed hard, closed her eyes, bit the tiny tip of tongue that protruded between her teeth.

"Uncle Eth?"

"In here, son," Ethan called back softly, stroking his sister's hair and whispering to her. "It's James, Della. James is home."

The boy came tentatively into the kitchen, his books hanging by a strap from his hand. Della studied him, lifted her gaze beyond his shoulder, and then extricated herself from Ethan's arms.

"Didn't get to the wash," she told him.

"Good day at school?" Ethan asked his nephew. He wiped his sweaty palms on his pants and fished another glass out of the sink. "Get some milk out of the icebox and I'll clean you up a glass."

"Your aunt Sissy dropped you off some cookies," Della said, passing James without touching the boy. "You save some," she warned him. "You hear me?"

"Yes, ma'am," the boy said, his eyes on her back as she left the room with her feet dragging against the wooden floor as if it was too great an effort to lift them.

"So," Ethan said, pouring some milk for each of them. "Good day?"

James looked at him with utter disgust. "Julia got a gold star for spelling, same as every day. Cara got to give out the papers. Bobby Whelan had to stand in the corner and he's got to bring a note home."

This last he mumbled. Since there was no love lost between the boys, Ethan was surprised that James wasn't happier about the beating Bobby was sure to get from his father. "What'd he do?" Ethan asked, sitting back down at the table and putting aside the drawing of Amelia Phillips. It was probably a stupid wedding gift anyway, a sketch of the bride's mother done by a man who was in love with her.

"Opened the door when someone was in the privy."

Ethan pushed the plate of Sissy's cookies at James.

It'd been good to see his oldest sister up and around. And how excited she'd been for him about Oliver's offer! She kept saying that she'd known something good would come out of such tragedy.

"Wide open for the world to see." James pushed his glass away and fingered the plate of cookies without taking one.

"Not by accident, I take it," Ethan said. He remembered Corny doing the same annoying things when he was a boy. But Ethan had had Bart to watch the door, or Charlie. "So who was it?"

James continued to fiddle with the cookies on the plate, silent.

"Oh." Damn, but nobody gave this kid a break. Nobody in Van Wert anyway. What if he did take him to California? Could he really be a father to the boy? Maybe Sissy was right about some good coming as a result of Worth's accident. And while maybe Ethan didn't deserve the chance to start over, James sure did. "How would you feel about coming to California with me, Jimbo?" he asked, picking up the pencil again and sketching the man in the photograph.

He glanced up to see the light in James's eyes. "I'd walk there if you'd let me come," he said in a whisper.

"Wouldn't be much good to me when you got there," Ethan said with a cough that let him cover the crack in his voice as he bent to his drawing.

No matter how hard he tried, the cheeks were still too full. He supposed it was the dimples that gave that impression. The chin, too, was deeply cleft, almost split in two. The nose was small, and he made a slight mark for it, ignoring for the moment the mustache. It was a waste of time anyway. Who wanted a picture of Cyril Phillips's driver? He laid the pencil down and got up to refill James's glass of milk. There was something about that face . . . something so familiar.

James turned the sketch around so that it faced him. "When you get done drawing the buckaroo," he asked, and Ethan felt the color drain from his face, "will you do me?"

* * *

"I don't understand why you think he has to stay in bed again," Sterling said as Benjamin tucked the sheet in tightly around Worth.

"I wanna—" Worth began, but the doctor put his finger to the boy's lips, careful not to disturb the bandage that still covered his chin.

"We can't always have what we want," Benjamin said. "Especially when we're young. Sometimes we have to wait and wait for things to turn out as we want them."

"But he was doing so well," Sterling said, trying to loosen the sheets slightly. It was too hot to wrap her poor honey lamb up like some Egyptian mummy. "You said you'd keep exercising him if I asked Ethan not to—"

"Where's Eth?" Worth asked. She covered her lips, but it was too late to take back the words. No matter how careful she was, she always seemed to bring up his name at the wrong time.

"Mr. Morrow's gotten himself in a little bit of trouble," Benjamin told her honey lamb. "And he's going far away until it blows over."

"Actually it seems he's going to California, too, like us. Only he'll be with Aunt Imogene and Uncle Oliver and you'll be with Dr. Cobb and me," Sterling said. "He's not in trouble at all. You remember that he was leaving when your accident happened. Now that you're so much better, he's ready to go."

"We gonna see him in California?" Worth asked, trying to reach his cowboy hat on the night table. "So he can see Honesty?"

"You mean so *you* can see Honesty, don't you?" she asked.

"No," her son said, shaking his head adamantly.

"Honesty's mine. The cowboy said. Or the knight?" He lowered his eyebrows in confusion.

Benjamin looked up at her as if both she and her son had lost their minds. "You don't really believe that your aunt and uncle are moving out there, do you? Your aunt's been saying that for years."

"They're really going," Sterling said. She'd seen the money spread out all over the bed in her aunt's room. She'd seen the deed.

"Your father know this?" Benjamin asked. He pulled at his mustache, and clumps of wax fell onto his lapel.

Worth squirmed in the bed, still trying to reach his hat.

"Don't do that," Benjamin said. "Lie perfectly still." He handed the boy the hat.

"But the doctor from New York said that exercise was the best thing for him," Sterling said, yanking at the sheets frantically until Benjamin stilled her hands, pulling her away from the bed and holding her wrists.

"Listen to me," he said, holding her to him until she quieted. "I spoke to the same New York doctor as your friend Morrow. Called him this morning. He wants to see the boy. And until he does, he wants him to stay flat and quiet."

"What? Did he say why? He's so much better, Ben. This treatment's been working." She tried to pull her hands away, but Benjamin kept a firm circle around each wrist.

He looked at the boy and then pushed her gently toward the doorway. Once they were outside the room, he shut the door behind him.

"Dr. Steinway says the boy won't get any better than this unless he gets special therapy." He looked up at her and frowned. "I thought I told you that I preferred flatter shoes. It irritates me to look up at a woman, and you do it to annoy me. Do you need to challenge me at every turn?"

"Don't be ridiculous. I just haven't had a chance to

buy new boots," she said, and bent her knees slightly. Her father had often accused her of trying to challenge him too. "I'm sorry. What do you mean he won't get better? He can almost stand."

"For God's sake, woman! Face the facts. What do you call those bruises on his chin and nose? Merit badges? Your father and I have discussed it, and the boy will go to New York with him. Then, when he is well enough, Cyril will bring him out to us."

Sterling gripped his arm, the hallway spinning around her. "Oh no! No, no, no! If Worth is going to New York, so am I."

Benjamin shook his head. "I can't just leave my practice, spend a month in New York, and then head out to California. I can't believe you would even suggest it."

"You can stay here," Sterling said. She didn't care what Ben did. She wasn't sending her son off with her father.

The man's face flushed. "Our wedding is set for Saturday, Sterling. And it will take place then. I'm not about to be made a fool of again."

"I only want to postpone it," she said, her eyes on the closed door to her son's room.

"You don't want what's best for your son?" he asked, tipping her chin up. "He may need lifelong care, Sterling. Care I could give him."

"Why can't you treat him now?" She lowered her voice. "You know I can't trust my father."

"You can trust me. You know you can. I've kept your secret, and I'll continue to do so. There's no reason for anyone to know that your sweet little boy is a bastard, or that his lovely mama made a tragic mistake, is there? And if your father doesn't bring the boy, we'll come after him. You do believe he wants the boy to get well, don't you?"

"No one will know your sweet little boy is a bastard."
"Don't use that—"

Benjamin held her shoulders and shook them slightly.

"It's what he is, Sterling. A bastard. And if you're not careful, it's going to come out. And after all that hard work to hide it. How do you think it's going to look, leaving me at the altar to follow your brother to New York? People are bound to jump to the obvious conclusion."

"But I've been taking care of him all along," she reasoned, a niggling piece of her knowing he was right.

"But now your father, *his* father, as far as everyone else is concerned, is here. You know, don't you, that the moment we're married, he plans to head back to New York?" He looked deeply into her eyes as if that should mean more to her than it did.

"And take my son."

"And bring your son to the doctors there. Don't be so melodramatic. My point is, he'll be gone from Van Wert, where he can hurt the people you love."

He meant Ethan. Benjamin knew that her father would eventually get around to Ethan.

"But I want Worth with us."

"Whole? Or lame? Sterling, honey, I wish I could fix him, but I'm just a country doctor. I don't have the tools, the knowledge, the expertise. We'll go set up my practice, and by then the boy will be ready to get on with his life."

"Do you swear to me that I'll have my son?"

Benjamin Cobb let go of her arms and took a step back. "You have to ask me that? It hurts me to say this, Sterling, but who's the one who isn't trustworthy here? Whose lie is it we're protecting?"

* * *

"Took nearly an hour to get that connection," Charlie said when Ethan found Mrs. Wells on the telephone in the mercantile. "Granddaughter's real sick out there in the Dakotas. Why don't you go up and say hello to your newest nephew while she finishes telling Sara Beth how to make a wet shirt?"

On a piece of brown package wrap on the counter, Charlie continued to take notes on Mrs. Wells's directions.

"A hay-flower decoction," Mrs. Wells shouted. "Cold, like it says in Monsignor Kneipp's book. Sari, stop crying! You're all she's got and you gotta have your wits about you. . . . Use one of Joseph's shirts. . . . Sari, stop that crying and listen to me!"

Ethan supposed that Mrs. Wells might be a while, so he nodded at Charlie and headed for the living quarters above the store. As he climbed the stairs, he tried to wipe the picture of Henry, Cyril Phillips's driver, from his mind. Telling himself it was none of his business hadn't changed the fact that without the mustache, without the small dark eyes, without the waves of dark hair, it was Worth's face he had drawn. Dimples you could hide raisins in. A cleft that would hold a penny.

Henry, not Cyril, was Worth's father. No wonder the man didn't want the boy around. He was proof of his wife's infidelity, and the child's face was a banner headline proclaiming his parentage, right there in the household.

None of my business, he told himself again as he knocked at Risa's door.

"Eth!" she squealed at the sight of him, hugging him to two boulders that stuck out from her chest like cannonballs waiting to be loaded. "Ow!"

"Sorry," he said, backing away as she rolled her shoulders forward in pain. What a woman went through! And over and over again. He thought of tiny Sterling, and the perfect baby she would present to Benjamin Cobb one day. "You got any carbo wafers?"

"What's the matter? You look a little green around the gills," Risa said, still moving awkwardly after Zach's birth as she lumbered over toward the sink.

"I've had to swallow a lot lately," he admitted. "But I'm going to California. For real. Leaving Saturday."

"And taking James, from what he says." Risa handed

him the medicine and put up a finger. "Uh! That's the little one, hungry as always, and thank goodness for that."

"I guess I'll go," he said, chewing on the tablet and waiting for it to calm his stomach. It was hard to imagine that he'd had an even worse taste in his mouth to begin with.

"Eth?" She was headed for the back room, her top two buttons already unfastened. "I'm glad you're going this time. It feels right. And I'm glad you're taking James. We'll be at the station to see you off."

"Aren't you going to the wedding? Ought to be quite the big affair." How often did the richest girl in town get married? The answer came back to him: once too often.

"I don't understand that girl," Risa said, disappearing into the baby's room and coming back in with his round little nephew, whose name once again was Zachary. "She was in here the other day asking after you, you know."

He didn't care. Not at all. Not a bit. Still . . .

"What'd she say?"

"She was buying a frame for some picture. Paid for it with pennies. I think it's the first thing she's ever bought for herself here." She had turned her back to him, juggling the fussing baby and talking over her shoulder.

"What'd she say?"

"Just wanted to know how you were doing, whether I'd seen you. . . ."

"Risa?" It felt like there was something she wasn't telling him.

"You really going to let her slip through your fingers and into the hands of that creep?"

He brought a chair up behind his sister-in-law and pushed gently on her shoulders. "That creep can offer her a lot more than I can, and that's what she wants."

"Well, if she's so well fixed, and he's doing so well,

why would she sell her mother's brooch?" Risa sat, and adjusted Zachary in her arms, then turned her head to stare at him.

"For twenty-eight dollars?" he asked—the money she'd given him the night he'd last seen her, touched her.

"About that. She bought the cheapest white satin—"

Ethan didn't hear the rest of what she had to say. He was too busy stomping down the steps and cornering his brother.

"Give me her damn pin," he said, not caring that several old biddies were on line in front of him. "I'll bring you the money tonight."

Charlie gestured with his head at the glass case at the far end of the counter. "Take it," he said. "Just don't break anything, huh?"

Ethan lifted the glass carefully, his eyes on the gold-and-pearl brooch that she hadn't wanted to die without.

Risa was right. If she was so well fixed, and he knew firsthand her daddy was, why did she need to sell her precious pin to help him leave town?

"Telephone's available now," Charlie shouted after him.

He'd almost forgotten all about calling the doctor in New York.

*   *   *

It had taken nearly an hour for Sterling to get Worth to sleep. An hour of trying to tell him a story while he asked question after question about Ethan and Honesty and why he couldn't ride his bike. An hour of talking without saying anything, fielding questions without answers, shushing the same fears she faced herself.

And now someone was banging on the front door with enough force to wake the dead, never mind the barely sleeping. She crawled off Worth's bed and tiptoed to the door. Just opening it a crack, she was able to hear Carl say that both she and Worth were not receiving.

Ethan's angry voice boomed up the stairs, knocking into walls and bouncing into her. "If she's here, she damn well better get her little bottom down those steps, or I'll come up after her."

"Sir, she specifically said that you—" Carl tried.

"I have something for you," he yelled over Carl. "And if you want me to get the heck out of your life, you'll come down here and get it so that I can return it to you and go."

"Sir, the boy is asleep and—"

"Still? Not if I shout a little louder, I wouldn't think."

She hurried down the stairs, trying to quiet him as she came. "Lower your voice," she tried to order him, but that good, kind face stopped her words in her throat. A few days without him hadn't made him ordinary, the way she had so hoped. Just the sight of him started that coil inside her spinning like a toy top out of control.

"Yours, madam," he said, holding out her mother's brooch in his open palm. As she reached for it, his hand closed around it. "Not so fast. You want to tell me why you sold it in the first place?"

"You needed money to leave here. I wanted you to go."

"So much so that you'd sell your mama's brooch? The one you wanted on you when you died?"

Her cheeks grew hot under his stare. How could they not? He was reminding her of the time she spent in his arms when she thought the world might end.

"You must want me out of your life pretty damn badly to go selling this heirloom of yours. I know Sissy's got a few of my mama's things and they mean the world to her. Why didn't you just ask your papa for the money if you were so desperate to get rid of me? I'm sure he'd have paid a damn sight more than Charlie to see me out of your life and the boy's."

"Because it was important to me," she said, her hands behind her back where she dug her nails into her palms harder and harder still. "Because I wanted to be the one to make you go." *To let you go. Because I had to know, in the years to come, that in my whole life I'd done something honorable. I'd kept you safe from my father and I'd set you free.*

He opened his hand, all marked with the ridges and dips of her mother's pin, but again when she reached for it, he closed his fist.

"Do you mean to tease me?" she asked, jerking her hand away from his.

He almost laughed. "I think that's your department, Miss Phillips, isn't it?" He stepped nearer to her and slipped a finger within the tight collar of her dress. "Let me put it back where it belongs," he said, and fussed with the brooch at her throat.

There were beads of perspiration on his upper lip. It was, after all, July, and the sun was hot and the air was close. He smelled of bleach and sweat, and heat seemed to pour from his body with the intent of making her dizzy. He was close enough that his breath lifted the tendrils of hair that had come loose while she lay with Worth on his bed.

How Worth would miss this man. Benjamin had insisted that he not be mentioned, just the way she had not been allowed to speak of her mother after her death. It had been a lonely, solitary mourning and had led to a lonely life.

"There." He patted the brooch and stepped back. "So then you love him?" he asked as if he couldn't resist the question one last time.

"I need security," she answered.

"Oh, my poor, poor Silver. When will you learn that there is no security without love. Without love, how can you know what tomorrow will hold?"

"I see it very differently. Love isn't something you should put much stock in. It can disappear in a moment, and if that's all that's holding two people together, what will bind them when it fades?" *When one of*

*them finds out the truth about the other and all the illu-
sions are shattered to bits?*

"You know, I told Sissy and Noah that I was worse off
for having had the dream yanked from beneath my feet.
I was wrong, though. It must be worse still not to have
the dream at all." There was more pity in his voice than
contempt.

One thing she'd never expected was his pity. She'd
been prepared for anger, ready for hate. His sympathy
was like a warm knife plunging into her frozen heart.
But she couldn't back down now. A door opened upstairs, but no footsteps followed. Well, she'd give her
father an earful of what he wanted to hear.

"Your wishes won't ever come true, Silver, because
you're afraid to even wish them."

"Oh?" she asked, swallowing hard, her chest so tight
she could hardly force a breath through it. "Better to
have some pie-in-the-sky view of nights on the prairie
in some dirt hut that love is supposed to transform into
a castle, I suppose? Well, I live in a real world where love
is an extravagance even I can't afford. It's not even
something that interests me. In fact you've nothing to
offer that interests me, so why don't you just go ahead
and finally get out of Van Wert?"

"I'll go." He said it quietly, all traces of anger gone
from his voice. "You know, I'd give anything, do anything, to make you happy. I don't know anyone who
deserves it more. And if the only way to do that is to
leave, I'll be on the train tomorrow."

She stared at him, stupid and mute, the pain in her
chest so sharp now that all she could take were the shal-
lowest of breaths.

"You'll tell the buckaroo to work hard at getting well,
won't you? You'll tell him that I'm waiting to hear that
he's riding that bike I got him?"

She might have nodded. Or it might be she was still
just staring.

"You know," he said, "more than anything except to be your husband, I wanted to be his father."

She watched his back, pains racking her chest in waves until she had to lean against the wall till he was out of sight. Upstairs a door closed. From somewhere at the back of the house Abigail appeared, taking Sterling around her waist and helping her up the stairs.

"It doesn't seem fair that a man's value is measured in what he can grab for himself and a woman's value is measured by what she's willing to sacrifice," the woman said to her as they passed Sterling's father in the hall and Abigail opened the door to Sterling's room. "I sure would like to find the man who was willing to do the sacrificing and the woman who was willing to grab."

Sterling rubbed at her arms, unable to stop the chills that sent gooseflesh up and down them. She could feel the cold sweat beading on her forehead beneath her bangs. The shaking started, and Abigail helped her to the bright yellow chair in which only a few years ago she'd nursed her son, cried herself to sleep, and wished on stars.

"I'll get you a basin, honey," Abigail said softly as the first waves of nausea assaulted her.

Ethan Morrow was leaving tomorrow. Of course it would be tomorrow. Her wedding day.

* * *

He was a man in a trance as he walked into Oliver Harrington's study, nodded his greetings at both Oliver and Genie, and sat in one of the plush leather chairs without speaking.

"I can't stop her," Oliver said with a shrug of his shoulders. "Never been any use to anyone. Now I don't even have the means to help her if she'd let me. And I've got to worry about Genie."

"The cowboy's not going to let her marry that plaid-covered excuse, Ollie, so stop blubbering in your beer." She pulled a fan out from her sleeve and looked at it with disgust. "There you are! Now that I don't even want you. But where's . . ."

She continued to hunt for something up her right sleeve, her left hand going farther and farther up until she looked like that Houdini fellow who did the magic tricks.

"I'm afraid that I'm not the man your niece wants," he admitted, rubbing at some dirt on the knee of his pants. "So I thought I'd head out for California tomorrow and get things started."

Lord, if that didn't sound ridiculous. He'd just leave tomorrow like he was going to Bellefontaine, or maybe as far as Columbus.

"Can't watch her do it?" Genie asked him, giving up on the right arm and switching sleeves. "What do you suppose makes men so stupid?"

"Too much scotch," Oliver answered.

"It's in the blood," Ethan said. It was what made them wild and reckless enough to do things for which they had to spend years repenting. It was what made them think with their fists or their privates and make mistakes. "It's a hunger in the blood."

"Nonsense!" Imogene answered, pulling an official-looking paper out from the shoulder of her shirtwaist. "Women have just as much hunger in the blood. That's how the problem started after all."

"You mean Adam and Eve and the apple?" Ethan tipped his head back, stretching his neck and wishing he could see through the ceiling and know what Sterling was doing at that moment. Probably trying on her wedding dress. He looked at the Persian carpet on the floor instead.

"Ppfft!" Genie said. "Men are so stupid. Can't see what's there in front of their noses. Now, women . . . they stick their noses in everyone else's business until they know the truth. But men—they want it on a silver platter, so to speak. And a woman just never knows what a man will do with the truth."

"Genie," Oliver said, his voice holding a note of warning. "A man knows the value of keeping someone's counsel."

Genie made another noise. "I want to give you this before Cyril comes back," she said, handing him the document. "It's a copy of Amelia's death certificate from New York."

"Genie!" Oliver stood, reaching for the paper, but she waved him away.

"He needs it to settle the deed on the land, Ollie. You just give it to the lawyer so that they can fix up the papers right. I don't want Cyril thinking that just because Amelia was stupid enough to love him and trust him, I'll do the same."

"So Amelia loved him?" Ethan asked, looking at Oliver doubtfully. If she loved him, then what had she been doing with Henry? "He's not an easy man to love."

"No," Oliver agreed. "But their life was all right, I suppose, as long as Amelia didn't cross him."

"He doesn't seem a man who would tolerate being challenged," Ethan agreed.

"Cyril? I swear he's got a book with every wrong ever done, and he ticks off his opportunities for revenge," Oliver said.

"Our list is very long," Imogene explained. "Because of Sterling of course. And then, well, there's no point in telling you. He's already done his worst to you, hasn't he?"

Had he? Just because he'd given Cobb an incentive to marry his daughter? It was Ethan himself who'd made a life that left him with nothing to offer the woman but hope and dreams. And there was no one to blame for that but himself.

"Son?" Oliver leaned forward, poking him across his desk. "Maybe if you told her you loved her . . ."

He smiled at Oliver and Genie both, getting to his feet. "It had occurred to me, but without a house and an income to back it up, it isn't worth much, is it?"

"Maybe you have more than you think," Genie said in her maddening way. "Maybe you've been looking at the wrong side of the puzzle pieces, cowboy. But it's not your fault. Not yet anyway."

Ethan held out the death certificate to Genie. "You'd better hold on to this. No one's gonna stop me from preparing the soil, and you can take care of the legal matters when you come out. If everything seems as good as it sounds when I get there, I'll write you and you can—"

"You take this," Genie said, pushing the paper back at him. "It's the only hope we've got left. You take it now. Later won't do us much good."

Chapter Twenty-four

For more than six years he'd been getting ready to leave Van Wert. He supposed he was as ready that Saturday morning as he'd ever been. More ready, when he considered that if he wasn't gone by three, he'd no doubt hear the church bells ringing for Cornucopia and Silver.

He'd sent James over to Harrington Manor with his fiddle and the picture of Amelia Phillips. The fiddle had been an afterthought. He'd meant to take it to California, but as he'd begun wrapping it for the trip, he'd remembered the music she'd coaxed from the old strings and knew that he'd never get any sounds from the violin again but lonely, heartbreaking ones. He'd no desire to torture himself, so he'd sent it with James to Silver.

Let her remember, he thought, every time she lifted it to play, how he had stood behind her and raised her hand with his. And every time hail fell, let her think of his hands on her breasts, and every time the sun kissed her cheeks, let her think of how he'd kissed her at the picnic.

To her he willed all the good memories, and kept the misery for himself.

He'd said good-bye to all his sisters and brothers. The various small fry had hugged his knees, his thighs, his waist. Peter had agreed to James's trip and had promised Ethan he'd give his marriage another, harder try. Peter'd hurt two women, he'd admitted, and the guilt was heavy on his mind.

Ethan knew the power of guilt all too well and had settled for asking that Peter simply try.

On Friday night Ethan had had a short talk with Miller and Tessie Winestock, wishing them well with the baby they were expecting. He'd admitted to Miller that he'd come to love Worth Phillips as much as any man loved a son. He'd gotten all choked up, and Tessie'd had to fix him a nice cup of tea, into which Miller had slipped a bit of brandy. They were good people, the Winestocks, who knew better than most how precious a child was.

In the morning he'd collected his bills for the roofing and fencing. There was only this one errand, the most important one, still left to be done.

Even on the landing above the infirmary the smell of carbolic acid was overwhelming. He supposed a doctor got used to the smells of medicine just the way a farmer got used to manure.

He knocked on Corny's door, and a faint humming grew louder as the doctor came to answer his call.

"Morrow." The smile on Corny's face faltered and then returned twice as bright. He gestured down toward his clean white shirt, his black dress pants, and shiny shoes. "Just getting dressed. Come to wish me luck on my wedding day?"

"What kind of luck do you think you'll need?" Ethan asked. After all, he was marrying Silver. Could a man be luckier still?

"You wish it was you, don't you?" Corny asked. Ethan noticed that his hair was thinning slightly on top after all. "A month or two and she'll be carrying my child inside her. She's even prettier with more meat on her bones. And her breasts!" He gestured with his hands like he was weighing summer melons. "You wish it was you, don't you, Morrow?"

"You know what it's taking not to wipe that stupid smile off your face, Cobb? Not to beat the crap out of you and—"

"All brawn, Morrow. That's all you ever were. You got height and weight on me, but then, she's just a little bit of a thing, our girl, isn't she?"

It welled up inside him, the hatred, the disgust—and he lifted Cobb from the floor by his lapels until his toes were barely dragging.

"If you hurt her, I'll know. I'll find you, and she'll never have to worry again about how big your parts are, if you get my drift."

"I'm not likely to hurt her. After all, she's going to be my wife."

He let the doctor down slowly.

"We'll have a nice life. A few kids, a rich daddy back east. Everyone will wind up happy. Except of course you." Corny rested his chin on his hand and smiled innocently at Ethan.

"Don't worry about me," he said. "I'll be just dandy. Long as I hear that Silver and the buckaroo are all right."

"Worth? Cyril'll make sure the boy's got whatever he needs. He's seeing Steinway next week. Thursday, I believe. Set up the appointment myself. Two o'clock. Costs a pretty penny, that specialist. Lucky thing the boy's got a rich papa, huh? And a doctor for a— He's going to need a great deal of care."

Ethan sat down in one of the doctor's comfy-looking chairs. "I thought he was doing so well. What happened?"

Corny raised his eyebrows and shrugged.

"Between you and me," Ethan asked. "He is gonna be okay, isn't he?"

"Would Cyril Phillips be interested in him otherwise?"

Ethan checked the clock on the doctor's wall.

"I promised him the dog, you know," Ethan said. "Noah says he'll hold him until you're ready to go to California."

"The boy's going east with the old man," Corny said,

shaking his head. "At least to start. And nobody wants your damn mutt."

"You don't care that the boy is counting on him?"

"That was your mistake, Morrow, wasn't it? What number does that make, or have we stopped counting?"

Ethan sighed. How could he have promised the buckaroo the dog without making sure the adults in his life would allow it? "You will get him a dog once you're settled, won't you? Every boy ought to have a dog."

"Yeah, and a bicycle, according to you," Cobb said, reaching for a white silk band bow. "Well, I guess we've both got places to be."

"Aren't you getting ready a little early?" Ethan asked. "You gonna sit around like that all day?"

Cobb looked down at himself and put the tie back on the table. "I suppose it's a little early," he admitted. "I guess I'm what you'd call eager."

"I don't blame you," Ethan said, rising. "But you take care of her, Cobb. And the boy. They deserve it."

Cobb smiled broadly, patting Ethan on the back as he showed him the door. "Not to worry, old man. She'll get just what she deserves."

* * *

"But you can't just have a man's dog," Sterling tried to explain to Worth. "A dog is like a child, honey. Honesty belongs to and with Mr. Morrow."

"But the cowboy said that the dragon was at the door with a note for Prince Perfect." He wiggled in the invalid's chair, trying to loosen the binding that Benjamin had used to strap him in.

"Dr. Cobb said you've got to be very still, honey lamb," she said, coming to kneel beside him. "He says that the doctor in New York thinks that there might be a piece of bone that could shift and hurt you." *Paralyze*, he'd said, wrapping the blankets around him and belting him into the chair.

"I want Honesty!" he said, hitting the arm of his

chair with his fist like a little king. "He's my dragon! Eth said that the knight left the dragon for the prince!"

"What would you do with a dog in New York?" she asked him as if it were ridiculous. "Once you get out to California, Dr. Cobb and I will get you two dogs."

She sank from her knees to the floor, resting her head against the chair. Worth put his hand on her head soothingly, stroking it gently. "Don't worry," he said softly. In the distance she heard the train whistle whine. "Cowboy'll bring me Honesty. He promised."

My, how the sound of a train could carry on a warm morning breeze. Right in through an open window to run right over a body's heart.

"Cowboy'll fix it, Ster," he whispered, petting her head with his tiny hand.

* * *

"Comfortable?" Ethan asked James once he'd stowed their cases in the rack above their heads, the shelf at the front of the railroad car, under their seats, and where one of James's feet ought to go.

The boy grinned up at him. He had a small valise under his arm, a sack of his aunt Sissy's cookies on his lap, and Honesty on the one foot that he'd managed to find a space for on the floor. "Yup!"

"You got anything to read?" Ethan asked him. He'd packed two of his favorite old books about the West for the boy, not knowing how long he could make polite conversation with a nine-year-old.

"You don't have to entertain me, Uncle Eth," James said, shifting in his seat to watch out the window as their family got smaller and smaller and Van Wert threatened to become a memory. "You gonna read?" the boy asked after a while.

"Huh?" He'd been thinking about Worth Phillips's father. His real one. It must have been awful for him not to be able to claim his own son. But not as bad as it was for the buckaroo. Two fathers, and neither of them

could parent the boy. "No, think I'll just sort things
through."

He couldn't remember when he'd last had time to
just think. He was too busy feeling to give anything real
thought.

At least the buckaroo had Silver. She mothered him
probably better than his own mother would have, what
with the way they raised rich kids in the city. And
there'd been his aunt Genie.

Poor, confused Genie. Ethan would have liked to have
seen her reaction to his drawing of Amelia. Of course,
she'd been mistaken about the photograph. Either it was
dated wrong or it was quite a while before Amelia's
death, considering that the buckaroo was barely three
and the note on the back of the photograph read 1891.

"Think we'll be stopping soon?" James asked him.

"Mmm. Fort Wayne's not far." He patted his pockets,
wondering what he'd done with Steinway's telephone
number. He'd meant to call him from Charlie's store,
but there'd been the brooch to distract him. The doctor
would have to accept payments over time, but Ethan
would be the one to bear the cost of Worth's care. He'd
been willing to do a lot more, but the boy's father
wouldn't let him.

He pulled the valise out from under James's arm,
tweaking the boy's belly as he did so. "Why don't you
have one of those cookies Aunt Sissy made you?" he
suggested as he dug for his envelope of important papers.

"I'm guessing trains," James said, unrolling the top of
the bag and sticking in his hand to see what shape
Sissy's cookies were.

"You're probably right," Ethan agreed distractedly,
fingering the death certificate Genie had pushed at him.
She'd had such faith in him, and he'd let her down. Let
them all down. He unfolded the document. *I hereby cer-
tify*, it read, *that I attended the deceased, Amelia Weldridge Phillips, from 9th November 1891 to 14 July 1892,*

*that I last saw her alive on the 14th of July 1892 about
four o'clock p.m., and that to the best of my knowledge
and belief the cause of her death was as hereunder written.
Cause: pneumonia. Contributing cause: bronchial infec-
tion. Witness my hand this 14th day of July 1892, in the
City of New York, Borough of New York.*

Eighteen hundred and ninety-two! He smacked his
forehead. "Idiot!" he said aloud, everything falling into
place at once. "Idiot! Idiot!"

"Uncle Ethan?" James's big brown eyes stared up at
him. So did several other pairs scattered throughout the
car.

Cyril Phillips had thrown her out, that bastard!

The word scorched his brain. *Worth? What kind of a
stupid name is Worth? Worth everything!*

Surely worth pretending she was the boy's sister.
She'd never called him her brother. Not once! No, he
was her "honey lamb."

She'd had to sell her brooch because her father
wouldn't give her a dime. Not unless it got him what he
wanted.

But what exactly was it that he wanted?

"Get everything together," he told James, hurrying to
gather their belongings. He nudged Honesty with his
foot. "Wake up, you stupid dog. We've got to get off this
train."

"What's the matter, Uncle Eth?" James asked, hurrying to close his cookie bag, put the soldiers he played
with back into his valise, and close it.

"We've got to call Steinway," he said. He'd bet there
was no appointment on Thursday or any other day.
They hadn't let Ethan see Worth because he was better,
damn it, not worse! And if he was fine, why the hell was
Cyril taking him away from Sterling and to New York?

* * *

"Stop fidgeting. Only hooligans fidget." It was an annoying habit the boy had developed, running his first

finger around his thumb, rubbing over the nails incessantly. No doubt he'd picked it up from some unsavory character in the Harrington household. Cyril took the boy's hand firmly and placed it on the arm of his invalid's chair. Confining him was actually an extremely efficient and appealing method of getting the boy to New York. In fact it was proving useful just sitting in his room waiting for the time to pass before leaving for the station. On the train there would be no chasing the ruffian in the aisles, no sitting him on his lap or other nonsense.

Once he got the boy to New York, he could turn him over to his driver, Henry, at the station, and let the servant see to the child. Sometime during the following week he'd get Steinway to pay a house call, since the boy wasn't fit for going out into society yet.

But there wasn't any rush. Cobb had tested him thoroughly and it was clear that the boy was on his way to a full recovery. Steinway had assured him over the phone that the boy was making remarkable progress and there was no reason to believe it would end short of a full and complete recovery. Hell, the boy was already so well, he needed to be tied to the damn chair so as not to ruin all the plans before Cyril and Cobb had gotten them in motion.

Of course if the doctors were wrong, Cyril could always send the boy out to his mother and her new husband. Wouldn't that pompous ass just love a surprise package along with his new equipment! His wife's accident.

"I want Ster," the child said tediously.

"You've made that abundantly clear," Cyril said. "And I've told you that she is about to leave for the church."

"But I—"

"When I tell you something, that is the end of the subject. Do you understand me?" He'd let Sterling have the boy too long. It would take months of training before he'd be able to so much as tolerate the boy in the same room.

"But—" the child started again.

"You have been a problem since long before you were born," he said to the boy. "And you will cease to be a problem now, do you understand me?"

The boy shook his head, wide-eyed.

"You will," he said. This time there would be no mealy-mouthed mother's interference as there had been with his daughter. This time he would set the rules and no one would countermand them. And this time there would be a product he could be proud of. "Believe me, boy, you will."

*   *   *

"Because no one checked the damn train schedule," Benjamin said, trying to take Sterling's arm. "And they've got an appointment in New York on Monday with the specialist. Surely you wouldn't be so cruel as to keep that boy confined to that chair for a moment longer than he has to be just so that he could see us get married, which he won't understand anyway."

He thrust a package at her.

"And put these on while you're up there saying good-bye."

"I can't just—" she began, and saw the warning in his eyes.

"I will not be late to my own wedding," he said, grabbing her arm and pulling her close to him. "Will I?"

Yanking her arm away, she stood her ground. "And I will not be rushed into saying good-bye to my son. Don't forget you have as much to lose as I do, Benjamin. I know how much you want that machine and I know that without me you don't have a prayer of getting it."

"Sit down," he said, shoving her toward the stairs and pushing her bottom onto one step. He yanked up her foot and began unlacing the white dress patent boot with the leather heel. "You think we're on even ground, do you?" he asked, towering over her and ripping the shoe from her foot.

"I can do it," she said, but he pushed her hand aside and roughly lifted her other foot.

"Let's see just what *you're* getting—a doctor who can care for your crippled son. A man who's willing to overlook your roll in the gutter. You think I'd be so easy to replace?"

He ripped open the package and showed her the flat black boots as if he cared whether she liked them.

"Put them on. Now what do I get? A woman who's known another man's touch, borne another man's child, and the result of that union. And I get a father-in-law who plans to own me like he owns everything else."

She sat with the boots in her hand, wondering if she still had any choices. Ethan was gone, and her aunt and uncle would have to fight their own battles, never mind hers. She was up against her father and this man, and her first concern as always had to be for Worth. Surely her father was more of a danger to her and her son than Benjamin was. "If you feel this way, why are you marrying me?"

"Tie them," he said, pointing at the shoes. "I don't want to be late." He crossed his arms and waited until he saw that she was obeying him.

"There are several reasons for our marriage. One—you're beautiful. Turn-and-stare beautiful. No one, no matter what I've accomplished, has ever envied me. Marrying you would change that. Two—you're shorter than I am, a matter of no small import to me. Three—you've retained your figure and your attractiveness despite motherhood. Since I plan to have several children and have seen my share of women who have gone to seed, that, too, is important to me. Four—you have a soothing voice. And I want that machine."

"At least you're honest," she said, standing and finding that her gown covered the awful shoes so that no one would see them.

"Say good-bye to the boy," he said. "And your father. I told Winestock I'd have you there early so that he could talk to you about the duties of a wife."

"Are you sure he can't come with us?" she asked, crouching slightly so that Benjamin would seem even taller and maybe give in.

"You don't want what's best for him? Fine. I'll go tell your father that we've decided we'd rather have him crippled but with us than give him up for just a little while." He moved past her, stopping a few steps above her. "Shall I?"

Silently she shook her head and took the arm he offered.

"I'll go with you." He patted her hand and waited for her to nearly reach him, then continued up the stairs, one step ahead. "That'll make it easier, won't it?"

In his room Worth sat with tears running over his fat cheeks and hiding in his dimples. Abigail stood by, a handkerchief at the ready. "He wants the dog," Abigail said, raising her shoulders along with her eyebrows.

Sterling sat on the edge of the bed and took her son's hands into her own. "I love you more than anything in the world," she told him. "And I would do anything to make you happy."

"I don't wanna go with Papa," he said between sniffs.

"But," she continued, "I have to think about what will make you happy in the long run, not just right now. It might make you happy today to eat a whole cake, or a dozen ears of corn, but I can't let you because it would make you sick eventually, right?"

The boy shrugged, not willing to agree.

"And I could take you with me, and not let Papa bring you to the doctors in New York. And you would be happy today. But tomorrow, when you couldn't get up to play, you wouldn't be so happy. And I want you happy always, not just today."

The boy sniffed, and held out his arms to her. She did the best she could to hug him despite the fact that he was bound to his chair.

"The next time I see you, I want you to be running as fast as the wind." She sniffed and stood. "Don't forget, I love you," she said with a bright smile.

"We have to go now," Benjamin said, taking her arm gently and steering her from the room. "It'll be all right. You'll see. Like you said, in the long run you'll be happy."

She leaned against the wall outside her son's room, fondling the door foolishly.

There were two people in the world she loved. One of them was already headed due west and out of her life. The other one was about to board a train east.

"I'm sorry, Sterling," Ben whispered. "It's time to go."

Chapter Twenty-five

He'd stood by the door the whole way back from Fort Wayne, as if somehow he'd get there sooner that way. James and Honesty had stood beside him, James patting his arm every now and then in an effort to calm him, Honesty seeming to know he was going back to the buckaroo.

Three telephone calls in one day. Almost as many as he'd made in his whole life. And each one had the power to change that life forever. If he was in time. He prayed Risa was up to the task, and nearly laughed out loud at himself. Risa? For him she'd move mountains.

The squeal of metal wheels on metal tracks ran up his back as the train slowed at the Van Wert station. Before it came to a complete halt, Ethan had already thrown out his belongings and was helping James down with his.

Honesty jumped from the train and headed on into the station like a hound on the scent of a hare. Of course even an old ham sandwich could bring that dog to life.

But it couldn't make him growl and bark and snarl, so Ethan rushed in ready to smack the dog soundly for making a nuisance of himself.

"Cowboy!"

The buckaroo was in the damn invalid's chair, a blanket over his lap and legs. Beside him stood his grandfather, held at bay by one angry dog.

"Going somewheres?" Ethan asked as casually as he could.

"We're taking that train to New York," Cyril said. "As you well know. Call off your mutt before I have him removed."

"Don't let me stop you," Ethan said amiably. "But the boy isn't going anywheres."

"You don't know whom you're crossing, young man," Cyril warned, "or what it may lead to."

"Keep your threats for the Cobbs of the world, Phillips. All I've got that's worth anything is hope, and there's no way you can take that away from me."

"Can't I?" He raised one eyebrow. "Want to put it to the test?"

"What I want is to find the princess and . . ." He knelt beside the buckaroo, who was in the midst of a shine by Honesty and a good head rubbing by Jimbo. "Where's your . . . where's Ster, Buckaroo?"

He saw the hawk catch his mistake, saw the glint in his eye, and knew he would use it against him if he could. But now Ethan was the one who held all the cards, who held the truth.

"The church," Worth said, reaching out two chubby little arms to him.

"The church! Well, what better place for a miracle or two?" he asked, grabbing the handles of Worth's chair and taking off at breakneck speed, the wind whipping the buckaroo's hair, his squeal carrying behind them and mixing with the sounds of running feet both young and old.

He didn't look behind him once. After all, his future was in front of him.

* * *

Aunt Imogene's wheezing filled the church, accompanied by the staccato clicking of Risa Morrow's heels on the wooden floor as she ran back and forth between the window and Aunt Genie's side.

"Hold on, Mrs. Harrington," Risa kept telling Sterling's aunt, whose gasps seemed predicated on Risa's movements, improving whenever Risa hurried to the back of the church, worsening when she returned to Aunt Imogene's side.

Sterling doubted that her aunt was fooling anyone. It couldn't be clearer that whether her aunt's attack was the real thing, induced by her genuine distress at Sterling's marriage, or just an act, stemming from the same reason, Imogene Harrington was doing anything she could to postpone the inevitable.

"Feeling any better?" Risa asked as she returned for the fifth or sixth time.

"I don't know," Aunt Imogene answered. "Am I?" To which Risa threw up her hands and lifted her shoulders.

"I really think you should be better in seconds," Risa said while Benjamin took Aunt Genie's pulse and sighed heavily.

"Maybe someone should take her home," Benjamin said. "And we can get on with it."

Charlie Morrow began to cough, as did several other guests. "Maybe there's something in the air," he suggested. "I don't think moving Mrs. Harrington would be quite the—"

"Finally!" Risa said from the back of the church, and the door swung open with such force that it smacked loudly against the back wall.

In the doorway, silhouetted by the sun, was Ethan Morrow, whose broad shoulders and straight back Sterling would know anywhere, blinding sun or not. In front of him was Worth, in that awful invalid's chair, and behind him she thought she saw James and Honesty as well as her father.

"What the—?" Benjamin began, gripping her elbow so tightly that it hurt.

"Oh, I feel much better!" Aunt Imogene said, coming to her feet and waving at Ethan.

He stepped into the church, ducking his head just slightly for the low doorway and then standing taller than she'd ever seen him. "I've come to cream the ruta-baga!" he yelled, holding up some paper in his hand.

"Hallelujah!" Aunt Imogene shouted, amazingly spry for a woman who was in the throes of an asthma attack just moments before.

"Thank God!" Uncle Oliver said, more to himself than to anyone else.

"Am I too late?" Ethan asked Risa, who was apparently in on his little scheme from the outset.

"No, but I wouldn't say you were a moment too soon either," Risa answered.

"Cream the rutabaga!" Worth shouted, just like he was watching one of those ball games and was angry with the umpire. "Cream the rutabaga!"

"You weren't invited to this wedding, Morrow, for a reason," Benjamin said, trying to pull Sterling behind him. "You've sniffed and snorted like a rutting boar around my—"

"Your nothing," Ethan said, coming toward the front of the church. "Sterling Phillips doesn't belong to you now, and she never will. Unless she wants a fraud and a jailbird for a husband."

The fingers that had been digging into Sterling's arm went limp, and she turned to find a white-faced man trembling by her side.

"Spoke to Francie this morning," Ethan said, turning to face the congregation. "That husband of hers is so literal. I mean, she kept saying how she just couldn't believe that Corny Cobb was a doctor. Not the same Corny who had stolen her unmentionables off the line and smeared them with—well, she just couldn't believe it, she said. Not the same Corny whose elbows always found their way—"

"I'm going to miss that train," Sterling's father said. "And this doesn't concern me, so I'll just take—"

"Doesn't concern you?" Ethan said, signaling Honesty, who sat with bared teeth between Sterling's father and the open doorway. "Your daughter's standing up next to a man who never passed his final exams at the New York Post Graduate School and Hospital—"

There was a collective gasp. Sterling folded her arms over her chest along with several other women, all of them no doubt thinking the same thing she was. He'd examined her. Everywhere, almost. He'd touched her in the name of medicine, his hands on her aching breasts, his eyes seeing things only her husband ought to see.

"—and it doesn't concern you? Well, it concerned my brother-in-law. Concerned him enough to bother checking the records while he was down at the school about his own children." He paused, seeking out his sister, Sissy, in the crowd. "Matthew's fine, and Michael's just about over the worst of it," he told her.

"Are you saying this man isn't really a doctor?" Sheriff Kear asked, standing up and coming forward.

"Not according to the College," Ethan said, shaking his head.

"Cream the rutabaga!" Worth yelled out again.

"I believe he just did," Sissy, who was sitting right near him, said softly. Someone laughed, and Honesty began to bark.

"You deceived me and my daughter," Sterling's father said, his hands on the back of her son's chair. "I'm outraged and appalled. I'll see to it that you are prosecuted to the full extent of the law. You treated my son! After we get back to New York, I—"

Ethan shook his head. "The boy isn't going back to New York with you," he said firmly. As if to prove it, Honesty bared his teeth and growled.

"He's my son and—"

Ethan shook his head again, and Sterling felt the room begin to spin. "I'm afraid I'm going to have to object to this marriage."

"Object to anything you want, but I'm missing the train!" her father shouted. "I've got to get my son back to New York so that the doctors can—"

"Steinway? Spoke to him too," Ethan said. "Miller, is it okay if we skip to the part about objecting?"

"Can you shut that dog up?" Miller Winestock asked, frowning at the dog in his church.

James waited for a sign from Ethan and then nudged Honesty with his foot. The dog quieted, but kept his teeth bared at Cyril Phillips.

"I assume you don't want to continue?" Miller asked Sterling.

Before she could answer, Charlie Morrow shouted out, "Miller, just get to the objections!" while Risa nudged him. "Before I get a hole in my side."

"Why is it every time the Morrows come into my church for a wedding, chaos reigns?" Miller raised his hands in defeat, then looked directly at Ethan. "I suppose you're waiting for this part: Is there anyone present who knows why this man and this woman—"

"I do," Ethan said. He paused to whisper to Charlie, who nodded and wheeled Worth from the church, gathering James with him as he went. Then Ethan climbed the two steps at the front of the church and took Sterling's hand.

"You want to state the grounds?" Miller asked.

"Not exactly," he said, "but I'd like to tell you all about a beautiful princess who lived in a big castle in the city."

"I don't have time for stories!" her father said. Of course not. He never had.

"Shhh!" someone yelled at him.

"And sit down!" someone else added.

"The princess was very beautiful, but very lonely. She had everything a princess could ever want, except love. Well, that's not wholly true. I believe that the queen loved the princess, but that only made things worse, because when the queen died, young and beautiful herself, the princess was left to mourn alone."

"My son and I—" her father started.

"Sit down!" It was Bart Morrow. He towered over

Cyril Phillips menacingly, and Sissy moved over to make room for him, displacing Hannah and Julia, who came and sat by their uncle's feet.

"And be quiet!" Mr. Hertel, the iceman Ethan had worked for, demanded.

"Yeah!"

Ethan took a deep breath and bowed his head at the reverend. Here it comes, Sterling thought. She could feel her cheeks redden, but Ethan squeezed her hand gently with a silent message that somehow everything was about to be all right.

"So the princess was all alone, and frightened. And one day, just after Christmas, she was standing outside in the snow and a man came up to her and said hello. Now, the snow was very bright, and her eyes were filled with tears, so she wasn't seeing very well, and she mistook him for her knight."

"What are you talking about?" she whispered.

"I'm telling a story," he said. "Don't interrupt me. So when the man asked for her hand, the princess foolishly said yes and married him and ran away with him."

"I have to catch that train!" Her father stood up. So did Honesty. Her father sat back down. The dog did not.

"So they lived happily ever after," Hannah said, getting to her knees as if the story was over.

"Not yet," Ethan said. "Because remember I told you that the princess mistook the man for a knight? But he wasn't really a knight. He was a cowboy! At least that was what he planned to be. For the time being, he was still just a farmer."

"Oooh. I get it!" Aunt Genie said. "So you're trying to say that was how she lost her pearls!"

He winked at her aunt and put his fingers to his lips. "And this farmer, after he married the princess, realized that he had no castle to take her to, no kingdom to offer her, and he panicked, which was very unknightly of him."

"I don't understand," she whispered again while the congregation began to put things together for themselves. "What are you doing?"

"I'm crossing the moat. You want to come in my coach? I don't have another family in there, Princess, like the coachman. There's room for me and you and the buckaroo, if you want to come."

"You don't understand," she said softly. "Worth is—"

"I'm taking my son and going," her father said, standing and kicking Honesty out of his way.

"He's not your son," Ethan said, signaling the dog to give the man all the room he wanted now that Bart was standing guard.

"He's not his son?" someone asked.

"Oooh."

"Oooh."

"Oooh!"

"Amelia Phillips died of pneumonia in June of 1892," Ethan said, holding up the piece of paper in his free hand and handing it to Miller. "Worth was born in September of '93."

"What about the princess?" asked one of the children who had gathered in the aisle.

"Ah, the princess," Ethan said. "Well, once again the princess was all alone, but not for very long. Shortly after her errant knight left her, she discovered that she was going to bear a little prince. For months she wandered and wandered, looking for her knight, and after she was delivered of her prince, she finally found him.

"But he was just a farmer, and ashamed. So ashamed that he hid from her, and didn't acknowledge her, and didn't take on the responsibility he should have."

"I can't let you do this," Sterling said quietly. "I don't deserve—"

"Does Worth?" He took both her hands and looked deep in her eyes, deep in her soul. "Isn't that what this was always all about?"

He dropped her hands and stepped to the podium.

"Once upon a time, I was young and wild. Everyone here knows that. I went to New York City and just went crazy. In fact I even wound up in one of those riots. Threw a brick and hit some man who'd thrown a brick at me. Stupid. Foolish. Then I made it worse by running away from responsibility, and went all the way to hell in a handcart when I tried to run away from love. Learned an important lesson: There are some things you have to learn to live with, and some things you shouldn't try to live without."

Sterling looked around at the crowd that filled the church. There was love filling the eyes of so many people—people she had expected to condemn her. They weren't fooled by Ethan's ridiculous confession. They were moved. They might not have believed, but they were willing to accept.

Ethan listened to the whispers in the crowd, desperate to save the reputations of both Sterling and the boy.

"You all remember how different I was when I got back."

"Yeah, Eth. We remember," Bart yelled as if nothing else short of the fact that he'd married and deserted Sterling could explain it.

"Yeah," someone else seconded.

"Can I have a minute with her?" Ethan quietly asked the reverend, who raised his eyebrows as if he didn't see how he could say no.

"This is insanity," Cyril Phillips said.

Genie Harrington stood up with her husband and answered, "I remember my mama saying the same thing when Amelia married you."

"You don't understand," Sterling whispered when Ethan cornered her at the back of the platform and blocked the congregation's view of her.

"I understand enough," he said, studying the floor. "And if you'll have me, I'll never ask you about it. It'll be the way I said."

"You must wonder . . ."

Stephanie Mittman

"Just one thing. Why didn't you just tell me? Didn't you know I'd love you no matter what?"

He searched in his pocket for a hanky while she sniffed.

Dabbing at her nose with the back of her hand in a most unladylike manner, she said, "I couldn't tell you. I knew how important honesty was to you."

"Heck," he said, looking over at the door. "He's just a dog."

"I wish—" she started.

"That's all it takes," he said softly, patting at his pockets again in the vain hope of finding a clean hanky for her.

The reverend cleared his throat and came toward them, his own handkerchief extended. "I don't suppose you've got a copy of the license?" he asked.

Sterling studied the ugliest black shoe tips Ethan had ever seen. No wonder she seemed even shorter than usual.

"There came a big storm," Ethan began.

"With wind," Sissy added.

"And hail," Bart said.

"And rain," Risa put in.

"And a tornado shook the earth!" Hannah said. Ethan was right about his niece. She was growing up.

"I see," Miller said, eyeing Cyril Phillips. "You know, a child is God's most precious gift. People can forget that. I know you two never will."

He said it as if it was a warning. And then he turned and addressed the congregation.

"Like our town, these children have weathered a terrible storm. And they have survived."

There were cheers from the audience.

"They have grown and matured, tall and straight like our oaks, and they—"

The back door of the church opened, and the buckaroo, supported on one side by James and hanging on to Charlie's lowered forearm for dear life, teetered into the church on shaky legs. Two steps and he was down, but he had walked into that church after Ethan and the dog, just as Ethan had promised Sterling he would.

"Oh!" she said, her hands covering her mouth. "Did you see him walk?"

Ethan watched her look to Corny, the man she had come to the church to marry, now sitting next to the sheriff with his head in his hands. He showed no surprise that Worth had managed to nearly support himself on his two tiny legs. He sat in silence.

"You knew!" she shouted, running over and kicking him in his shins with her ugly black shoes. "You let me worry and cry and you were going to let my father—" She pulled her leg back and kicked with all her might, hard enough to lose her balance and wind up flat on her little can on the bottom step of the riser.

Corny was screaming, holding his leg and claiming that she'd broken it, when Clyde Dow came storming into the church. Before the good doctor—Ethan smiled at that thought and corrected it—could scramble away, Clyde's fist connected with the fraudulent doctor's nose. Several women yelled out that Clyde should hit him again, but Sterling barely noticed that Cobb, or Clyde, or even the congregation were there.

"He walked," she said reverently, staring at her son, who was happily playing in Charlie Morrow's arms.

"Bring him up here where we can measure him for that bicycle," Ethan said, swallowing around the lump in his throat. It would take them a few days to find the right way to explain it to the boy, but when they started their new life in California, he sure hoped he'd hear the child call him papa as he went running by.

Miller cleared his throat loudly. "As long as we've a church full of people to whom I could preach an extra sermon, I don't think it would hurt anything to do this marriage up right in the eyes of God. Lord knows they don't know about God in New York!"

Ethan kneeled at Sterling's feet, taking her hand in

his. "Would the princess consider the farmer?" he asked.

"No matter what you think, you have always been my knight in shining armor," she said, sniffing back tears. "It would be an honor."

Ethan lifted the buckaroo and balanced him on his right arm. He stood with Sterling to his left.

"Dearly beloved," Miller said in his all-you-heathens-take-heed voice.

Behind them, Ethan caught a glimpse of Cyril Phillips being quietly escorted out of the Pleasant Township Methodist Church by Ethan's big brother Bart. When the old man was gone, Bart retook his seat in the Morrow pew, let Rory climb up on his shoulders, and signaled for the reverend to get on with it already, a big smile on his open face.

Miller Winestock nodded and continued. "We are gathered here together to witness the joining of these two people in holy wedlock, a state not to be entered into lightly, or without careful thought. . . ."

* * *

They got off the train at Terre Haute, James all bleary-eyed and disoriented, Worth asleep in Sterling's arms, still clutching his bag containing what was left of his Boys-on-Bicycles cookies. Ethan, her shining knight, managed to somehow carry all their luggage and still steer them toward the hotel without losing sight of Honesty, who was following along proudly, the handle to the basket that bore the turtle in his jaws.

"It's kind of irregular to have more than the honeymoon couple in the honeymoon suite," the clerk told her brand-new husband. He leaned over and whispered something to Ethan, who looked at James and nodded.

"I suppose you're right," he admitted, looking every bit as disappointed as she felt.

"Do have two small rooms up on the fourth floor with a connecting door," the clerk offered, brightening.

He looked at his watch. "Seeing how it's late and the last train's in, could let you have them for a buck fifty for both, instead of the usual dollar apiece. Nothing fancy, but they're clean and neat and well . . ."

The *well* was what got them. Ethan fished into his pocket and paid the man.

Ten minutes later both boys were under the covers and Ethan was telling them a story, which Sterling could hear in the adjoining room.

"So the dragon jumped up, swishing his tail," Ethan said.

"And breathing fire," James added.

"No," Worth explained. "He's outta fire. He just drips water now."

"You boys tired?" Ethan asked.

"No!" Worth said.

James was slower to respond. "Uh, sure, Uncle Eth. I'm tired. I could fall asleep right now."

"I'm not," Worth repeated. Sterling thought maybe if they hit him over the head . . . not that she was eager. In fact she was probably more fearful than most brides on their wedding night, she figured.

But Ethan knew. And she trusted him to treat her fairly. She wasn't asking for more than that.

"Okay, I'll tell you the end of the story, but only if you close your eyes," Ethan said. "Deal?"

The boys must have nodded, because the story continued.

"So the dragon came into the church, snorting and roaring, and he cornered the evil king, who had come to ruin the princess's life by forcing her to marry the evil troll, Mr. Rutabaga. . . ."

There was a pause, but then a soft voice demanded, "And then?"

"Then," Ethan said, his own voice much softer and quieter, "the cowboy came in and—"

"Don't you mean the knight?" James asked.

"Oh no," Sterling said, coming to the doorway in her

nightgown and robe, her hair loose around her shoulders. "He was a cowboy, because that was what he'd always wanted to be. And the princess above all wanted him to be happy."

He looked up at her and she noticed his Adam's apple bob, not once, but twice.

"And they lived happily ever after in a kingdom not far from the sea, where even the old duke and duchess came to live with them in the sunshine and fresh air, and if you guys aren't asleep now, I'll have to smother you both with pillows because I can't wait one more minute to get into bed myself."

And then she and the world's handsomest cowboy waited.

And waited.

And smiled.

Broadly.

And Ethan rose and turned down the lamp and tiptoed to where Sterling was waiting for him. "Lord, you are the most beautiful woman who ever lived. I swear it."

Carefully she pulled Zena Morrow's earrings from her ears and placed them on the bedside table. "Wasn't that nice of your sister to save them for me?" she asked.

"A gift from my mama," Ethan said. "For her newest daughter-in-law."

"Thank you, Mrs. Morrow," she said, fingering the pearl-and-gold earrings that complemented her mother's brooch.

"Oh no," Ethan said, tipping her chin until she faced him. "Thank *you*, Mrs. Morrow."

"Do you suppose," she asked, feeling the color rise in her cheeks, "that out there in California my skin might turn golden like your sister's?"

"Where?"

"In California."

"No, the skin where?" He untied her robe and helped her out of it. "Here?" he asked, touching her naked upper arm and then pulling at the strap of her gown until he'd rolled it down her arm an inch or two. He rubbed her shoulder with his thumb. "Or here?"

Now it was her turn to find it hard to swallow.

"I hope you won't be disappointed," she said, fingering the silky fabric that separated her from her husband.

"I was thinking the same thing," he admitted, sitting down on the bed and fighting to get off his boots. "I mean that you wouldn't be. I mean that I hoped you wouldn't be."

"Oh no. I'm sure you'll be perfect," she said, brushing the curl of honey hair off his forehead.

"I thought you were afraid of what that might lead to," he teased, pulling his shirt out from his pants and turning it inside out in a hurry to be rid of it. "Help me here," he begged.

And so she pulled at his sleeves, and lifted his summer balbriggan shirt over his head. And he pulled her close against his naked skin and sighed contentedly.

How slow did a man have to go? he wondered. He could make out the outline of her nipples, and could see them reaching for his touch.

They had all night. He tried to remember that as he rolled the straps of her gown farther and farther down her arms until they were even with her breasts.

"Would it be all right if I . . . ?" he asked, one finger pulling gently on the fabric between her breasts until one and then the other sprung free. "Holy Hannah! Do you have any idea how beautiful you are?"

She looked down at herself and blushed to her roots.

"I'm embarrassing you. I'm sorry. I mean, I imagined that you'd be lovely, but you take my breath away. And my restraint." He was ashamed to admit it. But he was bursting with his love for her, and if he didn't take her in his arms soon, he was afraid he'd die unfulfilled.

"Ethan? You don't have to restrain yourself. I'm your wife. You have every right to . . . to . . ." But even as she said it she was reaching for the covers and pulling them up to her chin.

"Love you?" he asked, turning down the lamp.

She didn't seem to think that was what was in store for her, despite the experience he knew she'd had. Far from being a woman of the world, she lay nervously in the bed, apparently awaiting his first move with terror.

And so he stretched out beside her, on top of the covers, and kissed her—no groping, no hugging, no touching at all. Except their lips. And he waited for her to put her arms around him.

And he waited.

Until he couldn't wait any longer. And he scooted under the covers and let his warm body touch her cold one.

"Do you have any idea how much I love you?" he asked, pulling her against him. "How many nights I layed awake in my bed, imagining you next to me?"

"I don't deserve you," she said softly, and he felt the wetness where her head rested against his chest.

"Are you crying?" he asked, sitting upright and trying to see her face in the dark, feeling her cheeks and cursing himself for doing something wrong. "Why? What did I do?"

"You deserve to be the first, the only."

"How very, very foolish of you," he said, shaking his head. "We owe Henry a debt we can never repay. Do you think I would erase the buckaroo's existence just to be the first?"

"I swear I'll be a good wife, Ethan. I'll do anything you ask. Anything that will make you happy. You'll never be sorry you married me and took my son and—"

"You'll do anything I want?" he asked, and saw her nod in the moonlight. "Then will you shut up? And kiss me?"

Again she nodded.

"And will you put the past behind you and think only of the future? And can the future start right now?"

"Oh, Ethan!" She sighed. "How do you always know the right thing to say? I wish I knew the right thing to say."

"That you're not afraid of me would be a good start."

She relaxed slightly against him. "I'm not."

"And that you love me, if you do." He tried to keep the confidence in his voice, but even he could hear the slight tremble.

"Oh, more than anything in the world. I love you so much! You and Worth and James mean everything to me. I—"

"Princess?"

"Yes?"

"The right thing to say now is nothing at all, because there's not much to say after 'they lived happily ever after.'"

"I just wanted you to know how much I love you. That I—"

He touched her lips gently, silencing her. "Show me."

There was the tiniest of gasps, and then she kissed him. She didn't wait for him to make his move, she just leaned over and kissed him hard on the mouth.

And oh, how he loved it!

He kissed her back, adding to it by tracing the seam of her lips with his tongue.

And she opened her lips for him, and he slipped his tongue into her mouth and coaxed her into following it back into his.

"Oh, Princess!" he said with a sigh, letting his hands roam over her back, slipping them within her gown and somehow managing to free her of the silken fabric so that he could touch her silken skin.

Softer than soft, smoother than smooth. She was really in his arms, just the way he'd dreamed.

And just like in a dream, she stretched out beside him

and let him touch her, while her own hands timidly explored his chest, playing with his hair, running gently over his nipples and sending waves of pleasure down his body.

And just like in a dream she was ready for him and welcomed him as he poised above her and took his love home.

Later, much later, their bodies sweaty and exhaustion about to overtake them, he felt the tiny woman in his arms—his wife!—stir against him.

"Tell me again," she said, pushing her body against his, fitting into his every bend with a soft piece of her anatomy. "How does it end?"

"Hmm?"

"The story. How does it end?"

It was late and they had a train to catch again in the morning. "All right, but this is the last time for to-night," he said, pulling her closer still. "After they creamed the evil rutabaga, the princess and the cowboy boarded the iron horse, bound for the sea with Prince Perfect, Sir Treetop, and the dragon—"

"Oh, yes!" Sterling said, her fingers creeping down his belly. "Don't forget the dragon."

"—where a vast kingdom awaited them. And the cowboy promised her a beautiful castle someday, if she could be patient—"

"Which she could," she said, capturing his manhood, and gasping over the fact that once again they could show each other just how deep their love really was.

"Yeah? It doesn't seem like you're very patient to me," he said, rolling her onto her back and leaning over her, his manhood brushing against her soft curls.

"Get to the good part," she said, spreading beneath him like a rose opening to the sun in June.

"I thought this was the good part," he said, slipping inside her and sighing at how right it felt, the boys in the next room, all of their futures waiting for them, Silver's fingers digging into his back. . . .

"You know what I mean," she whined, rocking gently against him.

"Where was I?" He kept himself very still. "Oh yes. So the princess and the cowboy and the members of their court all moved into the wondrous castle by the sea, where grapes grew and turned into wine enough to keep them all merry."

"And?" She sucked on his earlobe.

"Huh?" She wanted a story? Now? Right now? Rhythmically he rolled against her, tempting her, torturing himself.

She rolled with him, but refused to be deterred. "And?" she demanded.

"Oh, yes," he said, his hands pressing her bottom against him. "And they lived happily ever after."

"Mmm," she said, squirming down beneath him with a deep purr. "Very happily ever after."

Let best-selling, award-winning author **Virginia Henley** capture your heart...

☐	17161-X	The Raven and the Rose	$5.99
☐	20144-6	The Hawk and the Dove	$5.99
☐	20429-1	The Falcon and the Flower	$5.99
☐	20624-3	The Dragon and the Jewel	$5.99
☐	20623-5	The Pirate and the Pagan	$5.99
☐	20625-1	Tempted	$4.99
☐	21135-2	Seduced	$5.99
☐	21700-8	Enticed	$5.99
☐	21703-2	Desired	$5.99
☐	21706-7	Enslaved	$6.50